SOWING HOPE

Heather Wood

Finding Home Series

Until We All Find Home
Until We All Run Free
Until the Light Breaks Through
Until We All Share Joy
(stand-alone novella concurrent with Until We All Run Free)

A Gathering of Mercies Series

Weaving Roots
Sowing Hope

Printed in the United States of America.
Cover design by Hannah Linder
ISBN - Paperback: 979-8-9900837-1-4

To my younger sisters
Hilary, Hannah, and Bonnie Rose
I'm permanently inking "Ohana" here for you.
Individually, you're examples to me of patient, sacrificial love.
Collectively, you're my OG squad.

Why do you make me see iniquity, and why do you idly look at wrong? Destruction and violence are before me; strife and contention arise. So the law is paralyzed, and justice never goes forth. For the wicked surround the righteous; so justice goes forth perverted. Look among the nations, and see; wonder and be astounded. For I am doing a work in your days that you would not believe if told.

Habakkuk 1:3–5 ESV

Dear Reader,

Although I share more detail in the afterword of *Sowing Hope*, I wanted to take the opportunity to alert you to the history you'll encounter in these pages. While Patrick is a fictional character, he interacts with many real people in this book. The stories of James Birney and Elijah Lovejoy are real, and I did not add to them. If they were said to be in Cincinnati or sick in bed on a certain day, they were. The fictionalizing I did involved taking words from their writings and weaving them into their dialogue to make them come to life. Although mistakes happen, I did my very best to depict them and their friends as they really were as much as absolutely possible.

As with all individuals throughout all of history, my characters reflect opinions and beliefs in existence at their time, which were of course not the only opinions and beliefs present in their people group and social circles. One of my primary purposes in writing is to explore what God was doing at different points in history, and I'm overjoyed to have the opportunity to share the truth of that with you now.

Running together,
Heather Wood

1

"Duty appears plainly to call me West." - Elijah Lovejoy

January 1, 1836
Baltimore, Maryland

I've made my decision."

Patrick Gallagher lifted a ruddy eyebrow, leveling a steady look of challenge at his older brother Colm.

No, that looked more obtuse than necessary, like he was twenty again. With a hard yank, the bow he'd just tied on his cravat unraveled. Colm faded from the mirror and his imagination, leaving Patrick alone in his bedroom with the cravat dangling around his neck.

He shoved his fingers through the reddish-brown curls falling over his forehead, pushing them back where they belonged, and squared his shoulders.

"I've arranged it all and will be leaving in March," he announced to his own reflection. "There's nothing to discuss."

And yet Colm would have a retort. He would think Patrick was crazy and making some sort of rash decision as usual. Patrick had long since quit letting Colm's cautious nature influence his choices, but that didn't mean he relished the thought of breaking his news today at New Year's dinner. That alone was proof that his decision wasn't rash and he'd thought through the details, down to when his family would have the highest chance of being in amiable spirits.

With the cravat recentered, he quickly tied his normal sloppy bow and shrugged a greatcoat over his vest. "I've been preparing for months and believe in the rightness of this step. Everything's in order." Well, not everything exactly, but life was unpredictable and he could figure out the rest when he got to it. "And you don't have to like it," he added in one last muttered growl to Mirror Colm before turning on his heel and exiting the bedroom.

The common room of his house was chilly and quiet. His housekeeper, Elly, had today and tomorrow off to spend the holiday with her husband, Hector, so breakfast wasn't waiting for him. No matter—he'd prepared for this too. Patrick coaxed the coals in the stove to life and quickly had a blazing fire going. He could do fire. And really, anyone who could make a good fire could figure out the rest easy enough.

Making a pot of coffee wasn't difficult, and while it steeped, he set about looking for something to eat. Poking around in the barrels, shelves, and dried stores hanging from the rafters, he chose bacon and a couple of apples. A meal fit for the new year. The bacon went in a skillet, and he chopped up the apples to fry beside it. See? He could do this. Elly had been patient in her cooking lessons, even though he saw the fear in her eyes. When he left, she'd have to find a new position, and not many households in Baltimore would offer the same income, protections, and respect to a free Black housekeeper that he did.

Which was why he had to go. He'd faced one setback after another, but he wasn't going to quit until things changed for all of the Black community. Laws changed. Minds changed. Society changed. He refused to give into despair that such change was impossible, refused to accept the many compromises readily available to those of his persuasion. After all, God had changed his own heart. England had changed her laws.

Patrick took the first sip of coffee and leaned back in his chair as his rallying cry fizzled out. He stared at the frost on the window as the very despair he'd just preached against danced at the edges of his consciousness.

Things had been changing all right, and all for the worse. 1835 had been the lousiest year yet, with mounting mob violence on abolitionists and free Black neighborhoods pretty much everywhere. Whether he wanted to admit it or not, St. Louis was his last stand. His final hope that he could be a part of the change his soul ached for. *Total abolition.* The bacon sizzled, and he used a fork to flip it over and give the apples a quick toss.

At three days past thirty-four, he was so very tired. Hopeful enough to be willing to give one last shot to the cause he believed in, but tired enough that pushback from Colm might be the thing to put him over the edge.

Please understand. "Or at least, keep it to yourself."

When his stomach had been filled, pleased in his ability to have accomplished the task himself, Patrick gathered his hat and headed out the door to church.

The large Colonial-style family home was warm and fragrant that afternoon when Patrick held the door open for his mother and sisters. His sister Maisie's children were already running in and out of the doors to the main hallway, so she must have arrived ahead of them and set to work in the kitchen. Father headed straight for the gentleman's parlor to the left of the front door while Patrick's stepmother, Bridget, and the girls shed their coats and hurried to join Maisie.

The smell of roast goose caused Patrick's stomach to rumble. Glancing outside to see if his brothers were coming, he found Finn in the street, giving Reuben a good-natured elbowing. Reuben knocked his hat off in return. Their work as journeymen kept them tied indoors most days, and they looked to be needing some time in the fresh air. Patrick made to close the door when a buggy rolled up, carrying Ben and his wife. Behind them came Colm's family, and everyone was here.

Soon the hall was full of activity, piles of coats and hats, and a cacophony of voices. Colm's wife Betha unwrapped their son and daughter, and Colm reached to take Danny and Marian's coats from her.

"Happy New Year," Patrick said to him. He peeked outside one more time, but Betha's eighteen-year-old nephew Henry had stopped beside Reuben and Finn. Patrick clicked the door shut against the bite in the air and turned to Colm. "How was church?"

"Very nice. Where did you go this morning?"

"First, with the family." Since it was his last New Year here, he might as well spend time with them at First Presbyterian instead of going to the Black church where he often worshiped. Colm and Betha were members at Second Presbyterian, close to their Fells Point neighborhood.

"Not to the Quaker meeting?" Betha teased.

"There are Presbyterian abolitionists, you know." Patrick scooped Marian's stiff body into his arms. Patrick being a secret Quaker was a running family joke. It had taken too long for the Quakers' extreme ideas about total, immediate abolition to be picked up by other denominations. "In fact, Elijah Lovejoy is one."

"Who's that?" Colm asked.

The reminder that he hadn't been reading any abolitionist newspapers grated.

"He's the editor of the *St. Louis Observer* and a Presbyterian minister." Patrick's pulse quickened. He wouldn't share about his plan when most of the family wasn't around, and he had to be careful not to say too much. "He's become more outspoken about slavery and free speech in his editorials this past year." He was also younger than Patrick, part of the reason Patrick had to go meet him. He was being heard in a way that Patrick only dreamed of, despite his age, and his writings revealed that he had been developing similar convictions and zeal.

Colm seemed to think the conversation was over and moved to say something to Ben. Patrick turned his attention to Marian and nuzzled her neck, making her giggle. The four-year-old was clearly behind her cousins, and even her brother, in her functions. Patrick didn't know the details, but it had been several years after Colm's marriage before Marian came along, and her birth had been difficult. She would always need extra care, and her life expectancy was still uncertain.

Danny was a healthy two-year-old who toddled off after his cousins. Since Patrick was bouncing Marian, heavy and rigid in his arms, Betha was free to slip into the kitchen.

The door opened behind Patrick, and his youngest brothers crowded in with Henry and the bloke who'd been calling on Lyla. Henry came straight to his little cousin in Patrick's arms and tickled her under her chin before planting a kiss on her cheek. He'd lived with Colm and Betha since he was twelve, and Patrick had been glad to see him become a permanent fixture in the Gallagher family.

"What have you been doing these days?" Patrick asked. Last he knew, Henry had taken work for a farmer on the outskirts of the city, but he wouldn't be tending wheat this time of year.

"Weaving for my da." Betha's brother Seamus had been a linen weaver before the cotton mills forced him out of the business. He left his loom up, and both he and Henry worked it whenever they had time, more to keep the family legacy alive than to make great amounts of money. There were still families in Baltimore who preferred the quality of Young linen. "What about you?"

What, indeed.

"This and that. I'm a customs officer for now." Patrick felt a flood of embarrassment. Colm knew, and Patrick had assumed the word had spread. Customs was hardly what he had worked toward all his life, but soon things would change.

"Ah. I hadn't heard what you decided to do after losing the election and assumed you were back at the paper."

Patrick gave him a weak smile. Maybe it was all for the best that he'd lost his bid for reelection to the state senate. Of all the disillusionment that had been served up on life's platter, being in politics had been the worst. He'd never been so chronically rage-filled as he had those four years. His frame of mind hadn't been particularly sparkly since leaving it either.

Bridget appeared in the kitchen doorway, banging a pot to call them to dinner, and Hanna came to take Marian from Patrick. She was the youngest of his siblings at seventeen, and as Betha's primary help with the children, she knew better than most of them how to care for the girl. Everyone crowded to stand around the table, and Father spoke the prayer aloud, beseeching the Lord for His mercy, guidance, and provision in the new year.

"Amen," Patrick murmured. Before the meal was over, the family would know just how much he needed it.

2

"While I value the good opinion of my fellow citizens as highly as anyone, I may be permitted to say that I am governed by higher considerations than either the favor or the fear of man. I am impelled to the course I have taken because I fear God." - Elijah Lovejoy

Well, Maisie wasn't here. Patrick looked around the makeshift plank table set up in his father's hall, taking stock of who was present. All the children were at the table in the kitchen with Patrick's unmarried sisters and some of the mothers. Betha was here beside Colm, but Maisie, the sister just under him in the lineup, must have decided to stay in the other room.

Well. There was no way he'd get this much of the family together again, and his secret couldn't wait any longer. Lowering his fork, he cleared his throat.

"I've decided to leave the customs house," he announced without preamble to Colm across from him, loud enough that those on both sides stopped to listen.

"I didn't get the impression you loved it there." Colm swallowed his bite. "What are you going to do next?" He cut a piece of meat on his plate and sat with it speared on his fork.

"I'm going west in the spring to work for Elijah Lovejoy's newspaper."

Now the ends of the table quieted as well to see what had captured the others' attention. "What did he say?" Reuben whispered, and Bridget repeated it for him.

"West where?" Ben asked.

"To the *St. Louis Observer*. I've written back and forth a couple of times with Lovejoy, the editor." Patrick hadn't exactly told the man he was coming yet. But he would.

"Another slave state," Betha murmured at the same time that Colm asked, "Why St. Louis? I mean, there are abolitionist newspapers closer to home. William Garrison."

And this was the part Patrick didn't know how to explain. William Lloyd Garrison's *Liberator* in Boston was far closer.

"I have a lot of respect for Garrison, but his incendiary reputation keeps most of the population from listening to him. There's something about Lovejoy that I feel a greater kinsmanship toward for the way he writes and our similar progression of thought throughout the years." And he was a Presbyterian, while Garrison was a Quaker. "I'd like to go west to get a broader understanding of what's developing out there and explore abolition and slavery across the states. See it for myself."

Which led to his other point. "So I'll be walking."

"Walking?"

"*Where?*" Father peered over his glasses, obviously confused.

"From here to St. Louis in the spring."

"Is that why you've been walking everywhere and carrying that pack?" Ben again.

Patrick nodded. "I've been preparing for some time."

There was a beat of silence while that sunk in. "How long will that take?" Betha asked.

"It should only take two or three months, but I'd like to make some stops and detours on the way. There are other people I'd like to meet. I could learn a lot from the things I'd see walking across the country."

"I know losing the election was hard on you," Betha began. Colm was suspiciously silent.

Shaking his head, Patrick cut her off. "I think winning it would have been even harder. I hated it at the time, but it's not that losing made me decide to do something crazy." There, he said out loud what everyone was thinking.

But he didn't say, *This is my last chance.*

Nothing else has worked.

I need to get away. To have two months of walking to clear my head. To find myself again.

I don't know what else to do.

But no one would understand that, and if he said it aloud, they'd shake their heads in pity. He took a deep breath. "You all have seen the news." Or maybe they hadn't been paying attention. Patrick looked around the table as he spoke, but his eyes kept returning to Colm, because maybe as the oldest, Colm's opinion still mattered the most to him.

"Garrison was attacked by a mob of two thousand for speaking out against slavery in the fall. Amos Dressler was publicly beaten in Nashville. Black communities are regularly the target of mobs. Laws are tightening up, restricting the freedoms of free Black residents. But just because the cause seems hopeless doesn't mean it's not worth fighting for. It's still right, even if it is dangerous. And I think Lovejoy is the person I need to work with. I hope I'm the person he needs. At the very least, I'll spend some time with him and come back with a greater understanding of where to continue the fight next after having seen the country. At most, I'll stay to work with him."

"How will you make it walking? I mean, you're not a woodsman, and there isn't a highway to St. Louis," Reuben pointed out.

"Or a navigator," Ben added good-naturedly. "Any time I ever got lost in Baltimore, it was because I was with Patrick."

The family chuckled but quickly silenced, seeming to hold their breath for the answer.

"The National Road will get me a far piece—into Indiana, at least. And actually, I've been studying the rest. Elly's teaching me to cook, and I'm learning about outdoor survival from her husband. I walk ten miles a day after work these days. By March, I'll be ready." Hopefully. Maybe.

Silence fell as everyone around the table seemed to be chewing over his words. Patrick took the opportunity to take another bite of his goose and roasted pumpkin and to pray to the Lord that he wouldn't have to face a mountain lion. His brothers were right to raise concerns. The whole family knew that learning to build a shelter was not enough to make a woodsman out of someone as citified as he was.

"I think it sounds amazing."

Colm's voice broke the silence and lifted Patrick's surprised eyes to his face.

"If you have the opportunity to do something like that, you should take it. You're single and financially independent. Why not, right?"

Patrick chewed slowly to keep his jaw from dropping open. "Right."

"Do you have some of Lovejoy's editorials that we can read?" Betha asked. "So we can learn more about the person you feel so closely tied to?"

"I have them all."

"I'd take a steamboat if it were me," Ben commented. "I'd feel safer traveling with other people than alone through the wilderness and wouldn't have to worry about getting lost."

"If you get a letter from San Antonio, you'll know I took a wrong turn somewhere," Patrick joked instead of replying. Ben could do it his way if he wanted, but Patrick was doing it this way.

"Sam Houston would probably be glad to recruit you to his cause for Texas." Reuben laughed. "I still can't decide whether I support the Texans or not."

"Oh, the Texan War is ridiculous," put in Maisie's husband Ezra across from him. "I don't think they should be taking the Mexicans' land."

The conversation at their end of the table shifted to Texas, but Colm was studying Patrick with his steady brown eyes. He seemed to be trying to unpuzzle a deeper motivation beneath Patrick's words.

"Can I come with you?"

Patrick shifted to blink at Henry, who had been silent beside him.

"No!" Betha exclaimed as Patrick asked, "Why?"

"I've always wanted to go west. You said it makes sense to go while he's single and financially independent," Henry pointed out.

"For heaven's sake, Henry," Betha muttered.

Patrick pondered. He liked the boy's company, and they'd always had a good rapport with each other. But did he really want a companion? One who was going west for adventure and maybe to escape, but not for the same reasons Patrick was going? One he'd be responsible for? Patrick was a lot of things, but long-term caretaker was on the list with woodsman of things he was not.

"Do you really want to walk?"

Henry grimaced. "Not especially. I hope to take the railroad one day." The railroad had only recently reached as far as Winchester, a fraction of the distance Patrick was about to travel.

"That might take a while. You can prepare and pray about when God is leading you to leave, but it doesn't have to be this year," Colm said.

That clear thinking was what Patrick appreciated about Colm. He'd been good for Henry. Henry's father and stepmother lived just a few blocks from them, but Colm had done the boy's raising, and his steady mind and thoughtful faith were the best things that could have happened to Betha's nephew.

"Maybe next time," Henry said with a grin at the insinuation that this was a trip Patrick might take more than once. Patrick smiled back, even though he knew Colm redirected Henry because Patrick was the last person who could be expected to keep another human being alive out in nature.

"Do you think I'm crazy?" Patrick finally asked Colm what he'd been wondering for weeks. Now that he knew he didn't need to defend his decision, he felt bolstered.

"I accepted you as crazy about twenty years ago," Colm said seriously. "I wouldn't want to walk to Missouri, but I can see that it's important to you to do this."

Colm's life's work was here, though, and always would be. As schoolmaster to the boys at McKim's Free School, he was making a difference. Unlike Patrick, who had tried and failed to make the slightest impact in the causes he believed in, no matter how many iterations his attempts took.

"You could run for city officer if you were willing to soften your abolitionist message," Father said. "We have plenty of connections who would support a son of mine."

"I know," Patrick said softly. Over the years, most of the family had come to see his point of view about slavery, but they didn't all agree on how outspoken they should be about it. "Even a whiff of anti-slavery leanings is enough to turn public opinion against giving me an office, and after my term in the senate, everyone in Maryland knows where I stand. I couldn't get a position in the entire state now."

Even those who weren't abolitionists were publicly crucified for defending those who were. The chokehold slavery had on America grew stronger every year, and mob threats kept public discourse all but silenced on the issue.

"People aren't too keen on having their minds changed. I suppose that's the same in Missouri as Maryland. Are you selling your house?" Father asked as Colm resumed eating.

"I haven't decided yet. It's paid for." There was a lot more to that decision to consider than Father knew.

"I suppose you'll work all the details out."

"Yes, sir."

The sound of clanking silverware reigned, and then Ben asked Colm about the school. With his dreaded assignment for the day complete, Patrick turned his attention to the rest of the family while he ate. If he was eaten by a bear or mobbed on his adventure, today would be his last holiday with them. They'd put up with a lot from him over the years and loved him anyway. He'd never taken them for granted, even when their lack of understanding left him feeling isolated. The feeling had ebbed and flowed as he'd matured and changed, but their response today deepened the acceptance he felt. Patrick meditated on it as he ate, allowing the moment to burrow into his heart. He'd need the memory of this moment to strengthen him when he faced that bear or mob.

And maybe whatever love he showed them now could do the same for them in the trials they'd undoubtedly face this year.

3

"The cry of the oppressed has entered, not only into my ears, but into my soul so that while I live, I cannot hold my peace." - Elijah Lovejoy

S t. Louis is awfully far." Maisie frowned across the parlor at Patrick an hour later, and the sadness in her eyes made his heart lurch in a way that jarred him. Maybe Colm's opinion wasn't the only one that meant something to him.

"You really have to go?" Ezra sat next to her on the settee, his hand clutching hers.

Patrick swallowed, sobered. He'd been so focused on his plans, the cause, the pit he'd been in, that he hadn't put much thought into what he was leaving behind until the moment his sister looked like she might burst into tears.

And then he was an eleven-year-old standing at his mother's grave next to Colm, Maisie, and Mor again. It had always been the four of them—until it was him, Colm, and Maisie standing next to Mor's grave in their twenties. By then, Father had married Bridget and the step- and half-siblings had all come along. But as much as Patrick's heart had grown to encompass all of them, Maisie was still his only living full sister, and she and Ezra were some of his closest friends. He hated to be the one to put that pain in her eyes, but he nodded anyway.

"What planted the idea in your mind to join Lovejoy rather than support him from here?"

Patrick's vision unfocused, lost to the memory of that fateful article. " 'The truth is, my fellow citizens, if you give ground a single inch, there is no stopping place,' " he quoted. " 'I deem it, therefore, my duty to take my stand upon the Constitution. Here is firm ground.' Lovejoy wrote that in November. A brilliant, bold editorial."

He returned to the present, looking to her for a reaction. She sat with her head tilted, giving him her full attention, waiting for him to continue.

" 'We have slaves, it is true, but I am not one. I am a citizen of the United States, free-born; and having never forfeited the inestimable privileges attached to such a condition, I cannot consent to surrender them. But while I maintain them, I hope to do it with all that meekness and humility that becomes a Christian.' "

He stopped as the warmth he'd felt the first time he read those words returned. Lovejoy's words burned deep inside, stronger than anything he'd felt for a long time. " 'I am ready not to fight, but to suffer, and if need be, to die for them.' It was when reading those words that I decided to go."

The room was silent, the bold declaration reverberating in the air as he let his head fall. He'd known the first time he read them that they would change his life, but their gravity made him feel lighter, not weighted.

Maisie was still contemplating when her son flung himself into Patrick's arms. "Don't go away, Uncle Patrick!"

Patrick patted his back, lost for words. He hadn't planned an explanation that a seven-year-old would understand. "Hey, Hezekiah. I'll miss you, buddy."

"Will you come back for my birthday?"

With a little shake of his head, Patrick blew out his breath. "It's too far. But I'll send you a letter."

"But what about St. Patrick's Day? You can't be gone for St. Patrick's Day!" Hezekiah wailed.

Patrick looked helplessly at Maisie. She only lifted an eyebrow, indicating that he was on his own to fix the problem he'd created. "St. Patrick's Day isn't going to be the same without you. I don't even know if they celebrate it in St. Louis."

Maisie crossed the floor to tousle her son's brown head. "When are you leaving?" She sniffed, making an obvious effort to hold her emotions in check.

"March." He glanced at Hezekiah. "After St. Patrick's Day." Staying through the seventeenth was a sudden decision, but one worth making for his nephew's sake. He couldn't meet Maisie's eyes again. She wouldn't try to stop him, but he couldn't think about the possibility of never seeing her again. As mobile as Americans were, Baltimore to St. Louis wasn't a trip people usually made more than once. Even on a steamboat, it was a grueling distance.

"I don't know how to explain it, Mase."

"You don't have to."

Finn and Lyla came in behind her with some nieces and nephews, but they skirted around the edge of the room to avoid interrupting.

"But I truly hope you find what you're searching for."

Patrick opened his mouth to protest that he wasn't searching for anything and then closed it again. Hezekiah shifted and shoved out of his arms to go to his cousins.

The question pushed its way out against his better judgment. "What?" He finally dared glance at Maisie again.

She studied him, a thoughtful look on her face. "Hope, I think. It's started to slip away from you, hasn't it?"

The other conversations in the room grew louder and Patrick turned away from her, unwilling to either agree or disagree.

"Did your suitor leave?" he asked Lyla, feeling stupid for being unable to remember the bloke's name.

Lyla settled her lithe frame into a seat, smoothing her skirt over her knees. "John, and yes."

Maisie exchanged a look with Ezra that Patrick didn't miss, an acknowledgement that he had deliberately avoided the question. He had two months of walking to wrestle over her statement and wasn't going to waste his last precious months in Baltimore doing so.

A soft, rhythmic tapping on glass woke Patrick from a sound sleep. He'd gone to bed soon after sundown, playing the day's conversations with his family over in his mind, concerned with whether he'd communicated the purpose of his trip the way he'd intended. So often the passion he felt didn't come out in words that his hearers could fully grasp. But once he was asleep, his family fled from his subconscious. In their place came his usual dreams like unrelenting watchmen standing at their posts night after night.

Every dream featured people he'd hosted on the Underground

Railroad over the years, interwoven with varying levels of fiction. In one, a group of them were locked in his house while it went up in flames and he stood outside, pouring buckets of water on the burning walls to no avail. In another, he was tackled and tied up from behind while slave catchers led away recaptured fugitives, cracking whips against their bare legs as they went, leaving him to watch helplessly.

The other, more recent addition, featured the day he left the state capitol after finding out he'd lost the reelection. In the dream, a crowd of Black people he'd known over the years gathered around the capitol steps, raising fists and shouting in anger. They were protesting against *him*, and not for losing the election. "I would never vote for you," was the common sentiment of the angry crowd as they surged against him. "You broke the promises you made us."

He stood defeated on the steps, staring deep into the pain-filled eyes of John and Hester, one of the couples he'd assisted on their way to freedom, when the tapping on the window jarred him to the present. It took a minute to orient himself to his dark bedroom, remember that the dreams had little reality in them, and light a lantern.

"I'm coming," he called through the thickness in his throat, grabbing his housecoat as he stumbled to his feet. Birds chattered loudly to each other from the trees scattered throughout the street, but the sun had not yet risen. Patrick padded to the back door of his chilly house, checking that the curtains were all tightly drawn as he went. Elly always closed them to prepare for the possibility of nighttime visitors before leaving each evening. Pulling the back door open, he was met by three sets of black eyes peering at him in the lantern light.

"Come in, in Jesus's name. I am a friend, and you are safe." He repeated the greeting he always used, and the shivering trio crowded into his kitchen. Goodness but the wind outside sliced through his robe. Shutting the door and locking it, he turned around to find not three but four dark Negroes huddled together. The fourth was but a child who must have been hidden behind her mother until it was determined to be safe to enter. Having a family in his home was rare, the danger of traveling as a group exponentially higher.

Patrick invited them to the table, hurrying to coax a fire to life and put the kettle on. "Have you eaten?" Most of his visitors came by boat to Baltimore Harbor and stayed in a safe house by the docks their first day in the city, making their way across to his house at the north end that night.

Sometimes they arrived in Baltimore early enough to be brought straight to him. Those guests' need for beds usually outweighed their need for a meal.

"No, sir," the oldest, a woman, replied.

Patrick had hominy warming on the stove and cups of milk poured for each of his guests before he took the time to look them over. The woman was probably around his age, although she looked older, gray streaking the curls that peeked out from her headscarf. The other three were young enough to be her children—a girl and boy in their upper teens and a younger daughter no older than ten. A quick examination gave him an idea of which pieces of clothing would need to be replaced the soonest.

"I live alone. My help, Elly, will be here in a couple of hours, but she has beds prepared for you. Are any of you sick or hurt?"

He grabbed the bubbling kettle and poured out tea while waiting for an answer.

"My daughter, sir, her arm was injured. They wrapped it up, but it's hurt bad."

Only then did Patrick notice the way the youngest girl's arm was tied across her chest beneath the blanket around her shoulders. "What happened?"

The mother looked from the girl to Patrick. "Perhaps I'll tell you later."

Patrick nodded a quick agreement. No need to make the girl relive horrific memories. "I'm not a physician, but I can look at it and see what we can do here. I could possibly get a trustworthy physician here tomorrow, but I can't promise."

This was the worst part of helping fugitives. So often their injuries were grotesque or infected, all well beyond Patrick's expertise and comfort level. And being the one responsible for nursing injured children was the worst of all.

Once the family was eating, Patrick knelt before the little girl. "Can I look at your arm?" he asked almost in a whisper so as not to frighten her. In his experience, he was the first white man many slaves had known to treat them with kindness. Their skittishness around him was not without reason.

She stared at him with rounded eyes and gave a stoic nod. Keeping his movements slow, Patrick reached out and began unknotting the bandage.

"What is your name?" He rarely asked his guests this, and then only children he needed to build rapport with in similar situations. It was safer if they never knew each other's names, just like he didn't know who the station operator was at the Baltimore Harbor. The only connection he had with the Railroad was the coordinator for the whole area, who met with him on occasion and went by a pseudonym.

"Salome."

Patrick unrolled the bandage until it began to catch and stick to itself. "That's a beautiful name. Can I soak your arm in warm water to help unstick the bandage?"

Another nod.

Little by little, the warm water did its job and the bandage unpeeled. "Does it hurt?" he asked as it fell away, revealing a bloodied series of deep gashes. Patrick ground down on his bottom lip to keep from gasping or throwing up.

She'd been bitten, and Patrick wasn't an expert enough to be able to identify the animal based on the teeth marks. If he wagered a guess, it was a slave owner—or catcher's—dog, and Salome was beyond lucky to be here.

"It doesn't look infected," he managed. Some of the gashes had pink tinging the edges, but one had started to bleed again when the bandage was removed. "I do think you need stitches."

He looked to the mother. "Do you know how to stitch a wound?"

"Not rightly. If it's just the top layer, I could manage."

Patrick wouldn't even bother trying to find the physician. His stepmother, Bridget, could handle a job like this one. "We'll take care of it in the morning. For now, I'll clean it and wrap it back up."

He retrieved soap and a new bandage and scooted his stool up to Salome. "You know, I got stitches when I was a little boy. Twice." He talked while he worked, distracting her from the pain with an embellished tale of a badly gone walk atop a fence rail. It was nothing more than a stupid instance of one-upping his new stepbrothers, but the way he told it had Salome giggling by the time her arm was rewrapped.

His guests fell into their beds just as the sun was rising, and Patrick arranged the curtain hiding the door inside his bedroom. No one could get to the guest room without going through his, which helped them all sleep sounder. In his late twenties, he'd apprenticed with the man building the house, not only to influence where the false walls were placed but because he'd needed to stay out of the public eye for a while until everyone forgot about the little fiasco that had gotten him arrested.

Returning to the kitchen, he washed the dishes and hid traces of the meal in case any unwelcome visitors arrived. He never could fall back asleep after taking in new guests. Whenever he tried, he ended up lying awake, imagining the horrendous things they'd gone through to get to his house until rage against the perpetrators threatened to consume him. Keeping his hands busy did much to protect the state of his mind, especially after seeing little Salome's arm.

Someone had released their vicious dog on her on purpose.

Fifteen years ago, a story like that would have shocked him, but not anymore.

Now it was just one more incident thrown onto the huge pile of stories that sat heavy and crushing on his soul, adding to the hopeless, helpless feeling.

Men were still setting their dogs against little girls, and all he was doing was sitting in his safe home, slapping bandages over wounds too deep to imagine.

4

"I am not aware that any law of my country forbids my sending what document I pleased to a friend or citizen. I know, indeed, that moblaw has decided otherwise. I have never knowingly sent any abolition publication to a single individual in Missouri or elsewhere; I claim the right to send ten thousand of them if I choose." - Elijah Lovejoy

Patrick stalked home from the customs house with his collar turned up against the bitter January day and a rolled newspaper clenched in his hand, oblivious to the bustle of passersby around him. His jaw spasmed at the memory of the editor's words crumpled under his fingertips.

Words had been flying around the country ever since Lovejoy, in his role as a distributor for the Bible Society, had sent a crate of Bibles deep into Missouri. Upon its arrival, the crate had been opened to discover that the Bibles had been wrapped in the pages of *The Emancipator*, an abolitionist newspaper. A mob had quickly formed to teach Lovejoy a lesson. Tar and feather, probably. Patrick writhed against the tingle the words brought to his skin.

Thankfully, the clueless Lovejoy had been out of town when the news broke and escaped harm. It had provided him enough time to put out a statement about his ignorance of the mistake, but the man had taken the opportunity instead to dig in his heels and remind the angry nation that he did have the legal right to send printed materials anywhere in the country.

It hadn't done him any favors, but it was that editorial that had given Patrick deep respect for his boldness and changed his own trajectory. The rest of the country's response in the ensuing months was beyond infuriating.

"You look like you swallowed a cockroach."

Patrick started, whipping around to see Colm fall into step beside him.

"You know, it's beyond the pale the lengths evil men will go in their determination to retain their depravity," Patrick said without greeting.

Colm's outright laugh jolted him, and he stared at the mirth on his brother's face.

"I'm sorry." Colm chuckled. "Just funny to hear an Irishman use the phrase. You sound like one of the king's men, talking about the pale in Ireland."

Patrick frowned at him, and Colm sobered. "What happened?"

He held up the crumpled newspaper. "They're trying to pass laws against sending abolitionist publications into southern states. So intent are they on withholding freedom from their slaves, they're willing to take away their own rights and the freedom of speech of every American to silence anyone who might be a threat. It defies rationalization. And our own dear President Jackson supports it."

"That is indeed terrible," Colm said quietly. "I've been hearing about it for some time."

"Lovejoy continues to be outspoken in his defense of free speech. It shouldn't be viewed as only an abolitionist issue; it should concern all of us. But anyone who dares speak up for a free press is instantly labeled an abolitionist, so the truth can't gain any ground among the masses."

"Does it make joining Lovejoy more dangerous?"

An expensively-dressed woman came down the sidewalk, and they shifted out of her way.

"I hope it does," Patrick declared, the fire in his chest glowing hot. "If they take him down, I'm going next to him. There's no question about where the line is between right and wrong. It's no time to stay silent."

They had reached Patrick's corner, and Patrick rounded on Colm to say more, but his brother had stopped walking.

"There's a difference between standing up for what is right and looking for trouble."

He was the picture of unruffled stability. Patrick had always viewed Colm as a sort of rock, and he reflected that now, his hat squarely on his head, not a speck out of place in his person, not even hunched against the cold, meeting Patrick's eye.

But Patrick wanted trouble. "I want to break something," he ground out. Break the status quo. Break the hold complacency had on his culture. Too many, even in the church, had been lulled to sleep while the voices of slaveholders grew louder and louder in Congress. He'd hit his breaking point with injustice twenty years ago. How much more would it take before everyone else in his church and community hit theirs? How were they able to tolerate the ever-increasing divide between what the scriptures taught and what society accepted without a care?

"Or maybe burn it all down," he added as an afterthought.

"For them, or for you?"

Patrick's eyebrows pulled together in a question.

"Are you fighting for the slaves still, or for something inside yourself? Who are you really doing this for?"

Patrick rubbed his gloved hands together as his shoulders fell. He looked unseeing around the square as the answer formed in his mind. "For all of us, Colm. Sin hurts the sinner, too, not just the victim of it. Our country cannot be well if this disease continues unchecked. It's for all of us."

Colm's lips pressed in thought. "I agree," he finally said. "I only ask because I know that sometimes in fighting for a cause, the cause can become its own beast until it, not God, is the one directing our steps. I'm not sure that's true for you, but it is something to be mindful of. We might start fighting for causes instead of people."

"It's true," Patrick said.

Another thing to spend his walk to St. Louis agonizing over. Taking a steamboat got more tempting every day. He could spend the trip gossipping with fellow travelers and ignore all the disorder in his mind and heart. But he'd been battling a wildfire by swatting at little blazes around him until he was exhausted, wounded, and covered in filth, while the gusts picked up speed, roaring hotter around him. He needed a long, *long* walk through the middle of Ohio and Indiana to heal and prepare before the next fight.

"You look worn ragged," Colm admitted. "You know I'm never going to suggest that you stop your work. But maybe you should think about laying down the burdens. The weight of the world wasn't meant for your shoulders."

Patrick looked toward his house, ready to escape before Colm dug any deeper. "I would if I knew how." Tipping his hat, he spun on his heel and left Colm staring after him.

For the next two months, Patrick prioritized visits with his family amidst his survival training with Hector and lengthened hikes through the hills outside of town. Elly dried meat and vegetables for him to pack, and he sold some of his furniture to pay for supplies and trip expenses.

He resigned from the customs house the second week of March and came home to start packing. His new boots had been delivered from the cobbler that day, and he was examining them after supper when Hector arrived to walk Elly home.

Patrick ran his fingers over the leather, frowning in concentration. It was hard to know what to spend his precious pack space on. Should he tie a second pair of shoes to his knapsack for when this pair wore out, or should he just expect to buy a new pair when he got to Columbus?

"Have a good night, Mr. Gallagher."

Patrick snapped to attention, shifting in his chair to face them. "Ah. Oh, good evening, Hector. I wanted to talk to you two."

Hector and Elly stopped with their coats in their hands, a matching question on their brows.

"Would you want to live here when I leave? I don't want to sell the house to a stranger when it's a known safe house, so I'd like to give it to you if you want to continue the work when I'm gone. I know it's a lot to ask." Elly and Hector had always been invaluable with the work, but it was another matter to take on the whole responsibility of running a busy Underground Railroad stop.

Hector gave a side glance to Elly. "We're always happy to help, Mr. Gallagher. But I don't think it would be right for you to give us your house."

"Oh, nonsense." Patrick stood up and waved his hand. "You've done enough work for me over the years to earn it, and it's as much for them as it is for you."

"We appreciate it, but it's not that," Elly cut in, staring at the ground at Patrick's feet.

"It's the neighbors." Unlike his wife, Hector looked Patrick in the eye. "No one would take kindly to a Black man owning a house in this neighborhood."

Of course. Why did he still forget these things after all this time? Irritation at the reminder of reality rose in his chest. "You're not wrong." Patrick rested his hands on his hips, blowing out his breath. "Well, would you be willing to live here and be caretakers? I could maintain ownership and give you rent in exchange for upkeep of the place." He tipped his head. "With the understanding that I'm not planning to come back."

A wordless conversation passed between the husband and wife. Patrick pressed his fist against the corner of his mouth and watched for a minute before speaking again. "You could let me know your decision in the next couple days."

"We'd like it for certain, Mr. Gallagher," Hector interjected. "They wouldn't think anything of your staff living here while you're away."

Patrick smiled, even as his heart hurt at the compromise. "All right then. If you decide to move away, just let Colm know. But please, do treat it as if it's your own home. I'd hate for you to never feel comfortable here. And your willingness to continue hosting guests means a great deal to me."

They thanked him profusely, but the unsettled feeling remained after they left. Patrick could only pray that they wouldn't run into any trouble living here without him. He regretted the furniture and buggy that he'd had to sell, but he needed the money to get set up in St. Louis, or enough for a return trip if Elijah Lovejoy didn't want him to stay.

Turning back to his boots, he made a split-second decision. They were sturdily built, and he'd pass other cobblers on his trip. It didn't make sense to be weighed down with another pair when it was still March and he'd need to carry blankets and food to get through the mountains.

Sitting back down, he tugged the boots on. It was time to start breaking them in, and he had several miles to walk before calling it a night.

5

**"They are impatiently calling me to the West,
and to the West I must go." - Elijah Lovejoy**

The Monday after St. Patrick's Day, Patrick stood at his bedroom window with his hands on his hips and watched the rain beat at the window as a roll of thunder rumbled through the house.

He had determination enough to leave today despite the rain, but the thought of all his supplies being soaked the first day wasn't appealing, and he wasn't on a deadline. He'd arrive in St. Louis long before winter as it was, so it wouldn't hurt to wait a day, except for the aggravation of being in Elly's way. She and Hector had moved in on Saturday. The bedroom he lived in and was currently hogging wasn't the largest one in the house, and he could stay squirreled away to allow her to settle in.

A knock came at his door, and Elly's voice accompanied it. "You up, Mr. Gallagher? You have company."

He turned from the window with a lack of curiosity. He'd said goodbye to his family yesterday at Sunday dinner, expecting to leave early this morning. But the farewells to his connections and friends had all been said as well, and Elly would have announced fugitives differently. Besides, runaways never showed up in daylight. Which meant it had to be family.

Opening the door, he found Colm and Maisie by the fire, peeling wet coats off.

"You were right, Colm. He didn't leave yet."

Patrick couldn't help his grin. "How long are you going to stretch this goodbye out?"

"Would you have come to us if we hadn't come to you?" Colm set his dripping hat on his coat. "We have time to have coffee with you before work."

Elly immediately filled the kettle and set it to boil, and Patrick thanked her. This wasn't how she was supposed to be spending her first day as mistress of the place.

"Well, come on in then," he said, gesturing to his invading siblings who were already settling into seats by the fire. "At least it was nice for St. Patrick's Day."

"Thank you for staying for it." Maisie patted brunette flyaways from her face. "It meant a lot to Hezekiah."

Patrick shrugged. "It would have been too early to go through the mountains before now anyway." Thunder rumbled again, shaking the plates on the table, and he reached out unnecessarily to steady them. When it passed, he grabbed a chair and relaxed. Despite the hard time he gave them, coffee with his two favorite people was a welcome surprise.

They stayed only long enough to drink their coffee, and if there was anything earth-shattering about the conversation, it was merely the comfort of it, the old easy camaraderie. No one tried to leave him with any last profound words, and they hugged him when they left as if they'd see each other in a couple of weeks.

Patrick released Colm from his embrace, looking down at the pressure against his chest to see a small hardbound book there. He took it from Colm, turning it over to see the title. The corner of Patrick's mouth lifted and he gave a small nod, and then Colm and Maisie were gone.

Patrick retreated to his room with the copy of *Pilgrim's Progress* still held to his chest. Leaning against the closed door, he looked around the dim, now-sparse room. The sound of Elly's singing came from the back bedroom over the noise of the storm as she unpacked. He had the rest of the day to himself, and really, his journey started now. It wouldn't be remiss to start it on the right foot.

He crossed the floor to where his pocket Bible lay on the bed next to his open knapsack. The more he drank of God's Word today, the more he'd have to meditate on tomorrow as he walked. Sitting on the bed, he stuck his new book in the knapsack and picked up the Bible. Holding it between his knees, he stared at the stiff leather cover and tried to form a prayer.

But what was it that he was hoping for from God on this trip?

"Lord, I ask that I would see You."

The evil around him in the treatment of both enslaved and free Black people had filled his vision until it clouded. Maybe it would take getting out of a slave state for a while and climbing an actual mountain to clear it again and see that there was still good in God's world.

"Make of me a vessel unto honor, sanctified, meet for Your use, and prepared for every good work. Someone You can use."

Since running an Underground Railroad house, working in legislature, involvement in the Freedmen's Society, and volunteering with the *Genius*—Benjamin Lundy's defunct abolitionist paper—had accomplished a whole pile of nothing.

What was it about him that God wouldn't use him? He'd surrendered his entire life to the Lord's work—at least a dozen times—and it still seemed that everything he touched was worse off than before.

"And bring justice, Lord," he whispered. "Freedom for those in chains and relief for the oppressed." Even as the words left his lips, the impossibility of his earnest prayer struck him. Shaking himself back to reality, he cleared his throat and opened the Bible.

The first glimmer of dawn edged the top of nearby houses the following morning when Patrick closed his front door for the last time and took a deep inhale of the crisp air. His full knapsack dug into his shoulders, padded by his new coat, and a gleaming Colt revolver hung across his right thigh. His belly was full from Elly's breakfast, and he was in a good mood.

Breathing out a prayer for favor on his journey, he turned his feet west to the music of early birds in the trees and the rumble of dairy wagons on the cobblestones. The air was cold and damp after yesterday's storms, and it was a good day to walk to Missouri.

By the time the sun was up, he was out of the city, making his way over the yellow-streaked hills west of Baltimore, through fallow fields not yet plowed for early spring crops. He'd hiked these hills many times over the past months, but this time, every tree and farmhouse that he passed was a farewell. His first day on the road wouldn't be spent thinking about everything he was leaving behind. The sites of his many failures, as well as the people he loved, the church where he learned to read by following along in his father's Bible, the graves that held his mother and sister.

The air had warmed up to what he guessed was the high fifties, so Patrick took his hands out of his pockets and flexed his fingers. He really didn't know what to expect in Missouri or on the trip for that matter, so thinking about the future was as pointless as thinking about the past. Instead, he chose to spend his first morning on the road simply enjoying the scenery, taking interest in the passing traffic, and feeling the burn in his legs. The teamsters, buggies, and other pedestrians on the turnpike between Baltimore and Frederick provided distraction enough from the torrent of thoughts he kept at bay. There would be enough other days to think—today it was enough just to feel, for the first time in far too long, that he was glad to be alive.

His feet and shoulders were aching by the time he found a quiet creekbank where he could eat his midday meal. Dropping his knapsack, he stretched out on the grassy incline and gave his back the relief it demanded. Fifteen miles from home sat an inn past Ellicott's Mills where he aimed to bed down for the night. It was tempting to try to push further, but wisdom demanded he pace himself if he was going to make it all the way to Missouri without injury. So after he ate, he leaned back for a brief nap before continuing on his way.

Day 1, Ellicott's Mills, Maryland
Health: Good. Tired and sore but up for the task ahead.
Supplies used: Biscuits and ham for dinner, $1 for room & supper
Wildlife: A handful of odd human characters on the road and some robins at dinner
Verse for the day: Luke 9:62 No man, having put his hand to the plough, and looking back, is fit for the kingdom of God.
Personal notes: I wonder if Benjamin Lundy is still in Philadelphia?

6

"It is the easiest thing in the world to become a Christian—ten thousand times easier than it is to hold out unrepenting against the motives which God presents to the mind, to induce it to forsake its evil thoughts and turn unto Him." - Elijah Lovejoy

Thick black smoke streamed, starkly contrasted against the blue sky and filling the air with the acrid smell of burning coal. Patrick watched the steam engine choke its way up Mount Airy ahead of him and wondered again why he had chosen not to ride for the parts of his journey that he could.

He had woken up this morning in the Ellicott City inn, every muscle in his body aching. Once he pushed past the initial adjustment to long days on his feet and hard beds, he would surely start to feel better—right before he hit the mountains, probably.

He'd started the day reading a few verses from his Bible before going down for breakfast. But now as he pushed his way up to Mount Airy, his full attention was on taking the necessary steps to get up the hill and to a hot supper, his second day on the road with no thoughts to spare on anything deeper.

A jangle of harnesses and clip-clopping alerted him to another wagon working its way up to the small town. Still watching the train belching smoke across the sky, he stepped to the side of the road as the wagon rumbled past. A closed carriage was coming along behind it, so he remained motionless as the train chugged into the distance and the traffic rolled by. It wasn't until he heard his name that he turned to realize that the elegant carriage had stopped in front of him.

"Mr. Gallagher? Senator, is that you?"

His throat parched at the sound of the high-pitched voice. Snapping his jaw shut, he looked up to the sight of Mrs. Goldsborough hanging out of the carriage window with horror on her face, flapping her handkerchief at him.

"Mrs. Goldsborough," he blurted out, unable to cover his surprise with a more intelligent greeting. He doffed his hat, stuffing it off-kilter back on his head.

"I thought that was you, but I can't imagine what you're doing out here like a regular gypsy with that pack on." She opened the carriage door, and his vision was filled with yards of mint-colored silk.

Patrick still hadn't regained his composure when his eyes fell on the mute faces in the recesses of the carriage—the bald head and whiskers of Mrs. Goldsborough's illustrious husband and the whitened visage of Linnea Goldsborough. His breath left him as he went cold and then hot before realizing that Mrs. Goldsborough was still talking, her dark brown curls bouncing in time.

" . . . but where on earth are you going?"

Patrick's mind raced. Admitting that he was walking to Missouri hardly seemed wise under the circumstances. The Goldsboroughs had written him off as crazy two years ago, when Linnea ended his suit of her on no uncertain terms. "I'm just . . . going up . . ." He waved vaguely at Mount Airy. "Just walking to . . . heading to Pennsylvania just now."

"What has you running away in such a form?" Mrs. Goldsborough's tone was demanding, as if she couldn't imagine what would possess a man to leave Baltimore.

"Mother," Patrick heard Linnea murmur from the shadows.

Her question had rattled him, and he couldn't form a coherent reply. He mumbled something about work to do and stretching his legs, but not surprisingly, the woman didn't look convinced.

"We are going to my sister's in Frederick, so you might as well get in and come with us that far instead of standing on the road like a homeless person."

"Oh no, really, I'm happy to walk," Patrick was quick to reply. "Thank you anyway."

"Up you go, senator. Being out in the sun too long is not good for anyone, I'm sure, and we won't leave a man of your stature rambling around like a regular farm laborer. There will be stagecoaches in Frederick heading to Pennsylvania, no doubt."

The danger in acquiescing was unquestionable. "Don't concern yourself on my account. Thank you anyway."

"Come along, senator."

The final statement was a command with a hard edge to it. Patrick would rather crawl on nails to Missouri than get into that carriage, but Mrs. Goldsborough wasn't known for ever conceding once she'd made a decision. He would have continued to argue if he hadn't known it would result in the carriage rolling slowly along beside him while she pestered him all the way up to Mount Airy. Biting back a sigh, Patrick slipped the knapsack from his shoulders and hoisted it up to the coachman to tie down before approaching the door. A quick appraisal of the situation revealed that the only open seat was beside Mr. Goldsborough and across from Linnea, who wasn't meeting his eyes.

"I'll ride atop," he announced, quickly shutting the door and swinging up beside the coachman before Mrs. Goldsborough could protest again.

The man was silent when Patrick landed beside him, and a full minute passed before a tap sounded on the roof of the carriage and the coachman cracked his whip. Patrick gripped his seat on the incline, glad after all that his legs and shoulders were given a reprieve from the hills. He felt double the relief at the awkward situation he'd averted inside the carriage, closed up in the small, dark space with Linnea's silent judgment, listening to Mrs. Goldsborough's arrogant half-truths and nonsensical demands. It was a small reflection of the greater danger he'd evaded when the poorly matched relationship ended.

His judgment had slipped soon after his thirtieth birthday when long-term loneliness caught up with him at the same time as his sudden rise to prominence upon his election. Thrust into social events with the most powerful and influential people in the state, he'd made the decision that, despite being an abolitionist, it wasn't his only or most defining trait. If he didn't bring up the topic at the outset, the pool of interested, sophisticated young ladies suddenly went from zero to dozens. Fool as he was, he'd brazenly assumed that he could eventually sway the woman of his choosing to see reason and align her beliefs with his.

Fool, fool, fool. He'd learned quickly that abolitionists and slavery advocates weren't basically alike with a few differences in perspective. No, they were on two completely different planets, and it turned out that education wasn't the answer for bridging the gap like his youthful idealism had believed. The carnage of that season of his life included the frosty female specimen riding behind him and a rude awakening that spewed cynicism into every corner of his being.

A great blue heron startled out of a bush to his right and flew away across the field. Patrick's watchful gaze moved from it to the approaching town, where he would need to contrive an escape from the Goldsboroughs. Distance between himself and the persons in the carriage was the most prudent thing for them all. To even suggest that his departure from Baltimore was because he was running away! The last thing he needed was to be exposed to more ridiculous accusations. And unfounded. Completely ridiculous and unfounded, that accusation.

As a grown man and a former senator, he would not be cowed by Mrs. Goldsborough. Excuse himself to the outhouse and never reappear, maybe. But allow her to coerce him into something he didn't want to do, never.

Because his heavy knapsack was tied with the other luggage, there was no leaping quickly away and disappearing when the carriage stopped. Patrick was thus adjusting the pack back onto his shoulders in front of MacPherson's Tavern when the coachman opened the door. The Goldsborough family swarmed onto the street as the supper bell rang inside the tavern.

"You'll dine with us, Mr. Gallagher." Mrs. Goldsborough swept past without looking at him.

"Ah, no, I'm afraid I can't. I thank you for the ride, but I must be on my way."

She swiveled around and gave him a once-over with a dark eyebrow aloft. "Had we left you on the side of the road, you wouldn't be arriving here for another hour yet, so you can spare that much time on a meal in our company."

Oh, if there wasn't a shred of truth to that—and his rumbling stomach that had already been looking forward to supper for several miles. Mrs. Goldsborough marched through the door with her husband a half step behind her, so Patrick reluctantly acquiesced his knapsack to the coachman and held the door for Linnea.

"I hope you are well, Miss Goldsborough."

"Thank you, I *was*." Linnea kept her eyes trained on the back of her mother's dress as she strode after it toward the dining room. "What in heaven's name were you doing out there?"

"I'm afraid you wouldn't understand if I tried to explain it, and I'm not interested in the attempt." The smells of ale and cooking meat hit him, drawing him into the building.

"For mercy's sake," Linnea muttered.

"I would be perfectly glad to leave you to enjoy your supper absent my company, you know." Patrick halted on the worn planks of the foyer, his mouth grimacing at the view of her pursed lips, which he couldn't believe he'd kissed. Of course she hadn't been scowling when she melted into his arms, and that was quite enough of that train of thought. Linnea grabbed his arm and hauled him forward again. How did he ever think he could educate this woman into changing her mind about anything worthwhile?

"Just don't be embarrassing," she hissed.

A smile spread across Patrick's face at the thought of all the ways he *could* be entirely humiliating over the course of the meal, but the ideas would have to be entertainment enough.

"I'll think about it."

7

"The country seats along the road are most delightful, the farms in the highest state of cultivation." - Elijah Lovejoy

The hotel cooks barely had their kitchen fires lit in the pitch black morning when Patrick begged a bowl of porridge and a cup of coffee off of them. When his breakfast had been gulped down, he eased his way down the front stairs and out of town, putting the painfully awkward supper the night before out of his mind.

By the time the sun was up, he was settled on the far side of a decrepit barn with his head pillowed by the knapsack and his long body stretched out in the shade to wait for the Goldsboroughs' carriage to pass. They'd have heard that he left early, but if Mrs. Goldsborough expected to overtake him again and force him into her carriage, she was mistaken. Once they were ahead, he'd be free to walk unhindered, hopefully without unwelcome intrusions by anyone else he knew.

Nothing slapped a man into reality and reminded him why he was still single quite so distinctly as running into Linnea Goldsborough. Hadn't he suffered enough for that mistake, or was God so intent on forcing him to face his faults that He would put the reminder in the middle of his path?

Maybe there was more to him than his abolitionism, but the truth was, he couldn't be happy married to someone who didn't believe in freedom for all humanity as strongly as he did. In order to find marital bliss, he'd need a woman who wouldn't complain when he came home late from helping a family new to freedom set up house. She'd be flexible, able to prepare a meal and a bed at any moment that a fugitive showed up at the door needing shelter. She'd be tireless in the work, like he'd always been. Believe in him and encourage him in moments like this, when despair was a breath away. She wouldn't beg him to stay home for his own safety when the work became dangerous. If God ever wanted to give Patrick a wife, she would have to be tough, physically and mentally.

The only women he'd ever known who met that description were married to his abolitionist friends or were firebrands traveling on Theodore Weld's speaking circuit, completely uninterested in a romance with a failed politician.

Patrick rubbed his fist over his chest where the loneliness burned. Sometimes he was able to keep busy enough to remain distracted from it, but sitting alone on a Maryland hillside, hiding from his one failed relationship, the pain was inescapable.

"As much as I love my family and the Black community You've given me, they really don't take the place of a wife, Lord."

How was it possible to miss so strongly someone he'd never met? And how was it possible that even now, on the way to pursue his passion, he was here, feeling acutely his lack of a wife? A second. Someone to come home to. All the purpose and service in the world weren't replacements for such a thing.

Picking a piece of ryegrass, he rubbed it between his fingers, giving the conveyances on the road only the smallest sliver of his attention. He wasn't here to indulge in self-pity, but he'd never exactly addressed that grief either, which had led to the massive error of judgment with Linnea.

A horse galloped past with a boy in the saddle, carrying the mail for the Pony Express. Then a familiar team of horses came into view, and Patrick sat up, alert, as the Goldsboroughs' carriage rolled by. Lifting his fingers to his mouth, he kissed them and flung his hand after the receding vehicle.

"May I never see you again," he cheerily announced to the wind.

Digging an apple out of his knapsack, he gave it a little toss and collapsed back on the ground with it and *Pilgrim's Progress*. They could have a ten-minute head start before he took the chance of continuing on his way.

Day 3, Monocacy River outside Frederick, Maryland

Health: Considerably recovered after the events of last night

Supplies used: Apple and a biscuit for dinner, room and 25 cent supper at a fairly dirty tavern.

Wildlife: Blue herons, chipmunks, wild turkeys.

Verse for the day: Isaiah 43:18-19 Remember ye not the former things, neither consider the things of old. Behold, I will do a new thing; now it shall spring forth; shall ye not know it? I will even make a way in the wilderness, and rivers in the desert.

Personal notes: You can't change a woman's mind.

Also—there's no way in blazes I'm stepping foot inside Frederick city limits today or ever.

With the necessity of skirting around Frederick to avoid Linnea's aunt and then facing Braddock and South Mountains, his first two mountains, it wasn't until Saturday night that Patrick reached Hagerstown as a cold front blew in. But the Goldsboroughs were far behind him, literally and metaphorically, and that alone was enough to lift a man's spirits. Walking into town as dusk fell, he was joined by canal diggers and farm laborers coming home from work.

Day 5, Hagerstown, Maryland

First night staying as an invited guest in the home of a man I met on the road near suppertime, so no room and board expenses. The Woodhouses are a decent family who accepted my explanation of walking across the country to see the sights quite satisfactorily.

Verse for the day: Mark 9:41 For whosoever shall give you a cup of water to drink in my name, because ye belong to Christ, verily I say unto you, he shall not lose his reward.

Personal notes: I promised Bridget I wouldn't travel more than a biblical Sabbath day's journey on Sundays, which being less than a mile, really isn't worth moving locations over. The Woodhouses provided a bath tonight, which is not to be underestimated. I'll go to their Baptist church in the morning and rest up to be ready for an early departure Monday.

It was gray and uninviting out three mornings later when Patrick leaned on the window frame of the men's dormitory in Miller's Tavern in Clear Springs and considered his options. It was raining steadily but not pouring, and the rubber blanket he brought to double as a rain poncho would keep him and his knapsack fairly dry. Had there been anyone interesting to talk to at the tavern's suppertable, he might be tempted to stick around until the rain stopped, but as there was no one intriguing to visit with, he might as well keep going.

Traffic was light on the road out of Clear Springs, and with a destination to aim for, Patrick put his head down and pushed on through the weather. Mr. Miller had stopped him on his way out the door earlier.

"West, ain't it?" He leaned forward on the weathered desk with his hands clasped together.

"Yes, sir."

"Two miles west of Hancock is Widow Downer's tavern. It's surrounded by a holler full of pine trees, and a day's walk'll get you there in this weather. It's clean and the only place I'd recommend bedding down out that way."

Trudging along hours later, Patrick's stomach growled at the thought of the offerings in Widow Downer's kitchen, the cold ham and beans he'd eaten at midday long since passed from his memory. Over the rain, he could hear the murmur of the Potomac River on his left, and once or twice, Virginia came into view through the mist. His toes were numb with wet and cold, and he alternated between stuffing his hands in his coat pockets and using one to hold his cloak closed as his boots crunched over the gravel road. Water dripped from the brim of his wool cap and down the back of his neck while his family's accusations tickled at the edges of his consciousness.

I hope you find what you're looking for—hope.
I know losing the election was hard on you.
Are you doing it for them or yourself?

The questions played on repeat in his mind like a nightmare he couldn't wake up from. Losing the election hadn't been hard on him. The last ten years had been hard on him. And yes, hope was at an all-time low. So what if he was running away from Baltimore, if he was also running toward the glimmer of hope on the horizon? What was wrong with that?

Patrick became aware of the apparition ahead on the road right before he heard a horse's distant whinny and a man's shout through the rain.

There was some kind of trouble, which didn't surprise him at all, considering the weather. He hadn't been paying attention to the vehicles that passed. Now all sense of time and distance was lost in the sunless day and he couldn't remember the last mile marker he'd passed.

The closer he got to the carriage, the more dire the situation appeared, causing him to quicken his steps toward it. The carriage tilted sideways in the ditch, and a man stood at the open door, which angled toward the sky. His attendance to those inside was accompanied by panicked shouts. No one was with the horses, rearing and whinnying nervously while still harnessed to the carriage. Every movement they made jolted the endangered vehicle, which listed further down the incline. Patrick hurried forward, taking up the abandoned reins as he neared. The horses wouldn't know his voice, but he spoke to them as low as the rain allowed, see-sawing the reins in his approach. As soon as he was near enough, he set to work unharnessing the four Morgans. And then he heard the human moans.

Someone was in the ditch, and if Patrick could hazard a guess, it was the coachman. The man at the carriage door appeared to more likely be the owner of it. Patrick made quick work of the harnesses, taking the horses one by one to tie to nearby trees. He dropped his knapsack against a bush and hurried to the ditch to find the source of the moaning.

Whatever was going on inside the carriage, the owner seemed able-bodied and capable of handling. Patrick could only wonder who was traveling with him and hoped it wasn't children. But sure enough, half-covered in mud in the ditch lay the coachman, who must have been thrown from his seat when the carriage crashed. Patrick leaned over him, rain running off his cap.

"Where are you hurt, man?"

The creature pushed himself up to sit. "Everywhere. Head and foot, mostly, but it all hurts."

"Do you think it's broken or sprained?" Patrick asked, looking toward the mud-covered boot.

"Don't know. I'd guess the boot would have protected it, so more likely sprained."

"Can you try to stand? I don't know what's happened to the family. Is that your employer?"

"Yes, Mr. Wentworth. His wife and little daughter are with him. Help a man up. I think I can stand, but it hurts like the dickens."

"Let's take it easy." Patrick reached a hand out and mud squelched between them as he grasped the man's gloved palm. "No need to injure yourself further."

But the coachman tightened his grip and pulled himself to his good foot anyway. Lowering his injured foot to the ground caused another groan to pass his lips. Leaning heavily on Patrick, he allowed himself to be led to the protection of the trees, where Patrick deposited him on a large rock.

Patrick freed his canteen from around his torso and handed it to him. From the top of his knapsack, he pulled his blanket and settled it around the man's shoulders, taking note of the soggy linen collar and woolen broadcloth coat that revealed a salary that was probably higher than Patrick's.

"If you're not going to pass out, I'll go check on the situation with the others."

"I won't." The coachman shook his head, slumping against a tree. "Thank you."

8

"If in every step we take we see the proofs of the wisdom and grandeur of God, so do we that God made man in his own image."
- Elijah Lovejoy

Back at the carriage, Patrick found Mr. Wentworth extracting a girl around eight or nine wrapped in a large coat from inside.

"Can I help you, sir?"

The girl was crying, and Patrick ached at the sound.

"I think her leg's broken," the man said, pulling his daughter against his chest. Patrick caught sight of the wife in the carriage, blood trickling down her temple and staining her bonnet ribbons. "My wife has cuts and bruises, but nothing broken. The wheel looks irreparable. Do you know how far it is to town or the nearest tavern?"

"I don't. I'm merely a traveler like yourself. Could you take your daughter on one of the horses?"

Hesitation passed the man's face. "I've never ridden bareback and am reluctant to risk her safety. I can carry her if it isn't far."

"I'm afraid I wouldn't know unless I went on ahead. Your coachman seems to have sprained his ankle. Perhaps he'll ride ahead with me? I could take your daughter, if you're willing." He so hated when children had injuries, but no one had hurt this little girl on purpose, and her capable parents had her in hand. Glancing toward the horses, he wondered anxiously how quickly he could get her to help.

"No, I'll carry her." Mr. Wentworth eyed Patrick, a glint of suspicion in his eye. He probably didn't even want Patrick to take one of his horses for fear he wouldn't return. "Is Burns capable of riding?"

"I can ask."

Patrick offered a steadying hand to Mrs. Wentworth, who gingerly climbed out of the carriage, causing the vehicle to list further down the ditch. The rain left dark splotches on her abundant blue silk skirts, and she tugged her velvet jacket tighter around her torso. She joined her husband near the shelter of the trees, so Patrick returned to Burns.

Even through the dusky rain, the whiteness of the coachman's face was unmistakable. He shivered even under Patrick's blanket. "Mr. Wentworth seems intent on continuing to town on foot, although his daughter's leg is broken. Can you ride?"

"Possibly." Burns drew the word out. "This team isn't used to bareback riding, and there's the matter of mounting."

"It doesn't look like you can walk, and the carriage is out of the question. I could help you up and lead the other horses. Mr. Wentworth doesn't appear to be willing to let me ride ahead, and I'm not sure that I blame him. Which horse should I bring to you?"

Burns pointed one out, and with the help of Patrick's firm grip, he managed to swing up from the rock he'd been sitting on. The party started down the darkening road with Burns precarious on the horse, Patrick clasping the reins of the other three, and the trembling family following behind, the child tucked firmly against her father's chest.

"I'm Harold Wentworth, and I am indebted to you for your assistance," Mr. Wentworth said to Patrick.

Patrick glanced over, the words "You're welcome" slipping automatically from his lips as something dark and sour rose in his heart. What was he doing, spending his time and effort to help a ridiculously wealthy white man? For more years than he could count now, his life had been spent assisting enslaved and free Black people. The coachman was also white and in a prestigious employment, but was it possible that Mr. Wentworth's other help had darker skin? They were in a slave state.

There were so many in the world who needed assistance, people with greater needs, people without rights or advocates. Patrick never helped rich white people. Now prickles ran over his skin at the thought that in his instinctive reaction to help someone in need, he could be assisting a slave owner. Even if he wasn't one, the world was full of Mr. Wentworths who used their positions of power and influence to suppress the Black race. At best, they ignored the plight of slaves and freedmen in their cities; at worst, they caused great harm. All of them were sources of the injury and insecurity that Patrick worked regularly to rescue people from.

Clenching his jaw, Patrick tightened his grip on the reins as the memory of Salome's pained eyes and gritted teeth ripped through him. The relentless rain pounded against his skull, darkening his ability to reason through the strife in his heart. Never in his life had he felt guilty for assisting a person with colored skin. Not like he felt now.

Day 8, Widow Downer's tavern, Hancock, Maryland
Health: Well enough, though never more glad to be in a warm bed
Supplies used: Ham and beans, tooth powder, paid for room and board and a quarter to have my laundry washed after today's mud bath.
Wildlife: Did not pay attention to anything moving today.
Verse for the day: Acts 28:2 And the barbarous people shewed us no little kindness: for they kindled a fire, and received us every one, because of the present rain, and because of the cold.
Personal notes: I may have appeared to be a good Samaritan today because I helped someone in need, but inside, I was like the Levite whose judgmental heart led him to take a different route to avoid that particular sufferer. Just how unhealthy has my mind become? Jesus healed the rich, the poor, the oppressors, and the oppressed. But the thought of offering my assistance to a rich slave owner makes me ill.

The sun was bright in the Widow Downer's scrubbed windows when Patrick pushed out of bed. He certainly needed the sleep after yesterday, and there was no need to rush out the door this morning if his blankets hadn't finished drying. But they must have been positioned in front of a fire all night, because his folded laundry was in a brown paper parcel outside the sleeping quarters, waiting for him. His wool pieces were brushed clean, and his linen shirt was ironed. The sight broke his heart for whatever washerwoman had sacrificed her sleep for him. After dressing, Patrick moved a coin from his purse to his pocket for her.

Only Burns was at the breakfast table when Patrick descended with his knapsack. The coachman's foot was elevated on a pillowed chair across from him, and he appeared to be finishing off a plate of buckwheat pancakes. In the daylight, Patrick could see the bruises on his face and hands. He looked like he'd seen better days.

"How are you this morning?" he asked Burns as Mrs. Downer bustled in to pour him a cup of coffee. He turned his attention to the lovely middle-aged woman whose warm demeanor reminded him of Bridget. "Good morning, Mrs. Downer. I want to thank you for my laundry this morning. I wouldn't have expected it to be ready so soon. May I thank the washerwoman personally?"

"She's over caring for her baby at present, but I'll send her to you before you leave. Are you interested in pancakes?"

"Yes, please."

She topped off Burns's coffee before making her departure to the kitchen, and Burns answered his question.

"Parts of my body hurt that I didn't know I had, but I'll be good as new with a couple days' rest. Thank you again for coming to our aid."

The first thought in Patrick's mind was, "I would have done it for anyone else," and it stopped him. He would have too. Done it for *anyone* else except a wealthy Southerner.

"No need to thank me," he murmured instead. "Have you heard from the Wentworths? How are they faring?"

"The physician came last night and set Miss Wentworth's leg. I haven't seen them this morning, but Mrs. Downer took breakfast to their private room and told me they were resting. I suppose we'll be laid up here for a few days."

With such quick medical attention, Patrick had no doubt the girl would recover fully in time. "Where were you heading?"

"Salisbury, Pennsylvania. Mrs. Wentworth's father owns mills there, and she visits her parents every spring."

Patrick considered digging deeper about the family. It shouldn't matter. The thought that Mr. Wentworth might be unworthy of his assistance certainly shouldn't bother him. So he pressed his lips closed, keeping his questions inside.

When his bill had been paid and the washerwoman tipped, Patrick bid Burns goodbye without seeing the Wentworths again and pulled his knapsack onto his shoulders.

The view out Mrs. Downer's front door was stunning. Blue-gray mountains rose around him under a periwinkle sky dotted by cottony clouds.

Streams ran down the ditches alongside the turnpike, and down at the river, laborers unloaded wagonloads of coal onto boats. Patrick had to wait for a few wagons and stagecoaches to pass through the tollgate before he started on his way. Traveling on foot, he was allowed use of the road without expense.

Everything about the pleasant day stood in stark contrast to yesterday. With the rain gone, he could see for miles. The sour feeling from the previous night's quandary lingered, taking his attention from the picturesque surroundings. Was he wrong to help someone who normally experienced great comforts at the expense of others? Wasn't it right for a man to experience a fraction of the suffering that he caused other humans on a regular basis?

The correct answer came to mind immediately, given by Jesus when He was asked by his followers, "Who is my neighbor?" Replying with the story of the Good Samaritan, Jesus had all but stated that everyone God put across his path was his neighbor—even those with different political views. The answer chafed, irritating further with the series of memories playing in Patrick's mind of hurting, traumatized Black fugitives—including scores of children—who'd come to his home throughout the years for shelter. Surely Jesus didn't mean to include people who did *that* to others.

Glancing down at his hands, Patrick felt dirty for betraying his Black friends, for wasting his strength on someone so undeserving.

The sight of his hands triggered the thought of Jesus' nail-scarred ones.

"I suppose You wasted Your strength saving a bunch of undeserving sinners, huh?" he said aloud, a wry grin lifting the side of his mouth. "Thank You for that."

With a lighter heart, he straightened his shoulders, losing his breath again at the scenery all around him. He wasn't responsible for judging who was worthy of help. Colm was right. He needed to figure out how to lay down some of the unnecessary burdens he was carrying.

9

**"The atmosphere of slavery is an unnatural one
for Americans to live in." - Elijah Lovejoy**

*Day 10, Willison Stone House, Martin Mountain, Maryland
Health: Am feeling the effects of pushing too hard the last
two days, but am nearly to Cumberland. I should reach it by
early afternoon tomorrow and plan to stay and rest the
remainder of the day.*

*Supplies used: Tooth powder, 50¢ room and 50¢ supper. Shared the
midday meal with an old, half-senile traveler who stuck by my side like a
burr all day and insisted I partake of his jerky and dried cornbread.*

*Wildlife: Two whitetail deer together on the side of the road.
Hawks. A red-headed woodpecker.*

*Verse for the day: (Is it too soon to use this verse?) Isaiah 40:31
But they that wait upon the Lord shall renew their strength; they shall mount
up with wings as eagles; they shall run, and not be weary; and they shall
walk, and not faint.*

*Personal notes: I knew there was some lodging available along the
National Road before I left home but didn't expect the frequency of the
taverns. The wagoners know which to stop at and which to avoid. I may have
to start camping out, not because of a lack of options, but to save some coin.
I've been reluctant to give up the real beds, hot meals, and conversation the
taverns provide.*

Five days later, Patrick woke to the sound of birdsong—and something scratching near his head. He froze, feeling his blood drain away with his stopped heart. This was it. A mountain lion had found him, and he'd be dead before he could reach his gun. Or maybe a bear, because weren't mountain lions quieter than this?

He opened one eye, moving his head slowly until he spied a raccoon rooting around at the edge of last night's campfire. He'd eaten the last of the beans and ham Elly had sent, and now all the food that remained in his knapsack was jerky and dried fruit, which he intended to save for emergencies. They were safely tucked away in the knapsack under his head, leaving nothing for the raccoon to find.

Patrick sat up, relief warming his bones. Placing his palms against his lower back, he stretched, breathing deeply of the woodsy air. There really were some advantages to sleeping outside, but none of them involved actually sleeping well. The mountains were invigorating, and he felt accomplished for having slept alone outdoors for the first time.

He gingerly washed up and had a drink in a frigid stream before packing up the cloak and blanket he'd slept with. Last of all, he grabbed the handkerchief he'd tied around a tree, pointing in the direction of the road and guaranteeing his return to civilization. On the way down the mountain, he snacked on new hawthorn leaves and gorse flowers growing along his path, just as Hector had taught him. They didn't fill him up but would tide him over until the midday meal.

Back on the turnpike, the bustle of traffic soothed him. He was back among humankind, and he was safe again. He found himself following a colorful wagon he'd seen back in Cumberland. A tall, white-whiskered gentleman in a top hat and purple coat had a curious audience gathered on the street corner while he presented his cures for everything from dyspepsia to megrims. Now the wagon boasting *Doc Methuselah's Elixirs and Tinctures* rolled on, going forth to save the lives of the good people of Pennsylvania.

Patrick entertained himself, inventing new elixirs in his mind for Doc Methueselah to hawk. It felt like the old days of joking around the table with his young stepbrothers again.

"No need to nurse a nervous neck now! Prepare a pint of purple persimmon poison to protect your pancreas and promote a properly placed pelvis!"

Doc Methuselah had long since passed out of sight when Patrick returned to the present with the realization that he'd been walking along with a silly grin on his face for the better part of an hour, entirely fueled by his juvenile imagination. When was the last time he'd laughed at a brainless joke? Life had been far too serious for far too long to allow it, and even now he felt ashamed for having let his mind wander like a child. It had been enjoyable while it lasted, but today, he didn't need a distraction.

Patrick adjusted the cap on his head, tilting the brim to shade his eyes as he peered ahead on the road. The way he figured on his map, he only had ten miles to walk today before reaching the infamous limestone marker, the very thought of which quickened his heartbeat as well as his stride.

"Where ya going in such a hurry?" a wagoner called behind him.

Patrick turned and tipped his cap without breaking his stride. "Pennsylvania!"

"Climb aboard, and I'll take ya there."

He'd expect payment, money Patrick didn't want to spend. "I've got a good strong pair of legs here. It's just a few more miles, isn't it?"

"Not more than that, near the foot of Winding Ridge. Past the border is Major Paul's tavern, a good place to put grub in your gullet." He cracked his whip, the bells on his wagon clanged, and he moved past Patrick on the road.

At noon, Patrick stopped only to fill his canteen at a spring. The road was busy nearing two o'clock when he finally spied the marker on the side of the road ahead. He started up the Winding Ridge incline, stopping just short of the iron mile marker post driven into the ground beside a limestone rock carved with a large P. He stood unmoving, taking in the words on the iron marker.

State Line, Penna. 34-1/4 to Cumberland, to Frostburg, 23-1/4.

Traffic moved past him, wagoners and stagecoaches who saw this sign every day. It didn't hold anything close to the meaning for them that it did for him. And it didn't mean to him anything close to what it surely meant to the enslaved people who crossed this point—although most of them probably did so under the cover of darkness and away from the busy road.

Closing his eyes, taking a deep breath, and imagining what it must feel like for them, Patrick took a step and crossed the Mason–Dixon line.

He stood now in Pennsylvania, a free state.

Turning, he looked back the way he came.

Enslaved.

And then at his boots on Pennsylvania soil.

Free.

Free. What a word. What a powerful, powerful word.

He could not truly put himself in their shoes and feel what someone in a lifetime of bondage must feel standing here, but the lightening he felt must surely be a small taste of it.

Simply being away from the evil of slavery brought deep relief to his bones, and he could not wipe the smile from his face.

He didn't feel hunger and didn't rush on to Major Paul's tavern. It was enough for today just to have reached free soil, and he lingered by the limestone marker, one of hundreds stretching across the miles to denote the Mason–Dixon line. When he closed his eyes to impress it all into his mind, he could hear the Black church back home singing, *"Freedom, oh freedom . . ."* Oh what he wouldn't do to give both his enslaved and free friends this experience.

Break their bonds, Lord.

Christ had already broken their spiritual bonds. The Black church knew a freedom unencumbered by their chains in this world, but they ought to know physical freedom in this life too. True freedom, the kind that didn't leave a man with a reason to constantly look over his shoulder and which gave him the full rights of a citizen.

Words formed in his mind for a letter to Elijah Lovejoy, and he owed one to Hezekiah as well. Those thoughts were what eventually drove him from the state line to seek a table at the nearby establishment.

Patrick was still at the table, engrossed in his book after completing his letters, when the supper bell rang and a crowd of wagoners and stagecoach drivers swarmed around him. He glanced up at a suited gentleman who took the seat beside him.

The chap was clean-shaven, erect, his hands folded on his lap. He tilted his perfectly combed head toward the open book. "Is that a good book?"

Patrick closed it, revealing the cover embossed with *Pilgrim's Progress*.

"It is indeed." He felt dirty and tattered next to the gentleman whose toilet was similar to what Patrick's own had been not that long ago.

At every tavern along the way, his skin was tanner, his russet curls brighter, and his face more chapped. Soon he'd look like one of the wagoners.

"My mother's told me to read it, but I never have," the traveler said. "I rarely have time for novels."

Patrick smiled and slipped the book into his knapsack as the waiters came in with steaming platters of food. Some of the taverns used unique menus to win an edge over their competition while others merely focused on filling bellies. Regardless of which side this establishment leaned, the fried chicken set before him made his stomach growl.

His neighbor was talking politics with the drivers on the other side of him now, so Patrick tucked into his food, meditating on the pages he'd just read.

Christian had just started on his journey to the heavenly kingdom, so wearied of the heavy burden on his back that he took Worldly Wiseman's advice to turn off the path Evangelist had set him on and headed to the home of Legality and Civility to have his burden off. Why drag his burden all the way to the cross if he could get it removed now, in his own time?

In the end, Evangelist showed up and told him that no one was ever freed from burdens by Legality and to distrust anyone who directed him off the path or made the cross seem odious.

Dash it all. Patrick's burden wasn't the same as Christian's, who hadn't yet shed the weight of his sins and would go on to find salvation in the story—he felt burdened by his own inadequacy and the pain of the oppressed. But the relief for the burdens was the same. It was at the cross of Jesus Christ that he could lay down the burden he carried, the effects of slaveowners' sins.

Legality never removed burdens.

In the story, those who went to Legality for help were in danger of being crushed under his falling house. And wasn't that, more than a little, where Patrick had gone in the situation with the Wentworths? He'd raced straight to legalism, because that seemed easier than carrying the burden to the cross.

It was a long-grown habit, of course. One honed by years harboring bitterness against those who'd hurt his Underground Railroad guests, and then practiced to perfection in the senate.

If he could hold everyone else to his moral standard, they could all bypass the cross.

The fried chicken had lost its taste, and Patrick dropped the half-eaten drumstick to his plate. The Mason-Dixon line wasn't the point where he could find relief and have his burden cut from his shoulders.

It was the *cross*. It had been all along.

Day 20, April 7, West Brownsville, Pennsylvania, overlooking the Monongahela River

Health: I've developed a chest cough that has slowed me down & am grateful it's Sunday so I have an extra day to rest at Acklin's tavern, formerly run by an old soldier under Washington, a Mr. Owens.

Supplies used: Other than my emergency dried foods and cash, my consumable supplies are depleted and I must buy or forage what I need each day

Wildlife: An osprey nest on a bluff by the river

Personal notes: I was much moved today by a conversation with Mr. Acklin, following my stop at Fort Necessity two days ago, site of General Washington's only surrender. I have always found Washington's intelligence, humility, and devotion to his floundering country inspiring, and I was honored to stand on the same land where he fought. Mr. Acklin told me stories of the previous owner's service under Washington in the Revolution. He quoted Washington as once saying, "It is infinitely better to have a few good men than many indifferent ones." May I never be accused of being one of the indifferent ones.

Verse for the day: Proverbs 29:2 When the righteous are in authority, the people rejoice: but when the wicked beareth rule, the people mourn.

10

**"In the midst of so many enemies I have, it is true,
a good many friends." - Elijah Lovejoy**

Five days later, Patrick stepped off a ferry on the Ohio River onto the packed dirt of the state of Ohio. The tiny corner of Virginia he'd passed through was a beautiful piece of God's creation, but it had been painful to have to return to a slave state so soon. Now, all that was forgotten in the wonder of finally having arrived in the infamous west.

He went in search of Moses Rhodes's tavern at the recommendation of the ferryman, and sat down on his selected bed to examine the state of his boots. His boots hadn't held up as well as he'd hoped; already the soles were worn thin. His socks had holes, and he was due for a visit to the laundry, but his blouse had lasted well—being protected from the elements by his coat— and his trousers were sturdy.

The question of whether it was time to replace the boots now that he was entering the frontier coupled with the matter of which route he would take from here. The people he was interested in meeting were in southern Ohio, a path that would take him off the turnpike should he so choose.

Time was in great supply.

Patience, however, had always been scarce, and floating down the Ohio River to Cincinnati was tempting. Which brought to mind Passion and Patience, characters in *Pilgrim's Progress*. Patience was willing to wait for the good things in life, whereas Passion wasn't, and the prizes he claimed immediately were old and used up before Patience got his. Maybe rushing things wasn't the way to go. Patrick had chosen to walk for a reason, and he'd never get the opportunity again. He only had to get to Lovejoy before he ran out of hope altogether.

But first, boots.

He found Mr. Rhodes at the counter downstairs and waited for the entering crowd to pass through before posing his question.

"Could you tell me how far it is to Mount Pleasant?"

Mr. Rhodes cocked his dark head. "Not more than a dozen miles, I'd say. Half a day's drive."

Twelve miles north, entirely out of his way, but a detour that could be worth it if he didn't get lost.

"Do you ever go up that way yourself?"

Mr. Rhodes drummed his fingertips on the countertop. "I've been there in the past but haven't had reason to go in a long spell. What do you need up there?"

Patrick crossed his arms and leaned forward. "I'm wondering if Benjamin Lundy's store is still open."

"Well now, Lundy hasn't lived there in some time, but his store was carried on by the Quakers, last I knew. That was probably a couple of years ago. I reckon you could find whatever you need to buy either here or in Wheeling sooner."

But Patrick's old friend only sold goods made without slave labor or exploitation. If Lundy's store still existed and was this close, he might as well go buy a new pair of boots that he could wear with a clean conscience. The detour was worth the risk.

Patrick gave Mr. Rhodes his lopsided devil-may-care grin, his mind made up. "Thank you."

The dinner bell rang, and pushing off from the counter, he left to see about satisfying his appetite.

There was a sense about the Quaker home that told Patrick's gut he was in a fellow Underground Railroad house, and he found himself glancing around as if he could identify hidden doors and rooms. He couldn't explain how he knew, other than the fact that he, a stranger, had been welcomed in like a long-lost brother. Not since he'd left his community in Baltimore—and really, not even before then—had he felt the long exhale and complete ease of sharing a meal with like-minded friends.

He introduced himself to the clerk at the store as a friend and former assistant of Benjamin Lundy's and was received with joy and an invitation to stay over the Sabbath. Now, with a full stomach and heart, he leaned back in his chair at the table and listened to his host, Nathan Davis, share about life in Jefferson County.

"We've had an influx of former slaves make it across the Ohio and to our village in the past few years. Many choose to make this their final stop and end their journeys here. The healing's a long process, but when they experience the love of the Lord Jesus—real love for the first time, not just words—that's where their recovery begins."

"And ends," his soft-spoken wife put in.

"And ends." Nathan nodded. Nathan's brother Jacob and his wife were at the table, along with Nathan's oldest children, but all the little ones had been put to bed. The lantern burned low, and a fire flickered in the hearth at his back, occasionally fed and poked at by Jacob.

"How do the Negroes settle into society? Are they able to build a life here?" Patrick asked. The idea of healing and peace for former slaves seemed foreign, like a dream he'd always hoped for but never seen materialize. Imagine being the last stop on the Railroad and the place the passengers found a home!

"Certainly some struggle more than others. Our little community does what we can to give them a firm place to find their footing, but it's the Lord who does the work. They have pressure from Black leaders in the community to be good citizens, to work hard and not cause problems. Laziness, public drunkenness, and the like are disparaged, because any such instance reflects on their race as a whole. So they're good neighbors and we've found some to be sweet friends. They own farms and stores in the area, and many spend much of their time and income working to buy the freedom of family members still in bonds."

Patrick felt a burning behind his eyes and blinked quickly at the thought of each of his overnight visitors settled down on a homestead, caring for their families in peace.

"I—" He cleared his throat and took a chance, safely far from home. "In Baltimore, I did what I could with the Underground Railroad. I've met many on their way to freedom and know a number of free Blacks living in the city. But this—" Shaking his head, he swallowed hard. "I've not seen this side of it, where they go on to start new lives. I never hear from them again, of course." He shrugged. "It's something I've never been able to picture, and it's moving to consider it now."

Nathan dipped his head compassionately. "I wish I could say that their lives in freedom are easy. It's not usually anything close to the paradise they imagined, because their families are still broken apart. But they're *free*, Brother. No one's hurting them. No one's controlling them or kidnapping their children. Whatever you have done unto the least of these, you have done for our Savior. Every meal, every bed, every bit of dignity and respect and safety you offered, mattered to them and brought them to freedom."

"That's what love does." Jacob planted his elbows on the table and leaned forward, resting his beard on his clasped fists. "Love is a reflection of God Himself, who made each person His image bearer, regardless of skin color. He established our personhood, and it's in giving another those most basic human actions of eating, sleeping, conversing, and showing respect that we are saying, 'You are a *person*, and as such, you matter to God and to me.' "

Had he done it for love though? The question gnawed at Patrick. So often, he'd assisted fugitives with a greater sense of hate toward their masters burning in his heart than with actual love for them. They deserved to be free. Giving them what ought to be theirs anyway was just and right, but how often was his motive *love*?

He opted for changing the subject. "So the Negroes settling here aren't interested in creating a colony outside of America any more than the ones in Baltimore are?"

Everyone at the table laughed and shook their heads. Patrick smiled at their response. The large majority of those who opposed slavery still advocated for colonization rather than integrating Africans into society. It was generally agreed that the best thing for everyone would be to send the Negroes to live in a new colony somewhere else, such as Africa. The matter was a significant dividing issue among slavery opponents, and it was a relief to find that his present company opposed the idea as well.

"Colonization eventually became a source of division between Mr. Lundy and myself when I worked for his newspaper in Baltimore. Does he still advocate for it?"

His hosts glanced around at each other.

"We don't hear from him anymore," Nathan explained slowly. "I hear that even now, he is traveling around the country and down into Mexico in search of an appropriate location for a colony. I believe his intentions are good, but we simply can't agree. These slaves deserve to live in the country they built. Their sweat and blood is invested here. How distasteful would it be to toss them out when we have no further use for them?"

"I agree. I'm sorry to hear about Lundy. He's done so much to advocate for the Negro."

Patrick had been there once himself and understood why men like Lundy believed colonization to be a valid solution. The only problem was that everyone who thought it was a good idea wasn't Black. In all his years with the freedmen society and the Black church, he'd never met a Black person who wanted to move to an foreign, uncultivated land. And Nathan was right—they shouldn't have to.

Monday morning found Patrick reluctant to leave the haven of the Quakers' home, but he had his boots, new socks, a replenished food supply, and a destination to reach. There was no reason to impose on the hospitality of his new friends any longer. He tugged on the old boots that still had a bit of wear left in them and tied the new ones to his knapsack. Gathering up his hat, he stepped into the warm kitchen at first light and found Nathan in his shirtsleeves and suspenders at the breakfast table, newspaper in hand. His oldest son dropped a load of firewood in the woodbin, and Mrs. Davis labored over the hearth, amid the appetizing smells of frying meat and baking bread.

Nathan turned when he heard Patrick pull out the chair across from him. "Did you know about Birney?"

Glancing at the newspaper in his hand, Patrick saw the title *The Philanthropist*—the abolitionist newspaper that former slave owner James Birney published in southern Ohio.

"What about him? I was thinking about heading that way to meet him next."

"He moved *The Philanthropist* into Cincinnati last week. This is the first edition at his new location." He waved the paper at Patrick. Sure enough, the second line read, VOLUME 1. CINCINNATI, OHIO. FRIDAY, APRIL 15, 1836.

Patrick let out a low whistle. What was Birney thinking?

"Didn't they call a meeting of five hundred leading citizens to oppose abolition when he moved his family into town in January—and drowned him out when he stood to defend himself? What is he doing, moving his newspaper in now?"

"Cincinnati has always been so pro-slavery, they might as well be south of the Ohio River. You have to respect gumption like his. I heard him last month when he traveled around the state giving lectures, and he's a fair-minded, engaging speaker. You'll enjoy meeting him."

There was no question now. Patrick devoured the meal Mrs. Davis set before him, still anxious to get to Lovejoy. He would get there eventually. But with Lane Seminary and Birney both in Cincinnati? It was time to pull out his map and figure the quickest route south.

11

"Fortune has, in the main, hitherto looked unfavourably upon me since I left home, but I begin to hope for better things."
- Elijah Lovejoy

No thinking person could accuse Ohio of not having beautiful scenery or wonder what it was that had drawn so many pioneers to its valleys over the past hundred years. But as Patrick hobbled toward the hazy shapes of Columbus's buildings rising on the horizon, he would gladly trade every one of Ohio's endless farms for the relief of having his journey end.

A pike pounded into the back of his skull—that was how it felt—and his legs and back ached. The loneliness had attacked him full-force after leaving the Davises and had remained a constant companion over the past week. Daydreams of stagecoaches and steamboats flittered through his mind, and the thought of skipping the Cincinnati detour grew more tempting with every step.

Everything ever said about journeys being just as important as their destinations was hogwash. Why didn't Colm and Maisie talk him out of this harebrained idea? Didn't they care about him at all?

Columbus inched closer as his headache intensified. In Maryland and Pennsylvania, the road had been busy, full of other travelers to talk to and break up the monotony. Traffic was far more sparse in Ohio, and the scenery less diverse. The only company he had was his own mind, which, frankly, was terrible company. The Lord was there, but Patrick's mind felt too dark and muddled to pray.

Hoofbeats thundered in the distance, and a minute later, the Pony Express boy came galloping past. Patrick watched him retreat, amused at his hurry. Wouldn't it be something if a letter from his family just passed him, beating him to Columbus? Traffic picked up as he neared the town, which the pamphlets he'd read back home had estimated at nearly six thousand inhabitants.

Ten minutes later, a wagoner pulled alongside him. Patrick looked over at the man's greeting and saw the honest face of a very large, very Black man.

"Howdy. Can I offer you a ride?"

"No, thank you," Patrick responded automatically.

"It's free, and you look tuckered." The man handled the reins, keeping the horses back to a walk.

"I am rather, but I wouldn't want to be beholden—"

"If you'd be beholden to anyone, it would be to the good Lord for prompting me to ask and giving these here horses strength to pull you. Climb up." He halted the wagon, and Patrick offered him a smile before tossing his knapsack onto the seat.

"Thank you."

The wagoner waited for Patrick to settle in before clicking to the horses. "Westley Strother," he said in a mild tone. "Have you been to Columbus before?"

"No, sir. First time in Ohio, in fact. I'm Patrick Gallagher." He held his breath after sharing his very Irish name. Too often the Irish were the greatest antagonists of fellow Americans with darker skin. Mr. Strother either didn't mind or didn't notice, because his friendly smile didn't slip.

"I'll take you to my friends then. You appear to be needing some looking after."

"I'm quite all right," Patrick lied, then winced when the wagon jolted.

Mr. Strother laughed. "We'll get you some rest. Where are you walking?"

Patrick decided to tell the truth. "St. Louis, but I'd like to go down to Cincinnati and meet James Birney first."

"Is that so?" Mr. Strother turned, glancing up and down Patrick. "For positive purposes or nefarious ones?"

Talking to a Black wagoner gave Patrick a boldness to be honest that he hadn't been afforded for much of his journey. "Good ones. I'm a newspaper man myself, and I'm interested in talking to him in person."

"Heard 'e moved his newspaper to Cincinnati."

"That's what I hear."

"Just a few days before, there was riot in the Fourth Ward."

"There was?" That hadn't been in the paper Nathan had, and Patrick hadn't seen many since. Hadn't seen much besides widely spaced farms for the past hundred miles. "How bad was it? Is that where he lives?" His heart rate increased, fear for Birney's safety paramount. "What happened?"

"Not where he lives. Those are Black streets. How bad it was depends on who you ask, I suppose. Homes and businesses burned down, residents hunted down and beaten."

Patrick's jaw spasmed, his headache pulsing harder. "It takes a certain kind of coward to attack peaceable citizens like that. That's horrible."

"It sure is."

Silence fell between them, because there was nothing more to say. The doldrums of Ohio's wide open spaces had fled away in a moment. Patrick pressed his eyes closed in an attempt to ease the headache.

"The leading men of the city ought to act against mob violence." The *Philanthropist* editorial came to mind, and Patrick quoted, " 'Whenever any government shall make a practice of delivering over, in any case whatever, to the management of lawless and infuriated mobs, not only the "property," but the personal safety and lives of those it should protect, no great political sagacity is required to see that its own days are nearly numbered. '"

Mr. Strother made a growling noise in the back of his throat. "I beg pardon, sir, but it's those same leading men who are supporting and even setting off the mobs in their back rooms."

He was right, of course, but the idea that cities in even free states were led by slavery supporters and racists turned Patrick's stomach sour every time. He'd taken this walk to try to escape this kind of anger. To work it out, shake it out, or at least outrun it. But here he was in the middle of Ohio, still wishing he could hit something.

"How about these parts? Do central Ohioans lean more toward abolition than those in the South?"

"From what I've seen." Mr. Strother turned his team down a busy thoroughfare in the center of town. "Cincinnati has an abolitionist society too. Seems to me, however, that the one here in Columbus doesn't need to fight so hard for the right to exist."

He pulled up at a fine home situated next to a cleared parcel of ground, littered with stacks of building materials. "Looks like they're moving ahead with building the new church. I'll take you in to my friends, and then this load needs delivered before I find supper."

"It's kind of you to bring me here, Mr. Strother. It's been a pleasure to meet you."

Inside the foyer, Mr. Strother was greeted by the white family as if he were a long-lost friend. Jason Bull took Patrick's knapsack from him, immediately taking charge of the situation in a way that made Patrick identify him as the kind of person he'd want to have around in an emergency. He was a stocky man with a wide face and untamed hair, significantly taller than his trim, plain-faced wife.

"I'm suspicious that our brother here needs a good bed and some medicinal remedies," Mr. Strother announced. "He looked about done in when I found him on the road."

"Oh, I'm well enough," Patrick protested, his vision swimming. "Though I won't turn down the offer of a bed and will pay for all my expenses."

Mr. Bull led Patrick up the stairs, still carrying his knapsack for him. Down in the foyer, they could hear Mr. Strother speaking to Mrs. Bull, making excuses for supper on account of his load that still needed to be delivered.

Patrick remained oblivious in the bed for the next two days. Whenever he awoke to relieve himself, he found hearty broths and cups of tea and ale by his bedside with the previous dishes cleared away, but he didn't see anyone come or go. By the third day, he felt well enough to sit up in bed to read *Pilgrim's Progress*, about Christian's refreshment at the hands of Discretion, Prudence, Piety, and Charity in the Palace Beautiful. Between the Davises' and Bulls' hospitality, the portion felt timely, and once again, the anger faded.

There were evil men in the world. There were ignorant men in the world. But there were also very good men, if one opened their eyes to see them. He was not alone in his crusade against the persecution of Negroes in America.

The book fell to the coverlet as Patrick half dozed, the story of the prophet Elijah in the cave coming to mind. Elijah had reached the end of himself, too, insisting, "I, even I, am the only one left who hasn't forsaken God's covenant."

But God had fed him and reminded him that he had seven thousand others still devoted to Him. As lonely as Patrick's work felt, the Davises and Bulls were a reminder that he was only one link in the chain, and nothing began or ended with him.

By Sunday, Patrick felt human again, having bathed, shaved, and attired himself in freshly laundered clothes. The blisters on his feet had almost healed, and whatever illness had taken over him was a thing of the past. He was glad to remain another day with the Bulls, attending the Methodist church led by Jason Bull's father.

Well enough to be a contributing conversationalist, he spent the afternoon in the parlor, visiting with the family and sharing stories from his time on the road.

"I was hoping to see Mr. Strother again before I leave," he stated as he watched the fire lick the logs in the hearth.

"He was sorry to miss you too," Mrs. Bull replied, her warm features falling. "He expressed his reluctance to leave without speaking with you again, but we didn't want to disturb your rest." She shifted a navy and cream knitted shawl back onto her thin shoulder.

"Are you still heading to Cincinnati next?" Mr. Bull asked.

Patrick nodded resolutely. "If all goes well, I'll stay over there several days. By my map, it looks like it will take about a week to get there."

"A week on foot sounds about right if you take the turnpike through Dayton. They're building a more direct road from Cincinnati to here, but not more than twenty miles is finished. There's a wagon path along there, but I'd recommend the turnpike."

Patrick retired to his cozy room for the last time, reluctant to face the loneliness of the road again. He wondered about the great southern Ohio city and what awaited him there. Violent mobs, burning tenements, abolitionist newspapermen, meatpacking plants, seminary dropouts turned schoolteachers, a major coordinated exodus of the Black community to Canada . . . whatever he found there, it was sure not to be boring.

It also had a high chance of adding fuel to the passions in his chest that his cross-country migration had failed to soften. Was he ready to come face to face with it all?

12

**"I am now 250 miles from home, in a land of strangers
and but 80 cents in my pocket." - Elijah Lovejoy**

The road was quiet on the third day out of Columbus when a yawn broke that felt like it would split Patrick's head in two. The way he figured, he had covered about two-thirds of the distance between Columbus and Dayton, and rumor was there was an old Indian mound not far from the road. Well, if he was going to come all this way, he might as well see what there was to see, and Indian mounds promised to be interesting.

The late afternoon sun was blinding in the western sky, causing perspiration to bead under his cap despite it being early May. Another mile passed before a small wooden sign appeared by the side of the road, peeling paint directing the way to Knob Prairie Mound Farm. Tugging his cap lower to shade his eyes, he turned off to follow wagon tracks rutted into prairie grass. In just a mile, a lone conical-shaped hill rose before him, topped by a large tree. Humor quirked his mouth into a half-grin. The only thing interesting about the mound was its shape; the size was hardly worth going out of the way for.

He walked briskly around the mound and then climbed to the top. The view was nothing compared to the mountains he'd been in a few weeks ago, but at least he could lay claim to seeing Indian mounds now.

His sightseeing complete, Patrick dropped to the ground, inhaling a piece of beef jerky and the strawberries he'd picked that morning for a long-overdue dinner. After a refreshing draught of water from his canteen, he sprawled out with his knapsack as a pillow. If he could just rest for a few minutes, he'd be good for several more miles before stopping for the night. These days, he camped when the weather was fine and nightfall had him far from civilization, and he stopped at taverns whenever day's end brought him to a town.

He woke to the click of a gun cocking accompanied by a kick in his ribs. Patrick's eyes jolted open to human shadows moving in the dusk.

"Grab the bag," the man with the gun growled without taking his eyes from Patrick. Before Patrick could slap his hands over his knapsack, it was wrenched from under his head, and he landed on the soft grass.

"Hey!" He scrambled to his feet, which was stupid. The gun owner waved the rifle Patrick had forgotten about in his face as his arms were grabbed from behind, twisting his shoulders painfully.

"Leave me alone!" Anger more than fear rose in him, and his ribs throbbed from the kick. There were only three men that he could make out—the leader with an old brown wide-brimmed hat and a faceful of whiskers standing before him, the one he couldn't see tying his hands from behind, and the beefy man on the ground going through his knapsack, his face blocked by his hat. Patrick felt his Colt leave its holster as whoever was behind him helped himself to it.

There was no light but the fading sun, but the pillager made quick work of finding Patrick's moneypouch and holding it up.

"What else has he got?" Whiskers leveled his gun between Patrick's eyebrows, freezing him in place.

"Just clothes and a couple books."

"Check all the seams and pockets."

Patrick held his gaze without flinching, but dread swirled inside at what he knew would happen next. Sure enough, his second stash of hidden cash was found, and his captor released him from behind, pushing him to the ground.

"Let's go."

There was nothing to do but watch their shapes race across the field until they were swallowed up by the night. There wasn't much appeal in getting shot if he tried to pursue them without his gun, and he felt grateful to have escaped worse harm. No need to go searching for injury.

Loosening the knot on his hands was the work of a minute, clearly tied by someone who had what he wanted and was simply looking to slow him down. Patrick shook his arms out with a sigh. His belongings were scattered over the ground, but his matches were in his pocket. How did his pockets escape getting searched? By making everything of value much easier to find, apparently.

Lighting a match, he used the light to sift through his things on the ground in search of a candle. It wasn't immediately to be found, so when the match burned down, he lit another one. On his fourth match, he found the broken candle rolled away from everything else and lit it. With his free hand, he stuffed his clothes, books, papers, and food back into the knapsack, his heart sinking as the reality of the situation settled over him. There were a couple dollars that he always kept in his boot and a few more sewn into the lining of his coat for this very reason, but the entirety of his savings meant to be used for housing in St. Louis was gone.

The thought wrenched deeper than his arms had a few minutes ago. It was a good thing he hadn't sold his Baltimore house before leaving or the thieves would have that money too. There was no way he could get to St. Louis without picking up odd jobs on the way now, and he'd arrive destitute.

He could only pray that his gear and health wouldn't give out before then.

"Oh, Lord." The prayer came out in a defeated whisper. "Why do the wicked prosper?"

Pushing to his feet, he lifted the knapsack and threw it over his shoulder. There was no hope of making it to a town this late, and he had no interest in camping alone in this countryside with robbers about. If he could make it to a farmhouse inhabited by upright citizens and not the men who robbed him, he could report the theft and hopefully find company for the night. Patrick scrubbed his hand down his face and shook his head at the darkness. Holding his broken candle out, he peered along the wagon track back toward the road to Dayton.

Patrick struggled against the strong arms holding him back, feeling the click of metal handcuffs tightening around his wrists as the first lash of a whip came down on the bare back of the Negro woman in front of him. The one he'd just been smuggling to freedom before highwaymen jumped them, revealing themselves as slave catchers. A strangled sound broke out of his throat and he thrashed against his captors.

The blanket flew off of his bed, and he sat up as the scene disintegrated into the air.

His eyes fell closed and he expelled a soul-deep sigh, rubbing his temples in an attempt to scrub the memory from the edges of his mind. How he hated that dream. If only it were just a dream.

Something moved against his skin, and he flicked a tiny black bug from his arm onto the scratchy blanket covering his legs. His fiftieth night on the road was over, spent in a rather disappointing inn too near to the Reading meatpacking factories. It was time to get out of this crib and on the road, away from the horrible smells permeating the neighborhood and the dreams plaguing him. Cincinnati was in sight, and today, he'd finally arrive in the Queen City of the West . . . with only a few dollars in his pocket.

Deciding to forgo parting with any of his remaining money for breakfast at the questionable dining room, he was still half awake when he bid the little Irish landlady good day and exited onto the street as golden daylight blossomed over the hills. It really was a damnable shame what the meat plants had done to this place. Breathing through his mouth in an attempt to avoid the smells, he tiptoed down the rutted street, sidestepping suspiciously dark puddles. It was probably too late to avoid a bug infestation. Every little twitch or brush of his clothing had him scratching at the multitude he had surely picked up overnight.

Hopping and smacking erratically, he made his way to a wide thoroughfare leading over forested hills into the city until the smell of butchered hogs was swallowed up by the black smoke of steamboats and coal furnaces and the droppings of horses and free-roaming cows.

Tree-lined streets ushered him past tri-story brick buildings hosting every kind of business and shop. Jangling harnesses, creaking wheels, thudding freight, protesting animals, human shouts, singing laborers, and belching steam-powered machines welcomed him into the largest city he'd seen since Baltimore. It was nothing like the cities Patrick knew. For one thing, there was a disproportionate lack of Black people on the streets. They were everywhere on Baltimore streets, driving carts and carrying laundry and tending animals, but Cincinnati appeared to be very white.

It was late afternoon now, and he'd found food at a wagon stand several miles back but hadn't come away with a recommendation for lodging in the city. Since he didn't have to think about it yet if he didn't want to, he followed the directions of a hackney driver to a pastoral lot nestled in the green dales of Walnut Hills.

Patrick eased the knapsack from his shoulders and gazed around at the stately classically designed campus buildings and picturesque lawn. To think that this location captured the eyes of the country just a couple of years ago for its bold and controversial slavery debates. It didn't matter whether the participants were for or against slavery, they did what no one else was doing at the time: talking about it. Publicly.

He'd scanned every newspaper he could get his hands on at the time, curious as to what Lyman Beecher, the president of this institution, had to say on the matter. Dr. Beecher was a well-known colonizationist who worked hard to maintain unity in his school. His efforts to placate both sides had pleased no one.

Now Patrick peered around the still campus of Lane Theological Seminary, curious if he would get a glimpse of the famous theologian. A door clicked, and he turned as a lone student left a tall building and made his way down the path. Noticing Patrick trespassing, he hesitated before diverting from his route.

Once again, Patrick was self-conscious of his dusty, road-weary appearance as the student neared. His thick brown hair was combed, his face clean and white, and he looked at Patrick with inquisitive eyes. The seminarian was so young, and Patrick felt so very old.

"Can I help you find something?"

Patrick shook his head, relaxing with a smile. "No, but thank you. I just arrived from out of town and wanted to see the site of the famous debates. Play the tourist, I suppose."

"Ah. I wasn't here at the time, but I can show you the chapel where they were held. None of the current students were around then."

Patrick hadn't thought about the difference a couple of years would make in a student body. "Do you know where any of the participants live? The abolitionist ones, I mean. I hope to meet some while I'm in the area."

The young man studied Patrick. "What do you want them for?"

Oh good heavens, he'd been running his mouth again without remembering where he was. Being in a free state—and on a seminary campus—was hardly an indicator of one's values.

"I'm sorry. My name is Patrick Gallagher, and I've long been impressed by the stand the students took. Didn't nearly all of them side against slavery by the end of the debates?"

"Ellis Dinsmore." The young man reached out and shook his hand.

"Against slavery and colonization as well. Nearly the whole class left the seminary that year and ended up down in the Fourth Ward, where they live and work among the free Blacks. Some transferred to Oberlin, and others are on a lecture tour with Theodore Weld, the abolitionist who started the debates."

"The whole class left? Why?" Patrick had only known about Theodore Weld and that some of the students had withdrawn, not all.

Ellis looked around as if to ensure that no one was within hearing distance. "It was—" He took a breath and started again. "The trustees forbade the students from further discussions of slavery or membership in anti-slavery student organizations, claiming it distracted them from their studies. The students withdrew en masse."

Patrick stared at him, stunned both by the trustees' absurdity and the students' decisive action.

"Dr. Beecher tried to appease the students, but it was too late," Ellis hurried to explain. "Enrollment numbers have been very low since."

It begged the question of whether Ellis was here because he sided with the trustees. Patrick tried to think of a way to obtain the information diplomatically, but it really wasn't his business.

Ellis bobbed his head from side to side. "I'm here to keep a promise to my father," he said as if he'd read Patrick's question on his face. "I don't think the Lane Rebels were wrong to leave." He inhaled, conflict playing out on his face as his gaze traveled unseeing beyond Patrick. "Sometimes you choose to do what you have to do to get where you need to go, even if you don't agree with everyone in leadership. It's not looking the other way as much as it is having a different purpose to which you need to adhere."

"You don't owe me an explanation," Patrick said to reassure him. "If you're where God has you, then everyone else doesn't have to understand."

Ellis refocused on Patrick's face. "Thank you," he said after a moment. "It's myself who doesn't always understand, I think. Well, come along, and I'll show you the chapel before I go to supper. Where are you staying while you're in town?"

"I don't know yet," Patrick admitted as he matched the boy's stride. "I'd like to find somewhere inexpensive where I can stay for a week or two. But not . . . too inexpensive," he added at the thought of last night's accommodations.

On the far side of the campus, a pair of men walked toward the building Ellis had come from, but otherwise the seminary was quiet. Ellis turned pensive eyes on Patrick. "Normally I'd take friends to my mother's, but it's a ways north, outside of Reading."

Patrick worked not to shudder, feeling bugs crawl all over his skin again. "I just came from there. It's kind of you to mention it, but I would like something closer to the center of the city, if possible."

"There's a boardinghouse owned by a widow of good repute, if you want a recommendation." He climbed the stairs to a white chapel building and lifted the door latch.

"Thank you." Patrick stepped through the door Ellis held open into a dim room with rows of pews and a pulpit at the front.

They were silent for a moment together, taking in the room and the importance of it.

"They weren't really debates, in that no detractors spoke," Ellis said, his voice soft with reverence. "The meetings were held to discuss the two questions—whether the people of slaveholding states ought to abolish slavery immediately, and whether the beliefs of the American Colonization Society and its supporters make it worthy of patronage. They were held every evening over the course of eighteen days. It caused a firestorm in the city, and we talked of nothing else for months."

"For me as well. I have a dream to meet Theodore Weld."

"Everybody was there," Ellis went on. "James Birney. Dr. Beecher and his children. Dr. Bailey, Mr. Staunton, and Mr. Stowe—he married Dr. Beecher's daughter this year, you know. People came from all over the community. Several speakers shared convincing arguments that the enslaved do desire and are capable of freedom, even those who work for kind masters. Terrible stories were told about things they endure in captivity."

Patrick appreciated the boy's knowledge, but he felt impatient at hearing everything he already knew repeated.

"I won't keep you long, but . . ." He gazed around the quiet room, then gestured to the pews. "I'm going to take a moment."

Ellis stepped back, and Patrick moved up the aisle and slid into a pew with an overwhelming desire to pray. Clasping his hands into a fist, he leaned his elbows on his knees, imagining the moving stories and powerful words spoken in this room. It would have been amazing to have been there.

Lord, give Your people boldness to continue these public conversations about what's right, the way the Lane students did.

The thought of Ellis's supper waiting kept his prayers brief, but his heart remained heavy with the burdens of those still in bonds as he stepped out again into the fresh air.

"If you direct me to the boardinghouse, I can find it on my own. You've been so patient already."

Ellis studied him thoughtfully. "It would give me an excuse to see my friends there. It's not fancy, but the staff will take excellent care of you. That I can assure you."

It sounded like the kind of place one could go to escape from loneliness burning through their soul, and Patrick jumped at the chance to forget his for a few days. "It sounds like they must be believers."

"Oh, I know some of them definitely are. It's about three miles down into the city, so I'll grab a hired hack."

Patrick didn't protest as he tugged his knapsack on and followed Ellis's long strides off the seminary campus.

13

"Of all sins, it seems to me that the sin of unbelief is the most dishonouring to God." - Elijah Lovejoy

The setting sun illuminated the city spread before them with the great Ohio River snaking beyond as the buggy jolted down the steep road toward downtown. Cincinnati appeared to be built on terraces stairstepping up from the river, which curved dramatically toward the metropolis at this juncture.

Ellis cheerfully talked about his city for the thirty minutes it took before the hired driver stopped outside a three-story brick inn in a neighborhood overlooking the river. Patrick paid the driver before Ellis could and stepped around a rooting pig on his way to the front door.

The Black maid who answered Ellis's knock wore a smart gray work dress similar to what Patrick's sister Hannah might wear and smiled shyly when she saw Ellis. "Good evening, Mr. Dinsmore."

"Good evening, Mary. I brought you all a boarder. You have room?"

" 'Course we do. Come in. Miss Rachel's upstairs, but I can take your bag."

"Oh." Patrick blinked at her. "I can carry it. It's heavy."

A middle-aged Black man with round cheeks and long sideburns came down the hall from the back of the house, bringing the stench of a stable on his person. "Ellis! Good to see you. How have you been?"

"I'm well," Ellis said with a grin, reaching out to shake his hand. "Mr. Gallagher, this is Uncle . . . I mean, Charles—"

"Everyone calls me Uncle Charles. Welcome!"

"Thank you." Patrick relaxed at his friendliness. "Patrick Gallagher. I ran into Mr. Dinsmore when I stopped at the seminary and—"

"Beautiful campus, isn't it? Well, let's get you settled, because it's about suppertime. You're staying to eat, Ellis, aren't you?" Uncle Charles hoisted Patrick's knapsack without hesitation. "Which room, Mary?"

"Well, Miss Rachel is up there and can direct you, but the east room and blue room are both ready at least, and the east room is furthest from the missus. But Uncle Charles—"

Patrick had started to follow him, but both halted to listen when Mary put a staying hand on Uncle Charles's arm.

"Do be quiet, especially going up the stairs. You know the missus don't handle the clomping too well, and keep your voice down."

A guilty grimace crossed Uncle Charles's face, as if he'd forgotten. "She's taken to her bed again?"

"Her girls be attending her. Well, you know the rest. And your voice do carry something frightful in this house."

Uncle Charles gave her a chagrined look and put his finger to his lips. Motioning to Patrick to follow, he tiptoed up the stairs, leaving Patrick's questions about the bedridden mistress unanswered. They reached the second story as a Black woman close to Charles in age quietly stepped into the carpeted hall and clicked a bedroom door shut. Her hair was pinned up under a net, and she wore a simple work dress with a generous apron tied over it. Uncle Charles waited for her to reach them, as if waiting for orders.

"We have a new boarder here, Rachel. Where should I put him?"

She pointed the opposite direction from where she came. "With Mrs. Markland down, it's best he go in the east room. Are you a very quiet tenant, sir?"

"Mr. Gallagher," Uncle Charles informed her above a whisper as he eased down the hall.

Patrick didn't know how to respond. He'd never been asked in his life if he was a quiet person, but he felt rather confident that his sisters would answer in the negative.

"I can try to be."

"I'm afraid Mrs. Markland has taken one of her spells, and we all need to do our best to keep the house as quiet as possible until it passes.

I hope it won't be a problem."

"No, I can—I can stay quiet." What kind of weak woman demanded her staff run her business and stay silent while she took to her bed?

Rachel ushered him into the room furthest down the hall, having passed no fewer than four other rooms on the way. Patrick took in the simple wood furnishings and the thick quilt on the bed and instinctively nodded his approval. Everything in the house appeared very clean and in good condition, although not expensive or frivolous.

"Will this do?" Rachel asked.

"It's perfect, thank you." It was just the type of place to suit him, other than accommodating the delicate owner down the hall, from whom he was happy to be so far removed.

"Supper is in ten minutes. We keep a strict schedule here. How long do you plan to stay?" Rachel pointed to the corner for Uncle Charles to deposit the knapsack before looking to Patrick for the answer.

"I'm thinking a week or two. I am not sure exactly." That depended on how quickly he could find work.

Rachel clasped her hands. "I'm Rachel Williams, and I'll handle your payment and go over the meal schedule and house rules after supper. We hope you enjoy your stay, Mr. Gallagher. I'm sorry your introduction was less than ideal, but it just happened at a challenging time." Her face was lined, probably with the burdens of caring for her difficult mistress.

"Not at all." It wasn't her fault, after all. "Would it be possible to obtain a bath sometime while I'm here?"

"Charles can draw you one anytime you need it," Rachel said, turning her first affectionate smile on the man, who nodded agreement with a grin of his own. The look they shared revealed a familial relationship of some sort.

Rachel backed to the door. "We'll see you downstairs for supper in a few minutes then." Uncle Charles tiptoed after her, and Patrick painstakingly shut the door slowly and quietly. Hopefully Ellis decided to stay for supper and wasn't feeling abandoned by the guest he'd brought to the door.

Patrick slid out of his coat as he approached the washbasin and mirror, finding a still browner and more weathered reflection than he'd last seen. He undressed to the waist, making quick work of cleaning all the parts he could see and pulling on the clean blouse in his knapsack. A shave would have to wait, and there wasn't much he could do in a couple minutes about the mass of curls that was even longer and more tangled than usual. But at least he didn't find any bugs during his toilet.

He tied his cravat and gave his coat a few quick brushes before pulling it back on and slipping his nearly empty purse into his pocket. Holding his breath, he carefully opened the door. His eyes stayed fixed on the shut door on the other end of the hall as he worked his way to the stairs, ensuring that no floorboards creaked on the way. It wasn't until he was down in the front hall before he felt he could breathe again. And all for an invisible businesswoman he'd never met? Good grief.

Thankfully, Ellis was standing in the dining room along with other boarders. Another Black girl assisted Mary in bringing dishes from the kitchen, and Rachel was in and out with an exacting eye, ensuring everything was perfect. Uncle Charles was nowhere in sight, but at least one additional female voice came from the kitchen, talking to Rachel.

Patrick made the rounds meeting the other boarders, gathering their names and origins. There was a married Black couple, a white itinerant preacher and his fourteen-year-old son, and two single men in their twenties traveling together.

"Mrs. Markland is unable to join us tonight," Rachel told Mrs. Adams, the only female boarder. Her tone was apologetic. "If you'll excuse me, I'll prepare a tray to take up to her and the girls."

"Give her my regards." Mrs. Adams, a long-faced woman probably a few years older than Patrick, pushed her eyebrows together in real concern. "Do let me know if I can help with anything."

Rachel nodded in response, glancing at the girl who was filling the final water glass from a pitcher. When the task was finished, she quietly exited, and Rachel announced supper.

After taking a seat between the minister and Ellis, Patrick bowed his head for the reverend's blessing. At the "Amen," he looked around the table and exhaled.

He'd made it. Other than occasional trips to Washington, D.C., he'd never been outside of Maryland, and now here he, Patrick Gallagher, was in Cincinnati, Ohio—a place he'd only ever dreamed about. First thing in the morning, he'd get out to explore the city and start tracking down famed crusaders of their shared cause.

It was getting old, sitting in Giant Despair's dungeons in Doubting Castle, having long since lost sight of his friend Hopeful. Maybe he could gather notes from these fellow crusaders for how they escaped the giant and maintained their joy in the face of impossible odds.

At the very least, he'd tell them that their work mattered. If his own battle was in any way the normal experience, maybe they needed to hear it too.

14

"I know that I have the right freely to speak and publish my sentiments." - Elijah Lovejoy

The bedroom door creaked the next morning when Patrick opened it, and he winced despite himself. It hardly mattered if it did creak if the shout he'd made in his nightmare had been vocalized. He'd woken up the second after it happened and really couldn't be sure, but if he did utter it aloud, it would have been enough to awaken the entire house.

He froze at the sight of the open doorway at the other end of the hall. His eyes remained fixed on the mysterious cavern as he eased toward the stairs. The dressing table and lamp visible inside were much like the ones in his room, but heavy curtains over the windows blocked all light from outside. How oppressive.

A light smattering of voices reached his ears, and then two Black girls appeared in the doorway. They stopped, staring at him with big eyes. They couldn't be older than ten, and wore plainly adorned but bright matching dresses despite the three-inch difference in their heights, their hair in tight matching braids. Well, he had been staring first.

"Good morning," Patrick said with a friendly smile, but the girls didn't smile in return. "Are you coming my way?"

Not wanting to scare them, he set into motion down the stairs. The bedroom door clicked shut, and little footsteps behind him indicated he was being followed. At the bottom of the stairs, he turned to give them another smile, and they froze on their stair, blinking silently at him.

"Well, have a good day," he offered.

He entered the dining room, where some of the boarders had already gathered around a breakfast buffet, and the girls went through to the kitchen, setting off pleased exclamations that told him they were well received there.

Patrick looked around for Uncle Charles to thank him for the bath, but the sun was already rising and he was nowhere to be seen. A newspaper sat on the corner of the table, so he picked it up, and over buttered toast, early strawberries, and a bracing cup of coffee, read of the battles in Texas. It seemed too early to go calling, so after breakfast, he took his Bible and journal into the parlor to pass a quiet hour.

Day 52, Mrs. Markland's boardinghouse, Cincinnati, Ohio

Health: Physically well. Spirits higher than they have been for some time.

Supplies used: $2 room and board!! I have to find work TODAY— and maybe a cheaper boardinghouse.

Wildlife: The housewives surrounding us released their cows out their front gates into the street this morning to join the roving chickens and pigs. What in the world?

Verse for the day: Proverbs 17:1 Better is a dry morsel, and quietness therewith, than a house full of sacrifices with strife.

Personal notes: I do not know who Mrs. Markland is, but she must be terrifying, the way these people bend over backward to accommodate her.

The city was noisy with voices, moving freight, and clattering wheels by the time Patrick stepped out the door onto the broad street. Cincinnati had such wide roads, they really could almost accommodate the menagerie roaming them.

Slapping his cap on his head, he squared his shoulders, inhaled with contentment, and set off to explore. The busyness of the river drew him. Walking parallel with the wharves, he counted ten steamboats at dock and more Black laborers than he'd seen anywhere else in the city.

He meandered west, where a pillared building with a cupola and stone edifice caught his eye, looking out of place with the architecture around it. A memory ignited—he'd read about this in his pamphlets. It must be Trollope's Bazaar, built by a British woman who had spent some years in Cincinnati and then written a scathing memoir about it. He was curious, but not enough to offend Cincinnati by going inside it.

Leaving the river, he headed into the heart of the lower level of the city. His pulse quickened when after an hour of roaming the streets, he finally found the clapboard sign he was looking for: Anti-Slavery Office. Patrick didn't waste any time reaching for the door latch and heading up the stairs to the second story.

Two men stood together at the type cabinet; the printer wore a leather apron over his clothes and was bent over the drawers, selecting letters for the composing stick in his hand. The other was dressed like a gentleman, standing with his back to Patrick and waving a stack of papers, which he appeared to be speaking to the printer about. He turned when the printer tipped his head to acknowledge Patrick's presence.

"How can I help you?"

He was obviously a busy man to be interrupted in the middle of the day. Patrick well remembered the pressure of the paper's deadline each week and the long hours required to meet it. Perhaps he should come back at closing time rather than barge in like this.

His step backward was a nonverbal apology. "Mr. Birney. I'm Patrick Gallagher of Baltimore, an abolitionist and . . . newspaperman." His head bobbed sideways. "Hoping to return to newspapering soon. I was on my way across the country and was inspired to stop and gain an introduction."

His legs ached at the memory of how many miles he'd come out of his way to meet this man, and he silently prayed that it would be worth it. To his relief, Mr. Birney's face lit up immediately. His light brown sideburns peppered with gray almost stretched to his chin, and his parted hair sported a little wave. He was not a large man for the size of his reputation around the States, but his eyes looked pleasant, like the kind of person one would want to know more.

"A joy to meet you. What papers did you work with in Baltimore?"

"Mr. Gwynn's *Gazette* and later Benjamin Lundy's *Genius*. I went into legislature after that, so it's been a couple years now, but I read your pamphlet on colonization last year and appreciated it deeply." He wished he could communicate how stepping into the office had bloomed an ache inside his chest to return to the profession. Had he missed it this much all along, and was the thought of donning a printer's apron again part of what influenced him to take this trip and pursue Lovejoy?

Mr. Birney tucked his papers under his arm and approached the counter separating him from Patrick. The printer continued with his work but didn't conceal his eavesdropping.

"If you have time after work sometime this week, I would be honored to meet with you."

"I would be happy to make time," Mr. Birney said with enthusiasm that convinced Patrick of his sincerity. "Where are you staying?"

The question reminded Patrick of his errand to find a cheaper place to lodge. "I'm at Mrs. Markland's boardinghouse for now . . ."

Mr. Birney's brow furrowed. "Here in the city?"

"Yes, in the First Ward, I think."

"Oh, I don't believe I'm familiar with it. I know a Mrs. Markland, but not one inside the city. If you want to meet me here at six o'clock, I'll take you down to meet other friends in the Fourth Ward. We can have supper together."

"That would be greatly appreciated." Patrick allowed his gaze to travel around the room, which was lined with bookshelves stocked with pamphlets and bound books. "You wouldn't happen to need another pair of hands around here this week, would you?"

Mr. Birney glanced back at his printer, hesitating. "I have Mr. Pugh and Mr. Robinson, so I don't. I pay for editorials, however, if you had a piece of writing to submit."

Patrick stifled a laugh at the crazy idea. "Not at this time." The suggestion niggled despite his initial instinct to dismiss it. Could he come up with one in a few days? Would it be harder to do that or to earn cash loading steamboats all week? Maybe he should think about wrangling all the thoughts running through his mind onto a page.

He repeated his commitment to return that evening and took his leave, taking note of the cross streets so he could find the office again. Main and Seventh. Spotting a sign for another boardinghouse, he diverted to it to inquire about the price. To his shock, it cost even more than Mrs. Markland's.

He wandered down the street until he came upon a market bustling with vendors and buyers and peppered with roaming animals and barefooted children. His stomach was rumbling, so he browsed the booths piled with early spring fruits, winter vegetables, and bread, but the prices were astounding.

It was probably too late to get the midday meal at Mrs. Markland's, but he'd already paid for room and board there; if he was going to afford a meal, it would have to be there or nowhere.

The house was quiet when he finally found his way back to it, and the dining room was empty. Lighthearted conversation sounded from the kitchen, however, so he knocked gingerly on the door, holding his breath while he strained to listen. Mary pulled it open, blinking back at him in surprise.

"I know I must be late for dinner. Is there any way to get a bite to eat regardless?"

It was a foolish request; none of the taverns he'd stayed at would have provided meals outside the posted times. But Mary grinned at him and stepped back.

"Of course! Come in, if you like."

He found himself in the hot kitchen, staring awkwardly at the table covered with half-eaten dishes, around which six Negroes sat. They had fallen silent when he entered, confirming that he shouldn't have intruded on their space. Rachel pushed back from her seat and stood up, and Uncle Charles waved at him.

"I'm sorry. I didn't mean to interrupt . . ."

"Come sit with us," Uncle Charles bellowed. "Unless you'd prefer it all proper in the dining room."

"I wouldn't, actually." Visiting with this group was a far more attractive proposition, if they'd have him. "Thank you. I take it the other boarders aren't around?"

"The Adamses left this morning to visit his mother in Kentuck for a few days. Preacher checked out to go on to the next town. Not sure about the other men."

"We didn't know if you planned to be back for dinner," Rachel began apologetically.

"I didn't either, until I saw the prices in the market." He took the empty chair she offered him while she pulled out a clean plate and filled it.

"It ain't a cheap place to live, that's for sure," Uncle Charles agreed. "We have plenty here for you. Fish?" He speared a filet onto the plate Rachel set before Patrick.

"This looks amazing," he said in wonder at the amount of food on the table.

"Dorcas is the best cook north of the Mason–Dixon," Uncle Charles informed him, and a gray-haired woman groaned and snapped her towel at him. He laughed. "It's true, anyway. Have you met the others? There's Sam, my youngest, and the girl is Peggy."

The camaraderie in the kitchen was contagious, and Patrick fell into it easily. He took the first bites of his food and leaned back, moaning. "It's been days since I had food that good."

"Where'd you come from?" Uncle Charles eyed him curiously.

"I left Baltimore on foot over fifty days ago. There was some good food in the taverns in Maryland and Pennsylvania, but nothing like this." He pointed his fork at his plate, and Dorcas made a disapproving cluck of poorly-concealed modesty.

"And you walked all that way? Now what on earth made you wan' walk from Baltimore to Cincinnati?"

Patrick began his story, and everyone except Rachel fell back into their chairs to listen, so he went on from the basics into tales from the road. She cleaned up the meal around them, finally stopping by Uncle Charles's chair.

"I'm sorry to interrupt, Mr. Gallagher, but these here lazybones can't sit here yammering all day."

"Oh, I understand. I apologize for keeping you." He pushed back from the table.

"She my older sister, so I have to do what she say," Uncle Charles grumbled good-naturedly. "Well, come along, Sam, and let's get back to work. You be here at supper, Mr. Gallagher?"

"It's Patrick, and no. James Birney promised to take me down to meet his friends in the Fourth Ward."

"Mebbe I'll come along then and bring my greetings as well. When are you going?"

"I'm supposed to meet him outside the newspaper at six."

"You get your chores done first, afore you go anywhere," Rachel warned her brother. "Dorcas, do you have that broth for Mrs. Markland?"

"I boilt it up this morning, just the exact way she said last time. It's been stayin' warm here by the fire, but her girls haven't come down for it."

"I'll take it up to her. Make sure it's warm but not too hot. We can't have her burning her mouth. All right then, get on with you, Charles."

Patrick stood, having heard enough about Mrs. Markland's mouth.

"I'll be in my room a little while this afternoon, if it's allowable. I have some correspondence to catch up on, but I'll be quiet."

Rachel nodded sharply. "You're welcome to use the parlor, too, anytime you like."

After a couple chapters of *Pilgrim's Progress*, Patrick felt drowsiness overtaking him, and he almost surrendered, sinking lower on the bed. The thought of Dorcas's fantastic cooking jolted him into wakefulness. At this rate, he could only afford to stay in this boardinghouse another day or two, and there wasn't a cheaper option around. If he wanted to keep eating like he had today, he had to do something about it.

Pushing up, he reached for his writing paper on the bedside table and stumbled to the small desk. The memory of a recent defense of slavery by the governor of South Carolina in the papers came to mind. Arguments had been forming in his mind against the man's points over the last several days.

Leaning his tired head onto his raised fist, Patrick took the pencil in his other hand.

"Why are slave owners concerned about abolitionists sending incendiary pamphlets to their slaves who can't read?

"How can they claim their slaves are happy and content on one side and be afraid of them revolting on the other?

"Proteus himself in the ancient mythology was not capable of transformations more jarring than what their slaves appear to undergo with ease in order to suit the reasonings which their masters find it convenient to employ."

Around these statements, paragraphs took shape. As more thoughts struck, Patrick drew arrows to the margins to keep his points grouped by topic. The editorial had to be perfect if he wanted Mr. Birney to pay good money for it.

What about the governor's reiteration of the oft repeated sentiment that the Bible protected or even defended the institution of slavery? Patrick's unseeing gaze fixed on the wall in front of him as words wrestled each other in his mind, logic and clarity untangling his thoughts to gain the upper hand. His pencil moved rapidly.

"When mere statesmen and men of the world—men whose time and thoughts have rarely been applied to the Bible—when such men turn commentators upon the scriptures, they are likely to make sad work of it.

The Bible itself represents a certain moral preparation as necessary to the right exposition of its contents."

He closed his eyes, searching for the truth and the correct words to communicate it.

"Men who only undertake to examine the scriptures once or twice perhaps in the length of a lifetime and then only to hunt after props for some system which they already adopted—is it likely such men will arrive at a correct and sound conclusion, especially where interest, love of ease, lust of power, etc. combine to warp the mind and lead it astray?"

A loud moo outside his window made his eyes fly open. Were the cows returning home already? Long shadows stretched across the white walls and oak floors, and Patrick reached for his watch in a mild panic. Half past five!

Dropping his pencil, he quickly performed his toilet, all but ignoring the haphazard state of his hair. "This is why I have you," he told his cap as he tugged it on and opened the door.

15

"Our laws are unjust in the heavy load of disabilities which they impose upon the colored man." - Elijah Lovejoy

The bedroom at the other end of the hall was closed, and Patrick made faces at it as he soundlessly moved down the hall.

Uncle Charles was waiting for him at the bottom of the stairs with his coat and hat on. "I wondered if I should come up for you," he teased.

"Shh!" Mary hissed, looking toward the ceiling. "You right under her bedroom."

"My voice just be naturally loud," Uncle Charles said in a stage whisper as he opened the front door.

Out on the street, Patrick turned back to look at the upper window covered by black curtains. Two dark little heads were visible in the glass, the curtain hanging behind them like a backdrop. Patrick lifted his hand to wave to them as he walked away, but they didn't move, only staring at him with their big eyes.

"Do Mrs. Markland's . . . 'girls' . . . not eat with the rest of you?" Patrick ventured to ask Uncle Charles as they set out.

"They still warming up to us and prefer to stay wit' her. They are separated from their parents, and we don' know if they dead or alive."

What a shame for little girls to be closed up in a dark room all day. Patrick turned to asking Uncle Charles about his family, inwardly grateful the man had invited himself along, thus automatically becoming his guide through the city. They reached *The Philanthropist* at only a couple of minutes past six and found Mr. Birney locking the downstairs door. He hailed Uncle Charles with familiarity and didn't look perturbed when Patrick apologized for their tardiness.

"I think I'll have an editorial for you in the next couple days," Patrick added. "I started writing down thoughts opposing Governor McDuffie's statements about slavery."

"Have you published before?" Mr. Birney asked with curiosity, gesturing to a waiting carriage.

"Not my own work, no." Patrick climbed into the front seat with him, and Uncle Charles settled into the bench behind them.

"I didn't know you were back in town," Uncle Charles piped up.

"I returned in less than a week this time." Mr. Birney cracked the whip to start the horses and turned to Patrick. "This spring has given me ample opportunity to speak around the state. Last week I had the chance to be in Columbus, and rabble-rousers worked vigilantly to break up the meeting."

"What happened?" How did he miss that Birney was in Columbus around the same time he was? Patrick sucked breath through his teeth at the thought that he could have avoided Cincinnati altogether, even though now he was glad he'd come.

"During the hour I spoke, the mob crowded about the door, engaged in discharging lighted missiles at me. When I had finished and was returning to my lodgings a mile distant, they accompanied me a greater part of the way while they broke into the stillness of the night with their fierce and demonic shouts."

"Pro-slavery sentiment is so high in Columbus?" Patrick asked, remembering his time cloistered at the Bulls'. There were always extremists, regardless of what corner of the country one visited.

Mr. Birney nodded soberly. He guided his horses around a corner, and pedestrians scurried to the side of the street to allow them room.

"I share it so that the friends of freedom to the slave and the white man, friends of protecting law, of inalienable rights, of constitutional liberty, may be more and more awake to the conflict. Every day is revealing to us more evidently the dangerous condition of our country and how a God of justice is bringing retribution on our nation in the loss of our own liberty for having violated the liberty of others."

He'd been a slave owner once, Patrick remembered. The guilt of that must still linger for him to have such a perspective now. "Repentance is the only means of saving our country," he replied quietly.

"We must face the work even more industriously than ever. Perhaps those of us laboring in the field will perish at our posts, but we think nothing of it if our suffering will cause others to step up to fill our place while we retire to heaven to our reward and the eternal presence of the Lord."

The danger of the work had often prompted Patrick to consider whether it was something he was willing to give his life for. While the answer had always been a definite yes, it would be hard indeed to lose his life if the sacrifice was overlooked, or worse, celebrated.

Uncle Charles murmured an "Amen" from the back seat.

"Our strength comes from the power granted by the Almighty. It enables us to fight, not in despair, but with the calmness of certain victory."

"Certain?" Patrick found himself questioning without thinking.

The carriage rattled over a hole in the road, and he grabbed the seat to settle himself.

"We have the promises of God!" Uncle Charles declared in a deep singsong rumble. "He promised to set the captive free and establish justice."

"We don't know how or when, but the promises are ours," Mr. Birney said cheerfully.

"The key," Patrick muttered under his breath.

"Excuse me?"

Patrick shook his head. "It's nothing."

That was the key that Christian realized he already had and then used to break out of Doubting Castle. The Key of Promise. He, Patrick, already had the full extent of God's promises in Scripture—it was clear he needed to familiarize himself with them more. Especially now that he knew that *they* were the way out of his despair.

"After you left this morning, I sent a message over to Revrend Nickens to alert him to our visit." Mr. Birney pulled up in front of a little brick church building that appeared intact, unlike the half-burned buildings they'd encountered on a neighboring street.

"African Union Baptist Church," Patrick read the sign aloud.

"The first Black church in Cincinnati and the location of the night school we'll observe tonight. But first, supper." Mr. Birney climbed to the ground while Patrick looked around the street at the African American faces as well as white ones—laborers returning home after work, children herding chickens and cows, young ones at play. The dirty rags on their bodies, broken windows, and animal droppings littering the gutters spoke of poverty like that of the neighborhood where he spent most of his time back home.

Uncle Charles led Patrick to the house beside the church while Mr. Birney unhitched his team. The Black man who opened the door was in his mid-forties and wore a well-brushed brown wool suit. He brightened at the sight of Uncle Charles, and they exchanged a hug before Patrick was introduced.

"David Nickens." He extended his hand to Patrick, and Patrick took it without hesitation. "Welcome to our home. Supper is almost ready, but come meet Owen and Marius."

Patrick was ushered into a homey parlor sporting wooden stick furniture and a red and yellow rag rug on the plank floor. His nose alerted him to the presence of ham and apple pie in the kitchen, adding to his feeling of comfort and interest in this place. A white man in his early thirties was waiting, tall with thick dark eyebrows forming straight lines over his serious dark eyes.

"Marius Robinson." He reached his hand out, and Patrick shook it.

"One of the Lane Rebels, now in the employ of *The Philanthropist*," Reverend Nickens said proudly. "And this is my brother Owen," he added as a taller version of himself entered the room. "Marius has boarded with us since before the debates, but his time with us is coming to an end."

Marius bowed slightly and quirked a grin. "Just until my wedding later this year. It's a pleasure to welcome a fellow abolitionist I hear has traveled far."

"There is a certain relief in being in a free state after growing up in Maryland," Patrick admitted. "I'm heading to Missouri, though, so need to prepare myself for the pain of living among those in bondage again. I've observed that there are difficulties everywhere, however."

"Ohio is not the freedom many in slavery believe it is, that much is true," Marius agreed. "We have a long way to go to win the rights of citizens for all our Black brothers and sisters. And you'll find many enslaved on the streets of Cincinnati."

"How so?" The idea befuddled Patrick. How could slaves be walking around in a free state, yet still in bondage? The Quakers in Mount Pleasant hadn't mentioned it.

"Their owners are from Kentucky." Owen spoke in a deep, serious voice. "They come for business and bring their help with them."

"We can talk more over supper." Reverend Nickens stepped toward the doorway as Mr. Birney appeared in it. "My wife, Serena, and Miss Emily, Marius's fiancee, have everything prepared."

They were joined at the table by the women and the Nickens children, confronted by the sight of fried ham, crispy hoecakes, green beans, and sizzling apple pie.

Patrick observed the small talk around the table, startled by the deep mutual respect on display among his hosts. He waited until the meal was underway and small talk depleted before he lowered his fork and addressed Marius's statement from earlier.

"You mentioned that Black residents of Cincinnati still lack rights of citizens. Which ones are withheld from them?"

Reverend Nickens leaned back in his chair, looked at his wife, and sighed, as if asking where to start on a long list.

Uncle Charles's graying head was bent over his plate, but he let out an "Mm-mm." Owen simply stared at Patrick with deep, dark eyes.

"Blacks who enter the state have to pay a five hundred dollar bond," Mr. Birney began. "It's obviously meant to deter those exiting slavery from coming here. Those who have saved up enough money to buy their freedom can't conceivably pay such an outrageous sum or find anyone to stand surety for them."

"It's meant to ensure good behavior and cover the expense should the individual become unable to work," Marius added.

Uncle Charles looked Patrick in the eye. "Not that Black citizens can utilize the courts, hospitals, schools, or asylums. We cannot hold public office. We cannot defend ourselves. Those who escape slavery are in constant fear of being recaptured and dragged back to bondage. No one will induct a Black man into an apprenticeship, so the trades are all closed to us. We can work only menial jobs such as laborers, porters, and ships' cooks. A few of the more fortunate are barbers."

"The large majority of our men work on the river," Mrs. Nickens explained. "The women are mostly washerwomen. The work is as back-breaking and relentless as it was in slavery."

Patrick shook his head. "It's not freedom," he said, echoing Marius's earlier sentiment.

"We are not helpless." Reverend Nickens placed both hands on the table, his dinner forgotten. "A few years ago, over two thousand of the Black population of Cincinnati migrated to form a community in Canada. It was a difficult year, with riots and mob action against our people, but they went voluntarily, not because anyone forced them. It was before we moved here, but Charles's family is one of those who chose to stay at that time." He tipped his head to the other end of the table, and Uncle Charles picked up the story.

"Our mother was too elderly to make the journey, and Rachel and I had good jobs here, but most of our friends and neighbors left that year." There was a pause before he added, "Our friends who stayed did so because they were in the process of saving up to buy the freedom of loved ones."

His words pulled at the weight sitting like a rock on Patrick's heart. *Imagine buying your family members. Worse, imagine having to decide which one to purchase first.*

Patrick opened his mouth to speak, weighing his words. "I know it is a dangerous place to live, for Negroes and for anti-slavery activists. Like myself, I'm sure you have all counted the cost hundreds of times and deemed it worth staying the course. But how—" He inhaled and considered how vulnerable to be. What did their opinion of him matter at a time like this? He had literally walked across the country for this very conversation. "How do you maintain hope when it appears that evil prevails at every turn? Laws get stricter, mobs get bolder. Will things ever change?"

Sweat beaded on the back of his neck while he waited breathlessly for their answer. He might lose his mind if they fed him lines about eternity and justice coming on some far-off judgment day.

Reverend Nickens smiled first, and then smiles broke on the faces of the other adults at the table. Patrick felt almost woozy, as if he was on a different plane of reality than they.

"Evil isn't prevailing!" Reverend Nickens exclaimed. "We have our own churches now." He gestured in the direction of the church next door. "We have schools for children and night schools for adults. The Ohio Anti-Slavery Society is growing, and several members live in our community and provide much-needed education, including Marius and Miss Emily. Our God is with us. He has not stayed silent or abandoned us, so we press on in His work."

"We have been blessed to have these two." An affectionate smile covered Mrs. Nickens's face. "Did you know our Marius was just ordained by the New York Central Evangelical Association to be an evangelist to the churches here, to arouse them to their duty? And now Mr. Birney is publishing bold anti-slavery editorials in our very city. God is alive and awake, and He's moving, Mr. Gallagher. His people are ushering more and more souls to freedom on the Underground Railroad every day."

"It is not a time to be indolent." Mr. Birney looked ready to climb over the table and grab Patrick by the shoulders. "I have been threatened by men in high position. A citizen of Cincinnati, a high commissioned officer of the militia, informed me that I would be disgracefully punished and abused and my property destroyed if I persisted in my anti-slavery movements. If we stay silent, if we do nothing, the evil will grow. If it is left unchecked, our children also may wear the livery of a slave. We could not stay silent in such a moment if we wanted to. And if I fall in this cause, I trust it will bring hundreds to supply my place. I pray you press on, Mr. Gallagher."

Chastised by his plea, Patrick nodded like an obedient schoolboy as his throat thickened with emotion. These people lived through more difficulties than he could imagine, yet this was their perspective? How could he, too, see the ways God was moving more?

"Do you know Elijah Lovejoy?" He didn't know where the question came from, but maybe it had to do with wanting to hear personal references of a fellow fighter or recommendations of his work from those passionate in the same cause.

"Mr. Lovejoy is a faithful friend," Mr. Birney replied, his face lighting up at the name. "He's in Pennsylvania right now."

The room faded as everything in Patrick slammed to a deafening halt until all he could hear was the ringing in his ears. Lovejoy, gone from Missouri? It was the very last thing he'd expected to hear at the mention of the man's name. The entire journey out here was fruitless, and he was a fool.

"He is?" he managed, his voice suspiciously tight.

"Certainly. He wrote to me when leaving for the Presbyterian General Assembly."

16

**"He was a singlehearted man. He lived solely for God
and the public good. - Edward Beecher about Elijah Lovejoy**

I believe the Assembly starts a week from tomorrow, or somewhere thereabouts." Mr. Birney looked oddly at the incredulity on Patrick's face. "They last a few weeks, I suppose."

A few weeks plus travel time. So he would be returning eventually. There was no need to rush on to St. Louis, except that the only way to afford to stay at Mrs. Markland's was to find employment.

"I wrote to him but didn't expect a response since I was in motion." Patrick kneaded the napkin hidden on his lap. "I intend to go to St. Louis after this, although now I see there is no reason to hurry."

"To our benefit," Uncle Charles said brightly, unaware of Patrick's financial plight.

Patrick turned to Mr. Birney. "I will have the article for you, but if I'm to stay, do let me know if any of you are aware of other paying jobs I could do during my tenure."

"If you have references from Gwynn, you should be able to apply at the other newspapers, although I would keep Lundy's reference to yourself," Mr. Birney said wryly. "You mentioned legislature earlier. Have you done anything else?"

"A customs office most recently. The state senate term. And I spent two years apprenticing for the builder who worked on my house."

Patrick folded his napkin and looked at Mr. Birney's necktie, avoiding eye contact. His spotty resume screamed of a restless life, and it told no lie.

He lifted his knife and cut a piece of ham on his plate, and while he chewed, the others gradually resumed eating. Marius asked Emily about the class she taught that day, and the conversation moved to the primary school. The sternness of Marius's eyebrows softened when she spoke, as if her presence brought tangible relief to the burdens he carried every day.

Emily wore the plain dress of a Quaker but it didn't hide the dimples in her cheeks, and the dull bun she sported barely detracted from the silkiness of her hair. She was pretty, but that's not what put the pang into Patrick's stomach. It was the way she was wholly dedicated to the same cause Marius was, the way they spoke to each other as if entirely cut from the same cloth. Marius didn't have to explain himself to her or convince her of the importance of the class he was giving up his evening to teach in a few minutes.

He was understood.

Patrick's family never actively discouraged his work in abolition, but they had never fully understood it. The Black friends he made in Baltimore understood the importance of abolition, but they didn't understand what it was like to be a white person advocating for it against their entire culture. His abolitionist friends understood the passion, but Patrick was just a needed worker to them, not someone to get to know beyond the cause.

Jealousy wasn't worth coddling, but Patrick floundered for a moment, searching for a way to make sense of it. Only the Lord could do that, so he returned to his plate, finishing off his food while offering a silent prayer for peace to replace the unsettled feeling.

He had barely finished his meal when Reverend Nickens and Marius pushed back from the table.

"It's time to go over and unlock the door before our students start arriving," Reverend Nickens announced, so the others joined them on their feet.

Patrick thanked Mrs. Nickens for the meal and fell into step with Marius as the men exited.

"What can I expect tonight?" he asked as they left the warm house.

"We have three hours of classes, although some students leave after two. It can be hard to stay awake after a long day of work. We teach geography, grammar, arithmetic, natural philosophy, and Bible study." Marius fixated on the church he approached as he spoke, demonstrating a focus that Patrick had noticed about him throughout the evening. He was a single-minded man who gave his full attention to whatever was in front of him, which probably aided him in the valuable work he accomplished. If he had planned to settle in Cincinnati rather than St. Louis, Patrick imagined that Marius might have become a good friend.

"There are other Negro schools in the city," Marius added. "Some are taught by African Americans and others by white teachers, including some of my classmates from Lane. The schools can't afford to pay much, but it's a joy to give education to those who were previously denied it. Reverend Nickens charges students a dollar per month, but we don't turn away any who can't pay. But tell me more about your time in the state senate." Marius gestured to the other men in front of them. "We often talk about the importance of getting more abolitionists into Congress if we want to see change."

"It doesn't work," Patrick said shortly. "There's too much southern agriculture money in the pockets of congressmen, even ones in free states. It's a fruitless fight on that front."

One of Marius's eyebrows rose, triggering the ever-present frustration to rise in Patrick in kind. Marius had no idea. It would be worthwhile for him to know the truth so he didn't fault those he believed should run for office.

"One day," Marius murmured.

"It would take something extreme to get it to change. That kind of money runs deep, and men aren't going to unfist it by choice. Not without a fight."

Marius looked like he had arguments on the tip of his tongue, but Reverend Nickens had unlocked the door of the church, and they reached it as he pulled it open. Patrick set his jaw, meeting Marius's eyes under his furrowed brow. Perhaps he had already disappointed his new acquaintance. Well, Marius could get in line with all the others.

Patrick sat in the back of the school beside Mr. Birney, listening to Marius's lecture on the Magna Carta. The benches were filled with African Americans of both sexes from their teens up to three participants with snow-white hair. Patrick caught an occasional yawn, but the group had a desperation to learn that he'd rarely seen, and Marius was without doubt an engaging speaker. Patrick had never heard the story of the rebel barons and King John told this way before. It certainly made more sense now than when he'd heard it in school as a restless lad who had better things to do.

The rebel barons had done something unheard of at the time, standing up to their king to demand accountability and protection for the rights of the people. Now hundreds of years later, people formerly in servitude were hearing about the brave, desperate actions of these men. What would it be like to do something that was taught and celebrated hundreds of years later?

Like the Separatists, who left for a foreign land so they could teach their children the ways of God.

Like Patrick Henry, who inspired a revolution by declaring, "Give me liberty or give me death" to a church full of men questioning whether the events in Boston even affected those in the southern colonies.

Patrick lifted his eyes to Marius, who offered his closing statements to a spellbound audience. This? This was undoubtedly as righteous and revolutionary an action, yet who would read of Marius Robinson in the history books of future generations? Staying up after a long day at work to give an education to those previously denied one was hardly romantic and certainly not fame garnering. But really, this man was a hero.

Patrick felt Mr. Birney's heat next to him. Another hero. And Reverend Nickens, and all the Lane Rebels, and every African American in the room, dedicated to the hard work of stretching their minds after long work hours, and even Elijah Lovejoy. People who worked tirelessly for what was good and right, regardless of the cost to themselves.

He scoffed at the thought of himself sharing a bench with such people. Somehow he'd managed to do more harm than good in his efforts to earn his place among such men.

What would Marius think if he knew that because of Patrick's blunders, runaway slaves had been recaptured and returned to bondage?

That he lost reelection because he couldn't stay silent in an inopportune time?

That the only abolitionist newspaper he'd worked for went defunct a few months after he joined it?

He could go on.

These good men deserved to be remembered by successive

generations for their heroic deeds.

Patrick was just like a pesky younger sibling who kept crashing his older brother's society meetings but could never earn a seat at the table.

For all his efforts, he could never be a Marius Robinson.

Over the following days, Patrick polished his article, tiptoed around Mrs. Markland's boardinghouse, ate in the kitchen with the staff who he now considered friends, got a haircut, and went every day to visit schools, churches, and Anti-Slavery Society meetings. Sunday found him worshipping on a bench in the back of the crowded African Union Baptist Church. Sometimes on his outings, he got his map turned upside down and ended up a mile from his destination, but he'd simply find a local to get him turned back around and enjoy the longer stroll down Cincinnati's broad streets.

The abolitionist and Black communities welcomed him politely at James Birney's introduction, because no one knew about his poor record back home. Their kindness gave him an uneasy sense of undeserved freedom, as if he could finally reinvent himself and be someone different.

The recent riots hung like a shadow over many of those he interacted with. Cincinnati had a long history of violence against their Black neighbors, and last month's attack served as a stern reminder that such a thing could erupt again at any minute. The charred buildings remained standing, sobering Patrick every time he passed.

He stood in the doorway of the boardinghouse parlor after returning from submitting his editorial to Mr. Birney and debated whether to go up to his room for the two hours before supper and start a new essay, sit in the parlor and read, or go out and find a friend to visit. Some new travelers had stayed overnight, forcing Patrick to eat in the dining room with them, but he looked forward to returning to the kitchen and his comfortable meals with the staff now that he was the only guest again.

Rachel came down the hall, carrying a tray with a full meal rather than a cup of broth on it, and Patrick watched her ease up the stairs, widening her step to avoid the stair that creaked. The tray stayed perfectly level, but this was ridiculous.

He reached into his pocket and stared at the few coins that were left. Using his forearm, he measured the width and length of the stair and then turned and walked out the front door.

It didn't take long to find the sawmill and spend his last coin on a piece of solid oak and a few nails. Patrick had it cut to his specifications and planed smooth before carrying it back to Mrs. Markland's with it tucked under his arm.

At the first strike of Uncle Charles's hammer, Rachel came flying down the stairs to see who dared make a peep while her mistress convalesced. She stopped short at the sight of Patrick on the steps, hammering the last nail into the stair.

He lifted the hammer, pushed to his feet, and shot her a deprecating smile. "For one minute of noise, don't you think it's worth it to avoid regular intervals of squeaking?"

She stared at him in stunned silence before asking, "How much are you going to charge for that?"

"For the stair, nothing. But as I spent my last penny on it, I'm hoping you'll allow me to do more repairs for you in exchange for room and board for a couple more weeks."

He eyed the water stains on the wall on either side of the window, and her gaze followed his. Instead of responding, Rachel descended to the new stair and stood on it, bouncing slightly to test it. "It's a good stair. Don't make a sound, and looks like it belongs with the others." Her eyes narrowed at him. "Your last cent?"

Patrick swung the hammer in his hand and gritted his teeth at the memory. "I was robbed outside of Dayton. Lost nearly all my savings. The rest . . ." The grimace turned sheepish. "Kept me alive the last couple of weeks. Do you think Mrs. Markland would allow me to take care of a few projects around the place?"

Rachel had crossed her arms over her chest in a protective measure at the mention of the crime he'd suffered. "I'll ask her. Charles is supposed to get to things, but he hasn't had time. It would be best to wait until she's on her feet again, but if you need room and board now . . ."

"Do you expect her to recover soon?"

"She was up a little today, but you can't really predict these things." The corner of her mouth lifted. "Leastaways, I can't."

By tomorrow, he should have payment for the editorial from Mr. Birney. "I can wait a day or two. If you have an account at the sawmill, I can get what I need and have it cut while I wait."

Rachel let out her breath and gave him a nod. "All right then. I'll make up a list of what we need done and have it to you by tomorrow."

Patrick grinned. Rachel may put on a stern act, but he'd learned over the past few days how soft she was on the inside. The stress of running the boardinghouse under Mrs. Markland would put a scowl on anyone's face.

"Well, come along to supper now," she said, moving to precede him to the dining room.

Patrick pulled his pocketwatch out and looked at the time—5:59. There was no doubt the woman was very good at her job, and Mrs. Markland was lucky to have her.

17

"No one will be persuaded by naked denunciation or misrepresentations." - Elijah Lovejoy

Golden morning rays heated the parlor the following morning when Patrick entered it after breakfast. An envelope had been waiting for him at his breakfast plate with five dollars from Mr. Birney, warming him from the inside out. He was to be published for the first time, but more than that, he was accepted by one of the most prominent abolitionists in Cincinnati and extended a place in their circle.

A thought struck him as he set his books on the little writing table he'd used most of the mornings since his arrival. Elijah Lovejoy might very well read his editorial in the paper before ever meeting him. It would surely be a validating introduction.

A light footstep sounded behind him, and he turned around. The vision before him was so unexpected, he blinked twice to clear his eyes. It was a woman—a white woman he'd never seen before. Her brown hair was rolled over her ears, held in place by combs peeking up on the back of her head. Under a smooth white forehead and perfectly sculpted brows were a pair of blue eyes that turned down on the outside corners, giving her a sort of melancholy appearance. She wore long earrings, a brown and tan calico dress puckered at the front and covered by a large white collar that reached to her shoulders.

Although obviously not wealthy, she was a lady, and one in the picture of health. A voice in the back of Patrick's head tried to insist that he knew who she was, and he refused to believe it.

"Good morning," he said, because he didn't know what else to say. To excuse his gawking, he added, "I didn't hear anyone approaching."

"I believe that would be because the stair was fixed."

She came from upstairs—something Patrick could not accept.

"I'm Patrick Gallagher, a recent boarder," he said, hoping against hope to hear a foreign name on her lips in return.

"Anna Markland. I'm pleased to make your acquaintance and understand you're the one I'm to thank for repairing the stair."

Patrick swallowed and gave a short nod. Scratching his jaw, he moved his gaze to the door beside her as his mind raced.

What in the name of blazes was happening?

His throat rolled as he swallowed again. "I hope it wasn't too loud. The hammer."

She seemed unable to come up with a reply, which must mean it had been. "It was fine," she said after too long of a pause. "It was kind of you."

Her voice was light and airy but had a distinct southern twinge to it. Kentuckian, if he wasn't mistaken. The realization reminded him what her youthful, ladylike appearance had chased from his mind. This was, after all, the high-strung owner who had lain abed for several days while making oppressive demands of her staff and kept two little Black maids locked up with her. His discomfort increasing, he looked for a way to escape her presence.

"I'm sure you have plenty to attend to now that you're up, so if you'll excuse me, I'll stay out of your way," he said, indicating the table holding his Bible and journal.

She seemed taken aback and blinked at him for a long moment. "Yes, very well then. Good day, Mr. Gallagher."

"Mrs. Markland." He gave a short bow, and as she retreated from the doorway, he saw the little girls, previously hidden behind her. They stared mutely at him before turning to follow her, leaving him to register what he'd just said.

Mrs. She was or had been married. Since he'd seen no possible husbands about the place, it must be *had been*. God bless the poor man, may he rest in peace.

Day 57, Mrs. Markland's Boardinghouse, Cincinnati
Health: Quite well.
Supplies used: None today, with thanks to the stair yesterday providing for my sustenance today
Wildlife: Female, late twenties or early thirties, southern accent
Verse for the day: Proverbs 26:14 As the door turneth upon his hinges, so doth the slothful upon his bed.
Personal notes: Mrs. Markland's youth makes her position and behavior all the more unexpected and ill-suited.

Anna Markland left the enigma in the parlor and continued down the hall, confusion darkening her brow. All week, she'd only heard positive reports about the gentleman boarder from Rachel and Mary, and even Leah and Jane had told her about his kind smile. She'd been curious about the man who apparently went in and out without making a peep, but anytime she left her room, he'd been out.

What she hadn't expected was for him to dismiss her so summarily upon their first meeting with cryptic comments about all that she had to do. She did have things to accomplish, to be sure, but what did Patrick Gallagher know of it?

Rachel was in the kitchen, gathering tablecloths and dishrags into a washtub while Mary stood at the dishpan attacking breakfast dishes and Dorcas rolled out a pie crust on the worktable.

A chorus of greetings welcomed her and the girls into the warm space, and they were ushered to the table, where stacks of flapjacks waited.

Anna seated the girls, looking over their place settings, but they had everything they needed.

"What did you tell Mr. Gallagher about me, Rachel?" she asked as she pulled out her own chair.

Rachel gave her a bewildered look. "I don't know that I said anything at all about you to him. Mary?"

Mary turned from the dishpan, shaking her head. "No, Mrs. Markland. Only he was there when I told Uncle Charles you done took to your bed and to hush himself up."

"What makes you ask?" Rachel inquired.

Anna scooted Jane's cup of milk closer to her. "He acted a bit odd and said he would stay out of my way, even though I came into the room he was in and blocked the doorway. Maybe he's afraid of triggering another spell?"

Rachel exchanged a look with Mary, her eyebrows raised. "I have no idea. I can speak to him."

"Well, I'm going to take the girls over to the Nickenses' today to see the school and see if anyone knows about their parents, so he can make all the noise he wants. I need to place my order at the dry goods store so it's ready to retrieve tomorrow. We have dolls to distribute, but we have a few we're still finishing up first, so that might have to wait until tomorrow. I'm afraid I have to rush all my errands now since the sick headache took up so much of our time here."

The tightness in her chest clenched further. The sick headaches robbed her of so very much time. If only they hadn't also stolen of her precious few days in town. Grief took her breath away in the moments before she could refocus on something else.

Leah and Jane were eating well, and she smiled to see it as she sipped her tea. They knew a thing or two about grief and the disappointments of life, and the three of them stumbled along the path together, taking turns lifting each other up. Anna didn't know what she would do without them.

"How long can you stay?" Rachel had paused with the washtub on her hip.

Anna inhaled, longing for the answer to be something different. "No more than two more days. And that's pushing too far as it is. Mother Markland is taking care of the house for me, and it's too much for her."

"Dear Lord," Dorcas mumbled, and Anna swallowed back her agreeing sigh.

"How's Mr. Markland these days?" Rachel asked without moving.

Anna toyed with the handle of her mug as she thought of her father-in-law. "Progressively worsening. He doesn't recognize me at all anymore, and he often calls Mother Markland by his sister's name."

"Mmm. That's a hard thing." Dorcas and Mary mirrored Rachel's sympathetic expression. "Well, I'll let you all get to your breakfast."

Her words echoed Patrick's, but they came across vastly different coming from her. Anna smiled wryly to herself as she spread her napkin on her lap and cut into her flapjacks.

Rachel had reached the back door when the kitchen door swung open and everyone turned to see Patrick filling the frame. He hesitated, his eyes landing on Anna and then Rachel and back again. "I, uh, need to ask about supplies," he began, his gaze shifting constantly between the two.

Anna squinted at him, leaving it to Rachel to reply.

"Come out to the shed with me and I'll show you the tools," she said, opening the door with the washtub still in her other hand.

With one more pointed look at Anna, Patrick followed Rachel outside. When he shut the door behind them, silence reigned in the kitchen.

Dorcas turned on Anna. "What have you done to that man to make him look at you like that?" she demanded with humor in her eyes.

Anna shook her head, flabbergasted. "I have no idea. I met him for the first time ten minutes ago."

"You done something to him, sugar. He couldn't keep his eyes off you."

To be fair, Anna had been staring too, but she saw no point in mentioning it. The man was just so odd. He was tall but not too tall, thin but not skinny. He was as tan as a Miami, with hair the color of bricks that he apparently didn't own a comb for, and wore a poorly tailored brown suit that matched his eyes. He'd had a Bible, notebook, and *Pilgrim's Progress* with him in the parlor, which hinted that he was educated as well as devout, but he apparently cared very little about his appearance. And yet he had a magnetism to him, so maybe he knew he didn't need fancy clothes to draw attention. From all reports, he made friends in the Anti-Slavery Society and went to church on Sunday, and he even ate with the boardinghouse staff without batting an eye. He'd fixed the stair, for mercy's sake.

But beyond the way he acted shifty and uncomfortable with her, Anna pondered with perplexity the darkness in his eyes. The man had ghosts, but the shadow hanging over him felt ill-fitting, as if he was used to laughter and teasing but held them at an uncomfortable distance now.

Leah and Jane had finished eating, and Anna excused them so they could take their dirty dishes over to Mary. She had just laid her fork on her empty plate when voices neared and Rachel returned to the door with Patrick. He held a crate with tool handles and wood scraps sticking out of the top. He thanked Rachel, and she stayed in the doorway to watch as he glanced at Anna and crossed the room to the hallway. The door closed behind him, and Rachel returned to her wash.

"You done something to him, sugar," Dorcas repeated in a low voice.

Anna stood and handed her dirty dishes to Mary. "I don't have the time or energy to figure him and his problem out. Are you ready to go, girls?"

Leah and Jane came to her side immediately, and she brushed a tender hand over the back of their dresses. "We'll probably have dinner with the Nickenses, but do plan on us for supper."

"Yes, ma'am." Dorcas grinned at them. "We'll look forward to it."

18

"How mighty is truth! It triumphed even though wielded by so weak an instrument as I am." - Elijah Lovejoy

Anna Markland ate breakfast in the kitchen—at his place at the table—with her two little servants by her side. It defied explanation. The vast majority of the population treated abolitionists very harshly for eating with Negroes, so what made her take the liberty?

And she had stared blankly at Patrick when he asked about the supplies, leaving it to Rachel to handle everything. The way Rachel ran the place, she clearly didn't even need Mrs. Markland. What an incompetent owner.

When Patrick returned from the sawmill with the wood he needed, the only person in sight was Mary, sweeping the foyer. He shed his coat, placing it over the back of a chair, and dug the crowbar out of his crate to begin tearing the damaged wood off the wall. Several minutes later, there was a hole in the wall around the window, and a pile of broken boards sat at his feet. Patrick swiped his sleeve over his sweaty face and stared at the hole.

He'd spent the entire time he worked stewing over Anna Markland. Good grief. *You don't even know her, man. Get her out of your head.*

He shook his head, running fingers into his damp hair and standing it on end. That was what had gotten him into reform societies in the first place. He simply couldn't bear the thought of those in positions of power controlling those beneath them with violence, fear, or manipulation. It chafed to no end to know that people like Rachel, Uncle Charles, and the poor little girls had to put up with an employer like her.

He didn't see Mrs. Markland the rest of the morning and ate his dinner in the pleasant kitchen with the staff. When the window was waterproofed once more and the wall rebuilt, he stacked the old wood into the firebox and returned the tools to the crate. Tomorrow he'd paint the new wall and anything else Rachel wanted touched up. Before he could make his way upstairs to freshen up for supper, the front door opened and a young couple came through it, seeking lodgings for the night.

Patrick backed out of the room, out of sight of the new guests, and tucked the crate into a corner of the kitchen. Bother. He'd have to eat in the dining room and pretend to be interested in the lives of the travelers now.

At six o'clock, he stepped into the dining room in his spare clean blouse, brushed suit, a hastily tied cravat, and nearly tamed hair, thanks more to the recent haircut than significant effort on his part. Mrs. Markland was alone in the room, not a hair altered from her appearance earlier in the day. Her eyes darted to his at his entrance and then sank to the region of his waistcoat.

"Good evening, Mr. Gallagher."

He considered backing out and forgoing supper altogether rather than share a table with the insufferable woman, but the new couple entered behind him, and he was stuck. The Lelands were at least ten years his junior and looked like they belonged more in the schoolroom than on a journey across the country unchaperoned. They had barely exchanged expected pleasantries around the room before Rachel pushed through the kitchen door, announcing supper.

"Thank you, Rachel." Mrs. Markland turned to the others with a sugary smile. "Shall we?" Pulling out the chair at the head of the table, she seated herself, and the other guests followed suit.

Throughout the meal, she was a perfect, elegant hostess, asking Mr. Leland about his occupation and what brought them from Philadelphia. The conversation moved smoothly with her follow-up questions and the interest on her face. Patrick focused on Dorcas's impeccable pork chops while waiting for his opening, his impatience growing by the minute. He didn't care beans about the Lelands, but he had heaps of questions about Mrs. Markland.

It wasn't until strawberries and cream were brought out for dessert and Mary retreated back to the kitchen that the conversation lulled long enough for him to pounce.

"And how long have you lived in Cincinnati, Mrs. Markland?" He sat erect with his fork in his untasted strawberries, his expression a mask of politeness. Mr. and Mrs. Leland perked up, turning to her with eagerness to hear about her in return.

Mrs. Markland lifted surprised eyes. "Oh, I don't live in Cincinnati. I live up at the North Bend, in Cleves, and have for seven years now."

Patrick could only stare at her, and she held his gaze boldly. He coughed and blinked away, realizing the impropriety his stupefaction had caused.

"You don't . . . live here?" He ventured one more quick glance her way.

"Noooo." She drew the word out, lifting her eyebrows as if waiting for an explanation for the odd question. "I come to the city twice a year to get supplies for my inn in Cleves. Mr. Markland and I ran it together until his death, and he left the sole proprietorship to me."

"I'm sorry for your loss," Mrs. Leland exclaimed.

Mrs. Markland murmured thanks, and Patrick nearly exploded with questions. Holding his tongue, he stared at his strawberries, having lost all interest in them.

"How about you, Mr. Gallagher? I haven't heard what brought you to the fair Queen City." Mrs. Markland looked at him expectantly, the earlier question still in her eyes. She was trying to figure him out, and he couldn't for the life of him figure her either.

He couldn't answer her question, of course. One did not mention the names of James Birney or Elijah Lovejoy to anyone who wasn't Black or a known abolitionist.

"I'm a reporter," he blurted out. Apparently the answer was as unexpected to her as hers had been to him, because it set off another staring round until Mr. Leland cleared his throat loudly.

"Well, that's very interesting," he said. "I'm sure you find plenty to write about out here."

"I have," Patrick said casually. "There's a great deal of odd and mysterious things happening in these parts."

As soon as it was polite to excuse himself, Patrick stood, and rather than retreat to the parlor with Mr. Leland, he bolted for the kitchen. Mrs. Markland's little girls were at the kitchen table, mutely watching the adult staff clean up from the meal and share their regular evening gossip time.

Patrick grabbed Uncle Charles's arm on his way to the back door. "I need to talk to you."

Out in the dusky May evening, he released Uncle Charles and clicked the door shut behind them. Peering first at one, then the other window beside the door, he was satisfied that no one was straining to eavesdrop before swinging around to face the older man.

"Who is Mrs. Markland?"

Uncle Charles squinted at him, the same befuddled look Patrick had been getting from everyone lately. "She's a friend of ours."

He stopped, so Patrick waved at him to go on.

"Missus a real decent kind of lady. Owns an inn out near the Big Miami River. Comes to see us a couple times a year. Why you ask?"

Patrick mentally replayed everything he could remember that was said about the woman since he arrived. "She . . . doesn't own this boardinghouse?"

"This here?" Uncle Charles gestured to the building to his back with a chuckle. "No sir, this is Rachel's place."

"Rachel's," Patrick repeated.

"Why did you think it belonged to Mrs. Anna? Ain't a Black woman capable of owning a business?"

Why had he? Patrick's gut knotted with the realization that what Uncle Charles was insinuating was true. Back home, no boardinghouses were owned by Black women, and he'd jumped to a quick conclusion based on the color of Rachel's and Anna's skin. But other things had watered the idea in his mind. "You all keep calling her 'the missus.' Where I'm from, that's a word people use to mean their mistress. Their employer."

"Oh, no." Uncle Charles laughed, amusement twinkling in his dark eyes. "We just say that as a term of respect. But it's real funny after you saw Rachel ran the place all week and Mrs. Markland didn't do a thing."

Patrick scrubbed his hand down his face, still unwilling to believe what he was hearing.

"You're right, she didn't." How had he missed the truth? He inhaled, glancing around at the shadowy shapes of trees and the shed in the yard without seeing them. "The truth is, it was also the way you all treated her all week, going out of your way to—" His hand flew through the air as he tried to articulate his thought. "To do things just exactly the way she wanted."

Uncle Charles leveled a look at Patrick, and Patrick felt chastised before he said a word.

"Serve her, you mean?"

"Well, yes." Patrick's hands landed on his hips as the full strength of his idiocy caught up with him.

"Like Jesus commanded we all do for each other?"

Patrick couldn't move. The words were exactly the same as ones he'd always heard back in Maryland, but here, the meaning came across as something completely different. "Just so."

"Boy, we serve Mrs. Markland because she our friend and we love her. She's our guest, just the same as you, but one we've known for years. She's a dear woman who's been through a heap of suffering. It's possible to serve out of love, you know, even for Black folk." He lifted an eyebrow at Patrick, and Patrick knew he'd be lying awake later that night, taking a hard look at his own assumptions.

Shouldn't he, of all people, have known better, being an abolitionist, a Christian, and someone who worked with the Black community regularly? Everything was different back home, and he had a lot to learn about life in the west. Humiliated, he rubbed the back of his neck, wondering how he could climb out of the hole he'd dug for himself.

"Are you going to tell the others how stupid I am?"

Uncle Charles gave a huff. "Ain't no way I'm telling Rachel you thought she a servant. She'd probably never want to see your white face again. No sir, this ain't going past my lips."

"Well, I'm sorry to you and to her. It's uncanny how our preconceptions have a way of sneaking in and creating a new explanation for everything in our heads, even when what we see is telling us something else." Patrick grimaced sheepishly. It had been easier to believe the worst of someone he'd never met than realize that his way of thinking was wrong. "I did think it was odd all week."

Uncle Charles's face softened, but he still shook his head in disbelief. "It's all right, best I can tell. No harm done."

Patrick's questions weren't exhausted, but he'd embarrassed himself enough for one night. "Thanks for straightening me out." He made to back away as Uncle Charles continued to chuckle and mutter, but suddenly the older man stopped.

"The work you did on the wall and stair was real nice," Uncle Charles offered, and Patrick paused. "How long are you staying, again?"

Patrick blew out his breath, having switched from one confusing topic to another. "I had planned to stay a week, but now that I know Mr. Lovejoy isn't in Missouri, I don't have a reason to hurry away. I've met everyone I came here to meet." He shrugged. "So I suppose I'll stay as long as Rachel has projects for me. I'll paint the wall tomorrow."

He liked Cincinnati far more than he'd expected. It may not be any safer for people who shared his beliefs than Baltimore was, but the people here had left a permanent mark on his heart. He even liked Rachel's comfortable boardinghouse, doubly so now that he knew it was Rachel's. The little room had started to feel like home after so long on the road, sleeping in a different place every night. But the moment her jobs for him started to feel like she was offering charity, he needed to leave.

Going around to the front door a few minutes later, he headed straight for the stairs, blessedly avoiding Mrs. Markland. There was no way he could face her yet, and he'd be glad if he never did again. He'd tiptoed halfway down the upstairs hallway before he remembered that he didn't have to stay silent any more—whatever had laid the woman up had apparently passed, but the habits he'd developed here would be hard to shake.

In the safety of his room, he lit a candle and stared at the books and papers on his desk, feeling too distracted for any of it to take hold. Grabbing his journal and pencil anyway, he collapsed on his bed with them and reread his entry from that morning. Sorting through the week in his mind, he picked out the facts he'd perceived were true, rearranging and replacing them with the new information he'd been given. It wasn't an easy thing to do.

He was at Rachel's boardinghouse, because Ellis had deliberately brought him to the only Black-owned public lodgings in Cincinnati.

Anna Markland was a guest like he was.

All the effort and accommodation the staff had made this week on her behalf were because they loved her and wanted to, not because of any obligation to do so.

And Patrick had viewed their Christian service through far more prejudice than he realized.

19

The next morning in the dining room, Patrick hid behind a newspaper from Mr. Leland while eating his toast and jam as quickly as he could. He could hear female voices on the stairs as he folded the newspaper and slipped into the still-chilly parlor with his coffee and books, grateful to have escaped before Mrs. Markland arrived with Mrs. Leland.

Thankfully, Mrs. Markland didn't stop in to greet him again, so he took his time reading his Bible and several pages of *Pilgrim's Progress* in the stillness of the room as daylight overtook the flickering candles.

He waited until the Lelands left—to sightsee or shop, he didn't know—before braving the kitchen for his supplies and the bucket of paint Uncle Charles had brought home. He was on his haunches in the foyer, stirring the paint, when footsteps on the stairs told him Mrs. Markland and her girls were approaching. Patrick avoided looking up, although his senses remained highly aware of their presence behind him.

Mrs. Markland stopped before the front door for a moment, and from the corner of his eye, he saw her straighten the girls' shawls and open the door. There was a beat of silence. She sucked in her breath loud enough that his ears picked it up, then led them out while Patrick's paint whirled vigorously around the bucket.

By dinnertime, all his painting was complete and left to dry, and the house bustled with the return of Mr. and Mrs. Adams from their rendezvous in Kentucky. Patrick ate his midday meal with them in the dining room and accepted his afternoon to-do list from Rachel. He oiled door hinges, fixed a broken handle on the cellar door, and replaced a few roof shingles. From his perch atop the ladder set against the eaves of the house, he saw when Mrs. Markland arrived, driving a wagon full of crates and barrels into the stable. The little girls sat on grain sacks in the back, and Patrick's gaze followed them until the dark stable swallowed them up.

Shaking himself from the distraction, he pulled another nail from his pocket and returned to work. If she'd completed the shopping for her business, was her time in Cincinnati nearing an end? But the supplies had come back to the boardinghouse with her, not to a warehouse by the river to be loaded on a steamboat. The woman was one mystery after another.

He was dressed and ready for supper a couple of minutes early by his pocketwatch, so he stepped into the parlor to stay out of the way of the staff setting up in the dining room. Two crates by the fireplace drew his attention, having not been there earlier in the day. Patrick stepped toward them curiously and peered down at the contents.

Several sets of dark eyes stared back at him from brown felt faces. Dolls? Dozens of them, unlike any he'd seen before. His sisters had occasional dolls years ago, and sometimes little fugitive girls carried one clutched to their chest.

But none of them had ever been brown.

The light footstep he registered was now recognizable as Mrs. Markland's, and he instinctively backed away from the crates. The girls passed by the door, continuing down the hall, but the lady herself came toward him with two more dolls in her hands.

"Do you like our work?" she asked, her tone light, maybe teasing.

Embarrassed at having been caught snooping, Patrick didn't reply for a beat. "I've never seen anything like them." His honesty surprised him, and apparently her too, because she stopped at the crates with the dolls in hand to look at him.

"Black dolls?"

He nodded.

Mrs. Markland bent, placing her dolls gently on top of the ones in the crate. "For little Black girls," she supplied brightly, her face beaming.

Patrick had lost all hope of being able to act normally around the creature, but if she was leaving the boardinghouse soon, she could return to Cleves and her odd life.

"Do you sell them here?" He wasn't sure why he asked, since he didn't particularly care.

"We give them away." Still bent over the crate, Mrs. Markland stroked a smooth brown face with her finger. "To girls new to freedom traveling through the city."

Disbelief almost produced a laugh out of Patrick, but he reigned it in before she stood and faced him.

He wasn't tempted to tell the stranger that he ran a busy Underground Railroad stop in a southern city. But his experience told him that the needs of fugitives for basic survival—for food, clothing, blankets, medical supplies, shelter—were so great and so far from being met that it was foolish and naive for those who had resources and ability to spend time making luxury items to donate to the newly emancipated. It defied belief and only showed how clueless she was.

"I see," he said with all the politeness he could muster.

An uncomfortable silence fell for a full minute before the Lelands and Adamses arrived and Rachel announced supper.

Patrick stayed out of the supper conversation as much as possible, offering the occasional smile, nod, and response required to appear civil. When the Lelands and Adamses retired to the parlor afterward for a game of whist, he bowed and declined their invitation to join in. He waited until they had disappeared before slipping into the warm kitchen.

Annoyance twisted through him at the sight of Mrs. Markland, who had beat him to his formerly safe haven and was standing by the table talking to the little girls. Patrick turned away, rolling his eyes at the wall, before approaching Uncle Charles. He glanced over to ensure Mrs. Markland wasn't paying attention to him before cutting his voice low.

"Are you going to the Anti-Slavery Society meeting tonight?"

"Not tonight." Uncle Charles sighed. "I'm plumb wore out."

Patrick backed up. "I'm going to head over there now."

"I'm coming." The feminine voice sliced into their quiet conversation, and Patrick jerked his head toward Mrs. Markland.

She stood facing them across the room, her face all innocence, as if nothing was amiss. "I need to take the dolls. Would you be willing to help me with them?"

Patrick managed to chase down his escaped voice. "To carry them?"

"If you could take one of the crates, that would be wonderful."

It would go against all of his moral upbringing to refuse, but Patrick could think of a list of things he'd rather do than tote Mrs. Markland's toys through Cincinnati. Shovel coal on a train. Work a funeral detail on a battlefield. Attend a fancy dress dinner with politicians.

Well, maybe not the last one.

"Of course," he said, eying her with distrust. Maybe she didn't own the boardinghouse, but surely the members of the society could see through the Southern-bred woman who kept little maids and donated trifles to those whose lives hung by a thread. But then, apparently Rachel and Uncle Charles didn't. Still, there was a difference between being anti-slavery and being an abolitionist. Even colonizationists were against slavery.

Mrs. Markland withdrew to the parlor to retrieve her crates, saving Patrick from having to be the one to explain them to the other guests. He went up to his room for his coat and hat and passed Mary ushering the little girls up to Mrs. Markland's room on his descent to the foyer.

Mrs. Markland was there with the crates and a lantern at her feet, setting a feather and lace-covered bonnet over her brown hair and tying the ribbons under her chin.

Patrick stifled all the revulsion he felt toward escorting her out and summoned an impassive face. On his final approach, he gave his hat brim another tug.

"Are you ready?"

He bent down for a crate, lifting and handing it to her. The cloth dolls weren't heavy, but the wooden boxes would be enough to cause aching arms by the time they reached the meeting. He couldn't manage both of them on his own and wasn't about to suggest what she might or might not be capable of handling.

Anna thanked Patrick in a distant voice and stepped back from him as soon as she grasped the crate. He opened the front door before placing the unlit lantern atop his crate and hoisting it, waiting for her to pass into the golden evening ahead of him.

She was tempted to say something about the lantern squashing the dolls, but she didn't dare. He obviously had a low impression of her as it was. The last thing she wanted was to antagonize the proud man who donned a mask whenever she was in the vicinity and groaned with impatience upon hearing that she was going to the same meeting as he.

She kept to herself as they walked side by side down the street. Rather than give Patrick another shred of her sanity, she reviewed her to-do list for this trip and the purchases secured in her wagon in the stable.

There was a lot more she would have liked to do—friends to visit, inquiries to make on behalf of Leah and Jane, better prices to haggle—but the necessary things were finished, and she'd been stuck in bed far too long. Her conscience wouldn't let her stay another day.

Anna's arms burned by the time they reached the *Philanthropist* office and she stepped through the door to the downstairs meeting room. The room was warm from a coal stove and the twentyish people standing around. Anna released her crate onto the floor with a thud. Patrick placed his beside hers and immediately turned to greet Mr. Birney. With his attention off of her, she faced the wall and rubbed her sore arms in privacy.

"You brought them!"

Anna looked up at the exclamation to find her friend Margaret Bailey beside her in a navy frock. Margaret scooped up a doll to admire as Anna looked beyond her, spying her bearded husband greeting Patrick.

"They're so sweet, and the girls dearly love them." She reached out to clasp Anna's hand, and Anna returned her smile.

"Take as many as you need. How are you and the children?"

As Margaret talked, a spot danced across Anna's right eye. She blinked, trying to focus, and another moment later, it was gone.

Oh no. Rubbing her gloved hands down her skirts did nothing to alleviate their sweatiness. Anna took a deep breath and slowly blew it out. *Please, Lord,* she prayed to fight the fear rising in her throat.

"I'm going to fetch a drink of water. The walk over here left me a bit parched. But do let the others know they can take dolls too," she said to Margaret, who waved her away and turned back to her husband.

Anna slipped around an elderly clergyman wheezing through the door and hurried out to the street as more dots speckled her vision. It was growing dark, but the cool evening air was an instant relief. A few jerks of the pump handle on the corner sent cold water bursting out. Tearing her gloves off and cupping her hands, Anna took a couple of drinks and then patted her face and the back of her neck. It was too dark to stay out here alone, but the room was too stuffy. She took lungs full of the fresh air, pausing to close her eyes and calm her panicked heart before slowly walking back to the door.

It swung open as she reached it, and Patrick stood in the doorway.

"There you are." He stepped back to allow her entrance in a sudden attempt to appear nonchalant, but his eyes roamed over her face. He didn't look truly concerned, and she wasn't going to fool herself into thinking otherwise—but he must have felt some sort of responsibility for her to come looking.

Anna put on a look brighter than she felt as she stepped inside. "Yes, thank you."

Mr. Birney approached the front of the room, and she was out of time to make personal inquiries of her friends. Patrick Gallagher was forgotten. She slipped into one of the chairs set up for women as Mr. Birney called the meeting to order. After the welcome, he proceeded to give the first speech of the evening. His friendly demeanor and the way he carried himself reminded her of her father, and she enjoyed the rare opportunity to hear him speak. As a former slaveowner, he understood both sides of the matter of slavery and was able to speak for abolition with logic, clearheadedness, and compassion that made him likable and his talks easy to follow.

Dr. Bailey spoke next, and when he concluded, called Patrick Gallagher to the front. Anna jolted in surprise, twisting around to see him push off from the wall he'd been standing against in the back. The man really could work on his presentation. He was as brown as if he worked on the river all day, his clothes sloppily assembled. In short, he looked like half the city of Cincinnati—more precisely, the half that didn't attend society meetings.

He reached the front and turned to flash a boyish grin at the attendees, but it didn't match the gravity his eyes always carried. Who was he trying to put on an act for?

"I was asked to share what I've seen and experienced pertaining to the cause across the country. My experience is limited to one person, of course, and all names and details will be censored."

Anna straightened. He was smarter than his appearance gave him credit for. Her vision clouded, and she closed her eyes, waiting for the film to clear. Even with slow, deep breaths, the spots were still there, blurring his image, when she opened her eyes again.

Patrick spoke about the Underground Railroad in Baltimore with the authority of someone who was intimately acquainted with it, and how spending his life in a slave state had affected his thinking as an example of how societies become complacent with the evil in their midst.

The man was a surprisingly good speaker. He obviously knew how to hold an audience, to keep his stories succinct, engaging, and personal. Anna pursed her lips. He had experience. And a lot of it.

"I left Baltimore in March, taking the opportunity to traverse the new National Road on foot through the mountains to the Pennsylvania border," he continued.

On foot? Never mind his silver tongue—she was right in her original assertion that he was an odd duck.

This was followed by stories of slaves, fugitives, and freedmen he passed on his journey, Quakers he stayed with, and a pastor who nursed him back to health in Columbus. He mentioned Underground Railroad routes and the free labor store with the tact of someone who knew this meeting wasn't safe from spies.

"I've been honored to meet many of you this week, and when I depart shortly to continue on my journey to St. Louis and Elijah Lovejoy, I'll remember you and the good work you are doing in Cincinnati fondly, keeping you in my prayers."

He stepped aside, and the audience broke into applause. Anna clapped half-heartedly, but her mind was whirling. His leaving soon was news to her, and she hadn't known where he was headed next. He'd only talked for twenty minutes, and she found herself wishing to hear more of his stories.

Mr. Birney was back at the front. "The meeting is now open for news and updates. Slave catchers from Kentucky apprehended our friend Robert Jones this week and succeeded in returning him across the river. Another safe house of one of our friends here was compromised and raided, but no souls were taken. Yes, Mrs. Markland?"

Anna had raised her hand and now came to her feet. Dizziness washed over her, and she reached for the chair back in front of her as she spoke.

"We're continuing to look for the parents of Leah and Jane, estimated to be ten and eight. Their boat was capsized in the crossing last July and the parents are missing. The parents' names are Joshua and Sandra, and the girls believe they came from southeast of Nashville. Leah and Jane are under my protection until their parents are found, but if I'm not in town, let Dr. Bailey know of any information and he'll get the message to me."

Anna swallowed and sucked in oxygen, but the dizziness didn't pass.

"Also, the girls and I have brought more dolls to be given to any little girls passing through safe houses on their way to freedom, so if you oversee one, please take some dolls. Leah and Jane would be so pleased."

She sank into her seat and shut her eyes as the room tilted. Another name was called, and she heard the man's voice but couldn't focus on the announcement.

Jesus, have mercy. Pain pulsed behind her closed eyes. She knew she had to leave, but grief at what the pain meant kept her glued to the chair. One thing was certain—staying and visiting with friends afterward would not only keep her in the stuffy room longer and exacerbate the symptoms, but they would ask if she was unwell, requiring her to come up with an explanation. The last thing she wanted was to use her small strength to help others understand why it was small.

Drawing in a deep breath, she counted to three and exhaled, focusing on the measure of each subsequent breath as a distraction. One breath at a time. One minute at a time. One meeting at a time.

20

"I am sure it is doing good or the devil would not be so mad about it."
- Elijah Lovejoy

Mrs. Markland was not his responsibility or his problem.

He simply walked beside her to the same meeting, which meant he would probably be walking back the same way. Unless she had friends with a buggy who were also watching the way her eyes were closed over pale cheeks and her hands clenched around the bonnet on her lap. Her appearance now made her look even younger and more vulnerable than before, and his heart pricked with the knowledge of her real role in Leah and Jane's lives.

The meeting continued on around him, but Patrick couldn't tear his gaze from her. Hopefully she wasn't going to faint. What could he do to help? Would a drink of water suffice? He didn't have a cup, and his experience with her and whatever ailed her was almost nil.

This was why he had Elly. Because Patrick Gallagher had no idea how to take care of a woman.

And Mrs. Markland wasn't his responsibility anyway.

Mr. Birney called the meeting to a close, and the room erupted in conversation. Patrick stood tense, ready, watching as Mrs. Markland came to her feet, grasping the chair in front of her. In two strides, he was by her side.

"Are you ready to go?" he asked in a low voice, shooting out a steadying hand to her elbow.

"So soon? Don't you have people who want to talk to you after your speech?"

Patrick looked, finding several sets of eyes on them. It was true that some of them were probably hoping for a word with him; that would be better than discovering they were staring at Mrs. Markland.

"I don't need to stay. Do you?"

Mrs. Markland took a trembling breath, still without meeting his eyes. "No."

Which led to the next question he didn't know how to form. "Would you . . . prefer to walk out together or on your own right now?"

Mrs. Markland lifted the bonnet to her head and tied it on with stiff movements before answering. "Together," she whispered, barely audible over the voices around them.

"Mr. Gallagher, it was a fine talk you gave," a voice at his side declared.

With his hand still bracing Mrs. Markland's arm, Patrick pivoted toward the older man beside him. The spectacled gentleman was a local businessman Marius had introduced him to after church on Sunday, but Patrick couldn't think of his name.

"Thank you." Patrick managed a smile even as he felt Mrs. Markland slip her hand through his elbow. She must truly be bad off.

"We've been talking about forming a free labor store here, and I'd be interested in talking to you about the one you visited." The man blocked the aisle and Patrick's escape, and a glance around showed more people gathered, waiting for a minute with him. Patrick drew his elbow in, thus moving Mrs. Markland into his side.

"I look forward to doing so the next opportunity we get. I need to get Mrs. Markland back to the girls in her charge now." He stepped forward, and the man moved back.

With more nods and excuses, Patrick managed to part the crowd and usher her to the door. After lighting the lantern, he glanced back one more time to give an apologetic glance toward Mr. Birney but didn't see him.

Outdoors, they joined others separating toward their homes. The cool air was pleasant after the closeness of the meeting room, and Patrick became aware that he'd been sweating. His career as a public speaker wasn't ended, as he'd thought when he left the legislature, and he grimaced at the realization. Mrs. Markland was silent and stiff beside him as he returned farewell greetings on his escape to a quieter street.

At the first semblance of privacy, he stopped, releasing her. "Are you quite well?" He didn't need an explanation; he just needed to know if she'd be able to make it back to Rachel's. Then she'd go back to being in Rachel's care, whom Uncle Charles claimed loved her, and the odd night could end.

She looked even paler in the lantern light, her lips a thin line. "I need some water."

He would be in trouble if she fainted on him. He'd caused enough trouble by escorting her out to the dark tucked into his side like he did, but he planned on being long gone from the city before she was forced to give an explanation to any witnesses.

Patrick looked around the street. "There should be a water pump." He moved away from her and walked around, swinging his lantern, until the light bounced off a black iron handle. "It's over here." Grabbing the handle, he waited for Mrs. Markland to make her way over. He realized his mistake too late as she tottered over the street. Patrick stepped forward to meet her and give her his support again when she suddenly halted, bent over, and heaved her dinner onto the cobblestones. Or what would have been the cobblestones if Patrick's feet hadn't arrived in that location, protecting the stones from the onslaught.

Horrorstruck, he stared at his boots and what the lantern revealed of the residue splattered up to his trouser legs. *Unbelievable.* Out of all the sicknesses of his own and the fugitives in his house, never once had any of them managed to make his person their target. What was it about this woman?

Mrs. Markland remained folded in half for a long minute while Patrick stood like a statue, at a complete loss for what to do.

"I'm so sorry," Mrs. Markland finally whispered before falling backward, landing in a seated position on the street away from the mess. Her knees were tucked up under her skirts, and she leaned her forehead to rest on them.

Patrick gingerly stepped backward in disgust, shaking his feet to slide the damage off. In a couple of strides he was back at the water pump, yanking the handle harder than necessary. Water gushed over his feet, and he took turns lifting them from side to side to remove the worst of the gunk. If the water wasn't so cold, he'd duck his whole body under and take a bath. When he had to admit that his boots couldn't get any cleaner with the method, he cut the stream off.

Mrs. Markland hadn't moved from her seat on the street. Compassion twinged in his heart. He'd tried to help her leave the meeting with her dignity attached despite his discomfort around her, but he wouldn't wish this situation on anyone. If she wasn't well enough to be out of bed, she shouldn't have come to the meeting with him. Why hadn't Rachel insisted she stay in her room?

"Can I help you over to the pump?" he asked in a low voice.

She didn't lift her head or respond. Patrick's gaze bounced around the street. Should he go locate a hack for rent? With what money? The few dollars he'd earned were back at the boardinghouse. And he'd removed her from her friends at the meeting for this precise reason—he was the only one who knew of her humiliated state.

A buggy turned onto the end of the street, and Patrick bent over Mrs. Markland with more urgency, lifting his lantern higher to alert the driver of their presence. "Let me help you out of the street." With an insistent tug, he slid his arm under her elbow, helping her to her feet. The buggy slowed, and they limped around the puddle she'd left in the road. He pumped the water for her, and she cupped her hands, taking multiple drinks and patting her face and neck. When she finally stepped back, he closed the handle, and the street was quiet once more.

"Thank you. I apologize, Mr. Gallagher."

"Do you think you can make it back?"

There was an unmistakable hesitation before she said, "Yes."

"What would . . . how can I be of the greatest assistance?"

Her lips were white now, pressed firmly together, and her eyes didn't lift above his chest. She didn't answer for a long minute, during which time a wagon clattered past and faded into the distance.

"I get these headaches," she said. Her voice was so quiet, Patrick bent his head to hear. "It's not so much pain. Well, it is, but it's not like normal headaches. One doctor used the word megrims, but others call them sick headaches. I can walk, but I'm dizzy."

He pondered. "So it helps to keep your eyes closed?"

"Whenever possible." Her head lowered further, her bonnet blocking her face altogether.

"All right then." There weren't multiple options, and he didn't have to like it. He just had to get this ridiculous evening to end. "I'll support you, and you just close your eyes and hold onto my arm. Can you trust me?"

"I'd rather not."

He almost laughed at her unexpected answer. One had to appreciate people who were honest. "That makes two of us, but it's the best option for getting you back without making a scene."

After another silent beat, he extended his hand to her. Mrs. Markland took a deep breath, then sighed. Her hand reached out, curling around his bicep and gripping his shoulder, securing her tightly at his side.

"Now close your eyes," he said gently. He couldn't see whether she did or not, so after a minute, he slowly stepped forward. Within a few paces, they had found a matching stride, slow and easy. Patrick prayed for her sake that they wouldn't run into anyone she knew while she was attached to him like this.

When they got to Rachel's, he'd deliver her to the kitchen, in case the other guests were still up, and then set about changing and properly cleaning his boots. He went over his plan repeatedly as they made their way down the street.

"Your speech was nice."

He started when Mrs. Markland broke the silence. Assuming she didn't feel well enough to speak, he hadn't tried to make conversation.

"Thank you."

"I can imagine what you must think of me. I'm terribly embarrassed."

His mouth twitched. She had no idea what he thought of her, which was definitely a good thing.

"It's not your fault. These things happen."

"Are we almost there?"

"No. We've gone one block."

At that, her head fell against his shoulder and stayed there. Patrick let it.

The truth was, he'd been wrong about her twice—at least. He only knew of the two instances, but was it possible that there were more? First, assuming that she owned the boardinghouse and was a terrifying, shiftless employer, and second by his conclusion that Leah and Jane worked for her. Was she merely a caregiver to the two parentless children?

"How often do you get these . . . sick headaches?"

They'd reached a cross street, and Patrick lifted the lantern hand to tug his hat low, hoping to conceal his identity from prying eyes for the sake of Mrs. Markland's reputation.

"I don't know. Maybe two or three a month. I just had one earlier in the week and thought . . ."

Her voice trailed off, and a minute later, Patrick realized she was swiping at her face with her free hand.

"Hey, don't cry. That'll make it worse, won't it?"

"Yes." The word came out in a sob, and she covered her mouth with her hand.

Maybe he shouldn't have asked, because thinking about it had definitely upset her.

"Sorry," he muttered. How should he have known it would make her cry? "We can talk about something else. Are your eyes still closed?"

"Yes. Where are we?"

"Um . . ." Patrick looked up the busy street. He remembered crossing it before, but what was its name? "I don't know."

"You don't know?" She stopped walking, halting him as well.

"Don't open your eyes. It's the one with the church, but I can't remember the name of it." He tugged her forward, and thankfully, she moved.

"The one with the church?" She gave a little laugh. Cincinnati was littered with churches.

"I have been to the *Philanthropist* a few times this week, so I do know this route. Don't worry. We have a couple more blocks to go." She had stopped crying, so the distraction seemed to have worked. He didn't dare ask her any more of his long list of questions.

"What paper do you work for?"

He gave a humph at the irony. With questions like hers, maybe he'd start crying next.

"I don't work for a paper."

"You told me you were a reporter. Do you sell your articles to anyone who will buy them?"

"I don't—" He sighed. He didn't owe her an explanation, really. "I'm not currently employed, but Mr. Birney bought an editorial from me this week. I quit my job to come here."

"Not here. St. Louis."

"Well, yes. But Mr. Lovejoy isn't there at the moment, so I won't head there until he returns from Pennsylvania."

"He'll come through here on his way."

Of course he would; Patrick hadn't thought of it. Lovejoy would take a steamboat like a reasonable person, and it would be unlikely that he'd pass Cincinnati without seeing his friend Birney while the boat was at dock.

Maybe Patrick would meet him sooner than he thought—and they could simply ride the rest of the way together.

"What made you decide to walk?" she asked.

"I wanted to see the country."

"That's not a reason. Everyone who gets off a steamboat in Cincinnati gives the same answer."

Fine. He would never have to see her again, so what did it matter if he told her the truth? "I needed time to be alone."

"That's it?"

"It about sums it up. We're on Rachel's street now."

"I know."

"Hey, close your eyes!"

Mrs. Markland gave her little laugh again. "They are closed. I recognize the little dog that's barking. I could hear him through my window all week."

He'd be saved from more conversation now that the walk was almost over. Or so he thought.

"Did you just get out of a relationship?"

What?

"Excuse me?" Patrick sputtered.

"Oh, I'm sorry. It was the explanation my mind had for why someone would want to be alone for that long. You know, nursing a broken heart."

Patrick bit his tongue. Maybe she wasn't that far off from the truth.

"My last relationship was neither recent nor the sort that left me with a broken heart," he said evasively. Some might call the information personal, but it wasn't half as personal as admitting to what really had broken his heart.

She hummed as if she was still trying to untangle the truth, but the boardinghouse was in front of them.

"We're here. How are you doing?" Patrick stopped, allowing her to separate from him before they were seen.

Mrs. Markland opened her eyes and swayed slightly. "I wish this wasn't happening again," she whispered. The vulnerability he'd seen in the meeting returned to her face, and he didn't know how to respond.

"Can you make it around to the kitchen?" he asked, stepping forward and extending a hand back to her.

Ignoring his hand, Mrs. Markland took a steadying breath and followed him.

21

"Though of delicate health, she endures affliction more calmly than I had supposed possible for a woman to do." - Elijah Lovejoy

Rachel and Dorcas were at the kitchen table lingering over cups of tea, and Mary and Peggy stood at the door with their wraps on as if they were about to depart. Patrick opened the door and ushered Mrs. Markland into the tidy space, his eyes finding Rachel's. She came to her feet as he tilted his head toward his charge.

"Are you unwell?" Rachel rushed forward, her black skirts swaying.

Mrs. Markland's hand went to her eyes. "It's back." Her voice was soft but tight with pain, and Rachel's arm was around her in an instant.

"Oh, dearie. Sit down, and we'll bring the remedies."

Mary and Peggy remained uncertainly by the door waiting for orders as Mrs. Markland collapsed into the chair Rachel propelled her toward. Dorcas had a cup of water in her hand in a split second and the kettle returned to its hook over the hearth.

Mrs. Markland sipped her water before her head dropped forward onto her arms on the table. "Thank you."

"The girls are upstairs, and we should get you on up to bed," Rachel said, blowing the lamps out. Only Patrick's lantern and the hearth fire remained lit, but at Rachel's deliberate stare, he put the lantern out and returned it to its hook by the door.

"I can't. Where is Uncle Charles?"

"He went out to close up the stable. What do you need?"

Mrs. Markland sighed from under her arms. "I have to leave tomorrow."

"You can't travel like this, sweetie." Rachel stood behind her, running her thumbs across Mrs. Markland's shoulders. "Where does it hurt?"

"My eyes right now. Oh, do take care of Mr. Gallagher. He'll need cleaning up."

Patrick shifted awkwardly as the female eyes turned to him. "Just some warm water sent up to my room." His problems seemed suddenly unimportant and not worth leaving Mrs. Markland for, especially if she would need help up the stairs in a few minutes.

Mary was back at the worktable, chopping onions and herbs and placing them in a cheesecloth. Some kind of poultice, probably. Dorcas stopped by her to give instructions before plodding over and filling another kettle of water and swinging it over the fire Peggy was poking back to life. Rachel continued to massage Mrs. Markland's neck and shoulders, but she turned her attention to the door when it opened and Uncle Charles shuffled in.

"What's the problem?" he asked, looking around the room.

"The missus has another spell comin' on." Rachel ran the back of her hand over her forehead.

"I have to go home tomorrow," Mrs. Markland said without lifting her head. "I've been gone too long, and I can't stay away from my mother-in-law any longer."

"How do you plan on getting there?" Uncle Charles asked.

"I don't know. Do you know of a driver I can hire to take us in the wagon?"

Patrick moved his hands to his pockets and leaned back against the window frame.

"I can ask around, but it would cost you," Uncle Charles replied, scratching his chin. "It's a far piece to Cleves."

"About seventeen miles. I'll drive it myself if I have to."

"Why don't you just take a boat?" Patrick asked, stating the obvious.

Rachel and Charles stared at him, and Rachel gave a little shake of her head. Well, so much for his help. A boat would easily be the quickest and cheapest way to take a load of supplies downriver.

"You're going that way, aren't you?"

Patrick snapped to attention when he realized Uncle Charles was addressing him.

"Toward St. Louis. Cleves is on your way," Uncle Charles continued.

"Well, I . . . I wasn't going to leave Cincinnati quite yet since Mr. Lovejoy . . ."

Rachel straightened. "I don't have any more work for you to do here."

It was a lie, and they all knew it. But he had finished the projects he'd started, and she could choose not to hire him for any others.

"I don't have anything to do in Cleves either."

Rachel leveled a chastising look at him. Apparently he was wrong about that too.

"He doesn't have to if he doesn't want to," Mrs. Markland said quietly from under her arms.

"Between your inn and your mother-in-law, do you have any jobs that could use a man's hand?" Rachel asked.

"Of course. There's always plenty of work, but I hadn't budgeted for it."

"He works for room and board," Rachel said, and a gasp of protest left Patrick's lips.

He clamped his mouth shut. Mrs. Markland was clearly suffering, and now was not the time to be petty.

Dorcas shuffled over with the warm poultice, which she laid on the back of Mrs. Markland's neck, and Peggy placed some sort of hot liquid before her in a mug.

"You girls can go on now," Rachel said, and Mary and Peggy said their goodbyes and slipped out the door.

Rachel, Uncle Charles, and Dorcas all turned to Patrick as soon as the door was closed. Goodness, but they were a fiercely loyal bunch. What would it take to get them in his corner? He could use friends like this.

"Mr. Gallagher," Rachel began from her position behind Mrs. Markland, "would you be willing to drive my friend and her girls up to Cleves tomorrow?"

He pondered all the angles of the effects it would have on him. Would he wait out Lovejoy in Cleves then, or come back? Was his time in Cincinnati truly over—and was that something he could accept?

"Do you have work for me to do in Cleves, Mrs. Markland?" he finally asked.

Her form lay still on the table. "I do, actually. We have outstanding repairs that we haven't gotten to for some time."

"Would you hire me to do them for room and board . . . and two dollars a week?"

She was silent for a moment. "How much for driving us there?"

Uncle Charles was wrong; Cleves was west, but it wasn't exactly on Patrick's way. He'd planned to return north to Columbus and the National Road, or maybe cut across and pick it up in Indianapolis. Driving her to the North Bend wouldn't really hold an advantage for him.

"A dollar," he said. Rachel scowled at him in the dim light, and Uncle Charles rolled his eyes and shook his head in exasperation. "Nothing," Patrick corrected in a mumble.

"I'll pay you," Mrs. Markland said. "Rachel, the hammer is starting. I'm afraid I need to lie down. Are we done here?"

The kettle shrieked, and Dorcas swung it off the fire. "Here's your water, Mr. Gallagher."

"Thank you. Yes, we're done; I'll drive Mrs. Markland tomorrow, but I'm not sure how long I'll stay in Cleves." Had he done everything he'd hoped to here? If he was leaving in the morning, he should finish the second editorial he'd started for Mr. Birney and turn it in when he went to say goodbye in the morning. But first, he was itching to get out of his soiled clothes.

Rachel was helping Mrs. Markland to her feet. Her hair had half fallen out of her bun, and the confident woman he'd passed the last two days was gone, only a limp shell of her remaining. Uncle Charles moved to her other side to lend support.

"I didn't get a chance to learn anything about the girls' parents," Patrick heard Mrs. Markland sigh to them on the way out the door.

"I guess you're stuck with me then," Dorcas said to him, using a towel to retrieve the hot kettle when Patrick was alone with her.

"Don't worry. I'll take it up myself." Patrick reached out, and she surrendered the kettle to him.

"Well, thank you, sir. And if I don't get a chance to tell you tomorrow, you take mighty good care of Mrs. Markland, you hear?"

Patrick stepped toward the door, steam rising from the kettle in his hands. "I will, but why?" He dipped his head. "I mean, why her more than anyone else?"

Dorcas widened her eyes in a *because I said so* look. "She's one of the sweetest, most considerate people you'll meet and doesn't have anyone to fight for her. You understand me?"

Did he? All the sweet and considerate women he knew—Bridget, Maisie, Betha—had families to ensure no one took advantage of them.

But once upon a time, when he'd first met Betha, she didn't have that. Living with a brother who couldn't see past the end of his own nose and his child, whom she was raising, Betha had been forced to stick up for herself. Most of the time, she didn't bother. The militant protection of Mrs. Markland by Rachel and her staff made a lot more sense now.

"I do. Thank you." He took another step backward. "I know it's late and I apologize, but if I clean myself and my boots, is there any way I could get these trousers laundered before I have to leave in the morning?"

Dorcas's affectionate smile returned on her wrinkled face. "Set them outside your door, and I'll take care of them. Don't you worry about a thing."

22

"Truth is eternal, unchanging, though circumstances may and do operate to give a different colour to it, in our view, at different times."
- Elijah Lovejoy

The steep road leading up the terrace in the direction of Walnut Hills beckoned the next morning as Patrick eyed it wistfully on his walk back to Rachel's. Ellis was someone he would have liked to spend more time with, but now he was leaving without returning to Lane again, or the African Baptist church. His good-byes to Mr. Birney, Marius, Mr. Pugh, and Dr. Bailey at *The Philanthropist* a few minutes ago had wrenched more than he expected. The week had flown by, but the things he'd learned and people he'd met in this place would surely remain a part of him for years to come.

Maybe he'd return to the boardinghouse to find Mrs. Markland much improved. If so, he would choose to stay in an instant. Patrick fingered the banknote in his pocket, Mr. Birney's payment for the editorial he'd labored over by lantern light until after midnight. Mr. Birney hadn't even read it; he'd thought so highly of the first one that he gave Patrick five dollars on the spot upon receipt of the second one.

The determination to go on to St. Louis, when Patrick considered it, remained alive and well in his heart. He did want to continue his exploration of the state not only of the African American community but abolitionism across the country, and the longing to know Elijah Lovejoy beyond a conversation or two still burned bright. So if he had to leave sometime, well, he might as well make himself useful and go with Mrs. Markland now.

A tin wagon clattered past and Patrick veered out of its way, sidestepping to avoid a chicken pecking at crumbs in the dust.

Don't be so selfish. Maybe leaving early wasn't his first choice, but had he considered anything other than how it would affect himself? Had he given Mrs. Markland more than a passing thought, or how his escort of her would provide Uncle Charles and Rachel with peace of mind for her care?

Patrick cringed at the thought of Leah and Jane. He had the opportunity to offer them protection, and they hadn't crossed his mind at all when he resolved to be their driver. In fact, little had gone into the decision other than the very clear understanding that Rachel would kick him out and he'd earn the ire of all his friends at the boardinghouse if he didn't.

"Lord, if You'd be inclined, I'd be grateful for Your help today with the three of them. I don't know the way to Cleves other than to follow the river, and Mrs. Markland already got sick all over me once. I'm not sure how she'll handle the trip, but it would sure be a blessing if that didn't happen again and You provided comfort for her and the girls . . . and kept us from getting lost."

His long, quick strides took him past tailors, cobblers, and coopers that had become familiar over the last several days. He wouldn't be selfish, and he'd obey Dorcas and do his best to get her friend home safely, but that didn't mean he liked it. Being in Mrs. Markland's presence had been uncomfortable since their first meeting, and learning the truth about her had made that worse, not better. Now being around her brought embarrassment, reminders of his foibles. She still annoyed him, just without the justifiable excuse he'd had at the start, and that was even more annoying. The consoling thought that carried Patrick up Rachel's walk was that Mrs. Markland had humiliated herself all over him last night. Surely she would want to avoid him now as much as he wanted to avoid her.

Leah and Jane stood at the open front door, watching Uncle Charles tote Mrs. Markland's trunk to the laden wagon parked out front. After donning his laundered trousers that morning, Patrick had stuffed all his belongings back into his knapsack. There was nothing else he needed to do but grab it.

"Is there anything else to load?" he asked Uncle Charles on his way past.

"Nope, this is it," Uncle Charles called over his shoulder. Leah and Jane parted as Patrick jogged up the front stairs. Mrs. Markland was halfway down the inside staircase, descending slowly on Rachel's arm, her face bleach white.

"I'll just grab my knapsack," he told Rachel. "Do I owe anything more on my bill?"

"We're settled," Rachel replied.

As it should be. He took the stairs two at a time and returned with his knapsack before they were to the wagon. Dorcas stood at the back of it, spreading out a quilt between grain sacks.

"You girls can sit right up here and be snug and comfortable on the ride."

They nodded mutely and obediently climbed up, settling into the spot. Patrick found a place under the front seat to shove his knapsack. He looked up in time to see Mrs. Markland climbing into the seat and quickly dove forward to offer his hand.

"You don't need to lie down in the back?"

She clasped his hand and landed in the seat. "No, thank you. I imagine I'll manage about the same in either place."

He gave her a wry look, wishing as much as she did that the grueling day was already over. While she and her friends began their goodbyes, he walked around the wagon, checking the wheels, horses, reins, and bridles. Rounding the corner of the wagon, he came face to face with Uncle Charles. The older man's grizzled eyebrows lifted as he looked Patrick over.

"God brought you to us for a reason." He made no attempt to hide the way his glance traveled toward Mrs. Markland and back again. "We're grateful."

After a thoughtful pause, Patrick inhaled. "Thank *you*. I hope to visit again in the future." Everything he'd experienced in Cincinnati would go with him to St. Louis, coloring the lens through which he'd see the culture, both black and white. But no more profound words came to him now as he backed away and climbed up to the seat beside Mrs. Markland.

A minute later, he cracked the whip and the horses started forward. Mrs. Markland clasped her hands on her lap, staring straight ahead, and the girls were silent in the back.

"Is this your team?" he asked, admiring the sleek brown backs of the horses in front of him.

"Yes."

"How are you doing? Did you get any sleep?"

"Some, thank you. It did help a little, and I hope to not have a repeat of last night."

He could do without the reminders. "If you feel like you might, just lean in the other direction, out of the wagon."

She did not laugh, and he wished the joke back. Then he remembered that he needed to pay attention to where they were going and steer the horses in the right direction. He focused on his driving and Mrs. Markland remained silent beside him, her hands clenched tightly together. They reached the river road and Patrick turned west to cross the Mill Creek bridge. Beyond the creek, high tree-topped bluffs rose on their right, and the wide river teemed with activity on their left. It should be a straightforward trip now; just follow the river to the North Bend.

Patrick relaxed, giving the horses their head, while Mrs. Markland slumped beside him now that there was less chance of passing traffic seeing her. Behind them, Leah and Jane were silent.

No one spoke until Patrick stopped at midday to eat on the riverbank. Mrs. Markland nibbled at the chicken Dorcas had packed, but she watched Leah and Jane like a mother hawk to ensure that they were eating enough. Patrick watched her hypocrisy silently, observing her movements and wondering what she was suffering physically. It was impossible to know what she was experiencing at the moment and how much she hid from him.

The irony of the situation struck him with a sense of discomfort—here he was, helping another Southern white woman. Even after his epiphany at the Widow Downer's more than a month ago, what he knew and what he'd always done warred with each other. What was God doing by repeatedly putting him in these situations? There weren't enough people willing to help assuage the staggering amount of needs of Black Americans, and he was willing. The favor he was doing now was to Mrs. Markland. She'd have driven Leah and Jane anyway.

When they had been on the road again for an hour, he glanced back to find both girls sound asleep, propped up against grain sacks with their heads lolling to the side. Mrs. Markland was tight-lipped beside him, and he offered up a tentative prayer for her pain. From the corner of his eye, he saw her sway, and darted out a hand to the back of her coat.

"Perhaps we should talk to help me stay awake."

Patrick withdrew his arm gingerly and curled his fingers around the reins again. What she needed was a closed carriage so she could sleep in privacy while he drove. But in lieu of that . . .

One of his most burning questions burst out before Mrs. Markland had time to pick the conversation topic herself.

"How did you come to have the care of Leah and Jane?"

She twisted around, presumably to ascertain what he already knew about their state of unconsciousness.

"I was there when it happened and was the one who found them." She faced forward again with her bonnet hiding her face and spoke in a low tone despite the fact that the girls were out cold.

"When the boat—?"

"Yes."

"And you only found the two of them?" Patrick tried to picture the scene. Night, probably, since that was when most runaways were rowed to freedom. If she was there, she must be the Underground Railroad operator whose job it was to meet them, for why else would someone be on the riverbank at night? A miracle, then, to have found the girls safely after their boat capsized, since it was likely they couldn't swim.

"Yes."

Her short answers didn't convince him that this was a topic she cared to talk about, but he had plenty of his own to avoid. If he asked questions, she couldn't.

"It was after you lost your husband?"

She turned to him then, fingers pressed against both of her temples. "He died four years ago, so yes."

If she'd lived in Cleves for seven years, he'd been gone longer than they'd been married. Patrick couldn't summon the gumption to ask how he died.

"Do you really think their parents survived?"

"Someone did. I could hear other people. It was the most awful night. It was a new moon, of course, so I couldn't see anything, and pulling the girls out of the river and getting them dry and safe took all my attention. When I saw lights come on at the Matsons'—the justice of the peace—I took the girls and hurried home. I thought anyone else would work their way to my inn eventually or I could find them in the morning, but my connections knew nothing the next day."

"And if anyone else survived, they could have been uncertain who to trust, so they went straight into hiding," Patrick mused.

"They could have been swept goodness knows how far downriver. They had to have assumed the girls didn't survive if they didn't stick around Cleves to search for them. They have an older son who'd escaped several years ago that they were going to join, but the girls don't know much about him."

"How do you explain the girls' presence to your neighbors?"

"Well, I kept them hidden indoors for two entire months. You've seen them, though—they are still so frightened and attached to me, they'll hardly speak to anyone else. Only my most trusted abolitionist friends knew so they could search for the parents. I smuggled Leah and Jane out to Cincinnati with me late last year and when I returned, they were riding in plain sight so it would appear that I'd simply hired help from the city."

Patrick thought of the sadness in their eyes and his heart sank with sorrow on their behalf. There could hardly be hope remaining after all this time that the parents hadn't died or been returned to chains. So often runaways who were recaptured were sold to the Deep South, and at this point, the sad reality was that Mrs. Markland would probably have custody of them indefinitely.

"Staying with me is their choice, you know," Mrs. Markland said softly even though Patrick hadn't questioned her. "There are African families in Cincinnati that would welcome them in, but they want to stay where they last saw their parents."

The wagon jolted over a rut, and Mrs. Markland groaned. "Sorry," he mumbled. For so very much. He'd been patently unfair to her from the beginning and only hoped she'd never find out by just how much. Shifting in his seat, he wondered how much trouble he'd be in for his next question. She seemed to be opening up to him a little and wasn't falling asleep anymore.

"Is that why you don't take the steamboat?" The girls would likely be terrified of water now, after experiencing such a catastrophe. "Because of the accident?"

"No," Mrs. Markland said shortly. "Well, I mean, it's one reason."

But not the main one. So . . . she herself didn't want to take the boat either. Perhaps it was how her husband died. Patrick wasn't going to be cruel enough to touch that with a bargepole.

"Where are you from?" he asked instead.

He could feel Mrs. Markland's eyes on him during the several breaths that she didn't respond.

"Outside of Louisville."

Patrick mentally congratulated himself on identifying her accent correctly.

"I've never been. Is your family still there?" *And are they slaveowners?*

"Yes, sir. I thought about going back after Isaac passed, but the inn is what I have left of him. And I help a good deal with Mother and Mr. Markland."

Her words sank through him, surprising him more by her willingness to talk so openly with a strange man than her actual words. But, like she'd said, she did need to stay awake.

"So you're in Cleves to stay?"

She tilted her head thoughtfully for a minute, then gave a definitive nod. "I think so," she said slowly, emphasizing the last word.

A rider neared, and Patrick tipped his hat as they passed one another. The sun had gone behind a cloud, so when the road was empty again, he swiped his sweaty curls off his forehead, pushing his cap to the back of his head. A glance at the sky revealed dark clouds forming in the west.

"Do you know where we could shelter up ahead if that storm beats us to your house?"

Mrs. Markland looked up, massaging her temples. "There are farms in a couple of miles. They have outbuildings we could wait in."

"You'll have to direct me when we get close. Does the weather affect your head?"

"No, actually. Sometimes certain foods do, so I have a very bland diet. Sometimes they seem to be brought on by stressful days or situations. Closed, crowded spaces cause them too. But other times they come with seemingly no reason or warning."

There was shuffling in the back, and two black heads popped up in Patrick's peripheral vision. The girls were awake, and he was saved from the effort of making more conversation for the time being. He turned to shoot them a quick grin, but they stared back without smiling. He couldn't blame them for being wary of him after all they'd been through. All he could do now was assist Mrs. Markland in giving them the best care possible and pray fervently for the reunion of their family.

23

"I can die at my post, but I cannot desert it." - Elijah Lovejoy

Anna's head swam as she pressed her palms into the bench on either side of her in an effort to stay upright. God had been gracious in helping the little bit of food she'd eaten stay down, and she'd avoided any more of Mr. Gallagher's looks of disgust like the one on the street last night. He might not be used to women heaving their dinners all over him, but he also didn't know that she was long past being embarrassed over every little humiliation her sickness had afforded her through the years. If he couldn't get over it, it wasn't her problem. He'd be on his way and out of her life soon enough.

She chanced opening her eyes to peek at him in time to see him glance back at the girls and give them a large, friendly smile. He sat relaxed against the wagon seat, his knees pointed to the sky to accommodate his long legs and his cap perched on the back of his head. He saw her staring at him and the smile faded. Anna arched an eyebrow and slipped her eyes closed again.

The sooner he left, the better.

For a minute, she'd thought they were getting somewhere with his questions. Knowing he had an irrational distrust of her, she'd answered honestly and with more than usual openness. She'd been fooled into thinking that with one conversation, she could help him get past whatever his issue with her was.

"Leah and Jane are awake," he said unnecessarily.

"Do they need a drink or to relieve themselves?" she asked.

Silence met her, and she opened her eyes again to see him staring straight ahead.

"You're not going to ask them?" A roguish smile formed on her face as he ran the backs of his fingers over his lips and shifted his legs. The view she had of embarrassed Patrick gave her the sense she was looking at a younger man, and it was the most attractive version of him she'd seen yet.

She raised her voice. "Leah and Jane, do you need to stop?"

"No, ma'am."

"We're about an hour from home," she said to them, noting the scenery, "but we might have to stop up ahead because it looks like it's going to rain."

"Seems you did well asking them yourself," Patrick said, and Anna couldn't stop a giggle.

"I suppose if you ever became a parent, you'd soon be used to all these things and more. Perhaps finding yourself with someone else's dinner all over you wouldn't be so unexpected then either."

He jerked toward her then, eyes wide, but not with horror or gall. The man was shocked merely because she'd spoken the unspoken things aloud.

"You are quite the woman," he mumbled, shaking his head and returning his attention to the horses.

She sobered, her amusement fading at his cold response. Why did she want him to like her and feel disappointed every time his walls reappeared? His opinion should be the very last thing she cared about right now, yet his inability to accept the humor she offered still stung.

Anna hugged her middle with one arm, resting the opposing elbow upright on its shelf with her face in her open hand, blocking out the light and putting pressure on her throbbing eyes. He was here because he'd been compelled by Rachel and Charles to come, not because he wanted to. She was an inconvenience to him, not a friend. He'd asked all those questions because he was nosy and probably wanted to know what situation he'd be working in this week so he could prepare for it. Well, hang it all. Hang him and the stupid sick headaches that came at the most inopportune times. She didn't want him to be here either.

The temptation to retaliate by snapping back and asking who had hurt him was strong. But who was she retaliating against? Him, for getting her to share too much? The headache, for blurring her mind? Herself, for continuing to believe that his little gestures of compassion meant he cared?

God, for sending not one, but two headaches during the few days she had with her Cincinnati friends?

A tear made its way out onto the palm pressed against her face.

Sure, God in his great wisdom must have some reason for shackling her with this sickness, but it felt so very unkind. She should be confessing her lack of faith to Him but couldn't bring herself to own it yet. Right now, her head hurt, Patrick annoyed her, and God seemed more oppressive than gracious.

More tears fell, and her nose began to run. Now she'd done it. She'd have to reach for a handkerchief, and Patrick would know she was crying. The thought of his witnessing one more humiliation made her so angry that the tears multiplied.

The situation became dire, forcing her to action. Reaching into her sleeve, she pulled the linen square out and pressed it to her nose. She was almost done cleaning herself up when he spoke.

"Mrs. Markland? I didn't mean anything by it. You just surprised me."

"It's not you." A sob burst out with the words. "Well, mostly not you."

He waited a beat before answering, probably trying to make out what that meant. "I'm sorry. For my part."

Anna started all over again in trying to swallow back her tears and stop her running nose.

"I don't think very often about the possibility of ever being a parent," he continued. "The thought took me off guard, and I only meant . . .well, most of the women I'm around don't bring it up."

Anna cried harder, the memory of a still, tiny swaddled being making her arms ache and doing little to bring her heart to terms with what she knew of God's sovereignty.

Patrick had the good sense to go quiet. He had no idea the hornet nests—plural—he'd poked at in the last twenty-four hours. He didn't need to know either. A cold drop of water landed on Anna's hand, and she lifted her head. That wasn't a tear. More drops landed around her, creating dark spots on her dress.

"It's raining," Patrick said, his voice small. "Tell me where to go."

Anna took a deep breath and swallowed. "Turn right at the next drive. The Hayeses have a barn not far from the road that we should be able to pull into." Her knowledge of the family was limited and more secondhand than ever having interacted with them.

Patrick obeyed as the rain picked up and the barn appeared. A man materialized, pushing the heavy barn door open as they approached. He must be one of the younger Hayes generation, looking to be in his twenties with blond hair poking out from under a straw hat like wheat stalks. Patrick took the implied invitation and pulled the wagon into it, the wet, cool air immediately replaced by the warm barn and sharp scents of hay and animals.

Patrick jumped to the ground and grabbed the nearest horse's bridle as the man approached. Anna stayed on the seat, head swimming, and waited to see what would happen. The girls stared about them with wide, silent eyes.

"The name's Gallagher, and we're heading to North Bend. Could we wait out the storm here?"

The man had spotted Anna and pushed his hat brim up, his spine straightening. Could he be any more obvious? "You're welcome to come get comfortable in the house and have refreshments while you wait."

"We're content here," Patrick said, glancing from Anna to young Hayes. He had to have picked up on the way the man's face lit when he looked at Anna. "We should be on our way before suppertime."

"Sure. No hurry."

Patrick lifted a hand to her, and Anna clasped it to carefully descend from her seat.

"Can I get you anything, Mrs. Gallagher?" Hayes asked when she was on the ground before him. "To make your stay more comfortable?"

"Oh, no, we aren't married," Anna said without thinking. She regretted it immediately. What did it matter if this man thought she was Patrick's wife for two hours?

"I'm her bodyguard," Patrick said easily.

Anna's tears from a minute ago nearly turned to snickers as Hayes sized Patrick up. He couldn't have just said "driver"? She bit her tongue to keep from snorting and managed to keep her face impassive. Patrick looked almost bored, but behind his heavy lids, his eyes were sharp, watching Hayes just as carefully.

"So do you need anything?" Hayes asked with a false brightness.

"No, thank you," Anna said. "You're very kind." It really was generous of him to invite them in, regardless of his motivation.

"Well, I need to get back to chores then, but you can use the benches," he said, pointing.

They stood watching as he picked up a covered milk pail and stepped out into rain that came down stronger now. Hayes stopped to shut the door most of the way, leaving a sliver of daylight in the barn besides the little that dusty windows let in.

Patrick laughed then, an infectious, full-bodied laugh. "You can use the bench, my lady," he mimicked, bowing low as his arm swept toward the wooden seat.

"Thank you, *bodyguard.*" She looked at him with both eyebrows raised, waiting for an explanation.

"You didn't have to tell him we aren't married, you know," he said, returning her look of challenge with one of his own.

"I forgot in that moment. Do you think he'll be back? I'd rather lie down against that haystack than sit on a bench."

"By all means. You've earned a rest, and I can divert him."

Before Anna could move, Patrick had shrugged out of his coat and spread it on the hay for her.

"Thank you."

While she settled onto her makeshift bed, he headed to the wagon and said something to the girls. Anna slipped her eyes closed, listening to the rain on the roof and Patrick's gentle cadence as he conversed with Leah and Jane.

All she could think about were the words "I'm her bodyguard" playing over and over in her mind in Patrick's rich, deep voice. But somehow, here on a pile of hay in a stranger's barn, a sense of safety encompassed her. She could rest only because he was here, handling the situation, caring for the girls, and giving her what she needed most.

Whatever possessed him to lay claim to the title, there was something so tangible about the truth of it, the safety she felt because of *him* . . . she could touch it. With that thought percolating through her veins, she fell asleep.

"Mrs. Markland?"

Anna was awakened by the sound of her name in Patrick's low voice close by. A hand closed around her upper arm, and she felt his thumb stroke over her sleeve.

"Mrs. Markland, the rain stopped. We should be on our way before it gets dark."

She opened her eyes to his brown ones leaning over her, rust-colored waves falling forward over his brow in the dim light.

"How are you feeling?"

Anna blinked, then turned her head to find Leah and Jane sitting on the bench, chewing on something and watching her. "A little better," she said in surprise. "I didn't know I'd fallen asleep." She pushed herself to a seated position, and only then did he pull back. "How long have we been here?"

"About an hour." He straightened up, looking somehow taller in his shirtsleeves and waistcoat without his coat covering half of his trousers. Anna didn't know why he even bothered with cravats, as he obviously didn't know how to tie one.

She made to stand up, and his hand appeared in front of her, an invitation. She grasped it and allowed him to pull her to her feet, purposely turning her mind to getting back on the road and away from how his hand felt encompassing hers.

A brief pause allowed her to gain her balance before moving forward. As she approached the girls, he said, "I gave them some jerky from my knapsack. I hope you don't mind?"

"It's good, Miss Anna," Jane said, swallowing her bite and wiping her hands on her pinafore. "Do you want some?"

She shook her head in a lie. It probably had spices in it she shouldn't eat and, as she was feeling better than she had since before retching all over Patrick last night, it wasn't a risk she felt comfortable taking.

"Are you ready to go?" she asked instead.

The door creaked and opened, revealing young Hayes again. "How is everyone doing?" he asked, looking around at them with a big smile. His gaze reached Anna and stayed there.

"We're doing well and are about to leave." Patrick picked hay off of his coat before pulling it on. "Thank you for the trouble."

"No trouble. My mother sent this." Hayes handed Anna a tied handkerchief, which was heavy when she took it. His eyes roamed over her, and she realized how disheveled she must look. Her hair was surely mussed, and she could only hope no hay stuck out of it.

"Thank her for us." She gave him a sweet smile before stepping toward the wagon and Patrick's waiting hand.

A few minutes later, they were rolling out of the barn into a hazy late afternoon. Droplets coated leaves and grass, and the clouds rolled eastward, opening up a clear sky to the west. Anna took a deep breath and let it out slowly. The pressure behind her eyes remained, but it was significantly less than before her nap, and she no longer had to wonder whether she'd make it all the way to Cleves in one piece.

"Are you doing all right?"

She looked over to catch Patrick shifting his eyes back to the horses.

"Yes." She turned her face up to the dissipating fog and forced the words out. "Thank you for driving."

"You're welcome."

"Are you going to stay with us until Mr. Lovejoy comes through?"

The horses clip-clopped forward another minute before he responded. "I'm thinking about it. What all do you need me to do around the place?"

"Well, there are a lot of little things like what you did for Rachel, but it would be nice to get some of the walls whitewashed. Do you do outdoor work? I have a dead tree that needs to be taken down. My friend has a sixteen-year-old son who could help if you need an extra pair of hands. He's capable but needs someone to help him stay on task."

"I don't know."

Anna's shoulders sagged. She'd done it again, asked too much. It was an ongoing problem, but she still hadn't learned when her asking went too far. It so often scared people away.

"If I'm still here, I can try, but I'm not much of an outdoors person."

She squinted her eyes at him in confusion. "You just walked across four states. And are planning to walk through three more."

"Yes." He gave a laugh that sounded more uncertain than humored. "Yes, I have been walking for about thirty-three years. Very good at it at this point, but you did not ask me to walk. Not even from Cincinnati to Cleves, denying me the chance to display my very fine walking skills."

"That's fair." Her smile surprised even her. "Still, walking from Cincinnati to Cleves would be out of doors. I presume the walk from Baltimore was as well, but I've never been there to say."

"It is indeed out of doors."

Had he not been a very new, very odd acquaintance, Anna might have pointed out the conflict between his words and his actions, and her curiosity would have prodded her to push for an explanation. From all appearances, the man's decisions weren't made based on logic.

"What did the man give you?"

"What?" The change of conversation jolted her back to the present and the package on her lap. "Oh. I almost forgot."

Untying the knots revealed four hard-boiled eggs and a hefty chunk of white cheese. "Food. Are you hungry?"

"Who isn't?"

Anna chose not to remind him of the jerky he had partaken of with the girls or how it wasn't even suppertime yet. "Well, give me a minute."

She peeled the eggs, handing two back to Leah and Jane before giving Patrick the third. Taking the pocketknife he offered, she cut the cheese into three chunks and distributed it between them before wiping the knife on the handkerchief and handing it back. He ate his egg in two bites while she peeled the fourth for herself. The food had killed the conversation, to her relief. It would take a clearer head than hers to be able to figure Patrick Gallagher out.

But although she retreated back into her own mind to eat and then watch the scenery pass by, questions about the man she'd invited home plagued her. Time with him would tell, but that was the one thing she'd happily do without.

24

"I have kept a good conscience in the matter, and that more than repays me for all I have suffered or can suffer." - Elijah Lovejoy

Mrs. Markland was quiet for the last hour of the drive, leaving Patrick to wonder whether she was in pain. He watched the road, avoiding any ruts and rocks, since there was nothing he could do but get her home as quickly and safely as possible.

And nothing to think about but how this little jaunt he'd started to St. Louis had turned out nothing like how he'd expected. But then, he'd never been much of a planner, and this was why. Everything he'd ever tried to plan in his life had derailed. Just what did God have for him in Cleves?

The houses they passed became closer together on their right, leading to a small community with packed gravel streets, while on their left, the wide Ohio flowed. Somewhere around here, Leah and Jane had suffered their accident, losing their parents. The scene was too painful to imagine. Patrick diverted his eyes away from the river, toward the town stretching up the valley to the bluffs.

He followed Mrs. Markland's directions to the inn with a view of the river and flanked by two tall oaks. It had to be at least a fifteen-minute walk up from the river, and he could think of little else than the night Mrs. Markland ushered two half-drowned children up here in the dark. It could not have been an easy feat.

The white plank building was three stories high in a perfect square, lacking the double length of Rachel's boardinghouse. It posed an attractive, welcoming air, but as they drew closer, the peeling paint, sagging steps, and the dead tree visible in the back told him that it had weathered its share of storms. Were he to stay long enough to see the repairs through, he'd never get to St. Louis.

"Pull around back," Mrs. Markland instructed.

He turned into a short drive behind the inn, just before the first house on the street. Here clustered a stable, chicken coop, outhouse, and another small building, maybe a smokehouse. Laundry lines hung between the outbuildings and interspersed with garden plots of varying sizes, backed up to woods running along the left of the inn and behind the houses. He pulled on the reins and jumped to the ground, first going to the horses to rub their noses and give them a good pat. A short, thin Black man in his sixties came from the stables and started to unhitch the team, so Patrick headed to where Anna now stood at the back of the wagon, helping the girls down.

"Where should I unload the supplies?"

Mrs. Markland looked them over, mentally cataloging. "If you carry my trunk in first, then Donny can help unload the stores to the cellar."

She'd already started walking when Patrick lifted the trunk and followed her and the girls toward the inn. The door opened before they reached it, held open by a Negro cook in her forties, dressed all in black with a spattered apron over her dress.

"Welcome home, Miss Anna. You do look a fright," she added as Mrs. Markland passed her into the house. Patrick stepped through the threshold after the girls. "That goes up to the third floor," the cook told him, pointing to a small staircase off the kitchen.

He pushed through, leaving Mrs. Markland to get settled with her staff. He was panting by the time he reached the third floor and met an older white woman at the top of the staircase, her arms full of folded linens. She too was in black, her gray hair pulled tightly back into a black lace day cap.

Patrick stopped to catch his breath. "Where does Mrs. Markland's trunk go?" he asked, assuming the small Puritanical-looking woman was the mother-in-law. But he'd made wrong assumptions before.

"The door at the end," she said, leading the way rather than trusting him to find it.

She lifted the latch and he stepped inside, lowering the trunk to the floor and taking a quick glance around Mrs. Markland's living quarters.

The blue-wallpapered room was spacious for a bedroom, small when he considered that it was where she lived. Only one bed was visible, but the girls probably slept on mats that were tucked away during the day. A wooden secretary stood against the same wall as the door, and a bench sat under the window that was flanked by heavy black drapes, now pulled open. On the bench sat a large workbasket and two smaller ones, brown wool and black yarn protruding from the top of each. There was a washbasin, a bureau, and a bedside table holding a lamp.

The woman cleared her throat. "And who are you?"

Patrick turned back with an innocent smile. "Patrick Gallagher. I, uh, escorted Mrs. Markland from Cincinnati."

The woman gave him an appraising look. "I'm Mrs. Markland, the elder. Is there a reason my daughter-in-law needed assistance traveling?"

He hesitated while his mind raced. Would there be any reason for Anna to downplay her sickness to her mother-in-law, or would she expect him to to tell the truth?

The older Mrs. Markland nodded when he didn't respond right away. "She fell sick, did she? I'd best head down there then." She stalked off, linens clutched to her chest, and Patrick blew out his breath and followed, hoping Anna would forgive him. But surely she would have known he might run into her mother-in-law when she sent him upstairs.

Leah and Jane were at the table in the kitchen, steaming mugs in hand, while Anna stood leaning against the doorframe with her arms crossed over her chest, deep in conversation with the cook. She looked up when they entered, and Patrick's chest bloomed with the reassurance of her now familiar presence.

"Good afternoon, Mother."

Mrs. Markland strode into the room, looking Anna up and down. "Anna, are you sick?"

Anna sighed, opened her mouth, and then shut it and simply nodded.

"Do you need to get up to bed?"

"I'm managing for now. I'll go to bed early. Which room should we put Mr. Gallagher in?"

"One or two. The back rooms are occupied."

Anna glanced at Patrick, who had stopped at the bottom of the staircase. "If you'll get your knapsack, Mr. Gallagher, I'll get you settled."

"I can do it." Mrs. Markland bustled to the inside door leading to the rest of the house. "You put your feet up."

"My feet have been up for hours," Anna muttered to her retreating figure.

Patrick crossed to the back door she was leaning against. "Shouldn't I unload the wagon first?"

She paused, seeming to consider. "Very well. Donny can point you in the right direction if he isn't done caring for the team yet."

By the time the cellar was stocked with Anna's purchases, Patrick was more than ready to see the inside of his room. When he passed through the kitchen again with his knapsack in hand, the smells were enough to make his eyes roll back in his head. The egg and cheese felt like a thing of the distant past. He found Anna in the dining room, folding napkins for Leah and Jane to lay on the table.

"They like to learn how to help," she said apologetically, as if he would judge her for making them work. Not anymore.

"They're doing a wonderful job." He gave them an encouraging smile, and Leah ducked her head away but Jane smiled back. Well, that was an unexpected victory.

"Mother headed upstairs already, but I can show you up." Anna led him out and down the hall, past a small ladies' sitting room and larger parlor, to the main staircase beside the front door. Patrick stopped himself from looking around to note what needed to be fixed and instead took in the character of the place, its cleanliness, and comfort.

"You must be proud of this place. What do you call it?"

"Home," she said with a light laugh, gathering her skirts to ascend the stairs. She teetered, then grabbed the railing with one hand, leaving the other to manage her skirts. "It's called Riverview Lodge. And I am proud of it, but mostly grateful that I can continue to keep it, despite everything. I have excellent, generous help. But you've surely stayed at many different lodgings recently, and I'm afraid there isn't much fancy about Riverview Lodge."

Patrick trod after her. "Oh, I didn't stay anywhere fancy, and I'm truly glad to be out of the woods and have a roof over my head." Then, to make sure she didn't think it was only better than nothing, he added lamely, "Riverview Lodge is nice."

It wasn't his best speech, but he meant it. He could see himself settling comfortably into the place for some time. There was something about the light blue color of the walls, the white crown molding, the vases of fresh flowers that must have come from the bushes out front, filling the house with their scent—well, it was all nice.

Mrs. Markland was in the bedroom Anna led him to, depositing a handful of beeswax candles on the bedside table beside an iron chamberstick. An attractive quilt in greens and blues was stretched across the bed, and a breeze from the open window made the white linen curtains flutter.

"You can be in here for the duration of your stay," Anna told him from the doorway.

"Father will be waking up from his nap soon, so I'll head over now," Mrs. Markland told her as she stepped out of the room. For being such a small woman, her steps sounded heavy down the stairs.

When she was gone, Anna explained, "Mother and Mr. Markland live in the first house next door, but the other staff all have rooms upstairs, in case you need anything in the night." She glanced toward the washbasin. "Supper is at six, and if you ever want a bath, just ask Donny. It looks like Mother already brought your water, so I'll let you be. We can meet in the morning to go over what you'll be working on."

Patrick nodded, lowering his knapsack to the ground, and Anna shut the door behind her. She must be miserable by now, to arrive home and set to work right away when her head was still hurting. One thing was for certain—now that he'd seen her as the mistress of her actual domain, he could no longer accuse her of being either lazy or tyrannical.

Day 58, Cleves, North Bend, Ohio
Health: Good.
Supplies used: All but the last of my jerky.
Wildlife: Bluebirds in the woods right before we reached Cleves.
Verse for the day: II Kings 11:11 And the guard stood, every man with his weapons in his hand, round about the king.
Personal notes: Mrs. Markland (the younger) did not seem to mind very much having someone looking out for her today.

25

Cincinnati did not cross Patrick's mind at all during his first day in Cleves, and Elijah Lovejoy registered only the briefest consideration.

He awoke at dawn to the smells of eggs, fried ham, and coffee, and the sound of the neighborhood roosters greeting one another. Stretching out in bed brought the uncomfortable reminder that as a contracted worker of Anna's, he ought to be in staff quarters, not taking up one of her paying rooms. The negotiations had occurred when she was vulnerable and at a clear disadvantage. Guilt niggled at him, but he already knew his plan to mention it to her would be pointless. Even though she wouldn't be convinced to move him, he still had to say something.

His frown deepened at the memory of supper the night before, eating in the dining room with the other guests. The other guests and not Anna, who was on her feet, doing everything Rachel had done back at the boardinghouse. He'd chafed against her not working there, and he chafed against her working here. Somehow over the past day in the wagon with her, her presence had become—well, not quite as annoying as it had been. To be waited on by her now, when he alone of the guests knew she was unwell, was nothing short of embarrassing.

Pushing out of bed, he reached for his trousers and pulled them on.

It was anyone's guess what his first day in Cleves would hold, but he could choose to start it right, with time in God's Word. It would be worthwhile to get his head in a good place before starting on whatever jobs Anna Markland had for him.

Patrick was draining the last of his coffee when Anna entered the dining room, an apron tied over her blue dress. She looked rested, her hair back in order and the disarray of the previous day cleared away. How she knew the exact moment he'd finished eating, he had no idea.

"Good morning, Mr. Gallagher. Did you sleep well?"

Scooting his chair back, he came to his feet. "Very well, thank you. And please extend my compliments on breakfast to the cook."

"I will. I don't want to rush you, but I'm available to meet with you now."

Patrick dropped his napkin onto his empty plate and gestured to the door, nodding to the other guests as he followed Anna to the ladies' parlor. She pulled a list from her apron pocket before turning in the center of the room to face him.

"Before we get into that, I was wondering if you have any beds available in the staff rooms for me, as I'll be working for you."

Anna stopped, her mouth open and eyes wide. She inhaled to speak, but Patrick hurried on.

"I'd really be more comfortable to not be treated as a paying guest."

Anna appeared flummoxed. "We had an agreement, Mr. Gallagher. You would work for me in return for room and board." She tipped her head. "And two dollars a week. As I work in room and board, the accommodations I gave you are in keeping with our agreement."

"It's too nice," Patrick blurted out. "I can sleep anywhere. I don't need to take up a room you could be earning income from."

To make matters worse, she produced a banknote from her apron pocket and extended it to him. "Here is what I owe you for driving us here."

Shaking his head, Patrick took a step backward. "I said I would drive you for nothing."

"Not originally. I have a feeling you only said that under pressure."

If he'd known how embarrassed he would feel now, he never would have requested payment. Reaching out, he gently pushed her outstretched hand away. "Promise me that you'll move me if a guest needs my room."

The bill hung limply in her hand for a minute before she audibly sighed and tucked it back into the apron. "I'll think about it."

Patrick crossed his arms, tried to think of something that would convince her, and gave up. "What would you like me to accomplish while I'm here?"

She handed the list over. "We'll need to make a list to take to the sawmill of necessary lumber. First, I'd like the back stairs repaired, and then there is rotten wood on the exterior near the foundation that needs to be replaced. We have a couple of leaks in the roof. And the kitchen and hall need whitewashing."

He lifted his eyes from the list to meet hers. "And the dead tree?"

"You don't have to do it. I'll take care of it another time."

Patrick shifted his stance. If he stayed in Cleves long enough, he could attempt it, but he didn't want to make promises when his future was committed elsewhere. So when she'd finished her instructions, he went out to measure the stairs.

The day was sunny and warm, perfect for an outdoor assignment. With a pencil from his pocket, he made notes of necessary supplies on the back of Anna's list as he walked around the property. A shutter she hadn't mentioned hung loose, but a couple nails and maybe a new hinge would fix it. The rotting wood at the foundation was concerning when Patrick kicked at it with the toe of his boot, fearful of what he'd find when he started replacing it.

By midmorning, he'd taken the wagon to the sawmill and given the foreman his order. He saw Anna only briefly at dinnertime, when she made an appearance in the dining room to check in and refill drinks. He handed her his cup when she stopped by his place and informed her that he was ready to start work.

"Let me know if you need anything," she said, setting the full cup back in his hand.

She'd already shown him the toolbench in the stable, so he gave her a reassuring nod. She had enough else to worry about; he could handle these things, take a few burdens off her hands. It was funny how thoughts about his required income had been so quickly eclipsed by real interest in the work.

In the stable, Patrick found a saw and a dusty old clamp leaning against the back corner of the toolbench and hauled them out to work in the sunshine. Maneuvering a plank into the clamp, he measured the length of the stair, tightened the clamp, and started sawing.

Three finished stairs sat beside him, and he had lifted a handkerchief to wipe the sweat from his forehead when he looked up to see an older man approaching. The yard had been fairly quiet while he worked, the cook coming out to the smokehouse once and a maid retrieving towels from the line earlier. Otherwise, Patrick had ignored the traffic on the street and noises from the houses.

"What are you doing?" The man stopped before Patrick, dressed in worn, carefully mended clothes. His gray beard reached his collarbone, and a black hat shaded his face.

"Good afternoon." Patrick rocked back on his heels and pushed his cap up. "I have been tasked with repairing the stairs for the inn."

He received a frown in return.

"Young man, don't lie to me. Those are my tools you're stealing."

Patrick stood, holding the sharp end of the saw back, away from the man. "I'm not taking anything, sir. Simply using the tools Mrs. Markland directed me to so I could make repairs for her."

"I make the repairs around here." The man's face reddened, and he grabbed at the clamp, yanking the board out of it. "You give my saw back and get off my property before I make you regret it!"

He lifted the board, and Patrick stepped back, alarm rising. "We could go in and speak to Mrs. Markland together," he said, keeping his voice calm and raising a placating hand.

"You thief! Give me that saw!" The man swung the board toward Patrick's head, and Patrick backed away quickly. Keeping his eyes on the volatile man prevented him from looking around for help, although he was sure if there was anyone capable in the vicinity, they would have already intervened.

"I can't give you the saw in this state, sir. But I'll go with you to talk to Mrs. Markland. Just put the board down—"

"Give me the saw, thief!" the man barked, swinging the board wildly.

Patrick retreated backward as fast as he could toward the house, one hand clutching the saw, the other lifted to block his face from the swinging board. "I'm not a thief. Mrs. Markland hired me!"

He was almost to the stairs when the door flew open and Anna rushed past him. "Mr. Markland! It's all right. It's all right. Mr. Gallagher isn't stealing your saw."

The man charged forward with the board and Anna sidestepped, barely missing a blow as she grabbed at it. "It's all right. I asked him to use it."

He slowed and she dove, grasping the plank with both hands and forcing him to a stop.

"He is stealing my saw!"

"No, he isn't. He's only doing some work for me. See?" Anna reached back, and Patrick surrendered the saw to her, watching silently. "See, I have the saw. I'm going to put these away, and you can come have a cup of tea at the inn." She pulled the board away from him as she spoke, soothing him with a steady stream of reassurances. "We're done with the saw now. It's time to go take a break in the inn."

The heavy steps of the elder Mrs. Markland sounded on the stairs behind Patrick. "Come on in, Jesse. Anna can put the things away." She pushed past him, and Mr. Markland allowed her to take his arm. "Everything is all right, and we can go have a cup of tea. We'll let Anna handle it."

Mr. Markland's face softened, and he went with her without a fight. The back door closed behind them, and Patrick exhaled, his shoulders falling.

"I'm sorry about that." Anna set the end of the board on the ground, leaning her hand on the other end. She handed the saw back to him. "Are you all right?"

"Gratefully, yes. Your father-in-law?"

"Yes. He got past Mother without us seeing. I'm sorry."

Patrick took a deep breath, his heart rate slowing again. "I take it he gets confused easily?"

"He's pretty much confused all the time these days. He doesn't seem to know my name at all and thinks he and Mother have to do everything for the inn. It was never theirs, though. They have a farm, and Isaac is the one who started Riverview Lodge. They only moved to town a couple of years ago, but Mr. Markland has still adopted a sense of responsibility for it because he used to help Isaac with projects back when his mind was clear."

She sighed, lowering her eyes and then shifting them toward the river. "Are you sure you're all right?"

"I am. Now that I know to expect him, I'll be better prepared," Patrick said, watching her.

Her brows knit together with yet another burden. "I should have warned you, but I didn't think of it. We try to keep an eye on him, but sometimes he gets away."

Reaching forward, he laid his hand on hers over the board. "You came out in time, and no harm was done. I'm nearly done cutting the stairs, and then I can sand them down and cut the risers. The iron railing looks like it's still good, but I'll replace all the worn lumber. Do you think it's safe to take the saw behind the stable to use out of sight?" He removed his hand, returning it to his pocket.

"We'll keep him away, but you are also welcome to work on something else, if you need a rest after all that."

Patrick shook his head, smiling at her. "Are there any other surprises I should know about?"

"Probably quite a few." Anna pressed her lips into a thin line. "As a public house, you never know who might show up. And I told you about my friend's son, didn't I? He might come around and take an interest in you. His name is Franklin, and if you want to give him tasks to help, you're welcome to. He can be helpful and is always excited to participate, but he's someone else who always needs a set of eyes on him. If he's bothering you, you can tell him to come find me for some candy."

"If I bother you, can I have a candy?" Patrick's eyes twinkled at her in an attempt to add some levity.

"Molasses candies are included in room and board. You're welcome to one anytime you want one." Her sweet smile assured him that her offer was more than transactional. He held her gaze, thinking of Leah and Jane and Mr. Markland and Franklin and how this woman made Black dolls and ran a safe house on top of all of that, and how two or three sick headaches a month meant she must be laid up at least a third of the time.

"How do you manage?" he asked without thinking.

Anna's smile disappeared, and she blinked at him.

"How do you handle all that you do, and your condition on top of it all?"

A visible wall went up over her features, and he was looking at a stranger again. "Sometimes you just have to, Mr. Gallagher."

He shook his head, because few people would do all that she did and remain as generous and kind as she.

"One day, I will tell you that God makes a way for what He wants me to accomplish and that I've learned to let go of everything that I can't do. But as it's a lesson I'm still learning, I would be a hypocrite to say so now."

Her words hit Patrick with a physical force in his gut, and he couldn't form a reply or do more than ensure that he took the next breath. He became aware that she released the board when it knocked into his hand, and he grabbed it before it toppled. Anna had faded into the inn, shutting the door with a quiet click and leaving him in the yard with the saw, the board, and the truth of her words working their way through his mind.

26

**"If I know my own heart, I do now feel the necessity of resigning
myself into the hands of my God, to mold and guide me at His will;
tho I dare not say that I am, at present, willing to do it."**
-Elijah Lovejoy

Using a crowbar as a lever, Patrick pulled the old back stairs apart the next morning, careful to preserve the lumber and nails to be reused for smaller projects. Cutting and sanding the new steps and risers the previous day had taken so long, he hadn't had time to start building and hadn't wanted to leave the inn with deconstructed stairs overnight, especially if Mr. Markland was about and could get hurt.

The muscles in his straining arms throbbed. It had been a few years since he'd worked them so much in one day. And now that he was no longer walking, his recently toned legs would start getting soft in turn. He shook his head at the handful of used nails he deposited in the growing pile. He hated to think of having to build his leg strength back up when he left for St. Louis, after his body had finally adjusted to long days on the road before Cincinnati.

His mind worked overtime now, too, another muscle that had grown lazy when he'd been unwilling to think too hard on his long walk. Something about the physical labor awakened it to life—that and this curious place in a remote small town that roared with activity from the river.

Or that and the curious woman who brought him molasses candy and cups of water, stopping to watch the river with a distant look in her eye.

Whatever it was, his mind couldn't let go of her statement that God gave the strength to accomplish what He wanted her to and she was learning to let go of the rest. It made sense for her situation. But if the same logic was true for him, then his entire orientation was at risk of being shaken.

All his life, he'd looked at the vast sea of needs in the world and begged and pleaded for those around him to join the Lord's army in going out to meet them. And when that army didn't show up in the needed numbers, it meant that those willing—him—had to pick up the slack.

How could he now accept that God had specific tasks for him to do with the capacity He'd provided, and everything else—the things that made him so angry—were none of his business?

Patrick yanked the loosened boards apart and tossed them onto the grass. What made him angrier—that evil prevailed while those who should step up and fight didn't, or that God hadn't granted him the capacity to fight it all single-handedly?

"People are suffering, Lord. Horribly suffering. And dying."

Thump. The crowbar flew into the next crack and he pushed hard, pulling the stair sections apart with a groaning creak.

"How. Can. You. Let. Them?" He tossed the separated boards onto the others.

Thump. Creak. Smack.

"How can You let them, and not give those of us with the passion the capability to stop it?"

Thwack. THWACK. He swung the crowbar harder.

"Why won't You use me?"

THWACK. THWACK.

"What is so wrong with me that You won't use me?"

His chest hollowed as the words left his mouth. He'd never dared to ask the question out loud before, but now, all he wanted was the answer. Why did God limit him so much, when all he'd ever wanted was to do good, love mercy, protect the innocent? Sure, he was a mere sinner saved by God's abundant grace, but so was everyone else. Why was *his* work thwarted at every turn?

Should he even go on to St. Louis, or would his presence be Elijah Lovejoy's undoing too? Why had God allowed him to come across the country to hear the stories and see the suffering of so many if he wouldn't let Patrick change anything?

"What is it that You really want me to do, Lord?"

Anna leaned against the kitchen wall, watching through the cracked-open window at Patrick smashing repeatedly at the decayed stair. He appeared to be growling something under his breath, but she couldn't hear his words. His pain was palpable, though, and she ached, unable to turn away from the agony on his face as he swung the crowbar down on the wood, splintering it.

Leah and Jane sat at the kitchen table sewing dolls and quietly making up their imaginary story world together. Anna had never tried to invade on this world, but occasionally she heard snippets about elegant castles and abundant gardens. They'd been watching Patrick work earlier until Anna chased them away from the window. She was as bad as the children, spying on him now.

She waited for something to happen, for him to get the peace for which he seemed to be imploring the Lord. At the same time, it was a step in the right direction to see him letting out his hurt and doing something more than attempt to ignore it. He dropped the crowbar with a clatter, his shoulders caving as he lifted his closed eyes to the heavens. Anna saw the movement behind him before he did.

"Whatcha doing, mister?"

Patrick opened his eyes and spun around. "Good afternoon, Franklin."

The youth stepped closer, wearing the same baggy shirt and trousers he always wore, and tilted his face up, squinting one eye. "How'd you know my name?"

A half grin played at the corner of Patrick's mouth, a different person than he was just a minute ago. "Mrs. Markland told me she was expecting you."

"How d'you know Miss Anna?"

Patrick's hands moved to his pockets, and Anna waited, straining to hear his answer.

"She's my friend."

Franklin relaxed and paced around the boards on the ground, swinging his arms. Anna couldn't help her smile. "She's everyone's friend. Say, are you a guest at the inn? She said I'm not s'posed to bother guests."

"No, I work for her," Patrick replied quickly. "I am staying here, but you're welcome to help, if you want."

"Whatcha doing?" Franklin asked again, then, "What's your name?"

"Mr. Gallagher. Patrick Gallagher."

"Whatcha doing, Patrick Gallagher?"

"I am fixing Mrs. Markland's stairs for her." Patrick gestured to the boards on the ground. "I'd love some extra hands pulling these rusty nails from the boards before someone gets hurt on them."

"Oh, Joe Beatty stepped on a nail once and his foot got a big infection and then they had to cut it off!" Franklin's voice rose in the excitement of the retelling.

"We don't want that happening to anyone on Mrs. Markland's property. Once we get the nails pulled out, I'll start rebuilding the stairs with this new wood over here. I'll need someone to hold the boards level while I hammer the nails in. You look like just the person who could do that."

"Sure, Mr. Gallagher. I can hammer for you too."

"We'll see." Patrick lifted the hammer and pounded the old nails backward out of the boards.

Anna backed away, long overdue to return to work. Patrick clearly had the situation under control and knew intuitively how to handle someone with Franklin's capabilities.

As she picked up the broom and headed to clean out a vacated bedroom, she felt compelled to pray for Patrick. He needed God to meet him in his pain, but another pervading thought directed her prayers as well.

He needed a friend.

The arrival of Franklin cooled the hot lava coursing through Patrick's veins, and he refocused on the task at hand. The sixteen-year-old kept up a steady stream of conversation as he pulled out the nails Patrick hammered free.

"Gallagher is an Irish name. I knew an Irishman once, Mr. Campbell. He lived across the river and even let me ride in his fishing dinghy.

Mrs. Markland said Markland is an English name, but it's her husband who had it and she only married into it. She used to be a Cooper."

He proceeded to share with Patrick the origins of all the surnames he knew in Hamilton County, which was apparently a hobby of his.

Patrick stacked the last old board aside and stood, brushing his hands together.

"Can I keep these old nails?" Franklin asked, holding up his handful.

"No, I might end up needing some of them again."

"Oh, that's too bad. It would be really nice to have them. Hi, Miss Anna!"

Franklin jumped up, and Patrick twisted to see Anna approach from the front of the house with two cups in her hands.

"Water time!" she called.

Patrick had been content working with Franklin, but her appearance still felt like a breath of fresh air. He stepped forward, taking the cup from her and returning her pleasant smile.

"Thank you."

Reaching into her apron pocket, she produced a molasses candy for each of them. Patrick popped his into his mouth, and the sharp flavor flooded his senses. He'd never cared much for the strong molasses taste before, but after his joke to Anna about getting candy for bothering her, he couldn't turn it away now. She thought he liked them, so like them he would.

Franklin regaled her with everything he'd learned and done over the past week. Patrick set his empty cup on the pile of boards and wandered over to the stable in search of a shovel to scrape mud and dried leaves off the bricks he would be rebuilding the steps on.

Spots speckled his vision as he stepped into the dark stable, and a rustle met his ears. He greeted the horses, stopping to stroke their noses. Donny was nowhere in sight, and Patrick became curious if the inn had any animals in the other stalls.

The third stall was empty, but a flash of movement greeted him when he peeked into the fourth. Startled, Patrick jumped slightly as he stared into the eyes of a human huddled in the corner, trying to make themselves invisible under the straw.

A fugitive.

"Don't be afraid," Patrick whispered. "I won't hurt you. Does the owner know you're here?"

Habit kept him from using names with the Underground Railroad.

The young man's dark head nodded.

"Do you have everything you need? Food and water?"

"Yes, sir." His whisper barely met Patrick's ears.

"If you need to discard any waste, I'll be glad to do it. No one will suspect me."

He received nothing more than another nod in return.

There didn't seem to be anything else Patrick could do for him, so he offered "Be well," and quietly closed the stall door. As soon as it was dark, the young man would be gone.

Donny returned when Patrick was on his way out with the shovel, and with the shrewd look he received, Patrick suddenly saw him as the watchguard he was meant to be, not a mere stablehand.

Anna hadn't been lying when she admitted that surprises were to be expected around this place. Patrick had been aware that there might be fugitives, but springtime wasn't a popular time for passengers to travel the Railroad, especially when the river was high from winter thaw and spring rains. The young man in the stable was either brave or crazy. And only desperation made a person that brave or crazy.

27

**"Say what you please of the religion of the Bible, but without the
moral precepts it inculcates, all history and experience teach that
neither civil nor intellectual freedom can long exist."**
- Elijah Lovejoy

Anna poked her head in the dining room Sunday morning and spotted Patrick sitting removed from the other guests with his Bible on the table beside him.

"I'm sorry for the cold breakfast." She eyed the ham and biscuit on his plate. "Mother Markland is very strict about keeping the Sabbath."

She almost didn't recognize him. He'd shaved and scrubbed, and his dark reddish hair fell in controlled waves over his forehead. And the man had a properly tied cravat on above his waistcoat. Unbelievable.

"Oh no, she's quite right. Um . . . are you going to church?"

"Yes, we'll be leaving in about a half hour."

"Can I come?" His brown eyes dilated hopefully. "I mean, I'll come too."

"Everyone is welcome at church," Anna returned playfully. "You're lucky to have arrived on a week the minister is in town."

Thirty minutes later, she descended his new stairs, the sturdiness beneath her feet bringing a swell of pleasure. They were good stairs, and she caught Patrick glancing back at them with satisfaction on his face.

Leah and Jane followed in their matching dresses with the cook and two maids, one older than Anna and the other a teen. Crossing the yeard, they met Mr. and Mrs. Markland exiting their house. Mr. Markland was tugging at his cuff and grumbling about something, but he stopped when his eyes fell on Patrick.

"The thief! He stole my tools!"

"No, Jesse." Mother Markland took his arm and tugged him forward. "That's the builder Anna hired. He's a friend. He was just helping."

"My name's Gallagher, Mr. Markland," Patrick said, stepping forward with hand outstretched.

Mr. Markland scowled at his hand. "I will not shake hands with a thief."

"I'm sorry," Mother Markland said with a sigh. "Once he gets an idea in his head, it's there to stay."

"I understand." Patrick gave her a compassionate look that Anna didn't miss.

He attempted to step aside to allow the others to precede him, but the Black staff did the same thing, so he ended up beside Anna, following Mr. and Mrs. Markland.

"You're looking well, but I haven't asked how you've been the last few days," he said when they fell into step together.

"I have been well, thank you." Anna gave his presentation another appreciative glance. "You're looking nice yourself this morning."

Perhaps if she affirmed his choice to take care of himself, he'd keep doing it. He no longer looked like a homeless ruffian, but rather someone she wouldn't mind being seen beside in public.

"I used to do all this and more every day when I was in the senate, but I can't say I miss it," he replied absently as they strolled up the street.

"You were in the senate?" She wracked her brain for any memory of him mentioning it before, but hadn't he only told her he was a reporter?

"In Maryland, until about a year ago."

"I would never have guessed," she said, her voice soft.

"Because I don't dress up now?" Amused, he glanced over, as if to see her reaction.

"A lot of reasons. But you do look nice today."

"I tend to think it wasteful to spend a lot of time and expense on appearance," he admitted. "My attention and money is better spent doing things that actually help people. And I suppose all the pomp and show in the government gave me a stronger distaste for it than ever."

Anna's mind worked to make sense of the new information, remembering how natural he was at public speaking.

"Are you telling me that you perform an abomination on your cravat every morning as an act of protest?" she asked slowly.

Patrick laughed, and Mother Markland shot him a reproving look over her shoulder.

"That would give me credit for thinking about it more than I do." He grinned boyishly at Anna, and really, it was the only accessory he'd been missing. The man was well and truly attractive in this state, and Anna quickly directed her focus to the road before her. But *the state senate*? He'd evidently done a lot with his life, and the familiar pang tightened in her chest.

She could have done so much if she were healthy.

She very well could have saved Leah and Jane's parents and reunited the family, if she hadn't been plagued with a sick headache that interfered with her vision that night and weighted down her movements.

Her life, her entire ability to help people, was limited to the four walls of her inn, where she had staff she could depend on and all the tools she needed to bear up when the headaches inevitably arrived. Only occasional forays into Cincinnati gave her access to the wider world and involvement with the anti-slavery campaigners who were bringing change to society.

Patrick Gallagher had no restrictions. He could decide to wake up one day and walk across the country if he wanted to, and he did. He could sit in the senate and pass laws and write newspaper editorials that reached thousands, because squinting at words on a page didn't put him at risk of being bedridden for the next several days.

In just a couple of days, she'd gotten used to having him around Riverview Lodge, but she shouldn't fool herself. As soon as he could leave to go do the next great thing, he would.

They arrived at the meetinghouse, and Corydon was at the door in his preaching robes, welcoming parishioners. He greeted his parents in front of Anna and hugged his mother. When they passed through, it was her turn, and she leaned into him for a brief hug.

"It's good to have you here, Corydon."

"Thank you, Anna. Can we come over later to hear how Mother and Father are?"

"Please do." She indicated Patrick behind her. "This is Mr. Gallagher; he came out with me from Cincinnati to do some work on the inn. Mr. Gallagher, the Reverend Markland is Isaac's older brother, Corydon."

Corydon pushed his glasses up his nose, making his blue eyes more visible behind the glass, and extended his other hand to Patrick. "Glad to have you."

Patrick bobbed his head in return.

Inside, Anna started down the aisle to the Markland pew but realized Patrick had stopped following her. He stepped inside a pew near the back, where Leah and Jane were in the care of the staff and other Black worshippers.

"You're welcome to sit with the Marklands and me," she said, turning aside to him.

He lowered his eyes, hesitating. "Would that put you in an awkward place? If people assume I'm *with* you?"

Anna was tempted to ask if that would really be so bad. "Only if we were alone. As we're with Mr. and Mrs. Markland, you'll be viewed as a family guest. My sister-in-law and the children are there too."

Why did she want so much for Sarah to meet him, and would she feel as proud to introduce him if he looked the same as he normally did? He wasn't always worth showing off. Anna ignored the intruding thoughts and celebrated her small victory as Patrick proceeded up the aisle with her.

Sarah was wrangling nieces and nephews when Anna and Patrick arrived at the pew, but she looked up with affection and relief when she saw Anna. Anna scooped up her two-year-old niece and slid in beside her, leaning in for a hug.

"How was Cincinnati?"

"I was sick for most of it," Anna admitted, and Sarah frowned in sympathy. She looked at Patrick with interest so Anna introduced him, highly aware of his very masculine presence beside her.

"How are you doing?" she asked Sarah in return.

"It's been nice to have Corydon around this week. He brought some pullets that he was gifted at a church up in the hills, so we'll have our own fresh eggs soon. He and the boys built a coop for them yesterday."

"He said he wants to come over to catch up today. Come anytime."

Sarah nodded, and a deacon stood up to lead the singing. There were no hymnals like the larger churches in Cincinnati had, but everyone knew the common hymns. Anna shifted Eleanor in her arms and joined in the acapella worship, but the new male voice beside her proved to be distracting. How could she expect everyone else to believe that he wasn't there *with* her if she couldn't convince herself?

Patrick was finishing a letter to Maisie in the quiet smaller parlor that afternoon when Anna peeked in the open door.

"Do you mind if we join you?"

He came to his feet, shuffling his papers together, as Corydon and Sarah appeared behind her. "Come on in. I can relocate." Inn guests were chatting together loudly in the other parlor, which was why he'd escaped here.

"You're welcome to stay. We just like to visit on Sunday afternoons when Corydon is in town."

The morning's events had revealed that Anna's siblings-in-law were close friends of hers, so he was surprised to be invited to join them. The minister had shed his robes and wore a black wool suit now. He looked to be around Patrick's own age, sporting dark brown sideburns that stretched down his jaws. Patrick liked the gentle style of his preaching, so out of vogue but powerful in its kindness.

"How long is your circuit?" Patrick asked as they settled into seats.

"Ten churches, just under a hundred miles. I make it back home about once a month."

So apparently the whole Markland family made it a habit of overburdening themselves. Who would want a life with a wife and children they never saw? Only a deep, abiding passion would make a man sacrifice a comfortable family life like that. Which was, after all, why Patrick didn't have one.

Corydon asked Anna a series of questions about Mr. and Mrs. Markland, and Anna conversed as easily with the couple as if they were siblings she'd been raised with. She answered honestly about Mr. Markland's deteriorating condition and how it took more of Mrs. Markland's attention away from the inn every week. Patrick had seen how Anna and her mother-in-law depended on each other, and read the fear in Anna's eyes. Mrs. Markland's withdrawal added to the weight on Anna's shoulders, weight she didn't have the capacity to bear. Not unless it was true that God desired for her to lay down the burdens He hadn't equipped her to carry.

But if she couldn't afford to hire the help she needed, would she risk losing the inn?

Could she afford his work?

Patrick sat back, pondering.

Corydon stopped mid-sentence, his gaze swinging toward Patrick and away again. What had he missed while lost in his head?

"He's safe," Anna said without hesitation.

Patrick blinked. Did she mean him?

Corydon watched Patrick carefully but continued. "I got the first solid lead indicating that Leah and Jane's mother survived. A woman of her description came alone through St. Jacobs late last summer. She was searching for her son in his teens, who had escaped from bondage a few years prior."

"Do they know where she went?" Anna leaned forward.

"They thought she was going north, toward Columbus. She was distraught, often murmuring about her dead babies."

"Leah and Jane," Anna whispered. "I wonder if the grief of her losses weakened her even more. I hope she's still alive."

"I told my contact in St. Jacobs to reach out the next safe houses on the Railroad and see if she could learn anything from them before I return."

"Good. Thank you."

In his circuit, Anna could have had Corydon seeking cures for her condition, yet she only seemed concerned with information that would reunite one of thousands of broken families. Patrick thought of the men he'd interacted with in the senate, both lawmakers and their constituents, who thought they were so powerful. Yet those men knew nothing of strength.

Anna Markland, an obscure woman in an obscure Ohio town, was one of the strongest women he knew.

28

**"How long will it take the gospel to work a cure
if it is never applied to the diseased part?" - Elijah Lovejoy**

Patrick and Franklin were pulling rotten wood off of the inn's exterior foundation on Monday afternoon when a grizzled white man in patched trousers approached the inn's back door.

Patrick straightened, wiping his hands on his handkerchief, and watched him carefully.

"Don't worry. Miss Anna will give him some food," Franklin said when he saw that Patrick had stopped working. "She always does."

"Does he come around often?" Patrick asked as the back door opened and Mildred the cook appeared in the doorway.

"Oh, I've never seen him before." Franklin peered closer. "She gives food to everyone who needs it though."

Patrick sat in the small parlor with his journal that night after most of the guests had retired to bed, thinking about the hungry man and how he'd left several minutes later with a parcel of food.

It was far too dangerous for Anna to have so many suspicious people about when she was harboring fugitives. With every new individual prowling about the yard, the risk of discovery increased.

He tapped his pencil against his journal, toying with the moral dilemma the situation created. How would he prioritize assistance if he were the one in charge? There was no easy way to answer the question, but living in a slave state, he had made the choice to focus on helping African Americans, especially those who were still in bondage or who had recently self emancipated. Meanwhile, Anna helped everyone. She wasn't wrong in her choice. But he wasn't either, was he?

She appeared in the doorway as if his thoughts had summoned her. "Still up?"

Patrick stirred. "For a little while more. Are you closing up?"

"I was, but you don't have to hurry. Just bank the fire before you leave."

"I will." He hurried to think of a way to make her stay, but she asked him about the day's work first. Perhaps she wasn't in a hurry to leave either, although she remained in the doorway.

"Have a seat?" he invited, even though he knew she wouldn't fully enter the room alone with him.

"I'd best not."

He set aside his journal and stood then, which he should have done when she first appeared. "I enjoyed meeting your brother- and sister-in-law yesterday. They seem like good people."

Anna gave a soft smile in the lamplight. "They are good people. I don't know what I would do without them."

"Same for them. You're the one caring for their parents. Do they have other siblings?"

"Yes, they have sisters scattered around the region, married. One of the husbands currently runs the Markland farm. But I don't mind helping with Mother and Mr. Markland. Corydon would, but he's rarely here, and their hands are full with all the little ones."

"How did you come to know the Marklands?"

"Oh." Anna's hands fluttered. "Cousins. They have cousins in Louisville."

"Ah. Do they—the reverend—know about the fugitives in the stable?"

Anna froze, swinging her frantic eyes to his.

"Don't worry. I can help if needed." She'd heard him in the society meeting. Would that be enough to convince her to trust that he'd be careful with her secret? "I can make deliveries day or night without it looking suspicious," he added, watching Anna slowly relax.

She inhaled deeply and let the breath out. "Thank you."

He couldn't think of another question, and she was going to head to bed. But there was the issue that had been bothering him all week . . .

"I mean it—I'm available to help. I also wonder if it is necessary that I eat in the dining room. As a worker here, I think I ought to eat in the kitchen with the other staff."

He waited, hopeful. The request certainly made enough sense that she should be able to see the surface value in it and not look deeper at his real meaning: that it was lousy eating with travelers he didn't know and didn't care about when he could be eating with her.

Her hesitation sank his hopes.

"Mr. Gallagher—the truth is, it's simpler to feed you with my guests. Because were you to eat with my staff, I would question what it is that makes you prefer their company over my guests. I'm afraid I don't know you well enough to know."

She looked him in the eye as she spoke, but her hands were clenched together before her, revealing underlying strain. As uncomfortable as her bluntness made them both, he far preferred it to a vague answer that would leave him wondering about the truth. Patrick nodded in defeat, unwilling to admit to either of them whose company he really sought.

"I appreciate your commitment to protecting your staff. You're quite right to do so."

She waited, perhaps expecting him to provide what made him want to invade on her staff's space. He couldn't blame her for still not trusting him. Being responsible for the safety of so many must carry unimaginable weight, and after all, he was concealing his true motivation from her.

"Perhaps I can reconsider once I've gotten to know you better," she said finally.

Would you want to? Patrick bit his tongue before he said it out loud. It was a preposterous question, especially to a lady. Especially when he was planning to leave any day.

Instead, he bowed his head to her. "I am at your service. The meals you have provided have more than kept your end of our agreement. I have eaten—and slept—very well since arriving here, and I'm grateful."

Except for the occasional nightmare, but hopefully her room was far enough away that she didn't know about those.

Anna left, leaving Patrick to stare at the blank page of his journal.

Day 63, Cleves, North Bend, Ohio
Verse for the day: 1 Corinthians 1:27 . . . and God hath chosen the weak things of the world to confound the things which are mighty.

Personal notes: I still have questions, but I'm less inclined to believe the answers are elsewhere. There have been times this week when I have doubted the necessity of going on to St. Louis.

At the sound of Anna's steps in the hall, Patrick slid the newspaper he was reading under his Bible. After a couple of weeks at her inn, her tread had become familiar, although tonight it was earlier than expected.

He tried to erase from his mind the horrifying news he'd just read. It would not help her to hear about the attack in Zanesville that killed a white schoolteacher who had received Black students into her classroom. The familiar pit yawned at him, ready to swallow him, mind and spirit, if he let it.

But not with Anna in the room. She had more than enough to deal with without hearing every bit of awful news in the papers.

She materialized in the doorway; he stood. Her evening check-ins had become regular, although oftentimes they never got around to discussing his work. Which may be for the best, as he'd discovered a series of issues with the inn foundation and had spent the last several days well over his head, trying to stabilize it.

"You're early."

A grimace passed over her face. "I'm afraid you might not see me for a couple of days. I wanted to make sure you had what you needed before I'm laid up."

"I'm sorry, Mrs. Markland." His soft voice conveyed compassion, but the thought of missing her for a few days produced a twinge of self-pity as well. "I heard from Mr. Birney today, and he confirmed that Mr. Lovejoy has not returned from Pennsylvania. I expect I'll still be here when you've recovered."

Anna reached into her apron pocket. "Here's this week's payment ahead, just in case."

He took the money reluctantly, accepting that it might be easier for her to have one thing off her mind while she focused on recovering.

"The delivery went well today and didn't appear to raise any suspicions." There hadn't been any other Railroad passengers between the first one Patrick saw in the stable and the man that arrived last night. It meant more than he let on that she'd trusted him enough to provide the transportation to the next safe house earlier this afternoon. "Is there anything else I can do to help while you're unavailable?"

"I appreciate the offer." Anna's eyes were sad as she lifted her fingers and pressed them to her temple. "Acting as host to the guests would certainly help, and I'm sure Mildred would be glad to have assistance with hauling water and firewood when I'm not here. Thank you, Mr. Gallagher."

They were silent for a minute together before she added, "You've been a tremendous help. Your presence will be missed when you leave."

His pulse stuttered at her unexpected compliment. Having spent his life feeling like he'd overstayed his welcome everywhere he went, he could hardly conceive that she meant it.

"I'm glad to have the opportunity to be here. To be honest, I've learned a great deal. Your generosity and hospitality have inspired me multiple times."

It was her turn to look uncomfortable and dip her eyes self-consciously. Patrick swiped his now sweaty palms against his trouser legs.

"You spoke to me earlier about your limited capacity," he continued. "I've actively worked in anti-slavery causes for over a decade, doing whatever I can to assist our Black neighbors. But you . . . you help everybody, regardless of color and station."

Anna tilted her head, squinting slightly to watch him. Her focused attention made him squirm.

"I'm inspired by it, and perhaps convicted. But I can't help but wonder how, with the limits you have, you haven't chosen to limit your generosity to those who need it the most. My curiosity isn't to be misconstrued as judgment, for I respect you all the more for what I've seen these weeks. But as white people can find assistance anywhere, I've never wanted to spend resources that could have gone to an African American with far fewer options."

He stopped, donning a sheepish look, anxious to hear how she would respond. She blinked slowly at him. He rubbed his hands down his thighs again, but the sweat remained, so he stuck them in his pockets. His hand hit the money she'd just given him, and a coldness trickled down his spine.

All along, he'd thought he had come to Cleves and worked at the inn as a favor to Anna, but he had it all backward.

She'd spent the last couple weeks giving him a job and lodging to help him out.

And he was white.

29

Anna saw the widening of Patrick's eyes and the parting of his lips as some appalling thought slammed into him, leaving him aghast. What had left him so disquieted?

"Need doesn't come in colors and sizes." She moved her hand further up her face, blocking the lamplight from her throbbing eye. "Even the wealthy feel pain. It makes sense for you to prioritize giving to the neediest who have fewer resources at their disposal, especially living in a slave state, where so few are willing to help them."

The look of horror hadn't left Patrick's face, but he was listening. Lowering her voice, she continued. "I have been in great need before, and I'm in need of help very often. So I've never felt it right to judge between the people God brings across my door. Frankly, that's something I don't have the energy for. I have to trust that God brings me the people that He wants me to help and leave the judging to Him. Sometimes a person's difficulty is unseen to the human eye."

Anna leaned her aching head against the doorframe. "I do see your point. Yet I've never found us truly unable to help anyone who came needing food or shelter. God has always provided enough."

Her words hit their mark. Patrick gave a small nod and lifted his fist to rest his chin on it in thought. The day's hair growth left a dark shadow on his chin and jaw, drawing her attention as he spoke.

"You mentioned before the gulf between what God has enabled you to do and what I presume is the things you wish you could do. That constricted feeling is one I have experienced often."

"You?" Anna blurted out.

"Very much so. The fact that I cannot alleviate the suffering of the Black population weighs on me enormously."

Anna gave a hum as she considered his words, seeing again in his eyes the pain she'd seen that day in her backyard.

"When did it start? Where did it come from?"

Patrick scratched his jaw with his thumb. "Church, actually. It was after my mother died, so I was probably about twelve. There was a sermon on God creating man in His image and the good purpose He created us for. My mind pieced together that it applied to all of humanity, not just ones sharing my skin color. We left the service and watched fellow parishioners get into carriages with their Black grooms and maids. And I simply couldn't understand how they could walk out of that service and not see their slaves as humans made by God just like them. I still don't understand."

"That's how it began for you?"

"That was it." Patrick sported a wry grin. "I've seen Negroes mistreated horribly my whole life. Of course, I always hated it, but it was that service when the Lord truly grabbed my heart to fight for emancipation and care for the vulnerable. When I realized that they weren't created inferior to me."

Anna leaned forward. "If that is what God has called you to do and the people He has called you to serve, then I agree that is where you ought to focus your priorities."

"But?" Patrick lifted an eyebrow and leaned forward in kind.

His challenge pulled a small humored smile from her. "But we have Jesus's example to follow. He served the people in front of Him, of all ages, stations, and races. I would only hope that if a person that looks like you fell in your path, you would lift him up and not go around him to another that you've deemed more deserving."

Patrick's eyes remained serious. "It is one of the things God has been teaching me on this trip, actually. I still struggle to reconcile using my energy and resources to help someone who has far more opportunities available to him than others, but I'm intrigued by what you said that you've always found there to be enough for the people God brings to you. That you trust Him to bring across your path the people He wants you to serve. I've always thought that I have to go out and find the right people."

"Perhaps you do." He was so serious, so intent on doing what he believed to be right, that Anna didn't want to direct him away from what sounded like his particular calling. "In your situation, those who are the most vulnerable might not know that you are safe to approach if you didn't take the first step."

It was more clear than ever that he needed to be in a big city like Baltimore or St. Louis, working together with leaders in the cause for abolition, making his voice heard. This man could never stay in a small town with a trickle of refugees coming through and a woman who was regularly laid up for a week at a time. It would be putting his light under a bushel.

She backed up into the hall to distance herself from him. It wasn't a good idea to become dependent on him when he didn't have a permanent place here. When he arrived two weeks ago, she hadn't expected him to stay beyond a couple of days. Patrick Gallagher didn't strike her as someone who would sit still or stay hidden away in a small town for long.

"I'm sorry I'm keeping you up." Patrick straightened, dropping his hand. "You told me you were unwell, and I've been rambling."

Anna waved his words away. "Trust me, I'd rather be here than accepting my fate in my dark room. I only wanted to encourage you to not overlook the trees in your campaign to save the forest. The people needing rescue from bondage are many, but they're still made up of individual people, and as humans, they're more than their needs, positions, and race."

Afraid she'd stepped too far, Anna almost winced at her forwardness, but Patrick was nodding in agreement.

"That's an important reminder, and I appreciate it."

Patrick stood by the parlor window, staring aimlessly at the dark street after Anna left. A lamp remained flickering on the table, but the room was cold and dim without her presence. Her confidence both drew him to her and sent a pang of melancholy through his chest. He'd been confident in what he thought God wanted him to do once too.

Now, years later, the cynicism had become a chain that he was tired of dragging around. He couldn't be sure anymore if what he'd told Anna was the work God wanted him to do, or if he'd been wrong all along. She seemed ready to believe him, but he didn't believe himself anymore.

All he knew was that the fire still burned in his chest on behalf of the slaves still in bonds, and the thought of going to St. Louis without Anna felt physically painful.

Day 73, Cleves, North Bend, Ohio
Health: Heartsore.
Wildlife: Busy on the inn property these days, the only wild thing I see, besides a couple rabbits in the garden, is myself.
Verse for the day: Proverbs 13:12 Hope deferred maketh the heart sick: but when the desire cometh, it is a tree of life.
Personal notes: I'm a middle-class, recently impoverished white man, and Anna Markland provided me shelter and a job that could have instead gone to either of the recent refugees.

The only way to get the bricks Patrick needed to repair the foundation was to order them through the local bricklayer, whose supply came from Cincinnati via barge.

Patrick used the days waiting for the delivery to finally complete the whitewashing Anna had requested. The inn was quieter when she was indisposed, making it easier for him to move furniture and get the job done. Yet she was far more active while invisible than he thought she'd be. Every day, Mildred had new reports from Anna, answering various issues that came up. Leah and Jane didn't stay cooped up in her room here like they did at Rachel's boardinghouse. They came down every morning neatly dressed, with their hair fixed. When they weren't doing chores or playing in the backyard, they liked to stand at a safe distance and watch Patrick work, regardless of how boring his current task was.

Mrs. Markland took care of the front of the inn while Mr. Markland stayed in the kitchen with Mildred or sat in the small parlor, reorganizing the crop rotation charts he carried everywhere with him and agonizing over the almanac. Patrick's presence had become familiar enough that Mr. Markland had developed a begrudging acceptance of the intruder, and sometimes

Patrick set aside his work to engage him in a game of checkers when Mrs. Markland ran errands.

Patrick dutifully ate supper with inn guests, forcing himself to make conversation and listen to the stories of their travels, which they thought were so original. He didn't bother telling any of them about his long walk, because they weren't there to listen and couldn't be expected to understand.

The bricks finally arrived the same day that Anna reentered the world. Patrick was inspecting the delivery in the backyard when he heard her talking to Mildred through the kitchen window, and his heart rate skittered. Forcing his feet to remain planted on the ground, he counted and recounted the bricks mindlessly while straining to hear more of her voice.

"Is there something wrong with them?"

He whipped around to see her standing at the open back door, looking as fresh and healthy as the first time he'd laid eyes on her in Cincinnati. For a moment, all he could do was exhale as the dreariness of the past several days fled. He took in the sparkle of her eyes, the glimmer of afternoon sun on her sleek brown hair, her trim figure in that pretty blue dress of hers, and for the first time that he could remember, was overcome with the feeling that everything would be just fine.

"You're back." He was smiling like an idiot, stepping toward her like a fish being reeled in.

"You're still here. Thank you for managing while I was unavailable. The walls look beautiful, and Leah and Jane told me that you even made a friend out of Mr. Markland."

His hands were suddenly in the way, so he clasped them behind his back. "Well, I'm not sure that he would say *friend*, but we are on speaking terms. It's good to see you up."

She descended the stairs, and he kept his hands clasped to keep from reaching out. "So these are the bricks for the foundation?"

He cleared his throat and turned back to the stacks. "Yes. They look good, and all three hundred of them are here. Mr. Boyton is supposed to come in the morning to start laying them. I've never laid bricks before, but I can help. Hopefully the place won't fall down at the next gale if I do."

"I'll have to stop giving you candies if it does."

Anna reached into her apron pocket and tossed Patrick a candy. He caught it and popped it into his mouth, and never had a molasses candy tasted so good.

30

Patrick concentrated on the ripples surrounding his fishing line on the bank of the Great Miami River while Franklin kept up a steady stream of conversation beside him. It had been a good many years since he'd last fished, and even then he hadn't been good at sitting still when he went out to the Patapsco River with Colm and their friends.

Franklin was worse at it than he was.

It had made sense to suggest the activity to Anna at the time. With the foundation project completed and no word from Elijah Lovejoy, there weren't a whole lot of ways to keep avoiding taking the dead tree down. Taking time off to rest his sore muscles while promising his catch to Mildred sounded like the best way to spend such a hot day. Now he half-listened to Franklin while studying Anna's dead tree in his mind, mentally cutting it down using all the methods he could think of. None of them struck him as being both safe and enjoyable.

July was almost upon them, and he'd have to leave soon. The delay in Cleves became harder to explain in every letter he wrote home. He had earned enough to make it all the way to St. Louis. But most of all, every day he spent at Riverview Lodge implanted Anna Markland deeper into his heart and made the thought of leaving more and more suffocating.

He had to leave before it was too late.

"I'm helping Mr. Matson plan the Independence Day celebration," Franklin announced, his fishing line bobbing erratically in the water.

"Is that so? What can we look forward to?"

"Reverend Markland is going to read the Declaration of Independence, and some of the old soldiers will shoot their guns. Then we'll have shooting contests and races and a pie contest for the women. I told him I can help judge it. My cousin Oliver will win the shooting contest. Once he shot the eye out of a racoon at two hundred yards. My ma once said that he's a better shot when he's drunk. Then after we eat, we'll have a bonfire. What do you want to do for it?"

"Oh, I don't know. I suppose I'll come and watch."

"Do you know how to set up fireworks? Mr. Matson said he wasn't sure we could do fireworks, but I guess if Cincinnati can do them, we can too."

"I'd trust Mr. Matson's judgment on that. Someone can get hurt if you don't know how to set them up right. I've never done it." The thought of setting up fireworks sent a boyish thrill through him, and he had to remind himself that setting them up with Franklin underfoot would not be the exciting event he hoped for.

What he should do was go back to Cincinnati. From there, he could find out if anyone had heard from Lovejoy and then buy a steamboat ticket for St. Louis. If he still managed to beat Lovejoy to Missouri, no harm would be done. He simply couldn't stay here and keep taking Anna's money.

"Mr. Matson said that the fireworks in New York are so big, they cover the whole sky," Franklin said wistfully.

Independence Day was Monday. He'd cut the tree down this week and leave Tuesday for Cincinnati. It would allow him one more weekend and the holiday with Anna, and then he'd be gone.

The respite of the last couple of months had been nice, but the problems in the world weren't going away, and he had work to do.

"If Corydon is getting home on Saturday, maybe he could help you cut it down Tuesday."

Anna worried her apron in her hands on the back step of the inn, watching Patrick cinch a rope around his waist.

Corydon only got a few days home with his family, and he didn't need to spend one on the old hickory tree. Patrick didn't dislike basking in Anna's worry for him, but it was a reminder that he needed to tell her he was leaving.

"Do you have enough rope?" Anna asked.

Donny and Franklin stood by, ready to drag away the branches Patrick sent down.

"There's enough," Patrick said. "Don't let the girls out until I come in."

Anna backed into the inn doorway, and Patrick squinted up at the tree. He could do this. Tying an ax to the back of his belt, he slid a knife into his pocket and hooked the saw beside the ax. With one last long swig of water, he started up the ladder Donny had borrowed. By the time he was at the top rung, he was among the lowest branches, grateful that he'd avoided having to shimmy up. His arms would have been dead before he even started the job.

He tied the end of the rope to one of the thickest branches before continuing to climb the spindly limbs. When he reached as high as he could climb, he secured the rope again, but up here, branches were no thicker than his leg. Taking a minute to get his bearings, he lowered back down to the bottom limbs. He found a notch to settle into and selected his first branch to cut. Balanced between two limbs, he pulled out the saw, tightened his legs around the trunk, and got to work.

Already sweat made his shirt stick to his torso, and his head itched. At fifteen feet off the ground, having slick palms was not reassuring. The branch he had sawed through cracked.

"It's coming!" he called, watching it crash to the ground.

Franklin came running, and Patrick wished he had a pulley system to let branches down slower. He selected the next branch, shifted his position, and kept going. Leaving a series of stairstep branches on the side he was sitting on, he cut his way up the tree. The heat was nearly unbearable, the sun blistering the top of his cap without foliage to shade him.

By the time he'd worked all the way up and sent down the top of the tree, he was parched and ready for dinner. With how slippery his palms were, it was time to return to the ground. Shifting around, he prepared to climb down when the dead branch he was balanced on snapped. Patrick grabbed at the rope to steady himself, his heart lurching at the sudden jolt.

The rope yanked on the top branch it was secured to and the branch broke, sending him plummeting through the air.

Instinctively, he flailed at passing tree branches, scraping his hands on the bark as he flew past. There was nothing to do but grasp the rope and try to keep from flipping upside down. The ground sped toward him as the excess rope reached its knot on the lower limb, slamming him to a stop two feet from the ground and spinning his body around. The rope jerked around his stomach, taking his breath away, before scraping up to his chest and coming to rest under his armpits. The ax had fallen from its place, but the saw he'd secured for the descent still swung from his belt.

Franklin and Donny approached, cautious of other potential falling objects, and Anna ran out of the inn. Donny reached Patrick first, grabbing his middle to stop the spinning. Patrick's battered palms clutched the rope for dear life as he tried to catch his breath. The knife was in his pocket, but he couldn't summon the strength to reach for it.

"A stool," he managed with a groan. "Or a chair to stand on."

Anna bolted toward the inn and returned with a kitchen chair, which she wordlessly shoved under him. His feet stumbled as they landed on it, and then he straightened, easing the tension of the rope around his chest. His ribs throbbed and his breaths came short and fast as he seized Anna's shoulders to steady himself.

She'd started working the knot, but he reached for his pocket. "I have a knife," he gasped.

Anna stared at it and then at the rope around his chest. Patrick extended the knife to Donny and turned, holding up the length that was still attached to the tree.

"I declare," Anna finally said to Patrick as Donny used the knife to saw. "Are you all right?"

"My ribs will be bruised. But otherwise, I just need some time to sit down."

"Please don't go back up there. I think you've done enough."

"It looks worse now than it did before I started," Patrick protested. "It shouldn't take more than another hour."

"Do you really want to go back up there?" Anna cocked an eyebrow at him.

The rope broke apart, and Donny slipped the sheathed knife back into Patrick's pocket. Patrick collapsed to the chair with the remnant still tied around his chest and the saw clattering behind him. Donny freed the saw, and Patrick slumped.

"Not really." He fiddled with the knot, but his hands didn't have the strength to work it.

Anna extended her hand. "Come into the inn, out of the sun, and I'll get you a drink of water. We can take care of it inside."

It took a minute before Patrick could trust his legs enough to stand and follow Anna, leaving Donny and Franklin to retrieve the tools and clean up the mess in the yard.

31

**"But time is speeding; and the billowy waves
Are hurrying me away." - Elijah Lovejoy**

Patrick gulped down an entire cup of cool water and leaned back in the kitchen chair, setting the empty cup on the table with a clumsy clatter. Anna had been watching him with her arms crossed, but now she approached and resumed work on the knot in the center of his chest.

She was impossibly close, and there was nowhere else to look but at her furrowed brow as she worked. Without the restored muscle control required to push her away and attempt the job himself, there was nothing to do but submit and enjoy the process while hoping that his galloping heartbeat would be taken for an aftereffect of his fall. Patrick took a slow inhale in an attempt to discern what scent she wore, but the only noticeable smell that met his nose was bread yeast. Of course. Strong scents were probably another headache trigger that she avoided.

"There it is."

The rope gave way and she stepped back, but Patrick's hand on her elbow stopped her. He meant to thank her and then let go. Instead she looked at him with startled eyes and he found himself saying, "I'm leaving Tuesday. I decided the other day but haven't had a chance to tell you."

Anna stilled. The disappointment on her face didn't make him feel better. It only reminded him that he'd stayed too long, that he would miss her, and that both of them would pay the consequences.

She swallowed and stepped back. "To St. Louis?"

"Cincinnati. But I intend to go from there to St. Louis shortly."

Anna nodded without meeting his eyes. "Have you heard from Mr. Lovejoy?"

"Not from him, just that his newspaper office suffered some destruction on account of his condemnation of the murder of a half-Black man there."

Anna leaned against the table next to him. "The McIntosh case?"

So she wasn't unaware of the news. "The judge didn't convict anyone in the murder after an entire mob dragged the man out of jail and burned him alive on the streets of St. Louis." Even in the retelling, Patrick's veins pulsed with anger. "They left the body on public display and refused to bury it. Mr. Lovejoy shared some very strong words against Judge Lawless for living up to his name and is being attacked for it, even in his absence."

"Is that supposed to make me feel better about you going?"

Patrick released his breath and looked to the window, through which he could see Donny and Franklin eating their dinner on freshly cut logs. "I have to go," he said, almost in a whisper.

"I know. I'm glad you survived that fall so you can."

Glancing down, Anna spied the blood on his palms and reached to turn his hand over. The scrapes on his palms stung, but they would heal soon. She absently ran a finger over the cuts.

"We'll be one more story in your travel memoirs," she murmured. "But we are glad to have known you, Mr. Gallagher."

"You're more than a story, Anna." His fingers tightened around hers, and she stared at them.

The silence was thick, and Patrick wondered where the staff and girls were.

"Do you need salve for that?"

Her question jolted him from the melancholy he'd been lost in. "No. I'll just wash them."

"How are your . . . ribs?"

They hurt, but weren't an area a lady could doctor. He started to say he'd go to his room to check on them when the door from the dining room opened and Anna backed away from him.

"Dinner is ready, Mr. Gallagher," Mildred announced, entering with Leah and Jane.

"He'll eat in here," Anna said quietly. "He's recovering from a tumble."

Mildred stopped in her tracks, horror in her eyes. "From the tree?"

"I had a rope," Patrick supplied.

"Good Lord, child. You just sit right there, and I'll get you some vittles."

Leah and Jane slid onto the bench near him, their rounded eyes never straying from him. Of course he'd lost his hat somewhere, his hair must be a mess, and he could feel the sweat and sawdust coating his face.

"I promised Mrs. Markland I'd wash my hands," Patrick said and pushed to his feet to visit the washbasin in the corner.

It hurt to draw a breath, but as he pulled up his chair to the steaming plate of food Mildred set before him, his heart soared.

He'd scored a meal at the kitchen table at Riverview Lodge before his departure. It was a moment to enjoy and a victory worth celebrating.

The dining room was still dark and empty on Tuesday morning when Patrick slipped through to the kitchen and lowered his knapsack to the floor. Anna was already there among the bustle of the cook and maids, but she was idle at the washbasin, her hair tied up in a blue scarf.

"Come sit." She indicated the table, where the buffet dishes were ready to be carried to the dining room. "Breakfast is almost ready."

He obeyed but turned toward her in his chair. "You're not feeling well?"

"Not completely. I'm afraid I'll probably end up back in my room after you leave."

It was tempting to offer to stay another few days and help around the place while she was laid up, but she'd always be sick again, and he couldn't stay forever. A few more days wouldn't fix her problems.

Mildred placed a cup of coffee in front of him, and a maid handed him an empty plate. Before he could help himself, Anna was there, filling the plate with eggs, bacon, biscuits, and berry compote.

"Do you think the events yesterday set it off?" he asked of her headache. It had been a hot, noisy day in the sun, with the smell of gunpowder and roasting meat in the air. Anna had been on her feet for most of it, helping prepare the town picnic in the green beside the meetinghouse.

"It's likely," she said quietly. "Thank you for helping Corydon with the tree. The yard looks so much better."

Corydon had come over early, before the heat took over, and he and Patrick had the tree down in less than an hour, like Patrick had predicted. His ribs ached too much to split the wood into firewood for her, but the branches were stacked on the edge of the yard by the woods. Perhaps she could hire the next bloke to do it.

It had been a sweet Independence Day. Probably not as impressive as the event would have been in Cincinnati, but out of all the places he'd been on his journey, he was glad to have spent the Fourth in Cleves.

"Eat with me?"

Anna sat, placing tiny amounts of food on her plate and picking at it while Patrick fueled up for his journey, dreading the return to aching legs and the weight of the heavy pack on his ribs.

"Are you walking to Cincinnati?"

"I'll start out walking, but hopefully I can hitch a ride along the way."

"And then to St. Louis?"

"I haven't decided yet. I'm considering a steamboat." The walk had lost some of its allure in the heat of summer, and the time in Cleves had accomplished more for his soul than the weeks on the National Road.

Anna fiddled with her fork, and Patrick glanced over at her silence. "You don't like steamboats?"

"Isaac died when the one he was on exploded."

Patrick set down his coffee cup in dismay. "I didn't know."

"It happens sometimes."

"I mean, I knew there was a risk but not that it caused his death. I'm sorry."

Anna let go of her fork and pushed her plate back. "If your boat stops in Cleves, come by and see us."

"I will."

She picked up a dish to carry into the dining room, leaving him to finish his breakfast alone.

He was packing food from Mildred into his knapsack when Leah and Jane arrived from upstairs. They flanked Anna as he said his goodbyes to the three of them together. It was inconceivable to think that he'd never see them again, and he refused to entertain the idea. Would he ever know what became of them and if they were one day reunited with their mother?

He swung his knapsack over his shoulder and accepted the filled canteen from Mildred. It was time to rip the bandage off and go.

With a set jaw and one parting wave, he strode down the street to the river road. It took great determination to not look back at Anna, standing beautiful and inviting on the inn steps. If he did, he wouldn't be able to breathe, and then all his resolve would crumble.

She was so much more than just a story. Cleves had been a detour he'd never expected when he left Baltimore, but it had become a memory he'd treasure forever.

32

"Abolitionists believe that, as all men are born free, so all who are now held as slaves in this country were born free." - Elijah Lovejoy

Heat radiated from the stones beneath the wagon wheels carrying Patrick east. He'd trudged a full ten miles before being overtaken by a farmer willing to give him a ride, and now he sat watching the horses' tails swish in front of him, trying to fan off their sweaty auburn coats. It was too hot for this, for all of them.

He tried to think forward, to seeing his friends in Cincinnati and then his ultimate destination in St. Louis, everything waiting ahead. But memories kept dragging him back to Riverview Lodge and Anna standing inches away from him, untying the knot on his chest while the one inside him tangled even further.

Fine, he was attracted to her. So? It made him human. And now it was time to move away from his boyish infatuation and face the task he had to do. His heart was taking far more effort to budge than his head.

"It's as far as I go," the farmer announced, pulling the reins.

Patrick swiveled, realizing they'd just crossed the bridge over Mill Creek. A barge floated past on the Ohio, carrying a menagerie of protesting livestock. Across the wide river, the bluffs of Kentucky rose, covered with thick forests, and Cincinnati spread out before him. He hopped to the ground, gave the man a coin, and adjusted his knapsack over his shoulders.

It was a couple of miles to Rachel's, and he could only hope that she had an available room so he didn't have to wander around looking for one.

The Fourth Ward was too quiet when he walked through it, but the heat had made him too tired to stop and visit with Reverend Nickens and Marius. There would be time for that later. A Black family hurried by on the road, their heads down and bodies clustered together. At the next cross street, a handful of white men stood around on the corner, wearing laborers' clothing and shifting their eyes at everything that moved on the street. No wonder the Black family looked concerned.

It was four o'clock by his calculation when Patrick reached Rachel's boardinghouse and jogged up the stairs. The door opened before he reached it and Ellis Dinsmore appeared on the step, a fierce look on his face. He and Patrick both stepped back in surprise.

"I didn't know you were still around." The tension on Ellis's forehead relaxed.

"I wasn't. It's good to see you. Are you on your way out?"

Ellis jerked his head down the street. "I just came down for Independence Day and am heading home now."

"Oh, how was it?"

The strain returned to his visage, and he looked over Patrick's head before responding. "Uh—not good. There was an altercation and threats from freedom opposers."

Patrick ascended two more stairs toward him. "What happened?"

Ellis responded by opening the door again and backing into it, ushering Patrick inside. The foyer was empty and silent. Patrick hadn't expected the sight of it to hit him hard with memories of Anna or how the freshly cut stair would put a smile on his face as he dropped his knapsack to the floor. She probably still thought he'd fixed it out of the goodness of his heart, because he'd forgotten about it and had never corrected the misconception.

Ellis led the way through the house, leaving Patrick's unanswered questions tumbling through his head. His mouth watered at the scents of Dorcas's cooking lingering in the kitchen as they reached it. Uncle Charles, Rachel, the staff, and four of their friends—faces unknown to Patrick—were gathered around the room, wearing their best dress and somber expressions.

"Mr. Gallagher!" Uncle Charles stepped toward him, extending a hand.

"What's all this? What happened?"

"Nothing more than reminders that Africans have no independence to celebrate in this here country."

"What?" Patrick turned to Ellis, aghast.

"The African Americans celebrated Independence Day today instead of yesterday. I came down for it, and Birney was there too. A group formed and attacked the gathering, dispersing attendees."

Are you kidding me? His friends obviously weren't, but the extreme opposition to humans in free states celebrating the national holiday was too horrible, too evil. Humans who had worked and fought for their freedom more than any white citizen had ever had to.

"When they say all men are created equal, they don't mean people like us," Rachel murmured.

"They don't, but God do," Uncle Charles returned hotly. "When our Creator made us in His image, He meant us."

"Of course He did." Patrick crossed his arms over his chest. "I am sorry, friends." How could anyone live like this, in the constant shadow of these bursts of violence?

After several minutes of listening to them rehash the events of the day together, Ellis took his leave again and Rachel turned to Patrick.

"What are you doing here?"

He shook his head. "I really don't know. It was time to leave Cleves, and no one knows what's taking Lovejoy so long in Pittsburgh. I thought I'd come in for the news and to give Birney the last article I wrote before I book passage and leave for good."

"What's wrong in Cleves?" Rachel demanded.

"Nothing." It wasn't exactly the truth, but it would be disastrous if the Williamses knew how much of his heart he'd left there. "I can't stay there forever, though."

Uncle Charles stared him down. "You were there a lot longer than we expected, after you and the missus didn't exactly hit it off."

"I know a lot better now." Patrick shifted uncomfortably.

"You need a room just for the night?" Rachel asked.

"I—" He really didn't know. He also hadn't expected to arrive to the news of a new outbreak of violence. Perhaps he should stay for a few days until things calmed down. It wouldn't do to abandon his friends during a volatile situation. "Can I stay a week?"

Uncle Charles and Rachel lifted matching questioning eyebrows.

"You paying in cash or in hours?"

"I can pay in cash unless you have work you need done."

"Anna's money," Uncle Charles reminded his sister, as if any of them had forgotten.

"How is Mrs. Markland?"

Right now? Probably bedridden in pain. Patrick lifted a shoulder. "She's doing the same as what I gather is her usual. Tough, kind, determined."

The skeptical looks stayed on the siblings' faces for a long minute.

"Didn't expect you to fall in love with her, boy," Uncle Charles finally said with an exhale.

What?

"Running away again," Rachel added from the side of her mouth.

"I'm right here," Patrick said. "And the plan for the past year was to go on to St. Louis. Nothing changed."

"Anna Markland's not going to move to St. Louis," Rachel said to Uncle Charles as if Patrick didn't exist. Their friends remained silent, watching the exchange from their seats at the table. "The only thing is for him to stay in Cleves."

"I'm not staying in Cleves." Patrick waved his hands in front of their faces. "And there's no future for me and Anna. Which room can I stay in?"

"He called her Anna. I would have put him in the front room, since it's empty now, but now I see that will never do."

Uncle Charles nodded in agreement with his sister. "Not unless you want to keep him up all night thinkin' 'bout her."

"I do need my sleep," Patrick volunteered.

"A week?" Rachel looked back at him.

He took a deep breath, considering once more. "A week."

"All right then." Rachel pulled an apron from a hook on the wall and tied it on. "Come along."

First thing next morning, Patrick returned to *The Philanthropist*, exchanging his newest article for a warm welcome, banknotes, and tales of the positive reception of his previous articles. He settled in for another week of Anti-Slavery Association meetings, night school—in sweltering temperatures now, where he stood by the door more as a guard than observer—free maintenance for the Nickenses' home, and diverting every stray thought about Anna into dreams for the future.

"You know," Mr. Birney said on Thursday night as they walked to the boardinghouse after night school, "I'm beginning to doubt whether Lovejoy is taking the river from Pennsylvania. It's always possible that he took a carriage overland."

Patrick decided not to remind him that he'd lived the last two months making decisions based on the assumption that Lovejoy would be passing Cincinnati on his way home.

"When did you last hear from him?"

"Not me—Owen Nickens heard from him about three weeks ago, which I passed on to you in the letter."

If he traveled overland, three weeks was enough time for him to have reached home, and Patrick was lollygagging—

No. He was providing a level of security to his friends during a week of violent outbursts against Blacks across the city.

See? God has given you work to do. He hasn't abandoned you. His presence helped . . . what? Five people? When two million labored in slavery and hundreds of thousands more lived in a false "freedom" like this one.

"I told Rachel I would head out on Wednesday morning, so I expect I'll stick to that. Perhaps I'll arrive around the same time as Lovejoy regardless." His long strides matched Birney's. The man may be in his upper fifties, but his energy equaled that of younger men.

"They appreciate having you around this week. I know they might not always say it, and their safety is never truly guaranteed, but one does get a measure of mental relief from knowing they aren't alone in their suffering."

Patrick didn't respond. He may be contributing valuable time to people who needed it, but it was still not enough. He would never be enough.

33

**"I do, therefore, as an American citizen, and Christian patriot, and in
the name of liberty and law and religion, solemnly protest against all
these attempts howsoever or by whomsoever made, to frown down the
liberty of the press, and forbid the free expression of opinion."**
- Elijah Lovejoy

M r. Gallagher? Wake up!"

Patrick jolted upright to a pitch-black room—not the one Anna had stayed in. He blinked, wiping his hands across his eyes. The banging on his door continued.

"I'm coming." He cleared his throat and dropped his feet over the side of the bed. Robes had not made their way into his knapsack for the trip, so he wrapped a blanket around his bare chest and found his way to the door by memory.

Uncle Charles was in the hall, the flickering light of his lantern reflected in his wide eyes. "They're attacking the press."

"Oh no. I'm coming."

"Hurry!"

There was no way Uncle Charles could show up to defend the press without risking his life, but what could Patrick do against a mob? He threw on his clothes, grabbed his boots, and ran after Uncle Charles.

"You can't come," he said, stopping on the outside steps. Leaning over, he quickly tugged on one boot and then the other.

"It's too dangerous for you."

"What are you going to do?" Uncle Charles asked.

"I don't know." Be there. Let James Birney know that he wasn't alone against the mob. "I don't know, but you can't come."

Uncle Charles nodded and didn't argue, because Patrick was right. He thrust the lantern at Patrick, and Patrick took off down the dark street toward Mr. Pugh's house, which housed the press. The noise started reaching his ears when he was a couple of blocks away, causing his heart to pound in his chest. What was he doing? He couldn't stop a mob.

Reaching Walnut, he found other bystanders he didn't recognize in the shadows, peeking around the corner at the house. Birney and Mr. Pugh were nowhere in sight.

Patrick turned his lantern down to hide his own face and peered through the darkness at the blazing torches of the rioters. Men were at the upper windows, dropping heavy fixtures into the street below, and showers of shredded newspapers floated in the noisy air. Edging closer, he watched rioters in front of the building grab the fixtures, shouting, and drag them away down the street. Anger pulsed through him at the realization that they were parts of the dismantled printing press.

Where was Birney? Where were the police? Patrick circled the street, staying in the shadows as onlookers jostled him. He stopped suddenly, recognizing Marius's still form at his elbow.

"Where are the police?" he whispered, backing into the doorway of the neighboring establishment.

"I don't know," Marius returned over the din.

"Is there nothing we can do?"

There were at least forty rioters, and with the press already broken into pieces, what was there to risk intervening for? Surveying the gut-wrenching scene before him, something odd stood out to Patrick. These weren't ruffians like he'd seen on the street corner the other day. They were systematic in their work, controlled—and well-dressed.

These weren't good-for-nothings. They were gentlemen, probably well-known businessmen in the city or planters from across the river. And this event was premeditated.

"You can't reason with a mob. Birney is smart to stay away. I wanted to be here if he showed up, but I don't think he will." Marius calmly turned his back on the scene, preparing to leave. Another crash sounded as a metal plate landed on the cobblestone street and two men rushed toward it.

"How long have they been here?"

"About an hour, I think. Someone said it started around midnight."

Patrick's hands itched to pick up a rock and throw it, to do something rather than stand here like a silent approver of injustice. The fact that these men were probably community leaders turned his anger to rage. If Marius hadn't been there, the definition of cool and collected, Patrick didn't know what he might have done. Whatever it was wouldn't have brought either justice or righteousness to the situation. So when Marius walked away, Patrick followed him, trembling with fury.

Perhaps lashing out in anger would spark a series of consequences he would regret, but there was no way he wouldn't regret being on the scene and doing nothing either.

There was no winning when it came to a mob.

"What time does your steamboat leave?"

Uncle Charles picked at his breakfast across from Patrick, who had spent most of the night lying awake after returning from the night raid, furious and helpless.

It was the worst possible day to leave Cincinnati, after the attack on his friend's property. If only he had known yesterday, before he purchased his ticket. God knew, and He must think that Patrick would never make it to St. Louis if He didn't intervene. So ready or not, today he would begin the final leg of his journey. Across the room, Rachel and Dorcas were busy packing food in a basket for him, because deck passengers on steamboats didn't receive the fine dining of stateroom residents.

"Ten."

"I reckon you're going to the newspaper office before then?"

"I'm not going to leave until I've seen Birney."

"It's a terrible thing they done. And rich men just provin' that education don't make a man wise or good."

"What's next, Charles? What will they do next? This neverending cycle of evil just hurts my heart."

"Boy, do I know it. If we don't keep our eyes on the Lord, the waves will surely overtake us. The Bible say that having done all, we are to stand. Sometimes it's all we can do to just keep standin'."

Patrick fingered the idle fork resting on his full plate. "Sometimes that feels like the hardest thing of all. I certainly would have crumpled in a heap long ago without God holding me up by the scruff of my neck."

"Ain't that the truth. Well, I'm getting a mite tired of these long, drawn-out goodbyes with you. Next time you come waltzing into town, you're gonna have to leave without a goodbye. I'm done in."

His words pulled a smile out of Patrick, who came to his feet. "It's a deal."

"There you go." Rachel lowered the full basket onto the table beside him. "You should eat more of your breakfast though, because the chicken Dorcas packed is supposed to last you all week."

He hadn't been hungry before, but the sight of the crispy chicken made his stomach rumble. So picking up his toast, he stuffed it in his mouth and washed it down with coffee. He pulled out his purse and gave Rachel enough to cover the food and his board for the week.

"Next time you come, you'll be our guest," Rachel said, giving him a smile of affection that he hadn't known she was capable of.

He returned her smile but shook his head, exasperated. What made everyone think he was coming back? St. Louis was six hundred miles away by river, not somewhere he'd be popping in from.

The sun had just risen when he set off down the street with his knapsack and basket. At the corner of Main and Seventh, the *Philanthropist* office came into view. The building was still standing, miraculously having escaped attack. Passersby slowed, gawking, while some clustered together, straining for a glimpse of Birney. Ignoring them, Patrick strode purposefully through the crowd and let himself in the door.

Mr. Birney stood at the counter with Mr. Pugh, Dr. Bailey, and Marius. Leaving his things by the door, Patrick headed toward the circle of men.

"Marius said you were here last night," Mr. Birney said as he approached.

"I was." Patrick stuffed his hands in his pockets, giving him a grim look. "They were gentlemen, businessmen. And no police in sight."

"I heard this morning that they had all been summoned to oversee other situations."

Patrick frowned. "Was there so much crime in the city last night?"

"Doubtful. They were under the orders of the mayor, I expect. He all but encouraged violence against us at the citywide meeting in January."

"Perhaps he was behind this? He has said that he hoped we would be mobbed," Dr. Bailey reminded them.

Mr. Pugh shrugged. "Some of them had Kentucky accents and I think were here on business, staying in the big hotels. One of the boys followed them back to one."

"How much have you lost? Have you calculated the damage?" Patrick asked Mr. Birney.

The older man rubbed his fingers over the lines of his forehead. "Fifteen hundred dollars, I imagine."

Marius stood unruffled beside him, looking as if he'd slept for ten hours, his suit in impeccable order. "Should we expect to buy another press and keep going, or look at other locations?"

"I have every intention of staying and not being cowed by lawless men. We have done nothing wrong, and they have only made it clear that what we are doing is important enough for them to want it silenced. If I buy another press, though, I will need to have the Ohio Anti-Slavery Society put up a guarantee for it. We can't afford to keep replacing such an expensive piece every time a group of thugs decides to have a go at it, and the city has made it clear that we can expect no protection."

Dr. Bailey swiped up a newspaper on the counter. "What sort of government doesn't provide protection for law-abiding citizens? One that does not guarantee the right to free speech and a free press."

"It's anarchy," Patrick murmured. The weight inside his chest pressed hard, stealing the air from his lungs. *And having done all, to stand.* Birney was still standing. Lovejoy was still standing.

And by God's grace and a firm hand on the scruff of his neck, he would keep standing too.

Day 114, Ohio River
Health: Sunburned, but the ache in my ribs is completely gone now
Wildlife: Too many bird species to name, a coyote onshore.
Verse for the day: Jeremiah 12:1 Righteous art thou, O Lord, when I plead with thee: yet let me talk with thee of thy judgments: Wherefore doth the way of the wicked prosper? Wherefore are all they happy that deal very treacherously?

Personal notes: Standing on deck, watching Cleves and Riverview Lodge pass by, I could think of little else but how much I wished I could have stopped by one more time.

34

"If we cannot be permitted to do this, except at the risk of property, reputation, and life, we must even take the risk." - Elijah Lovejoy

The first two days on the steamboat, Patrick stood on deck, soaking in the scenery and the novelty of river travel. He watched the bluffs pass by, amazed that he had ever chosen to walk through hundreds of miles of isolated Ohio farmland alone and trying desperately to keep his thoughts focused ahead.

It wasn't easy when the steamboat passed Anna's instead of stopping as he'd hoped, and he was haunted by Uncle Charles's voice accusing him of being in love with her. All he could do was give the whole muddled situation to God and trust that if He wanted Anna Markland to have a permanent place in his life, He'd manage it somehow.

The third day was spent waiting for the crew to untangle a snag on the paddle that delayed the trip almost a full day. Louisville was reached at the end of the fourth day, and Patrick disembarked to set foot on Kentucky soil for the first time and spend the night on shore. They passed Cairo on the sixth day and moved into the muddy waters of the Mississippi. That night, the steamboat stopped at Sparhawk's Landing and Patrick took a room at a tavern up on the bluff, adding Illinois to his attainments in a letter to Hezekiah.

By the time St. Louis was in sight, the sun was going down on the eighth day of travel, and Patrick's fried chicken was long gone. As glad as he was be on dry land, he had to admit that it beat walking four hundred more miles overland on trails that the National Road hadn't reached yet. There stood a good chance that he would have gotten lost if he'd attempted the Illinois wilderness without the highway to guide him.

It was late and he was starving when he landed on the soil of Missouri, his new home. All he had to do was find affordable accommodations for the night, and in the morning he could finally go looking for Elijah Lovejoy.

Day 122, St. Louis, Missouri
Health: Healthy as a horse.
Supplies used: Last of my crackers from Dorcas, tooth powder, $1 for a hard bed and fairly skimpy supper at an inn owned by a Presbyterian couple.
Wildlife: I admit that I was too distracted to pay attention today.
Verse for the day: Isaiah 43:19 Behold, I will do a new thing; now it shall spring forth; shall ye not know it? I will even make a way in the wilderness, and rivers in the desert.
Personal notes: Even I would not have expected this trip to take from March 19 until July 21 to complete. It's a journey I'll never forget. What does God have in store?

Patrick was up at daybreak the next morning and took the time to brush his coat and hair and tie his cravat in a knot that Anna wouldn't sneer at. Picking up his hat, he left his knapsack and basket in the room and went in search of breakfast. As he passed the front counter, a stack of religious newspapers caught his eye, and he backtracked to peer closer. The large majority of the places he'd bedded down on the trip had been owned by unsubtle slavery supporters, and it was odd to see such a pile out in the open here.

There was *The Philanthropist*, with his newest article. Patrick couldn't help his grin as he perused it. Seeing his name in print didn't get old.

Laying the paper aside, he glanced through the others in the stack. There was a copy of last week's *St. Louis Observer*, with a fresh editorial from Lovejoy lambasting Judge Lawless for failing to indict any of the mob in the McIntosh case. So Lovejoy was back. It was going to be a good day.

The sight of yesterday's *St. Louis Observer* sent an additional thrill through him, and he picked it up to read over breakfast.

The middle-aged innkeeper's wife poured coffee into his cup on the table as he took a seat in the dining room. She looked over and clucked when she saw the paper he'd chosen. "It's such a shame what they've done to him."

Patrick remembered what he'd heard about the trouble at the *Observer* office when Lovejoy was away. "Do you mean the looting, or the damage to his reputation?"

Leaning over him, she tapped a stubby fingernail on his newspaper. Patrick looked down at the little square in the corner and read.

THE OBSERVER - REMOVAL

After much deliberation, and a consultation with a number of our friends, we have decided here after to issue the 'Observer' from Alton, Ill. There is no doubt the paper will be better supported there than it now is, or is likely to be, remaining in St. Louis.

Snatching up the paper, he leaped to his feet. "He's moving?"

"Not only that, but I heard this morning that the print office was attacked again last night after this was released."

"No." The memory was still fresh of the damage to Birney's print shop. Patrick dropped into his hard wooden chair and inhaled his breakfast while he read the rest of the paper.

Before the food had time to settle, he grabbed the paper and strode out the front door. Out on the chaotic streets of St. Louis, he remembered that he didn't yet know his way around. He burst back through the inn's foyer and found the innkeeper's wife clearing his dishes away.

"Can you tell me the way to the *Observer*?"

She stacked his cup on her tray and moved toward the kitchen. "I'll get my boy to take you."

The moment turned to several before a boy in his young teens finally came sauntering through and Patrick followed him out the door. It felt surreal to walk streets that Lovejoy walked and pass businesses that he passed. Soon he would meet the man himself, and his future would be determined.

Or had Lovejoy already left for Illinois? Was he too late?

What a wild turn of events, to finally arrive in time to find the object of his interest turning tail. Birney had chosen to stand firm where he was, but then, Birney didn't live in a slave state. Would moving across the river really provide that much more protection to Lovejoy?

Patrick took the opportunity to take in the sights of the burgeoning city on the edge of the frontier. A fraction the size of Cincinnati, the pace of St. Louis felt slower, despite the Friday morning activity on the streets. The boy guiding him certainly wasn't in a hurry. Like Cincinnati, there was the air of temporariness with travelers and traders coming and going, using the city as a launching place to the West rather than a final destination.

The Black individuals he passed on the street—driving carts, carrying packages, and balancing heavy bundles of laundry on their heads—were not free, bringing the McIntosh case to mind. How could a person with dark skin feel safe in a city that dragged out of prison and brutally murdered on the street free men of mixed pedigree? They couldn't simply leave as easily as Lovejoy could when things became dangerous.

The boy deposited him in front of the sign for the *St. Louis Observer* and remained gawking at the broken window and rubble inside. Patrick took a deep breath, offered up a prayer, and stepped through the door, months of anticipation sitting on his chest.

Stepping over glass splinters and spilled type strewn over the floor, Patrick worked his way through the office to the activity in the back of the room. One man pounded nails into the cover of a large crate, which could only be housing the printing press. Lovejoy must be wasting no time ferreting it to safety. Two movers stood nearby with ropes and a low wheeled cart, but it was the fourth man whose presence drew Patrick to his side.

Tall and stout, with black hair tufted out above both ears and dark, serious eyes, the silent editor stood in a suit, overseeing the proceedings with his hands clasped behind his back. Patrick joined him in his silence, watching until the press had been moved out the back door and loaded onto a waiting wagon.

"Ship it to Alton any day but Sunday," Elijah Lovejoy instructed as the movers clambered to the wagon seat.

"We'll see it done, sir. She'll arrive safe and sound."

Lovejoy remained at the door until the wagon disappeared from view before closing it and turning to Patrick.

"You are not John," he stated, giving Patrick a good look for the first time. "I was expecting my brother, but he would not have remained silent so long. Are you here to describe our defeat to the neighboring papers?"

"I'm here to seek a job. I'm Patrick Gallagher, of Baltimore. I wrote to you several months ago, indicating that I was hoping to meet and offer whatever assistance you could accept."

Recognition lit Lovejoy's eyes, bringing a measure of relief that was quickly dashed by his words. "As you can see, I have no business to employ you in at present. It will take some time to get a print office set up elsewhere."

"I'm glad to see the printing press survived. I was at *The Philanthropist* not a fortnight ago, where James Birney's press was dismantled and dragged through the streets."

Lovejoy must not have heard the news by the look on his face. "We have both had the honor of being mobbed at last. I have been expecting the catastrophe for some time, and now it has come. Are you married, Mr. Gallagher?"

"I am not," Patrick replied, and an image of Anna talking to him against the parlor doorjamb slid unbidden into his thoughts.

Lovejoy's gaze traveled methodically around the destroyed room. The back of the room where they stood was dim, but light streamed through the broken window by the street, shimmering over the glass on the floor. "I can now feel as I never felt before the wisdom of Paul's advice not to marry, and yet I would not be without the consolations which my wife and child afford me for all the world."

He gave a heavy sigh, lost in thoughts Patrick couldn't share. Shaking himself back to the present, he gestured to the debris with a sad smile on his face. "Still, I cannot but feel that it is harder to fight valiantly for the truth when I risk not only my own comfort, ease, and reputation, and even life, but also that of another beloved one."

"Has your wife been threatened?" Patrick leaned forward, anxious to hear all the news withheld from the papers.

"We have been, repeatedly. It precipitated our removal from this place. Mrs. Lovejoy and our son Edward are even now at her mother's in St. Charles for their protection and gratefully avoided the ransacking of our personal belongings at home last night after the miscreants finished here."

"I did not know you had entered the ranks of fatherhood. Congratulations."

The lines around Lovejoy's eyes softened for the first time. "In March, yes. Thank you. I'm grateful that the Lord has kept him well throughout my wife's and my recent illnesses. I will be glad to be reunited with them when the house has been prepared in Illinois."

"Are you leaving tonight then?"

Lovejoy bent to pick up a handful of type from the floor, which he dropped on the counter with a clatter. "We are. There will be equal facilities for circulation in the two states, and I hope to maintain the same connection with our subscribers in both."

Patrick scooped up a few more pieces at his feet and added them to the pile, watching while Lovejoy sorted through the letters. "I imagine it will be more comfortable there for you and your family. I would like to come and help you set up the office and resume the paper, if you'll have me. I understand that other employment will be necessary to procure for the time being, but I'm willing to do it."

Lovejoy's square jaw remained set. "So long as duty seemed to require our remaining here, we were determined to remain, at whatever sacrifice of personal reputation or safety. God seemed to open a way for our location to change to where it will be much more useful than the current arrangement has been. Perhaps your arrival just before our removal is another of His provisions." He dusted off his hands. "Come, let us leave this tomb and find a more pleasant space to discuss the future."

With a gracious gesture to Patrick to precede him to the door, Elijah Lovejoy stepped over the remnants of his livelihood and exited the *St. Louis Observer* for the last time.

35

"Scarcely a town site could have been selected on the Mississippi more unpromising in its appearance." - Elijah Lovejoy about Alton

Early that afternoon, Patrick was back on the river again, standing beside Lovejoy and his eighteen-year-old brother John on the ferry winding its way the twenty-four miles up the river to Alton, Illinois. Everything had happened so fast, he could scarcely conceive it.

Patrick's gratitude at being invited by Lovejoy to Alton was strong enough to overpower any dismay about the sudden change in locations. It wasn't the worst thing to settle into a free state, despite the set of troubles he now knew they came with.

Elijah Lovejoy was easy to talk to, with his honest, straightforward style of discourse, and even though their opinions hadn't aligned on every subject, Patrick couldn't help but like him.

For one thing, Lovejoy still refused to accept the label of abolitionist, and although Anna Markland and James Birney both considered him a friend, he insisted on distancing himself from the incendiary reputation of their movement. Lovejoy had taken Patrick to a quaint coffeehouse for a second breakfast, over which they'd discussed matters of faith, the free press, slavery, and gradual emancipation—Lovejoy's favored course of action.

"The abolition society uses overly confrontational language. They're too harsh and denunciatory to change minds," Lovejoy insisted. "I believe coming to reason together like men and women is a more profitable philosophy."

Patrick listened dubiously, even as he reminded himself that this thoughtful deliberation was what drew him to Lovejoy in the first place. But now his new acquaintance had been threatened and attacked multiple times for speaking out against slavery. What more would it take before he'd call a spade a spade?

Near the end of the meal, John had burst into the eatery, snatched a chair by his brother, and launched into a tirade about the events of the last day.

"I am completely disgusted with the West." He crossed his arms over his thin chest, not seeming to care who Lovejoy's guest was. "My trunk with my clothes and money were all packed in the print office to be shipped, and the criminals even threw that in the river. No one should leave the East and come here. Their property is not safe, their lives are not safe, and in fact, nothing is safe."

Remembering the recent treatment of Garrison in Boston, Patrick said nothing. Things were probably quieter and safer in Maine, where the Lovejoys were from, than most other places out east.

"You may expect some severe articles one of these days." John had noticed Patrick and directed his scowl at him. "The people here deserve it, and I think they will get it, for you know that Parish is perfectly able to give them a dose."

Patrick glanced from John to Lovejoy, surmising that the boy was talking about his older brother.

Lovejoy dipped his head. "The family calls me that," he explained aside to Patrick. "My middle name."

Having read the *Observer*'s recent articles criticizing Judge Lawless, Patrick certainly agreed that the man in front of him was able to "give someone a dose."

Lovejoy sat leaned back in his chair, his empty plate pushed aside. "John, meet Mr. Patrick Gallagher from *The Genius* and more recently, *The Philanthropist*. I believe all of us present are aware of the power of a well-aimed article. You may be seeing Mr. Gallagher in the new office in Alton."

Patrick soon became intimate with the heat of many of John's opinions, as he rarely felt the need to restrain them. At nearly his own age, Elijah

Lovejoy was much more level-headed, answering his brother's ranting and raving with well-timed words of wisdom that sometimes bordered on poetic. But he very rarely disagreed with John.

After breakfast, Patrick returned to the inn for his knapsack and paid up, to the chagrin of the innkeeper's wife, who was sorry to lose his business so soon. Before he knew it, he was boarding the ferry with Elijah, John, and the few belongings they'd salvaged from the ransacked rooms.

The wooded banks of Illinois were mostly level until they neared Alton around the time Patrick's stomach had begun growling for supper. Here, rocky bluffs appeared and the town became visible perched on the steep incline. The ferry neared the dock just past a large warehouse on the river with the words Godfrey, Gilman & Co. painted on the side. A third the size of Patrick's expected new home of St. Louis, Alton still boasted a busy riverfront, with steamboats, barges, and ferries at dock.

Patrick stepped onto dry ground, taking it all in. As he followed the Lovejoys in search of temporary lodging, it became clear that Alton was a boomtown, bursting at the seams and growing faster than the town could handle. They passed hundreds of houses, dozens of stores, four hotels, and two schools before they found an available room, by then weary enough to be willing to bunk together.

After supper and a promise from Lovejoy to see the building for the new print office on the morrow, Patrick sat down to write Colm of his location. The sheath of blank papers tempted him, and he hesitated, rubbing the smooth grain between his fingers, before pulling two sheets out. It was entirely appropriate to let Anna know that he'd arrived safely and provide information on where he could be reached, in case anyone in Ohio wanted to know.

Day 123, Alton, Illinois
Health: Well-rested after a week on boats and ready to work.
Wildlife: Still more deer, foxes, and hawks.
Verse for the day: Luke 10:10-11a But into whatsoever city ye enter, and they receive you not, go your ways out into the streets of the same, and say, Even the very dust of your city, which cleaveth on us, we do wipe off against you.
Personal notes: Naively believed my travel journal ended yesterday, yet here I am in a new, unexpected place with new friends and a world of possibility ahead, feeling better than I have in a long time. I reread the end

of Pilgrim's Progress, *where Christian and Hopeful arrive in the Celestial City, and all the struggles feel worth it.*

Saturday was spent touring the low stone print building, returning to the docks to see if the press had arrived, and searching for work while the Lovejoys met with the bank about houses for sale. News came at breakfast Sunday morning that the press had been delivered on the *Palmyra* at daybreak and was sitting at the docks waiting to be retrieved—against Lovejoy's express wishes that it be delivered any other day. Patrick couldn't blame him for honoring the Sabbath and leaving the crate where it was until Monday morning, when he could hire porters to move it into the new office.

Patrick joined Lovejoy and John at the Presbyterian church for service, taking in the names and faces of leading businessmen of the town who were introduced to him. Lovejoy had made connections during his scouting trip to the area, and now he was welcomed joyfully by the prominent men in the church. The surprisingly positive reception lifted Patrick's spirits. Maybe Lovejoy actually found somewhere that he and his family would be safe after all.

John was eating breakfast beside Patrick in the crowded boardinghouse Monday when the first sign of trouble appeared in Lovejoy stalking toward them, his brow dark. He'd been gone from the room when they awoke, presumably to see about getting the press moved immediately. Dread ate its way up Patrick's stomach as he dropped his spoon and came to his feet at the same time as John.

"What is it?"

Lovejoy came to a stop before them and caught his breath, swiping his hat from his head. "It's gone."

Patrick and John glanced at one another, tight-jawed.

"This morning before daybreak, the press was broken into and dumped into the river," Lovejoy finished.

"But we're not even in a slave state anymore!" John stared at his brother, confounded, but Patrick understood. Being in Ohio hadn't saved Birney's press either. "These mobs are outrageous, uncivilized, fiendish, and dangerous to the preservation of our government! Are the people here sending a message about your welcome, or did crooks follow us over from Missouri?"

"There's a great deal of speculation, but no one knows." Lovejoy dropped his hat onto the table. "The whole of the *St. Louis Observer* is destroyed now. We must start completely over."

"John and I are here, ready to help." Patrick's heart was in the pit of his stomach, but Lovejoy didn't look like he was going to wallow, and Patrick wasn't going to add to his defeat. "The miscreants will see that they haven't won. We can get started today."

"I can't believe this," John muttered, his hands in fists.

Lovejoy was as cool as Marius in the face of a mob as he snatched his hat up again and returned it to his head. "So long as I stand on the basis of eternal justice, all the hosts of hell cannot prevail against me. We will not allow ourselves to become discouraged."

They followed him out to the street, away from the din and listening ears at the table. They had barely reached the front step when a well-dressed man approached them on the street. As he neared, Patrick recognized the minister from the Presbyterian church, Frederick Graves. He stepped up to Lovejoy and asked about the news of the press, which the editor repeated for him.

"I came to invite you to a meeting tonight at the church to discuss your particular problem," he announced, stroking his moustache. "Many of us are interested to hear what your intentions are now."

Lovejoy slowly nodded and agreed to be there, and after a few minutes, Reverend Graves moved on.

Patrick watched his retreating back until the traffic in the streets swallowed him from view. "If money weren't an issue," he asked thoughtfully, "where would you get a new press?"

Beside him, Lovejoy let his breath out. "The ones I prefer, the cast iron hand-operated press that can be operated by one person—they're built in Cincinnati."

36

"We would provoke no violence from any portion of the community; the only weapon we would use is the truth, the only sentiment we would appeal to, the moral sense of the community. - Elijah Lovejoy

The darkness pressed in, the four walls of Anna's third-story bedroom holding her prisoner. Never had a sick headache raged so long and so intensely. The very fact that they always ended provided hope to help her through each one, but this one seemed to never end. For days now, she'd lain in her chemise in the sweltering room, the curtains tightened over the windows preventing any movement of air.

Mildred came in with broth twice a day, and Mother Markland brought any questions about the inn, but really, they didn't need her. She'd been here enough times to ensure that her staff was capable of managing in her absence, as long as Mr. Markland cooperated and disaster stayed away. Sometimes her headaches allowed her to be up and about at different points of the day, but not this one.

Every time she rolled over, the world tumbled about for several minutes before steadying again. The food she ate didn't stay down. Her eye and the back of her head throbbed sharply, all but stealing any rational thoughts from her mind.

Not enough of them though. Not the ones that would keep her blissfully oblivious to the passage of time. Not the memories of her failure to help Leah and Jane find their parents the night of the accident.

Not the thoughts of Patrick leaving to go do Big Important Things in Big Important Places.

It was foolish to have allowed feelings to grow for him. It would be wrong to saddle a man with so much drive and conviction with a woman who required so much care.

She could just picture herself on the Judgment Day. "Greetings, Lord, I'm the woman who kept Patrick Gallagher in the house, checking in guests and fixing loose floorboards when I couldn't get out of bed, after You'd created him to change the world."

Isaac had been a born innkeeper. He was a people person and a homebody, a phenomenally gracious host, and a thoughtful son who specifically wanted a place where his parents could safely spend their elder years. The inn in Cleves made sense for him. It made sense for Anna, who was usually well on enough days of the month to care for logistics and keep the place running and then had somewhere she could hide away on the days she wasn't. But it did not make sense for Patrick.

If only she could change bed linens or arrange flowers for the parlor or do anything except lie here alone with the memories of him.

If only she could wake up in a few days, when all of this was over.

If only she were big enough and important enough that someone would care enough to stay.

Thanks to the influence of Messrs. Godfrey and Gilman, partners of the largest business venture in town, it was just a matter of days before Elijah Lovejoy had received enough subscriptions to head to Cincinnati to purchase a new printing press.

Thanks to Monday night's meeting with the town's mayor, clergy, and leading businessmen, Patrick's face darkened in thought as they strolled together on the steamboat carrying them back down the Mississippi River.

Foremost in his mind was the interrogation Lovejoy had faced from the council about whether he was bringing trouble to Alton by continuing to publish incendiary remarks against slavery. As if it were his new friend's fault that his press had been mobbed! Worse, by his own admission to Patrick and John in the room that night, Lovejoy had denied being an abolitionist to his new neighbors.

"I stand against slavery, but in a free state where the evil does not exist, I feel myself less called upon to discuss the subject than when I was in St Louis."

Standing in their shared bedroom, Patrick had felt hot and cold at Lovejoy's retelling.

"I told them," Lovejoy continued, pulling his shoes off, "that as long as I am an American citizen, and as long as American blood runs in these veins, I shall hold myself at liberty to speak, to write, and to publish whatever I please on any subject."

"Hear, hear," John muttered.

Patrick had gaped at him, stunned.

"Do you really believe that slavery is less of an issue, less deserving of denunciation, just because we are not forced to see it in front of our faces every day?"

Lovejoy calmly slipped out of his coat. "The gentlemen needed to know whether or not to fear my bringing turmoil to their city. I was called upon to assure them of my intention as a new arrival to contribute to the peace while maintaining my freedom to write about whatever my conscience dictates."

His explanation had done little to make Patrick feel better. Now, in the muggy heat on the steamboat deck, Patrick couldn't help but wonder if he had been too hasty in offering his assistance to someone who was backing off from the fight he cared about the most. Or were the words to the townsmen simply offered to appease them and buy Lovejoy time to get settled? He wouldn't know until time had passed and the new *Alton Observer* started rolling off the press. He had no interest in returning to Illinois to simply print articles about Sabbath-keeping and avoiding drunkenness, if that's all Lovejoy intended to do now.

"I'm going in to lie down." Lovejoy pushed back from the deck railing.

He did look peakish, but the humidity was enough to sap anyone's strength. He'd left John behind in Alton to guard the new print office and what remained of their belongings, but Patrick had jumped at the opportunity for the trip. So much had changed since he left Cincinnati last, and he could easily imagine the gloating look Uncle Charles and Rachel would exchange when he materialized on their doorstep again.

Patrick stayed on deck, where there was at least the breeze from the moving boat. The Mississippi was almost a mile wide here and felt so exotic and interesting, a great highway through the middle of the country. If only the mosquitos didn't keep finding his skin beneath the netting over his hat and gloves on his hands.

"Where do you want me, Lord? Where will you use me?"

In Cincinnati? Providing a safe presence to his friends didn't pay bills. Birney was doing good work that Patrick believed in, but he was fully staffed, and Rachel's boardinghouse was in good shape now. He simply wasn't needed.

In Cleves? Dismantling trees and whitewashing hallways didn't register on his list of dreams and goals in life. The way Anna served her town was good for her, but Cleves was so out of the way, the work so small compared to the way his heart burned to fight slavery as a whole. If he didn't, he might burst into flames.

In Alton, with Lovejoy's promise to not offend his hosts?

Or somewhere else?

Had his trip fulfilled its purpose, and was it time to think about going home?

It had to be more than the August sun that made Elijah Lovejoy's face shimmer bright red as Patrick walked beside him up to Rachel's boardinghouse. Patrick had his suspicions about the toll the last couple of weeks had taken on him, despite the eternal optimism he always projected. From all appearances, the man was not well.

"Patrick Gallagher, what are you doing here?"

Rachel stood with her hands on her hips, scowling down at him from the doorway, until her eyes landed on his companion.

"Mr. Lovejoy!" Smiles replaced her playful scowl and she was all welcome then, ushering them into the foyer. "Come, let me take you to a room. How long do you intend to stay?"

"Two nights," Lovejoy said, mopping his forehead with a handkerchief.

Patrick swallowed. He shouldn't have expected to see Anna on this trip, but if he could figure out a way to make it happen, he would. But only one full day in Ohio made the idea simply impossible. The best he could do in a day was see what news he could glean from the staff.

"Let me get you settled so you can freshen up before supper."

Rachel practically shooed them up the stairs. Patrick obeyed, amused at the way the woman had changed from night to day at the appearance of Lovejoy.

The next morning, he accompanied Lovejoy to the press builders, wanting to stay close to the editor, should he collapse from his obvious fever. But Lovejoy soldiered on and managed to get the press ordered for delivery to the steamboat. Patrick would have stopped by *The Philanthropist* on the way back to the boardinghouse, but one look at his friend's face had him eliminating any unnecessary stops.

While Lovejoy retired to his bed, Patrick removed to the kitchen, impatient to hear any mention of Anna. What he received instead was far worse than he'd imagined.

Dorcas's knife flew on the counter, filling the room with the eye-watering sting of onions, while Rachel stood idle against the dishpan with her towel in hand, answering all his questions.

"Things changed right after you left," Rachel began. Notices started appearing around town offering a hundred-dollar reward for the capture of James Birney. Hundreds of people attended a meeting hosted by city leaders to decide what to do about *The Philanthropist*, concluding that if Birney continued to publish, they could not be responsible for the consequences."

Chills raced up and down Patrick's spine, and Rachel wasn't done with the telling. Uncle Charles's son Sam came in, dropping into a chair beside Patrick at the table to listen.

"Only a few days ago, the Ohio Anti-Slavery Society published a refusal to the city's request to shut the paper down. It's the freedom of the press." Rachel gestured with the dish towel in her hand. "They refused on principle. Mr. Birney's is the only paper in the city printing an opposing viewpoint. Well, that letter was a spark to a dry keg."

"What happened?"

"Another mob, larger than the last one. They started at the newspaper office, done tore it up, and then headed to Mr. Pugh's. After they destroyed everything they could there, they actually went looking for Mr. Birney. Went to his house."

Unable to keep still, Patrick rubbed his palms together.

"His son was the only one home. Shut the door on them and went to an upstairs window with a loaded gun in case they should try to break in. They went back to the office, looking for someone to hurt. And ended up in Church Alley, burning up Negro neighborhoods."

"No." The word came out in an agonized groan from deep inside him. Covering his face with his hands, he tried to breathe over the constriction in his chest. "That's so near to here." His friends had come so close to being hurt or killed. Who was to say tomorrow they wouldn't be?

"It's been a sad few weeks, Mr. Gallagher." Rachel exhaled.

Patrick ran his hands down his face and let his breath out. "I'm so sorry to hear about more violence. Are the Nickenses safe? What became of Birney?"

"The Nickenses escaped harm. We all have friends that didn't. Birney was out of town and hasn't come back yet. We assume he's heard the news and is lying low somewhere."

Patrick nodded, his whole body tense. Was there no end to the violence? No end to the evil?

"We're awful glad to see you and Mr. Lovejoy, Mr. Gallagher," Rachel added softly. "You haven't told me what brings you here."

Leaning back, he drummed his fingers on the table. "Things aren't much better out west," he said with a sigh. He told them about the attack, the move to Alton, and the destruction of their press. It was another ten minutes before he could finally move the conversation around to Anna.

Rachel met Dorcas's twinkling eyes with an amused glance. Patrick didn't care. They'd already decided he was in love with her, and he didn't have the fight in him to set them straight.

"Haven't heard anything from Mrs. Markland these weeks," Rachel told him.

His heart sank further. If only there was a way to stop by and see her and the girls. Just to lay eyes on her and ensure she was well, let her know she wasn't forgotten.

Fine, maybe there was more to it. Maybe she was the only bright spot in the oppressive world around them.

He just had to figure out what God wanted him to do about it all.

37

"I feel much more composed about Parish than I have for months past. I think the mobites will make an abolitionist of him."
- Elizabeth Lovejoy, Elijah's mother

A loud clatter outside brought Anna from the foyer she was sweeping to the front window. Moving the curtain aside, she peered out to see a buggy stopped on the street before her door. In a moment, she deposited the broom in a corner, ran a hand over her day cap, and pulled the door open.

The first thing her eyes landed on was the perspiring face of a man half bent over, coming up her stairs on the arm of his valet.

"Why, Mr. Lovejoy!" she cried when recognition registered. She'd never seen him with bloodshot eyes and sunken cheeks before, but it was definitely Isaac's old friend.

Quickly, she stepped aside, opening the door wider to allow them entrance. Only then did she regard the second man. She blinked twice, her heart unable to control its sudden stutter.

Patrick was next to her now, smiling boyishly down at her, so close that she could smell the outdoors clinging to him. Oh, she'd gotten way too fond of someone who would always leave again.

"Welcome back," she said, holding his gaze for a heartbeat. In the next second, she had slipped away to the staircase, leading Lovejoy up to the closest available bed.

Patrick deposited their bags on the floor of the room while Lovejoy sat on the edge of the bed, pulling his shoes off.

"I'll send up some tea right away," Anna said, thinking as she spoke. "And send for the doctor. How long has he been sick?"

"Four or five days." Patrick did not look amused. "He was hoping to make it home, but we can't continue on if he wants to arrive alive. Should I sleep in here too?"

"Oh, no, you don't want to bunk with someone who's ill. Since we're almost full, I'll have to put you in the small room at the end of the hallway."

"Whatever's best for you." Patrick stepped forward to hang Lovejoy's coat on a hook and pull back the covers. The poor man collapsed, shaking with fever.

Anna wasted no time hurrying off. On her way through the kitchen, she ordered Mildred to put the kettle on before continuing out the back door and down the stairs Patrick had built. In two minutes, Donny was riding up the hill in search of the doctor. Mother Markland stepped out of her house to see what the commotion was before disappearing back inside. Anna was pumping a fresh pail of water for the sickroom when Mother Markland returned with a pile of rags in her hand and Mr. Markland trailing behind her.

"I don't know who's going to nurse him," Mother Markland said in the kitchen, where she selected a large bowl from the cabinet. "You haven't time, and it's not appropriate. Jesse, you don't need candy right now." Mr. Markland snarled at her when she took the candy jar from him.

"I suppose Mr. Gallagher will have to." Anna stopped in the middle of the floor with her pail in hand. "Although I'm sure it will be awkward, as he's only just met him." Not to mention the fact that he didn't strike her as much of a nursemaid.

"Is he here too?"

"They came together. I've yet to hear what brought them. Mildred, can you send Leah up with the tea when it's ready?"

Back in the sickroom, Anna poured water from the pail into Mother Markland's bowl to soak her rags, then offered Mr. Lovejoy a drink from her dipper. He didn't open his eyes, but his lips moved, and he swallowed. The action prompted gratitude inside her that it wasn't her in the sickbed today. God was gracious to allow her to be up when the men arrived.

"I'll leave this here for when we need it," Anna told Patrick as she set the pail down. "The doctor's on his way, and I can show you to your room."

Mother Markland arranged a damp rag on Mr. Lovejoy's forehead, so Anna moved to the door to intercept Mr. Markland before he intruded. Patrick was by her side in an instant, shaking her father-in-law's hand. Concern for Mr. Lovejoy's condition couldn't dampen the delight Patrick's unexpected presence brought them all.

"I received your letter," she told him as she led him and Mr. Markland down the hall. "I expected you to be in Illinois now."

"I have much to relay since then, from both there and Cincinnati."

She turned in the narrow hall, her eyes wide. He'd been to Cincinnati? "I'll come to the small parlor after supper, when all the guests are taken care of, and you can tell me then."

"I'll be there."

His ready agreement shot anticipation through Anna along with another, more rational thought. Holding a bedside vigil for Lovejoy hadn't crossed his mind. She needed to see about hiring a nurse.

Patrick had been in the quiet small parlor for an hour before Anna finally arrived and sank into a settee across from him. She was a busy woman with a full house, but he'd still been straining at every little sound in expectation of the moment she was free.

"The surveyor, Mr. Peters, is reading in the other parlor, but I think everyone else has retired. The staff has all headed upstairs."

Patrick closed his Bible and set it aside. "Thank you for taking us in. We'll have to stay until he's fit to travel, however long that is. How have you been?"

"I've been well this week," she said, and sucked in her breath, looking uncomfortable. He waited, and she admitted, "Last week was difficult."

"Then I'm glad it's in the past." Patrick thought of the previous week and how hot it was when he was on the steamboat on the way to Cincinnati. How miserable to be sick then. It touched him that she had chosen to be honest with him. Anna Markland never tried to be anything more than herself, and he liked that about her. "I'm sorry it was hard. Is there anything you need me to do while I'm here—just as a friend, to keep me occupied?"

"You don't have to do anything unless it's to save yourself from boredom." Anna ran her palms over the textured fabric of the seat. "The only thing I can think of is chopping that wood."

"You're really intent on making a woodsman out of me, aren't you?" Patrick gave her a half smile. Really, he should have expected her answer. He'd done everything else on her list already.

"Only if you want something to do," Anna repeated.

Patrick drank her in, taking long, slow breaths in an attempt to calm his galloping heart. The effect her presence wrought on him was inexplicable.

"What brought you to Ohio?" She wasn't breaking the lock their eyes had on each other either, and he wished she weren't so far away.

"I wanted to see you."

Her eyes slit in doubt. "That's not why Elijah Lovejoy is here."

After a beat, Patrick let his breath out. "No. But I did accompany him in hopes of seeing you. He needed to replace the printing press his adversaries destroyed. We came to Cincinnati for it, and he was sick by the time we arrived. We were there long enough to get the press and hear about the mob violence against Birney and the Black neighborhoods last week."

"Oh my." The heat on her face turned to dismay. "There's no end to the hate, is there?"

Patrick realized his hands were tensed, squeezing his thighs, and he relaxed them. He shook his head, unable to think on it overlong. "They think they're the righteous ones. Lovejoy and Birney are enemies of the public peace. The status quo."

"There is no peace as long as people are oppressed and sin is left unchecked at the highest levels," Anna declared.

Patrick's mouth parched as his body went hot. Had she really just said a nearly exact quote of what he'd told Colm last winter? She was . . . amazing. How was it possible that God had led him past so many forks in the road to a woman so perfectly suited to him?

"Where did you go?"

Anna's soft voice broke into his thoughts, and he slowed his jiggling foot.

"Into the future," he said honestly. "I pray that one day our nation will be rid of this evil and know that peace."

"Do you think it will ever change?"

Patrick swallowed against the burning his previous line of thinking had lit in his chest. "I have to. I can't keep going if I didn't have hope that it will."

"Sometimes I doubt whether it will be our government that brings justice to this unjust world. It seems like wherever I look in history, in every century, injustice has prevailed. Yet God promises justice."

"He's also told us to do it," Patrick replied stiffly.

"Right. That seems to be normal—God's people doing justice in their own circles in the midst of unjust societies. And praying for it for the wider culture."

"So you don't think we'll be rid of slavery as a whole in our times?" Patrick cocked his head. Could he live with that? Could he do as Anna suggested, doing justice and praying for it but never being part of real change?

Anna's shoulders slumped. "I don't know. I just don't know. Nothing will change if we don't do the work, but at the same time, only God can change hearts, so we can't . . ."

She trailed off, her face scrunched in thought.

Colm had said what she was trying to. That the burden, the weight of the world, wasn't his—or hers—to carry. God wanted His children to take their burdens to Him. Do the work, yes, but let Him carry the weight.

"I know," Patrick said. "It's a struggle to labor toward something and leave the result with the Lord. I so desperately want His sweeping justice to happen in this life, not only the next one. I ache for it."

Anna fixated on him, angling her body and reaching toward him on the other side of the room, as if begging for him to hear her. "Your compassion is such a gift. You reflect Jesus's compassion to the world, and that's so important, Patrick."

"It so often feels like a curse." He smiled sadly at the fire.

"Don't stop," she whispered.

Patrick slid beneath the covers in his bed thirty minutes later, Anna's words playing over in his mind. In the course of the conversation, his attraction to her had shifted into startling clarity.

He wanted to marry her. The thought brought pure pleasure coursing through him like the first sip of sweet hot chocolate. He could park himself right here and send Lovejoy on to Alton with his press alone.

But . . .

He forced himself to blink in the flickering light of his candle, to consider the buts. But Anna might not be looking to replace her husband right now. She obviously thought of Patrick as a good friend, and rushing the good thing they had together could destroy it if he didn't do it right.

Besides, all his reasons for not moving to Cleves were still true. He couldn't do everything he longed to from here. Just because he could die happy here with this incredible woman by his side didn't mean he could die with a clear conscience that he'd done his best to fulfill God's purpose for him. The thought that he was hiding away in peace and security while evil continued on unchecked in the world would chafe.

He yawned and closed his eyes, his vision changed. She was no longer Anna Markland, the enigmatic inn owner. She was his potential wife. The thought made all the gloomy realities of life feel more bearable, and he breathed deeper.

He would take his time. Go back to Alton and help Lovejoy get established. Fight slavery with the press and use the power his white skin gave him to protect people who had no voice in a court of law. He'd begin a correspondence with Anna, over time revealing his intentions. He would bide his time and pray hard and wait for God to iron out the muddled, sticky things.

Because He would. Patrick had never been more sure of anything in his life.

38

"I should be false to the Master I serve, and of whose gospel I am a minister, should I allow my own interests, (real or supposed), to be placed in competition with His." - Elijah Lovejoy

Going west and meeting up with Elijah Lovejoy must have been good for Patrick, because he was noticeably different than he had been a month ago. It was as if something tightly rolled in his chest had unfurled for the first time since Anna met him.

He spent a couple hours each day chopping wood for her, which was as entertaining for the girls as it was for her. They pressed their faces to the window and giggled as he swung the ax and missed or caught the corner of the log he was splitting and sent slivers flying.

So he wasn't an outdoorsman and he wasn't a nursemaid, and he certainly was no lumberjack. But that never stopped him. Anna had rarely met someone who plowed forward with as much determination as he did, skill or no skill. His skill lay in his voice, and his pen. Anna knew. All of his published articles were in the bureau drawer in her room, tucked under her aprons and shawls.

But he chopped the wood anyway. He let Mr. Markland win at dominoes, even when Mr. Markland forgot what he was doing halfway through the game and got up and wandered away. He hid a fugitive under a load of winter wheat seed heading for the Markland farm and drove them to the next safe house on his way to deliver the seed. He emptied the chamber pot from Lovejoy's room. He spent hours attacking his sheaf of papers in the small parlor, writing what Anna hoped was more articles. And every evening, she sought him out in the same room, stopping for a short chat.

The difference was that the urgency was gone. He no longer worked like he was in a race against time.

And he laughed.

The first time Anna heard it, she was walking into the large parlor to call the guests to supper. The sound of his rumbling laughter brought her up short in the doorway in surprise. There he was, surrounded by the four adult Phillips sisters who had taken up residence in the inn while waiting for their brothers to arrive from Louisville. Anna had arrived too late to hear whatever had put the mirth on their faces, but it was the first time he'd ever found other guests amusing.

For a moment, jealousy sliced through her. The sisters spanned their thirties, Anna guessed, each one dressed in a different color and pretty in her own way. Shouldn't she simply be glad that he was happy and relaxed for the first time since she'd known him and not care whose joy he shared?

Anna's arrival had caught the attention of the room, and everyone was looking at her, waiting. Her eyes crashed with Patrick's humor-filled ones, and he pushed to his feet, still smiling.

Anna smiled back. "Supper is served."

He gestured, allowing the sisters to precede him from the room. Anna stood aside as Hatty, Harmony, Hortensia, and then Bernadette passed her. Mr. Peters was next, with Patrick last. Anna nearly gave in to the temptation to invite him to eat in the kitchen when he reached her. He would take her up on it, and the thought was enough to calm the jealousy.

"Our guests are delightful, are they not?" she asked instead.

"I've never met four sisters so different from each other. But they do know how to have a good time."

"I'm glad you have a nice diversion," she said, and meant it.

After supper, she helped Mildred prepare the bread dough for the next day and left Patrick to spend the early evening hours with the other guests. Mildred could do the bread, but the staff were tired after a long day, too, and Patrick wasn't hers to hang onto. Leah and Jane sat at the kitchen table, sewing button eyes on Black dolls and chattering together.

A knock sounded on the back door, and Anna wiped her dough-covered hands on her apron to open it. Rather than a passing traveler looking for a meal or a neighbor with a request, she found Corydon on her back step.

He took off his black hat, taking in the occupants of the room as she welcomed him into the kitchen.

"I got home this afternoon. Can I talk to you in the parlor?"

"Yes. Thank you for finishing up, Mildred." As she led him across the hall to the small parlor, Anna told him about Lovejoy and Patrick's presence in the inn. Thoughts of Patrick flirting with the Phillips sisters down the hall niggled, and it took effort to set them aside.

"I would like to see them before I leave." Corydon closed the parlor door behind himself. Anna waited in anticipation while he took a deep breath. "I found Leah and Jane's mother, Sandra."

Anna's stomach tumbled in a flurry of emotion. She pressed a trembling hand against her bodice and tried to breathe. "You're sure?"

"As sure as I can be. She was not open with me about where her husband is."

Questions and thoughts of possible effects of the news assaulted her, and she fell into the settee. What to ask first? "How is she?"

"She was . . . distrustful. Possibly paranoid."

"She's lost a great deal. At the hands of white men."

"Yes." Corydon let a ragged breath out. "I told her about the girls being alive. She didn't look like she believed me."

"Do you think she can provide for them?"

"I don't know enough to be sure. The brother was there. He's about twenty and looks capable. Anyway, we need to reunite them. Perhaps having her daughters returned to her will return some of her . . . sanity."

Anna sat up straight. "She's insane?"

"I'd say scarred. You'll need to tell the girls she's found, and I suppose we need to take them up to her."

This brought a frown to Anna's face. "They've been through a great deal as well. It's been fifteen months. I would rather she came here, to where they feel safe and comfortable. She can stay with us as long as it takes for them to bond again. I can't be gone from here for long, and I don't want to drop them off with her without staying to make sure they'll be safe and cared for."

"I know." Corydon rubbed his knuckles across his chin. "I'm not sure that she can be convinced to come with me. Slave catchers set traps like this."

"I'll have to think about it," Anna said. "It would be so much better for them to meet her here."

She'd talk it over with Patrick. Maybe he'd know what to do.

"How long have Mr. Lovejoy and Mr. Gallagher been here?" Corydon asked after a moment.

"Three days," Anna replied absently, her mind still on the girls. "Mr. Lovejoy is pretty sick still. They could be here a while, or his fever could break suddenly. Mr. Gallagher is in the other room now, if you want to see him."

"I'll give my greetings while I'm here, since he could be leaving imminently." Corydon hesitated with his hand on the door.

"He's enjoying an overabundance of female company in there," Anna said in what she tried to make a light tone.

Corydon cleared his throat. "Sarah and I wondered if anything would develop between you two."

Anna choked, flapping her hand at him. "He's not looking to settle down in such an out of the way place."

A long pause followed while Corydon ran his hand over the knob. "Would you ever consider leaving Cleves? We can arrange other care for Mother and Father."

"You don't have to do that," Anna said quickly, coming to her feet. "Our arrangement is working well. I need the inn, Corydon." Surely he could see that. They'd had so many conversations about it over the years. "It is doing good work here and allows for my condition in ways not many other situations would."

"What if the right man comes along, Anna?" Corydon searched her face. "Wouldn't he be able to help you settle into another, equally accommodating situation, where you wouldn't have to be the one managing everything? God is capable of doing so much more than we can imagine. Don't hold yourself prisoner by thinking there's only one way He can work."

"I love Riverview Lodge." Her heart wrenched at the suggestion of leaving her haven. She liked Patrick, but did she love him enough to leave her home? Besides, he needed a partner with vitality, not one with health issues that would hold him back.

"Sometimes we have to let go of what we love to find the life God has given us to live." Corydon spoke gently and deliberately, in the minister's voice that had helped her through so many painful things in life. "What was the right answer at one time might not be the right answer forever. I just encourage you to think and pray about it."

Then he was gone, and Anna fell into the settee again. She pressed her hands against her temples, her life suddenly upended. Corydon's unexpected visit had challenged every corner of her precarious life. She couldn't even think about his assertions about Patrick right now, with the news about the girls' mother.

What would she tell them? What kind of mental state was Sandra in? They'd been separated for too long already—she wouldn't steal more time from them while she hemmed and hawed about what to do. But she also didn't want to do anything until she talked to Patrick first.

But why? Patrick had nothing to do with it. Corydon had to be wrong that she had a chance at a future with him. Should she bring him into her confidence and decisions if he had no place in her life? Leaning forward, Anna moved her hands to cover her eyes. She needed to pray about it, like Corydon said.

"I don't know how I'm supposed to pray about all of this, Lord. I don't know what to ask for. But You promise wisdom to those who ask, and You promise Your Holy Spirit to those who don't know how to pray."

The urgency she felt to rush into an answer on both fronts wasn't from Him. Corydon had reminded her not to limit God. Anna took a deep breath and another one. God never hurried. When He did a thing, this kind of impatience and anxiety were unnecessary.

God had brought Patrick back to Cleves on His own good time, and He'd brought Sandra's location to her attention on His schedule. Could she trust Him to reveal her next steps at the right time as well?

39

**"I cannot surrender my principles, though the whole world besides
should vote them down—I can make no compromise between truth
and error, even though my life be the alternative."**
- Elijah Lovejoy

The parlor settled into a happy silence after the Phillips sisters bid Patrick and Mr. Peters goodnight and traipsed up to their rooms. The echoes of the evening's mirth still lingered in the empty space, leaving Patrick sitting for a moment in his content.

If only his friend Lovejoy was well. When he stopped in the sickroom earlier in the day, Lovejoy was asleep, still raging with fever, while the elderly Black nurse Anna had hired refreshed his poultices and changed out the damp rags on his forehead with fresh, cool ones. There was nothing else Patrick could do for him.

"Well, I'm going to move on too," he finally announced to Mr. Peters. He didn't say he was going to retire. He just didn't want to miss his late night conversation with Anna in the private room next door.

When he slipped into the little parlor, he was disappointed to find it quiet and dark. Perhaps he'd already missed her. It was funny how she laid aside the propriety she'd held to last time and came all the way into the room to sit alone with him these days. There was a good eight feet between them and no one else downstairs at night to see, but still. She must have decided that she could trust him and they were past the age of needing chaperones for quiet conversations about what was going on in the world.

He stoked the fire in the hearth and pulled out his Bible from the shelf where he'd stored his books. He'd try to read, though his heavy eyes felt more like dozing. Settling comfortably into his favorite armchair, he opened the leather cover and settled in.

Anna lay blinking at the sliver of moonlight falling across her bedroom floor and the sleeping faces of Leah and Jane on their mats. The thought of losing them ached. It wasn't only a sad ache; there was a happy ache, too, that their mother was alive and their family could be reunited. Would it crush them to find out their father might have died? Anna wasn't sure if they had already grieved the death of their parents or still held out hope that they were alive, since they hardly mentioned them anymore.

She lay praying and thinking for a long while until thirst drove her from her bed. In her distracted state, she hadn't brought up water at bedtime, and she'd have to go all the way down to the kitchen. Not that she was sleeping anyway.

Anna tied her dressing gown over her nightgown and pushed her feet into slippers before easing the door open and tiptoeing down the stairs with a candle. In the kitchen, she filled a cup of water and took a long draught before poking around, moving things into position for breakfast preparation in the morning.

She moved into the dining room, straightening vases and candlesticks as she went. As she stepped into the hall, the glow of firelight under the first parlor door caught her eye. Was someone still up?

Anna lifted the latch and poked her head inside. Patrick was in the shadows of the far corner, writing in his journal in his shirtsleeves. He looked up at Anna's intrusion, and their gazes tangled.

"You're still up." It was an inane thing to say, but she didn't have any idea how late it was, and more intelligent greetings had fled her mind.

He smiled, closing the book on his lap. The day's growth on his chin and cheeks accentuated the shadows on his face, and the firelight reddened the tips of his mussed hair so they almost glowed. "I was finding this more restful just now."

"Than bed? Why so?" Anna came further into the room.

She pushed the door behind her so it stayed cracked without latching shut.

He didn't respond right away, and she wondered what she'd stumbled into. "Dreams," he said simply. "Come join me?"

She shouldn't. She wasn't dressed, and her hair hung in a long braid down her back. If he were anyone else, she wouldn't even be tempted to stay.

But she lowered onto the settee anyway, and Patrick had the presumption to add another log to the fire. The action was a clear invitation, and she dove in headfirst.

"I do want to talk to you tonight. When Corydon came, it was to tell me that he found Leah and Jane's mother just west of Columbus."

Patrick straightened up from the hearth, brushing his hands together. "He's sure it's her?"

"Yes." Anna relayed the whole conversation and then found herself pouring out her concerns and fears about how the transition might affect the girls.

He sat on the edge of the armchair, leaned toward her with his elbows on his knees, and listened intently.

"I feel quite sure that it would be best for the girls to meet their mother here, but I don't know how to convince her to come," Anna finished.

He pursed his lips, steepling his fingers together while he watched the fire. "Perhaps the brother is the key."

Patrick spoke slowly, feeling out the idea as he talked. "If he's willing to meet you at a neutral location—a safe house that helped him or his mother on their way, perhaps—you may be able to persuade him to come down first and meet the girls. When he sees it's safe, we can leave it up to him to bring the mother down."

As far as Anna could see, it was probably the only plan that would work. "It's a lot of time for a young man to miss work. Each trip would take about a week."

"We can find someone in the Anti-Slavery Society who would be willing to sponsor it. Cover his traveling expenses and missed wages. If Corydon can convince the brother to meet with you or even to come all the way down, I'll write to bring the appeal before the society. I stayed with the Bulls in Columbus, a minister's family. They would be happy to host a meeting for you if the brother doesn't name a preferred location."

"If he won't meet with us, I'll just have to close the inn and take the girls up there when I can stay for a few days and help them settle in. And pray that I don't get sick while we're away."

"Hopefully you won't have to do that. I agree with you that it would be best for their sake to meet here." Patrick was silent for a minute while the logistics played through Anna's head. "Will it be hard for you to let them go?"

In an instant, tears pricked at the backs of Anna's eyes. "Yes. It will be significantly easier if I know I'm leaving them in a good situation."

"You've worked tirelessly toward this moment for so long. I can only imagine how divided it must make you feel."

"Thank you for understanding," Anna managed.

"I wish I could stay and help," he murmured, more to the fire than to her.

It gave her what she needed to change the subject to him, and she pounced on the opportunity. "What do you think of Alton?" It was rare enough to have a long conversation with a friend. Listening to Patrick talk would easily be the best way to spend an evening.

"Quite different than the situation I expected when I left home," he said and told her about its growing population and uncertain future. "We learned very quickly that it's not the safe haven Lovejoy was hoping for. I think we all came to the hard realization that just as nowhere is truly safe for African Americans, nowhere in America is truly safe for the abolitionist. Or even slavery opponents who won't yet claim the title of abolitionist."

"It's quite the weighty label," Anna said softly. "How many of us bandy it about outside of society meetings? I'd venture a guess that most of Cleves wouldn't identify me as one."

"Use of the name endangers those we're trying to protect. To most, the word merely means a rabble-rouser and draws slave catchers sniffing about. I can't blame anyone who chooses to distance themself from those things."

"Do you feel safer using it now that you're far from home?" Anna asked.

He gave her a little smile. "More precisely, I sought out anti-slavery activists on my trip and only used it with people I already knew were safe. But yes. My stint in the senate and the subsequent revelation of my beliefs brought greater scrutiny on my actions, so it's probably best for my friends' safety that I left Baltimore."

The clock in the hall chimed one o'clock several minutes later, in the middle of a story Patrick was telling about his sisters. Anna stifled a groan at the sound. If she stayed up much longer, she'd be inviting a sick headache, and with her full house and fevered guest, she couldn't afford one this week. This cursed illness never stopped stealing from her.

"I wish I could stay up all night and talk," she confessed, wanting to cry at the thought of cutting the conversation short. Uncurling her legs, she reluctantly came to her feet.

Patrick looked up in surprise, as if he hadn't realized it was the middle of the night. He stood because she did, clasping his hands behind him as he wound down his story. A wave of rust-colored hair had fallen over his forehead, and his vest hung unbuttoned over his rumpled shirt. Anna looked at his unkempt appearance with new eyes. She liked put-together Patrick, but suddenly, she realized that she liked relaxed and comfortable Patrick too. He never tried to impress anyone. It was refreshing.

She made her way to the door and stopped to let him finish what he was saying.

"Are your sisters all in Baltimore?" She had to go but couldn't bring herself to reach for the door and end the magical evening.

Patrick placed his books on the shelf and knelt to bank the fire. "Mor died of yellow fever in her early twenties, but Maisie is married now and lives in Baltimore. I write to her very often. And my step- and half-sisters are still at my father's."

"I'm sorry," Anna whispered at the mention of his loss. Patrick had spoken of his sisters as if they were such a part of him. What would it take to become someone he wrote to *very often*?

"They would like you." Using the fire shovel, he layered ash over the smoldering logs, leaving Anna alone with his statement. She'd never thought about whether his family would like her, but her heart warmed to think that they would. That they wouldn't judge her for spending half of her life indisposed.

"You're far from your family," he stated simply as he came to his feet.

"I am. My siblings are all married with children, and I do miss them. I love the Marklands, though, and living in Ohio. When I went home, I didn't quite fit in anymore."

Now the only light in the room was her candle burning low, with which she watched as Patrick retrieved his coat from the back of his chair.

She opened the door, pausing so as to not leave him in darkness.

"Because of the slavery?"

"That's definitely part of it." Her involvement with free Blacks and abolitionists was such a large part of her heart and life. How could she be close with someone she couldn't share that with?

Patrick's eyes had darkened in the light of the candle. She waited as he neared, realization dawning that their shared heart made him feel closer than her own family. When he left, taking his friendship and camaraderie with him, the pain would doubtless be excruciating.

40

"While I value the good opinion of my fellow citizens as highly as anyone, I may be permitted to say that I am governed by higher considerations than either the favor or the fear of man. I am impelled to the course I have taken because I fear God." - Elijah Lovejoy

Patrick approached Anna, standing still and quiet in the dim corner. But when he neared, he didn't pass her into the hall, as they both expected.

One moment, he was stepping forward and taking the candle from her, and the next, he reached to place it on the hearth while the hand holding his coat landed on her waist.

He locked on her sea blue eyes drawing him in, overwhelmed by how right she felt anchored in his arms and lost in the heat sparking between them. He had found what he'd been searching for. No force on earth could stop the dipping of his head, the trajectory of his lips toward hers.

Until Anna lifted a weak hand to his chest and applied the slightest pressure.

Patrick stopped an inch from her mouth, expelling a sigh. She had been standing there looking entirely soft and feminine and kissable, causing every other thought to flee from his mind. Now doubts closed in.

"Do you have a good reason why I shouldn't kiss you right now?" he whispered. He couldn't think of a single one.

"I do." She increased the pressure on her hand, where she had to feel his heart thundering in his chest. He obediently lifted his head until his forehead rested against hers, and waited for her to continue.

"Will you be leaving with Elijah Lovejoy?"

His heart plummeted. "Yes."

Anna's breaths came small and quick, betraying how his touch affected her. "I will not be."

But he'd known she wouldn't. He had nothing to offer her in Alton, and she had everything here.

"Would you want me to stay?" he finally asked, resisting the temptation to tighten his hold on her.

"I . . . I don't want to hold you back."

The little tremor in her voice and worry in her eyes brought a scowl to his face and his head rearing back to look at her. "What put that idea into your head?" He couldn't even wait for her answer to refute it. "Anna, you make me feel like I could go so much further than I ever thought I could alone."

She twisted her braid around in her hand. "What did you do when I was laid up before? You did chores around the house and entertained my father-in-law. You were made for so much more than that. Being with me would limit you. I couldn't be there to support your work for days at a time, with no warning."

Was that truly how she viewed him? Patrick's mouth hung open at the absurdity of it. As the shock wore off, the realization grew that it wasn't that different from what he'd thought himself. It just sounded worse coming from her mouth.

"I was wrong," he managed through his dry mouth. "Your work here, Anna, is incredible. You see people. You care for your father-in-law and every poor tramp who comes through Cleves every day, regardless of the color of their skin. And I've never once thought the work you do is too small or unimportant. If it's not too small for you, it's certainly no less for me. The newspaper—" Dare he say it? Could he believe it? "The crusading . . . it's not more important work. It's just different work." His stomach churned. Where had he gone so wrong to consider the type of service she did as beneath him?

"Do you truly think those things about me?"

"These days? Absolutely. Although it might be a bad time to admit that I thought differently of you when we first met."

Anna tipped her head back to where he could see her wide eyes by the flicker of the candle. "About that! It was clear that you did, but I have no idea why. I'd never even met you before."

Even after all this time, he was too embarrassed to think too hard about it. "Let's just say that I incorrectly pieced together the bits of information I was given. I was glad to be proven wrong, and learned an important lesson about making assumptions."

"When did you decide that I'm not the monster you thought I was?"

Patrick bobbed his head sheepishly back and forth. "Partly when the whole truth was revealed to me, partly by coming here and seeing who you really are for myself."

Anna frowned at his vague answer. "And what had a perfectly capable man like yourself so broke that you had to fix door hinges for room and board?"

He'd expected her to say something more about his change of heart, and was taken off guard by the twist in conversation. Patrick's eyebrows arched. "Rachel didn't tell you? I was robbed at gunpoint right before I arrived in Cincinnati. They took everything but a couple of dollars that I had hidden. And goodness, but things are expensive out here."

Compassion twinged Anna's mouth into a little frown. "I had no idea. But don't you see, Patrick? You fixed my stairs because you had to to survive. You said yourself that the press is different from the work Riverview Lodge does. And that's obviously what God made you to do." She paused, seeming to weigh her words. "Until you are very sure that He wants you here, what He has given us to do should come first."

"You need to reunite Sandra and her daughters. I need to help Lovejoy get established in Alton." Patrick grasped for hope as he felt her slipping away from him. She had left him no doubt that she, too, longed for a joint future to be within reach, but talking to her had confirmed what he'd figured on his own.

There was no way the two of them would work together the way things were. The mutual attraction wasn't enough to make up for two lives that were simply incompatible. At least now he knew that she had no designs to let go of Riverview Lodge anytime soon, nor did he want that for her.

Anna smoothed her hand across his chest when he didn't respond, then dropped it to her side. He hated the distance, but she was right.

"Come on." He couldn't stay a minute longer. Patrick lifted the candlestick from the hearth and placed it in her hands. If he didn't get out of here, he was going to end up kissing the frown off her face. Ten minutes ago, she had said she needed rest. Instead, he'd stayed and betrayed his determination to take his time before revealing his intentions to her. "If you get sick because I kept you up, I'll never forgive myself."

He stepped into the hallway ahead of her, backing toward the front staircase and a quick escape. The spark of hope that had lit in his chest last night smoldered under a cold dousing of reality.

Anna had almost reached the kitchen when he stopped. She couldn't go to bed thinking that her rebuff had him running away. "I agree that we shouldn't get ahead of the Lord," he said, his voice rumbling through the quiet hall. "But I don't regret asking. Goodnight, Anna."

Anna found each step away from Patrick harder and harder to take, overcome with a desire to rush up to him and bury her face in his chest. He had shown himself humble, correctable, and quick to set aside his own desires for the Lord's. Men like that were hard to come by. Why couldn't God bring her a man as special as Patrick but in a career Cleves could support?

"Sleep well, Patrick. Will you have better dreams now?"

She couldn't see his face in the shadows as he edged away. "Horrible nightmares about the prettiest woman in Ohio halting my romantic advances. But God and I will talk about it, and He'll remind me that He loves me perfectly anyway."

Anna gave a sad smile and turned away, letting him go.

41

"Politics, laws, and government are subjected to free discussion."
- Elijah Lovejoy

Elijah Lovejoy was still sick when Patrick checked on him the next morning. He'd hoped to see him well, for more reasons than to relieve man of his misery. How was he going to spend more time with Anna, knowing what he did now about how she felt in his arms and her hopes for a future with him, too, while keeping her at a proper distance? Until God tore down the barriers keeping him and Anna in different spheres, it would be best if he puttered away down the river to where his head could cool off.

As soon as breakfast was over, he retrieved the key from her and headed out into the foggy morning to the stable. It was kept locked now, both to keep the tools away from Mr. Markland and give further protection to any fugitives who couldn't be smuggled safely into the house. Patrick grabbed the ax and was soon attacking the downed tree again.

His muscles were still protesting the chopping he'd done yesterday, but his pent-up emotion needed someplace to go. Before long, shards of the logs strewed the ground around him, and he couldn't lift the ax one more time. Patrick stood heaving, staring at the mess he'd made. For all his asking, God still hadn't given him peace about staying in Cleves. Without something better to offer Anna anywhere else, he simply couldn't find a way forward for them. He could write to Colm, get his perspective, but the thought made Patrick want to scratch his eyeballs out.

The slam of a door nearby jerked his gaze across the yard. Mr. Markland stood on the steps of his home, glaring into the morning.

Taking a step backward, Patrick quickly slipped toward the stable with his ax, hoping Mr. Markland hadn't seen him. He locked it up and returned to find Mr. Markland at the chopping block, growling about the splinters littering the ground.

"Good morning, Mr. Markland. Lovely morning, isn't it?"

"Was there a storm last night? What's all this?" Mr. Markland pointed around at Patrick's chopping debris.

"Kindling! Lots of fine kindling. I'll get a rake," Patrick said, exuding false cheeriness.

The Marklands' door opened again, and Mrs. Markland called, "There you are, Jesse! I didn't know you'd gone out already. Are you ready to leave?" She had a hat tied on and held a covered basket, but her face looked bone-weary.

"Not until this young man cleans up this mess."

Patrick looked guiltily at Mrs. Markland as she approached. It did look rather like the scene of someone having a nervous breakdown, and her errands shouldn't have to be delayed on account of his wayward ax.

"We're going up to Corydon's to take them bread," she explained to him.

"Do you mind if I come with you? I can clean this up later." If he walked off with Mrs. Markland, her husband would join them, hopefully forget about the yard, and she wouldn't have to sit around waiting while he raked. "Or if you'd rather, he can stay with me while you go."

"You're welcome to come," Mrs. Markland said politely. Patrick wasn't sure what she really wanted. Not knowing what to do, he reached out to Mr. Markland.

"Let's go see Corydon and Sarah. It's a nice day for a walk, isn't it?"

"No," Mr. Markland said, but he bent his head and came with Patrick, hmphing and snorting all the way.

The walk was a short one, and soon they were coming up to a two-story house where Anna's oldest nephew, probably around eight, was feeding chickens in the yard. They found Sarah in the kitchen, chopping potatoes with her toddler daughter working beside her.

She laid aside her knife when she saw her in-laws enter with Patrick. "Come in! I'll put the kettle on."

Mrs. Markland deposited her basket on the table. "Is Corydon in?"

"He's in the other room," Sarah said, reaching for the water pail.

Mr. and Mrs. Markland settled at the kitchen table, but Patrick stepped through in search of Corydon. He was at a small desk with his Bible and papers arranged neatly around him but lowered his pencil at the sight of Patrick. Two children sat on the sofa copying letters onto slates. Morning sun filtered through the glass windows and fell across the clean plank floors.

"I apologize for disturbing you," Patrick told him. "I came with your parents."

The children looked to their father in anticipation. "Go on," he said with a wink. When they scampered off, he turned back to his guest.

"You're welcome anytime. How is Mr. Lovejoy today?"

"Unchanged, from what I can tell. It's hard to know how long we'll be here." At least the new press was safe; no one in Cleves knew it was here, stored at a warehouse by the river. Patrick lowered onto the sofa the children had abandoned and pulled his foot over his knee. "Anna told me about Leah and Jane's mother."

Corydon arched an eyebrow. Was it at the fact that it had to have happened after he left the inn at nine o'clock last night, or at Patrick using Anna's Christian name?

Patrick took the liberty to continue and relay the suggestion he'd given Anna for facilitating the family's reunification. He'd just finished when Sarah came in, handing mugs of black tea to each of them.

"I'm feeding your father in there and agreeing with him about the atrocity of the 1824 election," she told Corydon. "We're doing just fine."

They shared a smile, and Corydon and Patrick thanked her before she left again.

Corydon sipped his tea while Patrick waited for his response to the previous conversation. "I won't be back to that area for three more weeks, but I'll write a letter today to a friend at the church up there so he can present the idea to their brother, Max. I'm sure he can't read. I don't think any of us want to draw this out longer than it has to take, but they aren't nearby, and there's a fair amount of potential danger on both sides."

It could take months, Patrick thought in despair—and this was just one family of thousands torn apart. But he and Anna had just talked about this.

Do justice. Cling to the promises of God. Work done for one person is no less important. Pray for the wider culture. Give the burden to God. His heart rate slowed.

"How do you think it will affect Anna?" Corydon asked.

Patrick stilled, recognizing the trap instantly. "Why do you think I would know?"

"Something tells me that you know quite a bit about my sister-in-law and spend time thinking about how you can minimize negative effects in her life." His lips twitched, but the smirk couldn't be hidden.

Patrick took a sip of the tea to mask his facial expression. "I'd like to know her better than I do. But our paths aren't aligning, and I don't have anything to offer her."

"Poor and content is rich, and rich enough."

Patrick sent Corydon a quizzical look, and he shrugged. "Shakespeare."

"Ah. I've never read him. I may be poor, but content would be more than I can say for myself. Not about the poverty, per se," he added quickly, "but about not being settled. It could take a while."

Patrick pursed his lips and toyed with the handle of the cup. He'd jumped at the chance to come with the Marklands this morning for this very purpose, hoping for a chance to talk to a minister and a stand-in for Colm's brotherly advice. "You know her pretty well, don't you? What do you see that she needs? She seems very rooted here."

"Are you looking to settle in Illinois?"

Patrick shifted, rubbing his thumbs over the teacup in his hands. "For now, at least. I long to work in newspapers again, and Lovejoy has given me a place in his print office. I've been hoping for this opportunity for over a year."

"I don't think . . ." Corydon inhaled. "I don't think Anna has to remain in the North Bend in order to live a fulfilled life. But she doesn't seem to have accepted that yet."

"Because of its connection to Isaac?"

"Not necessarily. That may have been part of it once, but now it's probably more because she feels safe here."

"I want Anna to feel safe," Patrick stated.

"She feels useful here, too, which in my experience is something many people with ongoing pain and sickness struggle with. Everyone here knows about her condition and accommodates her. Anywhere else, she'd have to start the process all over of making people believe her illness is not imaginary and she's not simply a weak person."

Patrick cringed. Those were the things he'd thought when he met her. It had taken weeks to correct his thinking. How long would it take a whole community?

"Has she sought treatment? Is it possible that a cure exists?"

Corydon gave a mirthless laugh. "In Paris, maybe. We wouldn't know. All the treatments she's encountered in Ohio have either not helped at all or made things worse. As far as I know, she quit trying several years ago and has turned her attention to managing it as best she can."

A long silence ensued, giving Patrick time to process how that disappointment must have affected Anna. "I believe there is a large degree that we would complement each other, and we have the same values and priorities, although we live them in different ways."

What was he trying to say? Patrick chewed over the words. "I get the sense that your mother won't be able to step in at the inn much longer, and I would be glad to give Anna more stability when she's unwell. We work well together in common causes. And she . . ."

Corydon had sat back to listen, his steady gaze assuring Patrick that he would be understood, no matter what came out of his mouth.

"I left Baltimore while at a low place. The Lord used various things on my journey to encourage, correct my thinking, even convict. But nothing has been like the hope I embody when I'm with Anna."

There, he said it. His neck warmed at the rawness of the confession, and he studied the tea in his hands. "I'm of a mind that hope is something we get from the Lord, not a beautiful face. The last thing I want to do is put another weight on her by making her my ballast. But to be perfectly truthful, I have no idea how to correct something that feels so uncontrollable."

A minute passed before Corydon spoke, but Patrick had nothing more to add. There was nothing to say but to reiterate what he'd already confessed.

"Well, Anna is a servant of the Lord. I believe it's quite possible for Him to use one of His children to bring His hope to another. Particularly in a marriage union."

Patrick reared his head back, but Corydon continued, nonplussed. "Having that sense that you can draw a deep breath, that you can face anything, as long as you have that particular woman by your side—one that loves the Lord as well—I'd venture to say that is, or can be, one of God's gifts. If you continue to seek God's face about it, I have no doubt that He'll make the matter clear."

The concerns that had haunted Patrick overnight dispersed at Corydon's final statement. God wasn't out to trick him. And maybe he was even right that the calmness he felt around Anna wasn't misplaced. He'd finished his tea, and he had plenty to mull over now. It was time to let Corydon get back to his studying.

"I appreciate your insight. I'm dedicated to praying about our future, and having a fuller picture of the truth of the situation will aid in that."

"Please keep us in your correspondence when you go back to Illinois," Corydon said when Patrick came to his feet. "Sarah and I will be honored to assist in any way we can."

"Thank you. I will." Patrick held his teacup with one hand and returned his cap to his head with the other. "I am grateful for your help."

If Mr. and Mrs. Markland weren't ready to leave yet, he'd walk back alone and get the yard raked up before they came. It would be the perfect opportunity to think over everything he'd learned in the last two days—and what he still needed to learn before the river took him away again.

42

**"By the grace of God I will not, I will not forsake my principles;
and I will maintain and propagate them with all the means
He puts into my hands." - Elijah Lovejoy**

I shall watch it now, and the first person that attempts to come to harm it may expect a small piece of lead to be lodged in him," John Lovejoy declared, staring at the new press safely ensconced in the Alton shop. "It is of no use to trifle with those scoundrels."

Patrick and Lovejoy exchanged a look of amusement, but then Lovejoy shrugged. "I daresay I won't prevent you from guarding it. Have you heard from Owen?" He looked weary after his horseback ride up from St. Charles. After ten days fighting for his life at Anna's, he had insisted on stopping to see his wife and son on the return trip.

Patrick came on to Alton with the press and had overseen its installation in its new home. He'd spent Sunday going to church and writing to his family and Anna. Monday was devoted to getting laundry done, restocking his supplies at the dry goods store, and applying for jobs to supplement his income until the newspaper got underway. Now Lovejoy was here, and Patrick was finally ready to get started at the print office.

"He said he's coming shortly." John ran his hand over the cast iron crank.

"What about Elizabeth?"

Patrick had heard the names of the other Lovejoy siblings often in the past weeks and remained curious to meet more of the family. Best he figured, Elijah was the oldest, and Owen and Elizabeth landed somewhere between him and John in the lineup.

"You'll have to write and ask her. The whole lot hardly tells me anything."

"I will," Lovejoy muttered. "Is there any news about the house we looked at?"

"Yes." John brightened. "You're to go to the bank to finalize it when you return."

"I'll do that immediately. The sooner that's done, the sooner Celia and Edward can come." He turned on his heel and walked out, leaving John and Patrick to admire the press together.

"I suppose we should do what we can to set up shop," Patrick said. He glanced toward the windows of the low building. It was a darker space than he liked to work in for tedious tasks like setting type. The workbench would have to be set beneath the south-facing windows to maximize working hours. "Has he found a paper supplier?"

"I worked on that while you were away." John puffed his chest out, then it deflated. "But Parish is going to have to make the final decision about the size he wants. The ink was delivered." He pointed to a crate of large bottles.

Patrick took in the furniture and supply crates stacked against the wall. Some of it had been salvaged from the riot in St. Louis, but a few sticks of furniture had been donated by Lovejoy's connections in town, received and stacked up by John.

And this was what Patrick had been retained for. "Get the crowbar, and we'll start opening these crates up," he said. Reaching for a desk, he tugged it into a corner for Lovejoy's use and found a chair to sit behind it. Type cases were soon set up against the wall, and John helped him push the large workbench beside them, beneath the window.

Two hours later, their stomachs were both growling, and a unanimous decision was made to return to the boardinghouse for supper.

"I'll sleep in the back room of the print shop again tonight, like I've been doing," John told him as they trudged through the business district of lower Alton and up a steep road.

"Are you going to stay there after your brother buys the house?"

"I expect he'll want me to live with him, but the press will need someone to guard it."

Patrick knew better what one man could do against a riotous mob, but he stayed silent.

"So the room at the office will probably be available if you want to live there," John finished.

"Maybe I will."

Lovejoy arrived at the supper bell and sank into the seat across from Patrick. "It's done—the Cherry Street house is ours. It's on the road to Middletown."

"Are we staying here tonight?" Patrick clarified.

"We can tonight. Tomorrow I'll send for Celia and we can put together the beds. How are things at the print office?"

Getting a good night's rest tonight was imperative, as far as Patrick could see. It would take Celia several days to come up from St. Charles, which would give them time to get furniture set up in the house. There was no need to rush things and put Lovejoy back in bed before his wife came.

John caught his brother up on everything that had been accomplished while he was away. Lovejoy peppered him with questions, handed a slew of tasks out to him and Patrick, and vowed to place the order for paper the next day.

Patrick ate his meal while observing Lovejoy's resolve and energy. So much for taking their time. Watching Lovejoy, he had no doubt that in very short order, the new *Alton Observer* would be in action.

Elijah Lovejoy, the editor, was back in full force.

The first week of September saw Patrick at the workbench in the print office, setting type for the first issue of the *Alton Observer* alongside Thaddeus Hurlbut, Lovejoy's newest hire and an ordained minister. Patrick had become fast friends with the dark-haired associate editor a couple of years older than himself. Owen Lovejoy was expected any day, bringing the newspaper staff to five, with John acting as a part-time print assistant.

This morning, the editor had walked the fifteen minutes from his house to meet with Patrick and Thaddeus and turn over the final articles before leaving for his other job as a shoe salesman. Patrick had picked up shifts selling harnesses three days a week, which was worse even than bricking Anna's foundation. He could hardly wait until the newspaper could support them all full time.

Now two columns of the front page were set in the galleys, with room for four more. The large sheet size Lovejoy had chosen would surely attract the new subscribers needed to support publication. Patrick's back ached from leaning over the workbench, lining each letter up one by one, but this was far preferable to selling harnesses. He noted the familiar stiffness and revelled in its presence. This moment was what he'd been hoping and waiting for all year.

The inaugural issue he was laying out had much of what Patrick had expected from Lovejoy: concerns about Catholicism and Sabbath-breakers and an explanation of his move from St. Louis. But a sense of relief and anticipation overcame him as he slid the letters from Lovejoy's editorial onto his composing stick.

"It is the duty of us all to unite our hearty and zealous efforts to effect the speedy and entire emancipation of that portion of our fellow-men in bondage amongst us."

Regardless of what he'd told city leaders last month, Lovejoy was making the clear statement Patrick had hoped for. Slavery was too important a topic to leave it alone. The man was doing what he'd promised, after all— writing about what he felt compelled to write about, apart from what any man, abolitionist or otherwise, demanded from him.

Setting the type for a clearly abolitionist-leaning religious newspaper, reassurance that he was in the right place returned to Patrick's gut. Lovejoy was bold and fearless. If anyone was going to be part of a wave of change in the nation, it would be him.

The Friday before Christmas, Patrick pulled on his gloves and followed Thaddeus and Owen out of the print office. A gust of wind cut through them, swirling up the snow banked against the building, and a full moon was rising, yellow and massive, above the bluffs.

"I'm going to stop at the post office on my way," Patrick reminded Owen as Thaddeus separated toward home and his own wife and hearth.

"I'll come with you." Owen tugged his hat on and lifted his lantern.

Patrick had taken to eating supper at the Lovejoys' the past several months with the family and the boarders Celia took in. The house burst at the seams these days, but it carried the warm energy of family and home that he missed. The weather had been up and down earlier in the week, but now it seemed like the bitter cold was here to stay. It would be frigid when he came back to his little room later tonight, but it was worth it to not spend the evening sitting in his room alone, missing Anna.

"Have you heard from Birney lately?" Owen asked as they started out.

"No. Things have been quiet in Cincinnati. He's back to publishing *The Philanthropist* after the mob violence was so widely denounced, and is enjoying the same peace and quiet we've been. I don't think there's any news to be had."

The postmaster was about to close up when Owen and Patrick arrived at his desk, but he retrieved their mail, slipping Owen all the Lovejoys' correspondence. When he handed Patrick a thick parcel beside his weekly letter from Anna, Patrick squeezed it curiously.

"Who's it from?" Owen peered closer.

Patrick turned the brown paper over. "Colm." Was it a Christmas gift? He hadn't expected such a thing, but maybe it was. Now started the hard part—waiting through Friday night supper until he could get back to his room and read his mail.

"Do you want to open it?"

He did, but Patrick shook his head. It would keep, and the postmaster was waiting for them to leave so he could go home.

The packet and letter sat under Patrick's coat on a shelf in the Lovejoys' foyer as he joined in discussion about the week's fluctuating weather around the suppertable.

The Lutheran minister boarding with the Lovejoys didn't even lift his fork before beginning. "It wasn't our imagination that the temperature dropped severely and quickly on Tuesday," he announced as everyone else dug into their pork chops. "At the barbershop this morning, I learned that what we experienced was nothing like the eyewitness reports coming in a few counties to the east."

"I missed it all," Patrick said from his seat between John and Elizabeth, the sister who had recently arrived from Maine. Holed up at the workbench all day, he hadn't heard anything that wasn't on the slips of paper Lovejoy gave him to set.

Lovejoy wiped his mouth on a napkin. "I read a little bit about that. What did you hear?"

"They're calling it the Sudden Freeze. After temperatures were mild on Monday and the snow started melting, the temperature dropped forty degrees in a matter of hours in the middle of the day Tuesday. Further east, it was accompanied by high winds that came out of nowhere. It killed large amounts of livestock, and humans who were caught out in it lost their lives as well. Men started out for town in fine weather and never made it. They were found with the blood frozen in their veins."

"Have you heard of anything like it?" Celia exclaimed. She was a tall woman with dark blonde hair and large blue eyes that looked larger now, rounded with disbelief.

"I don't think anyone has," her husband responded.

In the parlor later, the minister read aloud some of the newspaper articles he'd obtained about the event while the family listened in horror.

"The wind in its fury and power blew the water into little sharply defined waves, which froze as they stood, leaving the ponds, creeks, and rivers crusted with a heavy coat of ice. The snow, slush, and mud were suddenly congealed into a mass strong enough to sustain the weight of a team and wagon."

Somber faces sat around the warm parlor, staring at the dancing fire and silently thanking the Lord for sparing western Illinois the disaster.

When Patrick pulled on his coat to leave, Celia handed him his hat, worry on her face. "Are you sure you'll be warm enough?"

"I'm already prepared for the cold," he assured her. "It's not like a freeze coming on quickly to people stranded out in fields. And it's only a fifteen-minute walk."

Gathering up his mail, he thanked her for the meal and received the trimmed lantern from John. The bright moon kept him company on his way home, his thoughts flipping between the men who were found dead, huddled together inside a horse carcass, and Colm's mysterious packet.

In his chilly bedroom, he stoked the fire to life and sat down on his bed with his coat still on. Anna's letter couldn't be properly savored until he knew what Colm was about, so he carefully slit into the brown paper with his knife. Shock rolled over him at the stack of banknotes that fell out onto his lap. Where did all this money come from, and how had Colm come to trust it to the Pony Express?

Thumbing through the stack, his initial count had the total somewhere around $800. Patrick set it beside him on the bed and reached for Colm's letter. It only took a minute for everything to become plain. Hector and Elly had decided to move to New York in search of better jobs, and Colm had sold Patrick's house.

"I did not think you would mind that I gave them a portion of the sale to assist them on their way," Colm wrote.

Patrick didn't care at all. Here was eight hundred dollars that he hadn't had a minute ago. What did the rest matter? He could . . . he could . . . well, he could do a lot with it, but more than anything, he could settle down and buy a house and have a life to offer Anna. If only he knew where that should be.

She was so close to getting Sandra to come to Cleves, had even out of frustration offered to bring the girls up to Columbus. Either way, Sandra would have to take a leap of faith, but communication had been slow and erratic, going through the Bulls and another safe house host that Max and Sandra trusted. Patrick prayed that the meeting would be able to happen by the end of the year.

He fanned out the stack of banknotes, seeing in them a key step toward the future he hoped to build. "Thank you, Lord," he breathed. Selling the house wasn't even anything he'd prayed for, but God had done it for him anyway. He always worked in ways beyond what Patrick could have imagined.

With a contented, grateful exhale, Patrick broke the seal on Anna's letter.

43

"I hold myself bound to devote my life to minister to the comfort of my dear, dear widowed mother." - Elijah Lovejoy

nna had never imagined it would take this long.

Finally, Christmas Monday, she refreshed a third-floor bedroom in a state of nervous anticipation for the arrival of Leah and Jane's mother. Had she known how drawn out the process would be, she would have put the girls in a wagon and driven them up to Columbus in September. It might have badly unsettled Sandra, but at least the girls would have had three more months with their mother.

"Help me to be a vessel of grace to this woman," she whispered as she fluffed pillows. There had been scores of broken, scarred people coming through her inn over the years, but had any of them been this skittish? She couldn't remember and couldn't be sure how to handle the woman when she arrived.

It had taken her two days after getting Jason Bull's most recent letter to decide to tell the girls that their mother was actually on her way. What would it do to them if she didn't show? But they had to be ready for the possibility, so Anna had the conversation and then begged God to let Sandra come.

Leah and Jane alternated between standing at the window and coming back to Anna. She had to stop straightening the room before her own nervousness made theirs worse. Plopping down on the bed, she reached her arms out.

"Come, girls. Why don't we pray for her? Remember, God cares about your worries. You can tell Him anything."

Jane immediately snuggled into Anna's side, while Leah gave one last look out the window before dragging her feet to the bed.

"Do you want me to pray first?" Anna asked, and Jane nodded.

"Very well. Heavenly Father, thank You for these months that you allowed me to spend with Leah and Jane. Thank You for granting them their freedom and that Max and their mother are alive and safe as well. Please protect Max and Mama from danger as they travel and help them to not feel afraid. I pray that You would calm our nerves and help us to be aware of Your presence with us when we feel uncertain. Thank You that You love us. Amen."

Jane prayed, copying some of Anna's phrases, but Leah sat stiffly with her eyes fixed ahead, terror on her face. Anna gave her a hug.

"Remember some of the stories you told me about your favorite moments with your mama? Remember how holding her hand as you ran to the boat made you feel safe? Your mama loves you and risked much to bring you to safety."

"And she can stay here with us for a couple days, right?"

"She can stay as long as she wants. All of you are always welcome here. But I am not the one who will decide when she wants to head back."

Leah shuddered, and Anna clasped her hand tight, fighting back tears. "Sweet girl. There is nothing to fear. The Lord is with us."

Voices sounded outside, and Leah ran to the window again. "They're here," she whispered.

Anna stood, smoothed her skirt, and tightened her grip on Jane's hand. "Then let's go make her feel welcome."

Leaving Leah and Jane in the small parlor with Mildred, Anna hurried out to welcome Sandra, Max, and Mr. Bull into the inn through the kitchen door. If she'd had her way, she would have happily brought them through the front door and given them the most comfortable guest room in the inn. But for runaways who could still have bounty hunters prowling around for them, the privacy the back door and third floor offered were best.

Max came first, and Anna knew better than to try to shake his hand after their first meeting at the Bulls' a month ago. He hadn't seemed to know what to do with her outstretched hand. He was tall, with Leah's flashing black eyes and a dimple on each cheek like Jane. His presence untied a knot in her chest, giving her a modicum of peace about the girls' future. Sandra came next, with her coat pulled tight around her and a dirty bag clutched to her chest, taking quick, shifty glances at all the corners and doors.

"Come in!" Anna held the door as the woman crept cautiously into the house. "Leah and Jane are in the parlor, anxious to see you. I'll take you to them right away. Good afternoon, Mr. Bull."

He removed his hat, taking the door from her. "I'll rest the horses for a bit, but then I will need to start heading home today. You said that Max can drive a livery horse and cart whenever they want to return?"

"Yes, and thank you."

"I'm a real good driver, and I never get lost," Max assured her. "I work as a delivery driver."

"Wonderful!" Anna shuffled through the guests to lead the way out of the kitchen. "Come see the girls."

Sandra clung to Max's hand as the group stepped across the hall into the parlor, where Leah and Jane stood frozen in the middle of the room with Mildred behind them. They wore matching blue calico dresses and new shoes, their neat braids tied with blue ribbons at the ends.

"My babies," Sandra gasped, rushing toward them. Falling on her knees, she opened her arms wide and gathered the girls to her. Leah and Jane responded instantly, grabbing onto her in return.

Tears of gratitude flooded Anna's eyes. They had found the right mother, and it hadn't all been a mistake.

"I haven't seen them since they were tiny little things," Max said in awe to Mr. Bull. "I'm not sure I woulda recognized them."

"You were so brave to come ahead by yourself and set up a place so they could join you." It was everything Anna could do to keep her hands to herself and not pat his arm proudly.

"I lost my pa though." Max's chin quivered, and he blinked quickly. Anna wiped her own tears away and grabbed the pile of ironed handkerchiefs she had prepared. She gave one to Leah and to Jane, but Sandra was sobbing too hard to notice.

"Mama," Jane said, curling into her lap.

Sandra rocked her back and forth, weeping loudly. "My baby, my baby!"

"The tea?" Anna asked Mildred. The cook slipped out, and Anna offered seats to Mr. Bull and Max, but both shook their heads.

"We've been sitting for days," Mr. Bull explained. "It feels mighty good to be on my feet."

Anna sat, since there was little else to do but wait. Mildred returned eventually with the tea tray, and Anna poured out cups and offered sandwiches to the men. Several long minutes later, Sandra released her hold on the girls and looked for Max for the first time. Setting down his cup, he joined them in the middle of the floor, crouching down to their level.

"It sure is something to see you girls all grown up. I've been hoping for this day for a long time. But there's something sad that you have to know. We lost our pa."

Leah and Jane stared at him with red-rimmed eyes from their perches on Sandra's lap.

"Now, we never got word that he died. But since he knew where I was and never made it up to us, it means he either died or got captured again."

Tears trickled down the girls' brown faces.

"My babies," Sandra cried, rocking.

Anna could have groaned aloud in despair at the news. If Joshua was recaptured, he'd likely been sold further into the Deep South, where his family would never see him again. So many considered death to be the preferred option. Both were too painful to consider.

Mr. Bull could not be convinced to stay overnight, and left around four o'clock. When he was gone, Anna led the family up to the prepared bedroom.

"Do you girls want to bring your mats into your mother's room?" she whispered, and they both nodded. Not knowing how the reception would go, she hadn't moved them into Sandra's room ahead of time. Now the girls hurried to their room and retrieved their mats, clothing bundles, and workbaskets.

"Look, Mama." Leah dumped her pile onto the floor and pulled a half-finished doll from her basket. "Look at what me and Jane been making."

Sandra ran a finger across the soft felt face. "It's beautiful, baby. You do this yourself?"

"Yes, ma'am."

"It's beautiful."

Alone in her room for the first night in a year and a half, Anna cried herself to sleep. She cried for more reasons than she could count and more emotions than she could hold. When she awoke the next morning, pain pulsed behind her eye, and standing up to reach for the chamber pot rolled nausea over her.

Leah and Jane crept into her room midmorning. "We missed you, Miss Anna. We was afraid you were sick."

"I'm so sorry, girls." A tear trickled down her cheek, and her head pulsed. "Tell me everything. How are you doing?"

"We're doing all right. We helped Mildred lay the table because Mama said we could, but when the guests came down for breakfast, she pulled us back into the kitchen," Leah said. "She won't let us go out and play."

"I understand. Your mama doesn't know how things usually are here"—or all the precautions Anna had taken to keep her daughters safe—"but you'd best listen to her since she's your mama. I'll try to get better as soon as I can, all right?"

"All right."

"How are you, Jane?" Anna felt around and patted her hand. "How is it going with your ma?"

"I don't feel as scared anymore," Jane whispered, "but I miss you. I think I want to love both of you."

"There's nothing wrong with that. We both love you too. What is your mama doing now?"

"She outside the door, listening," Leah said.

Anna went cold, replaying their short conversation in her head. Had she said anything that Sandra wouldn't like? Her head spun, and she couldn't be sure.

"She's real scared a lot," Jane added.

"Remember how scared you were when you first came here? Maybe you can remind her that Jesus loves her and He'll help her when she's scared too. Will you do that?"

"Yes, ma'am."

"That's a good girl. Now I'll get better just as fast as I can. You can come back if you need me for anything."

"Yes, Miss Anna. We'll see you soon."

The girls backed away, and a moment later, the door clicked shut. The tears returned, and Anna pressed the heels of her hands against her eyes.

She little imagined that it would be the last time she'd see the girls.

Anna awoke in her blacked-out room the next morning, an unexplainable pit in her stomach. Her attempt to leave the room had her falling back into bed, her head spinning. Mildred found her that way an hour later and told her what she'd already guessed. Sandra and Max had disappeared sometime in the night, taking Leah and Jane with them.

44

**"Truth will prevail, and those who do not yield to it
must be destroyed by it." - Elijah Lovejoy**

I f they're with their mother, why does it hurt so much?" Anna sobbed to Sarah.

After she'd spent an entire day lying in bed, crying and trying not to for the sake of her head, Mildred had intervened, sending for Sarah.

"It was painful, but I'd accepted that they had to leave me. But not getting to say goodbye and make sure they were going to be fine first . . ."

Sarah sat on the edge of the bed, her arms wrapped around Anna's shoulders as Anna blubbered into her sleeve.

"Of course you're worried for them. I think that you also hoped to have a chance to help Sandra heal, and she rejected that opportunity."

Had she hoped for that? It hadn't been a conscious thought, but Sarah was right. Anna had wanted the family to spend several days in her inn for more than to ease the girls into the change. She wanted Sandra to return to the old self the girls knew, someone who was well enough to care for children.

"Mildred said she left everything." Anna sniffed, her eyes refilling. "The dresses, the shoes, the hair ribbons. She didn't take a single thing that I'd provided for the girls. She still wouldn't trust me or be beholden to me."

The filled workbaskets hurt the most. Leah and Jane would never have left the dolls of their own accord.

"Oh no," Sarah breathed.

Anna could hardly form a new thought in her pounding skull, the same thoughts pummeling over and over. Everything she had done for Leah and Jane had been rejected by Sandra.

Her mothering had been rejected.

She had been rejected.

Her concern for the girls' wellbeing sat in the forefront of her conscious mind, but underneath it all, slicing into her deepest places, pulsed the other pain.

Once again, her infernal sickness had made her fail the girls.

She could have brought them all to stability before heading back to Columbus. She could have shown Sandra that she'd been a good guardian for the girls and helped her to overcome her distrust if she'd gotten out of bed on Tuesday. More than that, none of this would have happened if she'd been well enough to find Joshua and Sandra the night of the accident.

"I failed them," Anna whimpered.

"Sweetheart." Sarah ran a hand over Anna's sweaty forehead. "You can grieve and pour out your pain to the Lord and take the time to work through it all. But I wouldn't be a good friend if I let you lie to yourself. You did not fail Leah and Jane. The relationship you had with them and the things you taught them will go with them into adulthood. Sandra can't take that away from them."

She could, though. She could brainwash her girls over time into believing a false narrative about their time in Cleves. *Don't let her paranoia go that far, Lord. Please help the girls to remember the truth about You and the love they experienced here.*

"I know it's not about me. And I do only want to see them safe and happy and loved. The rejection and distrust and feeling like I failed them only compounds it. I know they're not the biggest thing, but they are present too."

"Oh, I know," Sarah soothed, leaning down to kiss her brow. "If the girls said that to you, you would tell them to take it all to Jesus."

"It's always a struggle to pray when I'm sick. But I will."

"Your body is weak right now, too, so don't push yourself. Right now just rest and remember that Jesus is here. You can think through all of this later. And, Anna, their leaving the other night had nothing to do with your sickness. She would have taken them then anyway."

"Maybe. But I would have gone after them in the morning."

"You know they wouldn't have been able to be found. Sandra wouldn't have taken the roads or a direct route. Next week, you can write to the Bulls and ask if they arrived back home safely. If their father knows their location, they'll not be likely to move except in extreme duress."

"That's true." Anna took a quavering breath, willing her tears to slow.

"We're only going to focus on and say things that are true." Sarah eased away to sit up. "Leah and Jane know that you love them. God loves them, and they know that too. Max is with them. Your role was to provide a temporary home for them, and you did that and did it well. In our weaknesses, God is strong."

"They were happy to see Sandra, and she was happy to see them." Anna's voice warbled. "They have each other, and they are capable. My sick headache won't last forever."

Further thoughts were lost in the swirl of her head, and she pressed her temple against the pain.

Sarah patted her shoulder. "When you're well, we'll add to the list and write them all down. Write to Mr. Gallagher too—that will help."

"Thank you, Sarah."

"I love you, sweetheart. Get some rest now. Do you want me to send anything up with the maid?"

"No. I'm going to go to sleep now."

"All right. Have Mother send for me if you need me again."

The door clicked shut, and Anna was soon lost to her dreams.

Lovejoy stopped by Patrick's workbench and slid a thick pamphlet over to him. "Finish the paper later. I need a hundred copies of this."

Patrick peered at the heading. "The letter by Reverend Channing? We put that in last week's paper."

"You saved the chase for it, didn't you? I adapted it and am sending a copy to every member of the Missouri legislature. They're trying to outlaw the distribution of abolitionist publications in their state. They all need to read this."

"I'll get on it right away," Patrick said, setting his composing stick aside. The letter, originally written to Birney, had been good reading one quiet evening. It came from an abolitionism critic who understood the importance of a free press, and yes, Patrick had saved the chase, which would make this job easier.

The bell over the front door chimed, and Lovejoy's friend Mr. Lippincott appeared, shutting the door against the cold blast. "Enjoyed your Sunday School lesson this week, Lovejoy," he announced.

"Thank you. Are you coming to the lyceum debates tonight?"

" 'Does the principle of the Right require the immediate emancipation of the slave?' I'd hate to miss a topic like that one."

Together they walked over to Lovejoy's desk to discuss whatever business had brought the storekeeper in, and Patrick picked up the pamphlet to flip through it. "Abolitionists are sufferers for the liberty of thought, speech, and the press; and in maintaining this liberty amidst insult and violence, they deserve a place among its most honored defenders," he read aloud.

Only in recent weeks had Lovejoy stepped more and more into being a full-fledged vocal abolitionist, speaking boldly in every new editorial against not only slavery but the nation's ministers who didn't decry it from their pulpits. Patrick loved every time the editor stopped by to give him something new to typeset. He didn't agree with every word, but it was always exhilarating.

It was true that Anna's work was no less important than his, but how could he leave something that excited him so much, something that pumped the blood through his veins? If only he could have her by his side through it all.

Patrick pulled out the chase frame holding the letter already typeset in place. He exhaled to think that a year ago, news that Missouri was considering laws like this would have been an oppressive weight on his spirit. Nowadays, it still made him angry, but he could do something about it. Relinquishing the burden to the Lord came quicker as well. The settling of his spirit was worth the trip, even if he did wish he could, like Lovejoy, convince his siblings to come out here too. There wasn't much about Baltimore that he missed, but it rotted to be alone and without a family.

Easing the tight grip he had on the chase, he refocused his attention from the sunny window as white spots blurred his vision in the dim room.

Here he was doing something tangible to turn the tide on slavery, but the helpless feeling remained, hounding him about Anna now.

Leah and Jane's sudden departure had hit her harder than he would have imagined. Overwhelmed with grief, she only sent short, sporadic letters anymore. Had the rejection of her role as the girls' temporary mother affected her deeper because of the baby she'd lost with Isaac? Fear prowled around the edges of Patrick's consciousness that the new interference by her sickness had cemented her belief that she would only be a setback to him too.

Whatever the real reasons for her silence, of which there were probably multiple, he couldn't fix them or change her mind. Letters and prayer were all he had. Blowing out his breath, Patrick released his frustration. The only thing he could do was show her that he could and would be the patient, accommodating friend she needed.

45

**"Though the chain which binds us together is lengthened
to such a degree, I do not believe it is weakened, and oh,
may nothing but death divide it." - Elijah Lovejoy**

Anna stepped carefully onto the flatboat, clutching her parasol and carpetbag as her eyes followed the man stowing her trunk with the other cargo. Her heart thumped, not at the long trip ahead, but at the prospect of the steamboat she'd have to take on her return trip. She could be brave and take this trip. And pray hard that she didn't get sick on the way.

"Are you ready, ma'am?" the captain asked.

"Yes, thank you."

"You're welcome to sit on the deck or in the cabin. Wherever you're most comfortable."

Anna seated herself on a crate at the front of the boat, the only passenger on the freighter. Why take the steamboat both directions if she could save that for upriver travel later? Opening her parasol, she settled in for the first long day on the river.

Thankfully, Sarah had been willing to take on Mildred temporarily, and the maids were happy to have a vacation to visit their families, so she didn't have to feel guilty about closing the inn. The days of leaving Mrs. Markland in charge for an extended time were over. It was getting more untenable for her to manage alone by the week, as her own energy deteriorated and Mr. Markland's erraticness increased.

Anna hugged the bag to her chest against the agitation pressing there over her uncertain future. If she were to put in a request to God, she would ask for a husband who wanted to run an inn. It would solve everything. But the only current candidate for the position was clearly meant for other things. So what was the answer?

Make a way, Lord. And make it plain. Please bring me someone who would be good for Riverview Lodge. If you have something else for me, help me to accept it as from You.

The hours ticked slowly by as Anna's thoughts and prayers swirled over one another as muddied as the water rushing beneath the flatboat.

On dry land three days later, desperate for a bath and a comfortable bed, Anna hired a cart and driver to take her to her final destination. The sun was on its descent, pulling the day's heat away with it, as Anna arrived at a large shingled farmhouse. Taking in the surrounding view, she saw the homestead with different eyes than the last time she'd seen it five years ago. It was as tidy and well maintained as ever, the fields already prepared for planting. The smell of fresh dirt brought back the memory of running through those fields as a little girl before her mother caught her and scolded her for dirtying her shoes.

"Anna?"

As if her memory had summoned the very voice, her name on her mother's lips broke through the stillness.

"Mama!" Lifting up her skirts, Anna climbed to the wide porch and was soon lost in her mother's embrace.

"Your father just brought your letter from town today. If we'd known when you were coming, he could have waited for you."

"It's so good to see you, Mama." Anna melted into her. Her mother had aged in five years, sharp joints poking Anna where flesh used to be.

When they separated, Mama cupped her face with her hand. "You didn't even come home when Isaac died."

There was no point in reminding her that Kentucky wasn't home anymore and hadn't been for a long time. "He died on a steamboat. I had a hard time convincing myself to take one, even now."

"Oh, love." Mama's thumb stroked her cheek. "I didn't know that was why you stayed away. Well, come on now. Supper is almost ready, and I'll have Mercy put another plate on."

The suppertable was just how Anna remembered, yet completely foreign. Only she and her parents were seated at it, because her family had never been hospitable, and Anna knew that the girls serving were unpaid and considered her father's property. How had all of this been normal to her once upon a time?

"Welcome home, sweetheart." Papa squeezed her hand after saying grace. "Have you been to Cincinnati lately?"

"Not since October. Normally I would go again about now, but I came here instead."

"It sounds like a most dangerous city, with all the Negroes living unguarded in neighborhoods together, and reports of mobs. One prominent citizen was just arrested for harboring a fugitive slave. Be careful who you trust there."

A shiver ran down Anna's spine. "Do you know who it was?"

"The newspaperman, James Birney. He claimed that the girl's skin was so white that he didn't know she was even Negro, but he's a known abolitionist."

"Lewis, the girl doesn't want to hear about politics," Mama soothed in her genteel way.

Politics? If only Mama knew how much the affairs of fugitives and abolitionists were a central part of Anna's life.

"I think it's best if you get your supplies here in Louisville on your way home and avoid going to Cincinnati altogether." Papa gave Anna a look of authority and took a drink of his wine.

"Aren't you ready to move back?" Mama entreated. "What is there to keep you in Ohio? Isaac has been gone a long time, and businesses are failing left and right in this economy. If you don't want to marry again, you don't have to. You can move in with us. How is your health?"

The food in Anna's stomach felt rock-heavy, and she lost interest in the rest of her serving. "I'm settled in Ohio, Mama." There was simply no good way to handle this conversation. If she told how the Marklands accommodated her health challenges, they would argue that her own parents could do no worse. "My health goes up and down, but I manage. The inn is my home, and we're good for each other."

While that had been true for the last several years, it now teetered on the edge of no longer being so if she couldn't find someone to step into Mrs. Markland's place soon.

"Please think about it," Mama said, as if the topic wasn't closed. "Your whole family is here. I can't think of why you would want to stay up there."

"I've come to love it, I suppose." The less she said, the less her parents would have to find arguments for.

"Well, I'm glad you've come now. What made you come in the midst of a financial panic? Do you need money? "

Anna stifled a sigh. "I don't need money. I came just because I missed you." She couldn't tell her about Leah and Jane and how the crippling of her mothering had made her ache for her mother's hug again. In her seven years in Cleves, Mrs. Markland had never offered one. The longing was strong enough to make Anna risk a steamboat ride to get it.

"Stay as long as you want. I'll send word around to the family, and maybe Francis will host a dinner so everyone can see you." Just like Mama, who never hosted a dinner if she could help it.

"Thank you. I can't stay longer than a week because of the inn, but I'll get my supplies from Louisville on the way home, Papa."

"Give me your list, sweetheart, and I'll send it around to the men I do business with. It will all be ready to go whenever you are. I can send a slave with you to see you home safely."

Anna pressed her lips together. If her father sent a slave with her, she would definitely make sure the man was emancipated the moment the boat docked in Cleves. Maybe her parents would know it was her fault, and maybe it wasn't such a bad idea at all.

By the end of the family dinner on Anna's fourth day in Kentucky, she was ready to be back home. A headache pulsed at the edge of her temple on the drive from Francis's, guaranteeing the rest of her visit would be spent confined to her room. Perhaps it was better to remain holed up than be out and about, being exposed to her siblings' arrogance and her parents' mistreatment of their slaves.

"I'm starting to get a headache, Mama," she announced, stopping at the bottom of the staircase in her parents' foyer.

"Oh, dear." Mama untied her bonnet and patted her silky brown curls. "Climb into bed, love, and I'll bring up tea and the tinctures."

For everything else, Mama sent her slaves, but Anna felt cherished when Mama oversaw her health herself. When she came up twenty minutes later, she sat on Anna's bed and braided her hair first, like she always used to. She fluffed the pillows up so Anna could drink the willow bark tea, and placed a ginger and arrowroot poultice on the back of her neck.

"I'm sure being around all the children today caused it," she said, taking the cup from Anna and setting it on the nightstand.

"It could be anything. Sometimes just riding in a closed carriage or going from a cool evening to a hot, crowded room makes one start."

She leaned back on her pillows, and Mama gently rubbed her temples with lavender-scented hands. She'd forgotten how lovely this could be. If Mama didn't think herself too good for it, she would have made an excellent caretaker or companion. For the first time, the thought of leaving behind all the responsibilities of the inn and moving back to be pampered by her mother was a real temptation. Why did she go through all the troubles and trials that she did unnecessarily? Everything making her anxious now would be gone.

She hummed in appreciation at her mother's gentle touch. "You've always been so good to me. Did you always know you were a good mother?"

"Certainly not!" Mama gave a surprised laugh. "I tried to be, of course, darling, but all you children had such different needs that I rarely thought I knew what to do. I depended on your nanny so, until we had to sell her."

"I always loved it best when I was with you."

"Thank you, love. But no, I never thought that I was good enough."

But a child knows when someone loves them. Anna snuggled deeper into her pillows. Did Leah and Jane know it? Surely they did. And hopefully they would always connect their memories of Anna's love with how often sh'de told them about God's.

"I hope one day," Anna said sleepily, "that I'll be as good a mother as you."

On the following Monday, Papa drove Anna to town to install her and her supplies on the steamboat himself. There would be no slave accompanying her that she could free, to her disappointment. The sky was overcast and temperature pleasant, so Anna pushed her cloak back on her shoulders as she sat alone on shore and watched her father finish the arrangements. Tucked in her bag was a newspaper with the news of the charges against Birney being lifted. The girl involved had not been released.

"Mrs. Markland!"

Walking up the street against the gray day were the four colorfully dressed Phillips sisters. Anna came to her feet, shaking away her trepidation about the trip and responding to the cheer their appearance brought.

"What a joy to run into you! I've just been visiting my family and am returning home now."

"We're on our way to the market." Hatty lifted her empty basket from beneath her orange cloak. "How are you? Did you have a lovely visit?"

"I did." It was the truth, if she didn't think about the way her parents' slave ownership turned her stomach. Taking a steadying breath, she indicated the *Campte* at dock. "It's my first time aboard a steamship since my husband lost his life on one, so I'm a bit jittery just now."

Hortensia reached out, her green cloak reminding Anna of a fresh spring day. "I'm sorry to hear that. We can walk with you. Do you want to hold my hand?"

Her kindness caused a lump to grow in Anna's throat, and she grasped the offered hand. "That would help. Thank you." They made their way to the huge, gleaming white boat, Anna surrounded by the sisters' compassionate presence.

"I know how hard this must be for you," Hatty said by her side. "I'll be praying for you."

At the gangplank, Anna gave each of them a quick hug.

"You can do it," Harmony whispered as she let Anna go and gathered her purple shawl around herself. Bernadette gave a final wave of her black-clad arm, encouraging Anna to take the final step that was no longer as terrifying as it had been even a minute ago.

Her father found her on the crowded deck a minute later and planted a kiss on Anna's forehead. "Everything is taken care of. Have a safe trip, darling." He pressed a wad of banknotes into her hand.

"I don't—" she protested, but he was already gone, weaving his way down the gangplank. Anna sighed, tucking the money away with shaking hands. She refused to look at the big black smokestacks already shooting smoke into the air.

"Ma'am? Your cabin is this way." The steward stood before her, indicating the staircase.

Lord Jesus, give me Your peace. Anna gave a quick nod, bolstered by the Phillipses' encouragement, gathered her skirt, and faced her fears.

46

Marius Robinson was tarred and feathered." John Lovejoy slammed the office door behind him and stalked up to Patrick's workbench, throwing the newspaper down on it.

Owen pushed back from his desk as Patrick snatched the paper, his skin crawling in empathy for his friend. "I know him."

"What happened?" Owen asked, coming over to read over Patrick's shoulder.

"He was speaking on a lecture circuit when a slavery-loving mob attacked him, slicing his leg and beating him before the tarring," John furnished. "This, my friends, could happen to any of us."

Patrick's vision blurred. It was one thing to talk bravely, but the thought of actually facing a mob intent on harm . . . A shiver raced through his veins, and he took a step back before it betrayed him.

"Emily?" he croaked, thinking of Marius's beautiful . . . she'd be his wife by now. He wiped his hands, sticky with sweat from handling tiny pieces of type, on his trousers. The summer heat made it almost too hot to work, even in the stone building.

"She'd stayed in Cincinnati. He's been in bed recovering all month since the attack. It could affect his ability to walk again."

"A crowd wouldn't have hurt her though, would they?" Owen took the paper from Patrick and perused the article. "The way Parish worries over Celia Ann, you'd think these mobs were out to harm women and children."

"She has gotten threats, Owen," John said in a low voice. "But if anything happened to Parish . . . She's so delicate. They don't have to lay hands on the wife to harm her."

And there was Anna, back in Patrick's thoughts. Anyone who harbored fugitives knew the work was dangerous. Anna wouldn't ever limit Patrick's work out of fear, he knew—Celia didn't either—but could he do that to a wife? Celia was terrified. Even though Lovejoy adored her, he never softened his message. But they all saw the way it weighed on him.

Taking care of a wife must be a terrific strain on the mind.

Owen lowered the paper. "The Market House meeting the other day just made everything worse. She took to her bed after that."

Thaddeus and Owen took guns into work the day after the meeting, assuring Patrick that if he stayed close to the press until things quieted down, they'd bring meals in for him. He'd been happy to do his part, but remaining at the office had left him on the outside of supper conversation. Now he pounced on the opportunity to hear the rest of the story.

"So the town met together and decided that your brother broke his promise to them when he moved to Alton—and didn't they send a group to bring their complaints to him? What happened when they showed up?"

"It was just the town leaders, and no, they sent a letter instead of coming in person. It was just a copy of the meeting minutes with all their resolutions, which can be summed up so: that he told them he wouldn't publish about slavery, and he does, and they want him to stop." John gave an amused huff and backed toward the press. None of them wondered whether such a letter tempted Elijah Lovejoy to change his course.

"Or what?"

"Or they can't guarantee his protection." Owen snorted. "Watch out, Gallagher. Next you know, that letter will end up on your desk to be plastered all over the front of the *Observer*."

He likely wasn't wrong. "Lovejoy didn't answer them, did he?"

"He was working on a letter last night, thanking them for their courtesy and assuring them that the points he disagreed on were not because he lacked respect for the men themselves." Owen walked over to his desk and tossed John's newspaper onto a stack.

"What he said," John called from across the room, "when the letter was delivered, at least, was that they weren't authorized to decide what should appear in his paper. He said the freedom of speech comes from our Maker and couldn't be subjected to public opinion."

Patrick studied the article he was in the middle of composing without seeing it, his head buzzing with how he would word everything to Anna later.

Lovejoy is his usual self, gracious but firm. Everyone in town who really knows him likes and respects him. Now the clerk for the new Alton presbytery, he's being called on more and more to perform ministerial duties, like the funeral he's at right now. No one calls someone they don't like to perform their loved one's funeral. But will they stand up to defend him if his detractors become violent? Some of his initial friends were among those at the Market House meeting, feeling betrayed by his vocal stance against slavery. Maybe having friends here isn't enough.

Patrick took a deep breath and let it out. For once, he was glad that Anna was far away and unattached to his name or that of any abolitionist publisher. Her support and long-distance friendship kept him going, but he wasn't sure that he would have the fortitude to press on with Lovejoy's boldness right now if he had a wife and family to think about. Not everyone was as fearless as Elijah Lovejoy.

Patrick leaned against Lovejoy's desk a month later and tossed a crumpled wad of paper at John's head. With Celia sick and Lovejoy off preaching somewhere, he'd gone out with Owen and John for supper earlier. They'd returned to the dark office together to finish their work and then stayed visiting, which had since deteriorated into ribbing each other.

Patrick relaxed in the camaraderie, glad for the distraction and a reason to not sit alone in his room. Anna hadn't written in weeks. He longed to have the kind of relationship with her that Lovejoy shared with Celia and Marius with Emily. But he'd meant it when he wrote expressing gratitude that she was safely distant, where he didn't have to fear bringing her harm by his involvement with Lovejoy's bold campaign. "I want Anna to feel safe," he'd told Corydon.

Maybe there was something to her fear of holding him back. Because suddenly the plight of the millions of slaves in bondage warred with this compulsion to make sure she was safe. It didn't matter, because she didn't write, and that felt lonelier than before he'd met her.

A loud crash sounded, broken glass shattering into the quiet night. Patrick leaped to his feet in unison with the brothers. He had expected trouble after the first meeting of Alton's Anti-Slavery Society the other day, chaired by none other than his chief. The moment they'd long feared burst upon the cozy office. The Lovejoys weren't supposed to be here, sitting around with their jackets long ago tossed over chairs and ties loosened. Any other night, Patrick would have been alone and in bed.

Through the broken glass came the light of torches blazing and the sound of raised voices. Mr. Godfrey, one of the *Observer*'s stakeholders, had insisted that Owen leave his guns at home, and now they were unarmed. Patrick tensed, his heart thundering in his ears, glancing at Owen to see what he was thinking.

"Hey! Get out of here!" John shouted out the window.

Patrick and Owen sidled up to peer out as a volley of rocks flew toward the window, breaking the jagged glass that was left and blasting into the room. They ducked, but a rock the size of a lemon smashed into the side of Patrick's head as he dove to the floor. Pain temporarily blinded him. Instinctively, he groaned, grabbing his head and feeling stickiness.

"Are you hit?" Owen rolled over and must have seen the blood between Patrick's fingers, because he sucked in his breath.

"I wish I'd kept my rifle here," John growled. "Why did we listen to that man?"

"We couldn't very well shoot anyone." Patrick's head began to throb, and he lowered onto his back.

"Just to fire into the air and scare them off. Don't fall asleep, Gallagher. Are you all right?"

"I could use . . . something."

More rocks shot into the room, and the shouts increased. Patrick shut his eyes against the blazing light in the window that burned his eyes as his head swam.

"We need to get out of here." Owen scooted to the wall and sat up. "Are you able to walk?"

"Get him a wet rag, stupid." John crawled over to the water bucket and came back with a sopping handkerchief. Patrick pressed it against his head, taking deep breaths.

"We can help you," Owen said. "But we need to go."

Patrick pushed up, and the room spun. "I can walk. But the press—"

John was there as he stumbled to his feet, grabbing an arm and throwing it over his shoulder. Owen darted around the room for coats and his hat before cracking open the back door and peering out. Discovering the alley was quiet, Owen fell into step on Patrick's other side, guiding them all into the shadows of neighboring buildings.

Sweat clouded Patrick's vision, and he stumbled through the streets, fighting to stay upright. If they'd been spotted, the crowd didn't seem to care. There was a loud crack and a cheer, which could only mean that the front door had been breached. *Oh, God.* Fear for the press registered a faint thought behind the blood pounding in his skull. He could get over a knot on the head in a matter of hours, but the press . . .

"Should I go for the mayor?" John asked, breathless.

"It's probably too late, but you can try." Owen shifted Patrick's arm around himself. "I'm going on to find Parish."

All Patrick wanted was to sit down. "Leave me here and save the press. I'll manage."

But Owen tossed John his coat and tugged Patrick forward. "There's no saving the press, and you're coming with me."

"I'm sorry to intrude when Mrs. Lovejoy is ill." Patrick struggled to sit up from the couch in the parlor, pressing his fingers lightly on the bandage on his head.

"We're just relieved everyone's safe." Owen lowered beside him. "They were out for blood tonight. They had Parish, and I'm still not sure how he escaped harm."

"They what?"

"The Lord delivered me from those who sought to do me hurt. Blessed be His name. I lifted up my heart to God, and He kept it in perfect peace."

Patrick and Owen jerked their eyes up to Lovejoy standing in the doorway, the peace he spoke of emanating from his face. "I told them I had to take medicine to my sick wife. One of them took the bottles I had and brought them to her. Then I told them that I had never injured them and they could only do to me what God permitted them to do. They dispersed soon after. I am indeed sorry to see they harmed you."

The lump on Patrick's head now seemed merciful, considering how the night could have gone for all of them.

"I'm afraid they destroyed your press, sir." It was embarrassing to admit after hearing how Lovejoy had calmly faced the mob and escaped harm. Maybe if they'd had a gun, the expensive equipment could have been protected—but would anyone have listened to him if he'd gone out to reason with them like Lovejoy did?

There was a bang in the hall, and John materialized, hatless. "They've broken up the large press and tossed it in the river. It was done before I knew it." He pushed both hands into his hair and expelled a frustrated sigh. "I couldn't find the mayor."

Patrick's heart sank, and his head fell back against the arm of the couch. Tonight they got away with only one little rock to the head. What would happen next time, when the town realized they hadn't succeeded in silencing Lovejoy?

Lovejoy frowned. "I shall certainly speak to him. There were doctors I know in the crowd lying in wait to tar and feather me. I must know where our legal protection was tonight as upright citizens of this locality."

"What are we going to do about the press?"

Subscriptions had skyrocketed to above two thousand lately, but would it be enough to pay for a whole new press? More importantly, would Patrick be allowed to escort it from Cincinnati?

"I can go get one," Owen finally said to the silent room.

"I'll have to talk to some people, and we need to raise funds first," Lovejoy replied after thinking it through. "Perhaps the *Telegraph* will allow us to print an appeal for assistance on their press. And I'll write to Joseph, because he can fundraise in the East."

How was it possible that they were in this place again? Patrick lifted a hand to his forehead, unable to escape the truth. Everything he'd always feared had followed him here.

Every good thing he tried to do failed, leaving it catastrophically worse off than before he got involved. Somehow Lovejoy was a man of God who could face down a mob and walk away unscathed, but the press Patrick was responsible to protect sat in the bottom of the Mississippi River.

The *Alton Observer* was silent, and it was Patrick's fault.

47

Miss Anna?"

Anna stopped on the bottom step of the staff staircase, her arms full of sheets fresh from the outdoor line. Mildred sidled up to her with a half-peeled carrot in her hand. "Two packages came earlier when you was next door, and I set them upstairs."

Anna nodded in understanding. "How big were they?"

"One was big, and one was little."

"Do I need to do anything with them?"

"I done checked them out, so they don't need anything done just now."

"Thank you, Mildred." Anna smiled and headed up the stairs in anticipation of meeting the adult and child who were now free from their bonds and on their way to a new life. In the third-floor workroom, she dropped the sheets into a basket for the maids to iron before stopping across the hall to check on their hidden guests.

Tapping lightly on the door, she whispered, "It's just me," and let herself in. A tall, dark woman sat tense on the bed in the tiny room, keeping vigil over the child asleep on it.

"I'm the owner here and wondered if you need anything. Are either of you in need of medical care?"

"No'm. Just rest."

"You can have as much of that as you need. We'll move you on tomorrow night if everything goes well."

"Yes'm."

Anna had moved into the room to keep their conversation low, and as her eyes fell on the sleeping child on the bed, she gasped. At first glance, the girl looked just like Jane. She had the same coloring and the same style of braids. But as her eyes fluttered open and she scooted into her mother's side, Anna could see that it wasn't Jane. Still, her size and wide eyes made Anna's arms ache for the other little girl of a similar age.

"We can find you new dresses in our boxes tonight, but I have something for you now. I'll be right back."

Anna hurried away, returning shortly with a Black doll, which she pressed into the girl's hands. "Some sweet girls stayed here last year, and they loved to make these dolls for other little girls. They'd want you to have it."

Anna's eyes filled with tears, but the girl and her mother only stared blankly at her.

"Thank you," the little girl whispered.

Anna wanted to wrap her in her arms and, for a moment feel like Jane was here again, but she forced herself to retreat to the doorway. "Supper is being prepared now, so we'll bring something up in a little while. Welcome to Ohio."

She gently closed the door before dragging her heavy heart to her room and dropping onto the bed. The days of feeling like every movement was pushing weighted limbs through molasses were largely over, but then little moments like this one brought the grief back again. She only made enough dolls for her own house anymore and didn't take extras to Cincinnati. But it would be letting Leah and Jane down if she ever quit making them, even though every stitch injected pain into her heart.

Corydon and Jason Bull had both agreed that it was best that she didn't show up on Sandra's doorstep uninvited. To do so would likely frighten the family into hiding, which would put undue strain on all of them. The Bulls' connection in Sandra's town sent occasional reports that the girls were well and helping their mother with the laundry she took in.

But Sandra and Max were autonomous adults now, and Anna needed to allow them to be that. She had no claim on Leah and Jane or the right to require that they stay in touch with her.

Hugging her middle, she took deep breaths and willed the tears away, lest they trigger a sick headache. As usual, she used the opportunity to pray for them before standing and smoothing her hair. It did no good to wallow, and her work was waiting.

In the kitchen, supper preparations appeared to be on schedule, so Anna reached for the kitchen door right as it swung open.

"There's an Owen Lovejoy here," Mrs. Markland announced as soon as she saw her.

"Owen?"

"He's here for one night at his brother's recommendation."

Anna's heart rate picked up. Owen had appeared in several of Patrick's letters, back when he still sent them. When she'd stopped responding, his had tapered off, and now she couldn't remember the last time she'd heard news from Illinois. With effort, she kept her pace down the hall demure, despite the urge to hurry. She found Owen standing in the hallway, a younger lookalike of his brother Elijah.

"Mr. Lovejoy, welcome! I'm Mrs. Markland, and I'm pleased to have you."

He gave a slight bow. "Thank you. I came to Cincinnati to retrieve a new press, and Parish encouraged me to spend the night here."

"Did you come alone?" Anna asked, looking behind him as if he were hiding a tall Gallagher man in his shadow.

"Yes."

"Come, let me show you to a room." Anna led the way to the stairs, masking her disappointment. She couldn't very well ask him why Patrick hadn't come. It might have been Patrick's choice to avoid seeing her, and it might not have been. At any rate, it was a long trip to take for a one-night visit to a woman he might not have a future with.

"I'm sorry to hear that you have need of another press so soon," she said quietly, stopping inside the bedroom. "They were here just exactly a year ago to purchase one."

He gave a tired smile. "Things have been tenuous lately, between the strong messages the *Observer* prints and the creation of our new Anti-Slavery Society. Add rumors that my brother said things he didn't . . ." He shrugged and took in the accommodations. "The room is lovely, Mrs. Markland. Thank you."

Anna found herself suddenly thirsty for news that pertained to Patrick.

"What happened?"

Owen set his satchel on the bed and tugged his gloves off. "A mob came to the office when we were there one night. We managed to escape out the back door with only one of our assistants injured by a rock in the head. After that, they broke in, dismantled the press, and threw it into the river. It was . . . encouraging to see the outpouring of support by our friends. They believe so strongly that we must carry on that the funds were raised quickly for another."

Anna's trembling hand flew to her neck. "What a mercy no one was hurt worse. How is the injured man?"

"He's had lingering headaches but no memory loss or anything of the sort. Gallagher's a tough nut, and he seems to be recovering."

It was him. Anna fingered her collar in an attempt to control her shaking hands. How close they came to a much worse situation. A rock to the head, indeed!

Her life had gone on in Patrick's absence, although she often thought of him and wondered how he was doing. She still cared about him, even though time and distance kept him from the forefront of her thoughts most days. A concussion was a miserable thing to experience, and she wished she had been there for him.

She tapped the doorjamb and backed up. "I'm glad to hear he's on the mend. Supper will be in the dining room in a few minutes."

Closing the door behind her, she leaned against the hallway wall and closed her eyes. The slightest difference in the rock's impact, be it location or speed, could have snuffed out those beautiful brown eyes forever. She could still see the gold flecks in them as they dipped toward her that night in the dim parlor.

Straightening up, Anna shook the thoughts away and hurried down to the kitchen.

Patrick stood on the dock with John, Thaddeus, and a dozen others of Lovejoy's friends as the early autumn breezes whispered across the water. Owen descended the steamboat's gangplank to back thumping and a buzz of enthusiasm. Only Lovejoy himself was missing, but he'd been in and out of town with the recent fundraising, not-quite-clandestine meetings organizing an anti-slavery society for the whole state, and visits to his friend

Edward Beecher, Dr. Beecher's son and the president of Illinois College.

No matter. They would protect this new press and have it installed and ready for him when he returned. Watching the crated press as it was rolled off the steamboat, Patrick didn't realize that Mayor Krum had joined them until he turned to follow the crate's progression into Gerry and Weller's warehouse. From the other side of the street, hecklers shouted half-hearted insults, but no one dared advance.

Patrick ended up behind the mayor in the crowd following the press up the street. He was young and had always seemed rather naive to Patrick's jaded eyes. Patrick didn't wish cynicism on any young person, but shouldn't a mayor have a good handle on reality and risk?

At the warehouse door, Mayor Krum turned and lifted his hands to the crowd. "I will see that the press is protected by the law. Let us all go peaceably, each to his own home."

With the other staff of the *Observer*, Patrick waited reluctantly until most of the crowd trickled away.

"He's set up a constable to guard it," Thaddeus said without peeling his eyes from the building. "I suppose he's keeping his word, so we should do as he says."

"I'd feel better if I had an armed militia here," John declared.

Owen removed his hat and tugged it on again. "I'm tired and hungry. First thing tomorrow, we'll get it moved into the print office." Shifting his satchel over his shoulder, he marched up the street, so the others slowly turned and followed.

Patrick was hungrier than he'd thought. Sinking into a chair at the Lovejoy table, he inhaled the smell of chicken pie and waited impatiently for the kitchen staff to serve it up.

"Oh, I have something for you," Owen said. Reaching into his pocket, he pulled out a cream envelope and slid it across the table to Patrick.

One look at his name in the feminine handwriting, and his mouth parched. He tucked the envelope away and fumbled for his glass of water.

"I didn't know Mrs. Markland was your lady friend," Owen said, watching him closely.

Patrick shook his head, aware that his neck was probably red beneath his collar. "A friend. But she's two states away, and new presses don't need to be retrieved every day, so . . ." He gave a weak shrug, hoping his explanation would keep any ribbing away.

John started to quote some romantic nonsense, but it was soon muffled by the food he shoveled into his mouth, and Owen didn't push further. Patrick accepted his plate and began eating with nervous anticipation at what the letter might say. After a couple months of silence, he'd despaired of hearing from her again.

"Did she seem well?"

Owen considered. "She's a lovely woman, to be sure. She did appear . . . sad. As if she'd been crying before she came into the room. But she seemed very interested to know about the paper and the happenings here."

Patrick nodded to appear nonchalant, but the invisible thread that somehow still held his heart prisoner in Ohio stretched taut.

48

"I have no doubt that four-fifths of the inhabitants are glad that my press has been destroyed by a mob, both once and again. They hate mobs, it is true, but they hate Abolitionism a great deal more."
- Elijah Lovejoy

The Lovejoy parlor stayed busy that night, with local friends congregating for the news and staying for hours. The clock edged near midnight when the last guests left, leaving Patrick with the Lovejoy brothers and two male boarders.

Owen turned to Patrick. "Are you staying here tonight?"

"I didn't realize how late it was. I've been back at the print office these days since the door was fixed, and things have been quiet, but I may as well stay here tonight if we'll be up early."

"What are you going to do when the press is installed?" John paced to the dark window and peered out. "It won't be safe to sleep there." The last attack seemed to have changed his perspective on a single man's ability to guard the press, especially when asleep.

"I don't know." Was it time to buy a house with his money? John was right—Patrick would never be able to sleep soundly at the office once the press was there, for fear of awakening to flames in the doorway.

"Don't worry about having an answer now," Owen cut in. "Just stay here tonight. John, what did Thaddeus mean when he mentioned Parish offering to resign?"

"Oh, you were away for that." John fell into a chair. "He sent a whole letter to the stakeholders, saying that he was willing to step down as editor if that's what they wanted. They had something like three meetings about it but eventually the nays outvoted the yays."

"You also missed Joel Parker, didn't you?" At Owen's blank look, Patrick crossed his arms over his chest. "A preacher up from New Orleans came passing around a pamphlet, spreading the message that slavery is blessed in the Bible. Some of our supporters started questioning which side was right after that."

John leaped back out of his chair, unable to sit still. "And Enoch Long told Parish he couldn't preach on Proverbs 31:9!"

"What?" Owen leaned forward, sending a confused glance between Patrick and John. "Which passage is that?"

" 'Open thy mouth, judge righteously, defend the rights of the poor and needy,' " John rattled off. "He said the way Parish prays for slaves is offensive to some of the church."

Patrick watched the frustration he'd wrestled with over the course of the month flash across Owen's face. "Enoch Long is a minister and Parish's friend! He ought to know better. It's enough to make a man want to go back to Ohio."

"Things aren't better there," Patrick said, more mildly than he felt.

"Well, there's plenty of work cut out for us then." Owen slumped back into his seat. Patrick was envious of his ability to hear the disheartening news and dig in his heels to the work. Truly, the other option was to give up, and that seemed equally impossible. There simply wasn't anything to do but to buckle down and put one foot in front of the other. But it was tempting to sit and stare at the wall in a stupor for awhile first.

"I'm going to bed." John stretched, and the other boarders joined him on their feet. "Come on, Owen. You must be tired after your trip."

"I'm exhausted." Owen pushed to standing and stumbled, bleary-eyed. "Need anything, Gallagher?"

"No, I'll just grab my usual blanket out of the cabinet and sleep on the couch."

Patrick laid his coat across a chair when he was alone, fell onto the couch, and was asleep in a minute.

The parlor was completely dark when a thump in the hall roused Patrick from a sound sleep. Pushing up on his elbow, he'd not yet rubbed the sleep from his eyes when Owen materialized behind a lit lantern in the doorway. Patrick shook the sleep away, blinking against the assault the light made on his eyes.

"Good morning."

"Is it?" Patrick cleared his throat to waken his voice.

"Not especially, no. The press was attacked around midnight."

"No." Patrick was on his feet in a second, his blanket falling to the floor. "There was a constable."

"Who figured it was safe to go on home. Guess where the press is now?" Owen deposited his lantern on a table and dropped heavily into the chair he'd vacated only hours ago.

Patrick didn't move. "Please tell me it's anywhere except the Mississippi River."

"No, my dear boy, you're quite mistaken. It is indeed in pieces in the river."

Patrick couldn't breathe. He itched to grab the nearest item and throw it as hard as he could against the wall. Or double over from the pain in his stomach. Or pull his boots on and run as far and as hard as he could and never stop. Or scream at the top of his voice. *Breathe in. Breathe out.* He almost couldn't manage the basic action, let alone any of the others.

"What are we going to do, Owen?" The question came out strangled.

Owen didn't answer for so long, Patrick almost repeated the question. "Wait for Parish, I suppose. I guess he'll be home today."

"Mayor Krum promised to protect it."

"I think he was there."

"*What?*"

"I heard he showed up and told the vandals to disperse. And I guess they didn't. I only heard one initial report. I'm sure there's more to the story that will come out when Parish gets here."

"It's an outrage," Patrick said with a deadly calm that came from outside himself. "It should outrage the entire country. There is no freedom of speech or freedom of the press by God-fearing men in free states. I don't understand."

"I don't understand either," Owen finally whispered. "That's what I keep telling the Lord. I'm at a loss of what else to say to Him." Leaning forward, he buried his head in his hands.

At some point, Patrick collapsed back onto his couch without being aware that he'd done so. They sat together in a fog as the darkness surrounding them slowly turned to gray early morning. Patrick might have dozed on and off—he really wasn't sure. Every time he returned to reality, the urge to escape, either by physically running or retreating deep into the recesses of his mind, overwhelmed him.

He was still there when Lovejoy returned later that morning. The editor didn't make it past the foyer before his brothers met him with the news, and he responded by going straight upstairs to his wife. Owen, Patrick, and John had nothing to do except field more friends and associates who came to hear what happened and offer their opinion on the matter. Patrick felt like a caged animal, unable to sit still but not wanting to leave before hearing from his employer.

When Lovejoy finally materialized, his sallow skin and the dark circles under his eyes were evident. He stopped in front of the couch Thaddeus and Owen were on, which Patrick had vacated a while ago to pace the room.

"James Birney is moving to New York."

Patrick stopped short, spinning around. "Was he forced out?"

"No." Lovejoy pulled out a letter, which he handed to Patrick. "He believes it to be a strategic move, to continue his work in a more effective location. Dr. Bailey is taking over editing *The Philanthropist*."

"What about us?" Owen asked quietly, gesturing around the room. "Is it time for the *Observer* to relocate?"

"We have broken no laws nor harmed anyone. Should a man such as I flee? We have a right to be here. If I leave here and go elsewhere, violence may overtake me in my retreat, and I have no more claim upon the protection of any other community than I have upon this one."

His silent employees remained motionless, with somber faces and pursed lips. He had a point. Patrick skimmed Birney's letter and handed it back.

"Yet it is wasteful to continue to lose presses to the Mississippi River," Lovejoy continued, slipping the envelope back into his pocket. "We shall see what to do when the convention meets."

John crossed his arms over his chest. "You're still continuing with the Anti-Slavery Convention?"

"God has devolved upon me the responsibility of maintaining my cause, and I am determined to do it." Lovejoy looked him steadily in the eye. "In the meantime, I believe it is best if I take my family to St. Charles for a short reprieve. Mrs. Lovejoy is unwell. I am unwell. We shall have a short rest and devote ourselves to prayer ahead of the convention."

Thaddeus voiced his agreement, and Owen slowly nodded. John looked rather like he wanted to go blow something up. Patrick just knew that if he didn't escape, he was going to end up punching through a wall, regardless of how much he agreed with Lovejoy.

Patrick spent most of the afternoon pacing aimlessly through the streets of Alton under an oppressively dreary sky. There was nowhere to go, like Lovejoy had stated. And the last thing Patrick wanted to do was go sit and stare at the river that now was home to three of the *Alton Observer*'s printing presses. It was hard to avoid doing so, since the town was set on bluffs overlooking it.

At one point, he ended up in the courtyard of the Upper Alton Presbyterian Church and sat for a while on an uncomfortable iron bench, trying to pray and make sense of his thoughts.

Lovejoy not only refused to give up, but he was the picture of inner peace. Everything was so black and white to him, his confidence in being on the side of righteousness unfaltering. Even before he'd fully identified as an abolitionist, those character traits had drawn Patrick across the country to him. But now? After nearly a year working with the man, Patrick loved him like his own brother. He couldn't leave if he wanted to.

But to stay meant to continue staring injustice upon injustice in the face. Whether it impacted his personal or job security was irrelevant. After all, so many others continued to suffer so much worse, with no voice.

He couldn't explain the injustice away or ignore it. To stay meant that he'd choose to keep standing in light of it, like Elijah Lovejoy. Maybe that was all they could do. Merely keep standing and keep facing it.

Even if God didn't answer the cry of his heart to be part of a wave of change in the nation. He'd answered no so many times now, maybe Patrick just needed to accept it instead of getting offended every time it happened.

Walking back to the print office in the near-dark, the hopelessness threatened to consume him. He wasn't going to turn tail and run or spend his life feeding on the anger. Neither accomplished anything. But truly, *nothing* they did accomplished anything.

After all this time, nothing had changed.

49

Letting himself into the dark print office, Patrick stood for several minutes, staring at the place the printing press should be. The rest of the destruction had been cleaned up weeks ago, his type neatly returned to their drawers.

He lit a lantern and found himself drawn to his workbench. He would have been back to work today if things had gone differently. Would he ever set type here again? He sure missed it.

Pulling out the last chase he did, Patrick ran his fingers across the columns of metal letters, desperate for the feel of type pieces again. With each letter and word set backward, it was unreadable, and he couldn't remember at first which article it was. His hand stilled on the cold, rough surface.

Was this a picture of how his life was? To him, everything looked backward and upside down. None of it made sense. But when the printer rolled ink across the chase and loaded it into the printing press, the paper sheets that came off the press were filled with legible, enriching words.

Could he dare to hope that God was doing something with his life that was incapable of being seen or understood yet?

Picking up his lantern, Patrick withdrew from the workbench, thinking. *The key to Doubting Castle is the promises of God.* Could he afford to believe anything less than that God would keep His promise to bring to completion the good work He had begun in Patrick's heart? He wanted to.

He had no sense of how much time passed before he finally stirred. After ensuring that both doors were well locked, Patrick dragged his feet to his lonely room. As he set the lantern down and closed his bedroom door, it dawned on him that he hadn't eaten supper. He had a stale heel of bread from a loaf he'd picked up the other day tucked into a handkerchief, so he pulled it out and took a bite. Without thinking, he went through the motions of taking his coat off. When he dropped it over the back of a chair, a paper in the pocket crackled.

Anna. She'd written to him and sent it with Owen. With everything else over the past twenty-four hours, he'd forgotten about her letter.

Patrick stripped down to his shirtsleeves and trousers, leaving his braces hanging down his thighs. The rest of the bread sat forgotten on the desk. With the letter in hand, he sat on his bed and considered the envelope. After spending the last several weeks trying to put her from his mind for the last time, now she was reinserting herself into his life. To what purpose? An entire year had passed since he'd seen her, and he was no closer to figuring out how they could possibly have a future together. Was it worth the inevitable ache his heart would undergo to read her letter?

Apparently all his sense of self-preservation was long gone, because he broke the seal and unfolded the paper. Closing his eyes, he could once again feel her trim waist beneath his palm and her forehead pressed against his. Well, there was no need to harm himself *this* much. He opened his eyes and began to read.

Dear Patrick,

Owen Lovejoy is here, and I'm grieved to hear about the destroyed press. As deeply as I know you love your work, I can imagine how you must feel the loss. I've spent a good deal of time reading the prophet Jeremiah this year. I've felt a sorrow similar to his. He was one of many prophets who spent their lives urging their people to repent of their sin and return to the Lord and never saw the answer come. I ask you—their life, their work, did it matter? In the same way, I believe that seeing great results is not an accurate indicator for us of whether we are being used by God.

You are the Lord's, Patrick. Find your rest in Him. Are we the beloved children of our Savior Jesus Christ? Yes. But we are also His unprofitable servants who are only doing our duty to our Master. (Luke 17:10).

In Jeremiah 18 (I read yesterday), the leaders of the people said there was no longer any hope, and they would in turn follow their own devices and live their lives according to their own evil hearts. But that's not us. We have hope in Jesus Christ. And remember, they killed even Him.

Don't despair. This is not the end.

The reminder is for me as much as it is for you.

Anna Markland

Patrick reread the letter four more times before falling back on his pillows. How did she know? More importantly, how did God love him enough to have her write this letter a week ago with the exact message he needed to read right now?

Picking his Bible up off the nightstand, he opened it to Jeremiah but sat with it open, praying. And thanking. And resting. Something of the peace that Elijah Lovejoy always carried now trickled, drop by drop, into Patrick's spirit.

Before drifting off to sleep, an old, long-dead prayer resurrected in his heart.

Please, Lord, give me a future with this woman.

For the next two weeks, Patrick returned to selling harnesses and tried not to hate it. It was just temporary; as the absent Elijah Lovejoy had repeatedly said, "We will see what happens at the convention."

Lovejoy wasn't content to merely speak out against slavery through the press and pulpit but had determined to organize abolition advocates around the state. If they could band and work together, not only could he find the protection he sought for his family, but they could turn a grassroots movement into a recognized body with a voice. He'd been working with Edward Beecher toward that end and expected to hold Illinois' first Anti-Slavery Convention sometime in the coming weeks.

While everyone waited to hear whether it would be held in Alton, Jefferson, or someplace else altogether, the town crackled with tension.

Even Lovejoy's friends gathered at his house and Thaddeus's in the weeks he was away to discuss whether they thought he was going too far. Maybe the state wasn't ready for an anti-slavery society yet.

Patrick was too caught up in his own battles to have an opinion. All he knew was that he would follow wherever Lovejoy went, and *how could he and Anna possibly be together?* He penned a letter to Corydon one night, sharing some of what God had been doing in his heart. By the way, how was Anna doing?

None of it gave him pause anymore. His entire life was a lit powder keg. Something was going to blow up soon, and at that point, none of the rest would matter. He'd just . . . see what happened at the convention.

And then the Lovejoys returned from St. Charles with the news that they'd been mobbed more than once in Celia's childhood home. Men had broken into the house and grabbed Lovejoy before Celia ran in, beating at them and shouting that they would have to take her first. She'd fainted on the floor as soon as they left and was unable to rise when they returned and took hold of Lovejoy again. Only by the merciful arrival of friends and defenders had the family escaped harm.

"So we're to be attacked in our own homes," Thaddeus said through whitened lips. None of them had thought their opponents would go this far.

Lovejoy didn't even turn his head. "Mrs. Lovejoy is exhausted and unfit to leave her bed. She continually starts from fitful slumber in cries of alarm."

Patrick stood with Owen and Thaddeus in the stunned silence of the Lovejoy's full parlor and neatly tucked the desire for marriage away from his mind once again. The faces in the room reflected a range of emotion from grim despondency to tender compassion to stern resolve. Despair threatened his own heart, but he'd started compiling a list of the promises of God in his journal in the evenings. Every night now, he went back to his room to scour the pages of his Bible for more, as if his life depended on it. After all, hope was a matter of life and death.

What were they, now that he needed them?

I will receive you, and will be a Father unto you, and ye shall be my sons and daughters, saith the Lord Almighty.

In desperation, Patrick began mentally listing as many as he could remember.

Come unto me, all ye that labor and are heavy laden, and I will give you rest.

There was his favorite—*In the world, ye shall have tribulation: but be of good cheer; I have overcome the world.*

And *I will instruct thee and teach thee in the way which thou shalt go: I will guide thee with mine eye.*

Thaddeus led prayers of thanksgiving that the Lovejoys had been spared harm, and the friends gathered joined in. Lovejoy had stood up to mobs intent on bodily harm twice now, after Patrick had concluded that there was nothing a single man could do against one. God did indeed hold the lives of His saints in the palm of His hand, and never had Patrick seen the truth more clearly displayed.

50

**"Every person may freely speak, write, and print on any subject.
The truth is, my fellow citizens, if you give ground a single inch,
there is no stopping place. I deem it, therefore, my duty to take my
stand upon the Constitution." - Elijah Lovejoy**

Dear Anna,

Give, and it shall be given unto you; good measure, pressed down, and shaken together, and running over. Luke 6:38

May the blessing you have bestowed on me by your timely missive in our dark hour return to you in kind, and may the God of all hope show Himself your ever-present and faithful friend.

Not many people here are aware that Lovejoy has sent for another printing press, at his own expense. I regret not being able to retrieve it myself and perhaps see you on the way, as God has used you greatly to increase my trust in Him. I can't tell you what a difference it has made.

We continue to face opposition at every step. Edward Beecher is in town, having come for the first Illinois Anti-Slavery Congress held at the Upper Alton Presbyterian Church. The meeting was bushwhacked by our enemies, who outnumbered abolitionists, grabbed votes for leadership, and once their party was installed, passed a series of anti-abolition resolutions in direct opposition to the entire purpose of the convention. Truth was suppressed and right was silenced.

Most of the town blames Lovejoy for the unrest; the other newspapers and pulpits are silent on the matter.

Today, we met at Thaddeus Hurlbut's, where Enoch Long deputized a number of us so that we could rightly defend ourselves if the town does not provide the protection we deserve. Everyone is sleeping with guns by their bedsides, which we all hope to never have to use. Beecher will be preaching in church tomorrow, so I think he will be staying around for a few more days. I'll wait to see what he and Lovejoy decide to do. I trust them, but I trust God more.

The convention is in ruins and the new press is on its way. Lovejoy is calm and resolved and credits it all to the Lord. His unwavering faith is doing much to hold the rest of us up. The scripture your letter referenced has done the rest. I have no idea what we will be facing in the days to come, but whatever happens, I am committed to seeing it through.

We are troubled on every side, yet not distressed; we are perplexed, but not in despair; persecuted, but not forsaken; cast down, but not destroyed; always bearing about in the body the dying of the Lord Jesus, that the life also of Jesus might be made manifest in our body.

With you in hope,
Patrick Gallagher

By Friday, Patrick didn't have it in him to sell one more harness. The printing press would be arriving by Monday, and nothing but Elijah Lovejoy and his disruption of the quiet life in Alton had been the topic of conversation in the entire region all week. Patrick packed his knapsack and vacated the print office, heading to the Lovejoys' in search of lodging.

"Is Mr. Beecher about?" he asked Elizabeth as she led him back to the parlor after leaving his bag in a room.

She turned to him with worry lines on her face and flapped her apron. "He hasn't left his room this morning. Parish is in there now."

Patrick rubbed the back of his neck, debating what to do. "Maybe I'll stop in for a bit."

"I'm sure he won't mind seeing you." Elizabeth smiled tensely and led him to a closed door. She gave a light tap on it and left, leaving Patrick to lift the latch in apprehension of what he would find.

Beecher was on his knees before the bed, his head bent over folded hands as he prayed aloud. Lovejoy sat in a chair, leaning forward with his hands clasped between his knees and eyes closed. Patrick didn't question his next move as he dropped to his knees beside Beecher.

There had been a series of meetings nearly every day since the end of the disastrous Anti-Slavery Convention. Some were hosted by the Colonization Society, and others were public events that Beecher attended, meant to help the two sides reach a resolution. The only resolution that the ever-growing number of opponents of freedom would agree to was Elijah Lovejoy quitting Alton and silencing his press.

Beecher's prayer suddenly tapered off, and when he reached for his handkerchief without lifting his head, Lovejoy took over. Patrick was struck by Lovejoy's sense of the presence of God. With quiet confidence, he entrusted his cause to the Lord.

"And we beseech you, Lord, for the best good of the community in which we dwell." Patrick heard little else of the prayer, struck by the complete, simple trust of that line. A minute later, Lovejoy said "Amen" and stood.

Patrick and Beecher came to their feet in response, Beecher's eyes unmistakably red. Lovejoy silently shook both of their hands and turned to go. Reaching the door, he stopped.

"I'll be at the meeting this afternoon. If they will allow me to speak, I think I ought to lay out our case before the people."

Beecher nodded cautiously, more an acknowledgement than agreement, leaving Patrick to wonder what he'd missed at yesterday's meeting. What was expected to happen today?

Patrick arrived at the meeting hall early that afternoon to find it nearly packed. Making his way through the crowd, he found a seat that Thaddeus and Owen had saved for him and settled in. Everyone was there, Lovejoy the picture of tranquility in front of them, by Beecher's side. Beecher leaned toward him, laying out the arguments he'd prepared to make. Patrick had no plan of speaking himself and had come to prevent the voices of lawlessness from having a majority.

The meeting was called to order, and immediately a resolution was presented that only citizens of Madison County have a voice on matters pertaining to their locale.

When it passed easily, the first trickle of fear crept up Patrick's spine. Edward Beecher was out. In one minute, the crowd had deftly silenced Lovejoy's most eloquent supporter. Patrick's thoughts clung to the prayers he'd witnessed that morning as a lifeline. Evil could not win the day.

A committee formed earlier in the week reported, proposing a resolution that Lovejoy leave town, a sentiment the chairman defended. One of Lovejoy's friends sprang to his defense, demanding freedoms for all citizens.

Patrick's view was suddenly blocked when Lovejoy came to his feet in front of him and walked to the front of the room. Beside him, Owen clenched his hands on his thighs, holding his breath. The room was surprisingly silent of the heckling Lovejoy had received on the street lately. Laying his coat aside, he turned to the crowd and began to speak.

"Mr. Chairman, I do not admit that it is the business of this assembly to decide whether I shall or shall not publish a newspaper in this city. I have a right to do it. This right was given me by my Maker and is solemnly guaranteed to me by the Constitution of these United States. What I wish to know of you is whether you will protect me in the exercise of this right."

Please, let him be heard, Patrick prayed fervently. Thaddeus's lips moved silently, and Patrick knew he was praying too.

"These resolutions are spoken of as a compromise. But if by a compromise, it is meant that I should cease from doing that which duty requires of me, I cannot make it. And the reason is that I fear God more than I fear man."

Owen's hands had relaxed, and now he rubbed his palms up and down his thighs, leaning toward his brother.

"Where can I be safe if not here? There is no way to escape the mob but to abandon the path of duty. And that, God helping me, I will never do."

For weeks, Patrick and his friends had been saying these things to each other in private, but it was marvelous to hear Lovejoy take the opportunity to lay out his defense so clearly to the public for the first time.

"You may hang me. You may burn me at the stake, or you may tar and feather me, or throw me into the Mississippi, but you cannot disgrace me. I—and I alone—can disgrace myself, and the deepest of all disgrace would be at a time like this to deny my Master by forsaking His cause."

Beecher's handkerchief was back out, and a lump grew in Patrick's throat.

"I am a husband and a father. I am made to feel the wisdom of the Apostle's advice: 'It is better not to marry.' I do not expect my wife will ever recover from the shock she received at St. Charles. Yet think not that I am unhappy. Think not that I regret the choice that I have made. I enjoy a peace which nothing can destroy. I have counted the cost and stand prepared freely to offer up my all in the service of God."

Lovejoy stopped for a long moment, and the first tears slid down Patrick's cheeks at the sight of his friend too choked up to continue. Thaddeus surreptitiously swiped at his own face.

"It is because I fear God that I am not afraid of all who oppose me in this city. Before God and you all, I pledge myself to continue the contest that has commenced here—if need be, till death. If I fall, my grave shall be made in Alton."

Elijah Lovejoy picked up his coat and strode out of the building in the silence that followed. Edward Beecher buried his face in his hands and broke down, his shoulders shaking. Patrick tried to swallow his emotion away, but it was pointless.

The gauntlet was thrown down, and only God could help them now.

51

"Whatever may be the consequences, I think, I trust, that through the grace of God, I am prepared to meet them—even unto death itself."
- Elijah Lovejoy

The air was still and heavy around Patrick as he stood against the stone warehouse with his collar up, listening to the breathing of thirty other men under the waning light of the setting moon. On the river, the unmistakable sound of a boat approaching kept them tense and observant.

The steamboat eased up to the dock, and when the gangplank lowered, the cluster of protectors moved as one body toward it. In surprisingly short order, a large crate was moved down the gangplank and onto rollers on the ground.

Low voices alerted him to the fact that Mayor Krum had arrived to once again oversee the safe installment of the press into Mr. Gilman's warehouse across the street. Patrick glanced nervously around, but no disturbances or mobs met them as they escorted the crate to the end of the stone building that faced the river. From the third-story window above, a beam appeared. Wordlessly, men set to work arranging ropes under the crate. Slowly, slowly, the press was lifted to the window high overhead and disappeared inside.

Patrick hurried into the warehouse with his friends and Mr. Gilman to wait for the arrival of Lovejoy and Beecher. Rubbing his hands together, he shivered against the chill of the November night. It was completely dark when the two men slipped inside and conferred with Mr. Gilman—it had to be after three in the morning now that the moon was gone.

"We can stay," Lovejoy told those that remained. "There is no need for all of you to lose your sleep when Beecher and I can stand watch."

There was little chance of sleeping anyway, but no doubt it would help to be rested for the following day, when the town discovered the press had arrived. Patrick reluctantly joined the others ducking out the door and tiptoeing soundlessly to their homes.

Now that the fourth press for the *Alton Observer* had arrived, would he get the chance to use it?

The following evening, Patrick counted the defenders gathered in Mr. Gilman's warehouse, concerned to discover the number was less than half of the night before. A collection of weapons sat with them, because every report in town that day had indicated to expect trouble tonight.

"I met with Mayor Krum today," Mr. Gilman said in a low voice to Patrick. "He told me that we have a right to arm ourselves and would be justified in defending our property if necessary. And if we need help suppressing any riot, he will be available to come."

Lovejoy was speaking to Enoch Long, who seemed to be the unofficial leader of the ragtag self-appointed militia.

Beecher had returned to Jacksonville and his post at the Illinois College after gathering the Lovejoy household for devotions and prayer that morning. Patrick's heart still wrenched at the memory of collecting around Mrs. Lovejoy's bed, and how very white she had looked against her pillows. Lovejoy kissed her hand, but his face held no fear. The man's conscience was clear, and he was completely at peace. Still, he'd left Owen and John to guard his wife at a friend's house tonight.

"It's ten o'clock," Thaddeus whispered to Patrick. "Can you tell what's going on outside?"

The only windows were on the ends of the building, so Patrick could see little than that a crowd had gathered and smashed a few windows.

Mr. Gilman strode to the door and stepped out. Bright moonlight streamed in the open door around him, and the sound of tin horns outside intensified. "What do you want?"

"We want that printing press!"

"We will not give it to you. We should regret hurting anyone, but we are armed and are authorized to defend our property."

Patrick couldn't hear what was shouted next, but Mr. Gilman dove back inside as bullets pinged on the door.

A murmur of voices rose inside, and Elijah Lovejoy stepped into the center of the room, hands raised. "My friends, we can not, we must not, we shall not surrender. I, for one, am willing to lay down my life here in defense of the right."

More glass shattered, the remaining windows destroyed by flying rocks and bricks. Patrick stood ready with one of Owen's shotguns as the first crash was made by a battering ram against the front door, making his heartbeat lurch. From the upstairs window, a member of Mr. Long's hastily appointed militia dropped rocks and then stone jugs down on those trying to break in. Silence fell from time to time, more concerning than the shouts and flying missiles. There was no way to know what the rioters were plotting next or from where the assault would come.

Gunshots shook the building, and a spray of bullets flew into the room without hitting anyone.

Everyone remained on edge and ready for several more minutes. "Fire into the crowd and scare them away." Mr. Long's words sounded weak, more like a suggestion than an order. Patrick clutched his shotgun, peering around the pillar he'd taken up residence behind as the blast of gunfire reverberated through the building.

"Who fired?" Mr. Gilman asked.

"I did," came three different voices around the inside of the room.

Patrick had no idea how many men were outside, but there had to be over a hundred, and at his best count, the press had nineteen defenders. Things fell quiet outside, but Patrick's shoulders remained tight, his jaw clenched. A minute later, a knock came at the door, and Mr. Gilman admitted the frantic mayor and justice of the peace.

"You need to give up the press," Mayor Krum exclaimed, and Patrick saw the fear in his eyes. "I cannot hold them back. They're completely out of hand. Protect your lives and property and surrender while you can!"

Mr. Gilman stepped toward them, and Patrick peeked over to see Thaddeus move protectively in front of Lovejoy. "I will not surrender," Mr. Gilman announced calmly. "I charge you as mayor to call on the citizens and prevent damage to the warehouse."

"I cannot stop a whole mob." Mayor Krum threw up his hands. "Even now they are sitting out there, drinking more."

"And setting a ladder on the south side of the building," the justice of the peace added.

Turning on their heels, the men left, welcomed back outside by jeers from the crowds.

"There are leaders of our town out there directing this," Mr. Long muttered, marching back to the others. "I saw at least three respected doctors in the crowd."

"If they set up a ladder, they're going up to burn the roof." Mr. Gilman swept worried eyes around the room. "Someone needs to go out and push the ladder over."

"I will," Lovejoy said immediately.

For heaven's sake! Patrick and Thaddeus stepped forward as one. The man whose blood the crowd wanted the most could hardly go out alone. "I'm going too."

Two others joined with their guns, flying on Lovejoy's heels out the door and around the corner. Gunfire exploded in Patrick's ears as he lunged at the ladder with Lovejoy, sending it and the boy climbing it with a torch in hand toppling. Racing back to the door, they slid inside and banged it shut, panting to catch their breath.

"They must have been too drunk to shoot straight," Thaddeus gasped. "We're all here."

"They're already shouting to try again." Mr. Long stood pressed against the wall by the window, taking furtive glances outside. For the first time, Patrick heard church bells tolling and realized they'd been sounding for a while, but he hadn't attended to them over the shouts, tin horns, and gunfire.

Patrick used the lull to check his loaded gun and pray that he wouldn't have to use it. How had he gotten to this place? Suddenly the thought of cutting down trees at Anna's felt like a picnic.

A lanky youth dashed in the door with a box of bullets, which he pressed into Mr. Long's hands. "They're getting up the ladder again. If they were sober, it wouldn't take so long," he told them.

"We're going to have to go back out there," Mr. Long replied. "If they make it up the ladder, they'll burn us out."

Patrick couldn't believe his ears when Lovejoy volunteered again. This time, Royal Weller and Amos Roff stepped forward, following him to the door.

How long is this going to go on? Patrick held his breath, straining to hear what was happening on the streets. Was there any way the night would end with their lives and the press intact? Would they all be burned alive?

What had God promised that would matter in a moment like this? *Come, behold the works of the Lord, what desolations He hath made in the earth. He maketh wars to cease unto the end of the earth; He breaketh the bow, and cutteth the spear in sunder; He burneth the chariot in the fire. Be still, and know that I am God: I will be exalted among the heathen, I will be exalted in the earth.*

Lovejoy opened the door, and Patrick's gaze fixed on the back of his friend and leader as he stood silhouetted on the step by the bright moon. Then a series of gunshots blasted through the night, and Elijah Lovejoy's body shuddered violently.

52

"For what is there desirable in life, to one deprived of his civil and religious liberty?" - Elijah Lovejoy

I am shot!"

Lovejoy ran into the building with his arms clutched around his middle as bright red spots sprang up across his body. Turning to the stairs, he hurried up them, collapsed on the floor of the counting room, and stilled.

Dashing up the stairs after Lovejoy, Patrick barely registered Royal Weller returning inside with blood trickling below his knee. He couldn't comprehend the sight of Lovejoy falling to the floor or the way Thaddeus dove to the body. This was not a time to stand around stunned, when their lives were all still in danger, but he could see nothing but the way Lovejoy lay limp on the ground. The editor did not stir—no spark of life remained.

Another man helped Thaddeus lift his body to a cot, and the two took up court on either side. Patrick stumbled backward, sliding his back down the wall until he sat with his arms over his knees, suddenly exhausted.

"They're still trying to set the roof on fire," someone said. No one knew why it hadn't been successful yet and when it would be. A different report said that it was indeed alight. Someone else shouted out the broken window to the crowd below that Lovejoy was dead and they could have the press. Royal sat washing his leg in the corner. Amos Roff came limping up, shot in the ankle after stepping out to try to broker peace. There was discussion about whether to continue to protect the press and questions of whether everyone else could safely exit the building yet.

Time slowed, separated from reality. Patrick leaned forward, pressing a comforting hand on Thaddeus's back. Celia and the baby came to mind, and the lump in his throat was too large to swallow around. How was it that in one minute, his friend who was so full of life and even joy had left the earth, never to return? How could something so permanent happen so quickly?

One of the defenders came running in. "Leave the building and let them in, or all the property will be destroyed!"

"Let's go while we can," Mr. Gilman finally announced. "They're promising not to shoot if we leave, and I'm not going to wait until they burn us out."

Thaddeus had his head buried in his hands at his place beside Lovejoy.

"Are you coming?" Patrick asked softly.

"They won't hurt me. Go on with the others. Please."

Patrick hesitated, then stumbled to his feet, joining Mr. Gilman, Mr. Long, and the others who hid their guns and gathered at the front door. Royal stayed with his leg propped up across from Thaddeus, but everyone else followed Mr. Gilman out the door.

One by one they slipped out, and when the bright moonlight hit them, took off at a run for the river. Patrick heard the gunfire and felt the whizz of a bullet as it went past, but didn't slow or change course. When they were beyond danger, some of the group veered off together to a nearby building and went inside while others scattered through the streets. No one had been hit.

Patrick pressed against the outer wall of the building his friends had gone inside, breathing hard. Inching to the corner, he stuck his head out to see men surging into the Gilman warehouse. *Lord, protect Thaddeus, and please don't allow them to do anything to desecrate Lovejoy.* The few flames licking at the roof extinguished, so someone must have made it up the ladder with water. A few minutes later, the printing press came flying out of the upper story window and the crowd pounced, dragging it down to the river. For pity's sake.

Too heartsick to keep watching, he pushed off from the wall. Even though Owen had Celia at a hidden location, Patrick still felt too much of an intruder on the family's grief to go to the Lovejoy home just now.

Thaddeus wasn't at his house, and anyway, Patrick wanted to be alone. Somehow he ended up at the Upper Alton church and fell heavily into a pew.

He couldn't think about everything being over. He couldn't philosophize. He couldn't bear one more second of sitting around parlors talking to friends and supporters. And he certainly would lose his sanity if he had to spend time in his own thoughts.

For a long time, he sat with his head between his arms, doing everything he could to not think at all. The air stayed dreadfully silent until scratching of mice in the corners broke the silence. Some time before morning, Patrick dropped over onto the pew and fell into a tortured sleep.

The first light of a new day crept in the windows, waking Patrick to a stiff neck and a heart too heavy to carry. He didn't move from the pew at first. The very presence of the hardwood beneath him confirmed that the nightmares of the previous evening were real. What was there to get up for? He had no work to get to, no cause to labor toward.

He always tried to make it a habit of praying before getting out of bed, so he thought he should pray now but had no idea what to ask for. Eventually he settled on, "Lord, help me face today."

Hunger and the need for an outhouse sent him stumbling from the church into the offensively bright morning. The Hurlbuts' home was the closest, so Patrick made his way there after using the church's well to freshen up of sorts.

The maid led him to the dining room, where Thaddeus sat at the table looking like he hadn't slept in a week. Breakfast was laid out, but he wasn't eating. Later Patrick learned he'd spent the night in the warehouse, guarding Lovejoy. Patrick joined the few friends gathered in adding a couple of flapjacks to a plate and taking a seat.

"We're going to take a buggy down to take the body to Cherry Street," Thaddeus told him.

"How is Mrs. Lovejoy?"

Thaddeus lifted his eyebrows. "She collapsed when she heard the news and hasn't moved out of bed since. Elizabeth has the baby."

"I suppose we should prepare for the funeral." Had the news reached Edward Beecher yet?

"I'm not sure that the town that murdered him would take kindly to there being a funeral," Mr. Lippincott returned. "It would add insult to injury if they showed up to protest eulogies of him. It might be better to simply let him rest in peace."

It wasn't until Patrick followed the hearse bearing Elijah Lovejoy's body through town and heard the heckling and jeering along the way that he felt the wisdom in Mr. Lippincott's opinion. The town seethed with hatred toward the abolitionist editor. So many of their former friends and supporters had moved toward neutrality and the opinion that Lovejoy had brought the attacks on himself. Very few loyal friends remained.

Owen, John, and Elizabeth were waiting at the door of the house when the body arrived to be laid out in the parlor. Celia was nowhere to be seen. Patrick stepped into the room with Thaddeus to find Owen's eyes searching for them. He'd forgotten how young Owen really was until he saw him now, only in his mid-twenties. Meeting him halfway across the room, Patrick wrapped his arms around him for a long minute before moving aside to allow Thaddeus to do the same.

"I should have been there," Owen whispered, his face stricken.

Patrick shook his head, and Thaddeus laid his hand on his shoulder. "He's the one who told you to guard Mrs. Lovejoy. Maybe he knew and didn't want your mother to lose two sons in one day."

"But he didn't have any of his family with him when he died! None of us were there."

"I was there," Thaddeus said simply. "He wasn't alone, Owen. And it happened so fast, I'm sure he didn't have time to think about it."

"He has gone to a world where hatred cannot disturb, nor violence injure." Owen turned back to the body and took a tremulous breath, hopefully taking Thaddeus at his word.

By the time Patrick stood at the silent gravesite the next day and watched dirt fill the hole over Lovejoy's body on the editor's thirty-fifth birthday, he couldn't take another day of sitting helplessly around. Thaddeus was a minister; he still had his church and his wife. Owen had his own theological studies and now his brother's home and family to manage. John was still young with endless education and career options ahead of him. Edward Beecher was back at the college he presided over. Everybody else from the *Observer* could keep going. They had other things to do.

Patrick alone had his entire existence tied up with a print office that had no press and no editor. It really didn't matter what everyone else did when they were ready to look at their futures. Patrick had come to Alton for one purpose, and that purpose had abruptly ended. If he was going to leave anyway, what was the point in delaying his departure? He had no property to sell, and the later in the year it got, the higher the risk of ice on the rivers. If he didn't leave now, he could be stuck here until spring.

"It's not running away," he told himself as he packed his knapsack in the Lovejoy home. This time, staying would be the impulsive, emotional choice delaying his future.

Still, Owen's face fell when he saw Patrick step hesitantly into the parlor with his knapsack.

"I knew you'd go." He expelled a sigh. "I was just hoping it wouldn't be immediately."

Patrick felt for him. It was too much change at once. "I know. And if I had a job to keep me busy, I'd put it off. But I have somewhere to be and nothing to do here."

Owen cut his eyes away, and Patrick gave him time. When he looked back again, he wore a sad smile. "Tell Mrs. Markland I send my greetings."

Patrick reached out and clasped his arm, trying to hide his smile. "I will. And if you ever need anything at all, Owen, I'll do it for you. I'm sure you'll be hearing it often in the coming days, but your brother was an incredible man. This year with him changed me."

Owen's throat rolled and he nodded. "Go with God," he managed, opening his arms.

Patrick embraced him one last time, feeling like he was leaving his family all over again.

53

**"The gospel, the gospel of the Son of God, with all its glorious hope, its
rich promises, and its bright anticipations, can alone minister true
consolations under circumstances such as yours."**
- Elijah Lovejoy

Patrick barely spoke in the eight days that it took for the
steamboat to carry him down to Cairo and then up the Ohio
River. Only by necessity's demands that he answer passengers
or crew members who directly spoke to him was his voice
prevented from falling into disuse. For most of the trip, he stood at the side
railing wrapped in his overcoat, watching the water pass by beneath him,
foot by tedious foot.

Even if he hadn't been too numb to converse, he bore the weariness of
talking that came from months spent debating every opinion and piece of
news that came into the print office. And he couldn't begin to put words of
how he felt in a letter to Colm. Maybe one day he would be able to talk
about what he experienced. Since none of it made sense now, nothing made
its way onto paper.

Trapped on the moving boat, the idleness felt less strangling than the
idleness of sitting around Alton. He was able to just be without having to
justify it to himself or make a single decision. Occasionally, his thoughts
roused to his arrival on land and what he would do after setting foot in Ohio,
but going through his days as if half awake, his thoughts sluggish, no effort

went into actually answering the question.

The day it happened was gloriously fine. The boat deposited him on the dock under a cerulean sky, and Patrick hitched his sack over his shoulder, no closer to knowing what he was supposed to do or would say.

He went through the motions of climbing the hill, because it seemed like the thing to do. Riverview Lodge, that dear, dear place, stood like a lighthouse drawing him to safety and comfort, and he followed the light obediently. He halted at a distance to simply take it all in and pull himself together before approaching, but at that moment, Anna came out on the front step with a broom. The fall colors must have peaked only last week, because the trees still hung onto the last vestiges of color and the ground was littered with a drying carpet of leaves. Anna's pretty brown hair was pinned up just so, and she stood tall and graceful in her blue dress. She set to work on the stairs without seeing him.

There was something so profoundly beautiful in the scene that he never could rightly explain afterward. Nothing about the picture had anything to do with the horrors he'd just lived through and was completely unrelated to printing presses and friends' silent burials. And maybe that was exactly why. Perhaps the very beauty of it allowed him to feel again.

The deep, deep fracture, something almost completely beyond himself, seemed to slowly rise to the top, to where his heart could access it. He couldn't have willed it up if he'd tried, but now the absolute anguish at the loss of Lovejoy was there where he could touch it—now at the surface— now spilling over of its own volition.

Tears rolled down his face, blinding him. He couldn't stay on a street corner in this condition, and he certainly couldn't approach Anna now. He had no haunts or hidden coves in this town. So he strode to the woods at the edge of Riverview Lodge's yard, not knowing where he was going except in pursuit of solitude. Someplace where he could feel the sorrow and shed his first tears for his friend.

The movement of a tall figure in a dark coat across the street captured Anna's eye, and she stopped sweeping in bewilderment. The man stalked toward the woods with Patrick's purposeful stride, which even after a year, she would recognize anywhere. Had he just arrived, and had he really come all this way to visit her . . . *woods*?

Setting her broom against the doorway, Anna hurried down the steps and across the yard in pursuit of him. At the treeline, she slowed, suddenly plagued with a list of reasons why a man might go into woods, none of which were appropriate for women to witness. But then he stopped fifteen feet into the shelter of the trees and brush, revealing his purpose when he dropped his knapsack and hat onto the ground with an anguished groan. Bending in half with his hands on his knees, he gave a low, guttural cry that froze her in place. After a long moment he straightened, and pressing his arm against a tree, leaned his forehead on it as his shoulders began to shake.

Anna remained rooted to the ground, unable to leave or drop her eyes. Half hidden as he was, his grief reached her, choking her. Lowering onto a stump, she settled in to allow him as much time as he needed. It was encouraging to see him shedding tears, when the Patrick she'd first met had been so ill at ease with his emotions.

Eventually his sobs slowed and she couldn't hold back any longer. Rushing forward, she reached him, sliding her arms around his middle and hanging on for dear life.

Patrick turned from the tree, dropping his arms to gather her close, and buried his face in her neck. Oh, she'd missed him. He felt so good, his embrace both sorrow and comfort, love and joy. The news of Mr. Lovejoy's death had kept her up at night praying, fearful for Patrick's mental wellbeing. When he struggled so with despair, would the murder of the man he worked with devastate him? He could react any number of ways, or run any number of places. But he had come here, and was hanging on to her, and the first hint of hope sprouted in her heart.

When he finally pulled back to face her, he rested his hands on her waist and she lifted her palms to his tear-dampened cheeks.

"I'm so sorry, Patrick. He was the very finest of men."

He took a shaky breath, and two new tears trickled out, which Anna wiped away with her thumbs.

"You're here," she added with a teary laugh.

"I didn't have anywhere else to go."

Her hands started to slip off of his face. What—

"Nowhere else I *wanted* to go," he corrected, tightening his grip on her.

"How long are you here for?" she asked, even though she knew she shouldn't. It wasn't really what she was asking anyway.

"At least until I've changed your last name. And then . . . well, that depends on you, I suppose."

"Really?" She certainly hoped he meant what he said, but his emotional outburst of a minute ago had her viewing him cautiously. The last thing she wanted was to become another emotion-driven decision of his.

"Is there anyone I need to contact to ask for your hand before I ask you to be my wife?"

"My father would appreciate a letter. But Patrick—"

"It's so dangerous, Anna." He pulled her into a tight hug again, wrapping his arms around her. "There's nowhere that is truly safe to take a stand for right, but we don't have any other option. There's no other way to live. I hate the thought of asking you to join me in this kind of life, but . . ."

But he knew she would. "Life's too short for safe. But my sickness, and the newspaper . . . what are you going to do?"

"I'm going to love you with my whole heart. Birney left Cincinnati, Anna. With the changes at *The Philanthropist*, maybe there will be an opening for me. But I'm not going right away. Waiting to hear from your father will give me time to rally—I need that just now—and just spend time with you. I won't rush you out of here, I promise. Not until you're ready, and not without the help you need."

Anna leaned against his chest, desperate to feel him and smell him and keep him as close as possible. "Mr. Markland is dying. I'm not sure if Mother would rather move in with Corydon and Sarah or come along with me. If my staff doesn't want to move, we'll have to hire new ones. But I'll come wherever you want to go."

"You will?" Patrick ran his hand slowly back and forth across her shoulder blades. "We don't have to have all the arrangements figured out today."

"What do you have figured out?"

Patrick didn't hesitate. "That I can't bear the thought of going through this life without you. That I will not allow Lovejoy's sacrifice to be interpreted as evil winning. He did not give his life for us to act like it did. We're going to be louder and bolder now that every man in the country will be called upon to question the firmness of his own convictions in light of the martyrdom of a God-fearing minister."

Anna stepped back in amazement, staring wide-eyed at the blazing light in Patrick's brown eyes. She had never seen him like this before. Was this who he used to be? It was certainly who he was supposed to be. He was fully alive, no longer looking like he was on his way to his own funeral, the way he looked all of last year.

His voice had risen, but now he lowered it again, looking at her fiercely. "We're going to oppose slavery at every turn, Anna, until it's wiped out of our land. But in the meantime . . . I learned from you about the importance of loving the individuals in front of me, regardless of the color of their skin and whether there's one or there's thirty. And that includes loving you."

He must have seen the pensiveness on her face, because he placed both hands around the back of her neck, gently caressing her jaw with his thumbs. "If I could perform miracles and change the culture single-handedly, and yet never loved deeply, I would not be a better man. From what I've seen of my brother Colm—certainly my brother-in-law, Ezra—even Thaddeus and Lovejoy . . . their positions as husbands and fathers have contributed to their character. So why wouldn't I allow your health to limit me as well, if it means that I, too, could learn to love in a richer way? You love so beautifully, in spite of your limitations."

Anna reached up one hand, clasping his in hers and folding their intertwined hands up between them until she kissed his knuckles. "Where did all this hope come from?" Because honestly, it seemed like things were worse than ever, now that opponents to freedom were willing to murder even law-abiding white men to keep others in chains. No laws had changed.

Patrick stood blinking at her, working out the answer before he spoke. "Lovejoy's death isn't the end; he lives yet. It's as if the worst has happened and now I know that it can be faced with so much grace, dignity, conviction, and peace . . . The fear is gone, taking the burdens and nightmares with it. I feel as if . . . now I'm free to love and work and give without concern for the outcomes. Not that I don't long for them or work toward them, but I'm learning to leave to God the things that are God's."

Anna studied him for a long time, feeling a painful twist inside at the thought of Leah and Jane and their outcome, so different than her desired one. Maybe as much as she loved Patrick, she needed him too.

"I'll be ready whenever you're ready to ask me."

"I'll ask you when I get your father's reply."

And then his lips were on hers, all his life and passion zipping through her, fairly tingling down to her fingertips. Anna's hand still clutched his between them, but her other arm went around his neck, hooking him to herself as she kissed him back. She nearly lost herself in the delirium of God bringing this perfectly matched man back to her and the changes that the last year had wrought in him. She had loved him when he was low and now loved him when he was high, and had confidence that God would provide the grace to see them down whatever road He would lead them together.

When she pulled away to gasp for breath, Patrick's lips moved to her cheek, her temple, her forehead, her nose.

"I love you too," she murmured.

"I don't think I ever really doubted that. Oh, darling, I doubted whether God would ever bring us together. I doubted whether it was a good idea to put you through what Mrs. Lovejoy has suffered. But I just couldn't have come before, and I don't regret staying as long as I did."

"I missed you dreadfully, but I wouldn't have wanted you to abandon Lovejoy or the *Observer* either. Good things are worth waiting for."

Patrick slowed in the kisses he was trailing up her jaw. "I suppose you're right."

Anna felt his sigh. He was so impatient to see other good things like the ratification of emancipation in the Constitution. "One day," she whispered. "Please, Lord, let it happen one day soon."

54

"There is One who can minister to a mind diseased—One in whose hand are all the issues of life and death."- Elijah Lovejoy

H i, Mr. Gallagher."

Patrick stepped out of the Riverview Lodge cellar, blinking to allow his eyes to adjust to the bright December day even as the chill pierced through his coat.

Franklin stood before him with a pile of newspapers in his hands, grinning. "I've brought your newspapers."

"Thank you. So the mail's arrived?"

"Yes sir." Franklin loved to help by bringing Patrick all the news, knowing how much he wanted it as soon as possible, but he or Anna still had to go back to the general store for the rest of their mail anyway.

Patrick clapped his cold hands together and took the newspapers from him. "I'm sure Mrs. Markland has a candy for you."

Franklin bounded to the back door, and Patrick hesitated, then walked purposely toward the store. He returned to the inn as Franklin was leaving, waving a cheerful farewell.

Patrick stepped into the warm kitchen and swiped his hat from his head. Mildred paid him no heed as he sank onto a seat at the kitchen table and laid the stack of mail out. His eyes landed on the postmark from Louisville, and he snatched the envelope up. When Anna returned to the kitchen a few minutes later, he looked up with a large grin, waving the letter at her.

"The letter you sent to your father with mine convinced him to give us his blessing. When will Corydon be back in town?"

"Next week, I think." Anna neared, peering over his shoulder. "What's that in the newspaper?" She pointed to the front page, where the words **ALTON TRIALS** appeared in bold. "Are they finally charging the men who killed Lovejoy?"

Patrick grabbed the paper, skimming the article quickly. "Um, no. They're charging . . . us. For inciting the riot and disturbing the peace." He ran his finger down the list of names. "Winthrop Gilman, Enoch Long, Thaddeus Hurlbut, Patrick Gallagher, Amos Roff, Royal Weller . . ."

Anna fell into the chair beside his. "You can't be serious."

"Apparently we 'unlawfully, riotously, and routously and in a violent and tumultuous manner resisted and opposed an attempt to break up and destroy a printing press . . . against the peace and dignity of the people of the state of Illinois.'"

Anna giggled, clapping her hand over her mouth. "I'm sorry, but if I don't laugh about it, I'm going to cry. Are you going to spend the first days of our marriage in prison?"

"I should certainly hope they find us innocent in court, but they'd have to come and get me themselves. It looks like Mr. Gilman is requesting to be tried separately, as he was merely defending his own property. I feel for Thaddeus though." Patrick laid the paper aside soberly. "He's been through the wringer already."

Anna stroked his hand on the table. "It's just so wrong."

Mildred hummed at her work behind them, and Patrick and Anna sat with her hand clasped in his as they pondered the news.

"How are things downstairs?" Anna finally asked.

"Coming along. I finished the wood frame."

They would all sleep better at night once he finished building the hidden room in the cellar for the Underground Railroad. It gave Patrick something to do with his hands while waiting for the letter from Anna's father, which he now possessed.

He gently squeezed her hand. The lady whose house he'd taken a room in down the street had a curfew of nine o'clock. His favorite part of the day, kissing Anna goodnight, was always shortly followed by his least favorite, when he had to let go and walk away. But tonight in the Riverview Lodge parlor, after the staff was gone and before he had to leave for the night, he'd officially ask Anna to be his wife. He already looked forward to that kiss.

The following Friday, Patrick was applying a thick layer of mud over the bricks of his hidden room to disguise it when a shadow blocked the open cellar door. A moment later, Corydon descended the creaking steps.

"Mildred told me I'd find you here. Sarah gave me your message to come over as soon as I returned, so you must have heard from Mr. Cooper."

"Indeed we did. Anna wanted to have you marry us as soon as possible after you arrived so that if sickness struck her, we'd have time to reschedule before you leave again. But then she did get sick today, so it might be a couple of days before we'll be ready for a wedding."

Corydon's grin stretched wide. "I'll be around all week. Send word when you're ready, and I'll grab my collar and Bible and be here in no time. Congratulations."

"Thank you." Patrick scooped mud from a barrel with a trowel and slapped it against his wall.

"How's Mother doing?"

"I think . . ." Patrick carefully smoothed the mud out. "She's quiet but seems to be doing well. On the one hand, she doesn't seem to know what to do with herself without your father here to take care of, and on the other hand, she seems to be enjoying the rest."

"She cared for him for so many years."

"I don't know what she'd do without the inn right now," Patrick added. "It gives her purposeful work where she can help as little or as much as she wants each day."

"I'll stop over and see her next." Corydon turned to go, then spun around. "Oh, I was hoping to see Anna. I have a message for her from Leah."

"You do?" Patrick froze with his trowel in midair, and mud plopped to the ground at his feet.

"I don't suppose I can give it to you in your condition, so maybe I'll leave it on the kitchen table," Corydon said, but Patrick was already pushing past him to the stairs.

"She'll want to hear it right away. Let me clean up."

He scrubbed his hands in the icy pump water in the backyard and dried them on a towel while Corydon waited. When he was ready, Corydon passed the paper over.

"It's from Mr. James, the pastor in Franklin County who originally connected Mr. Bull with Sandra and Max. He sent a note of explanation and then the message Leah dictated for Anna."

Patrick clutched the paper in his reddened, numb fingers. "I'll take it right up."

Corydon headed next door to see his mother, and Patrick dashed up the staff staircase to the third floor. Necessity had sent him to Anna's bedroom on rare occasions over the past month, so he didn't hesitate when he reached her door and tapped lightly on it. "Anna?"

"Come in."

The room was as dark as midnight when Patrick opened the door. "Darling, Corydon arrived. I have a special delivery for you," he whispered.

"Oh, we can be married as soon as I'm well." He heard a rustling as she shifted in bed and then groaned.

"I'm going to have to light a lamp."

"All right."

He fumbled through the dark to her nightstand and managed to light the kerosene lantern. Anna's blue eyes squinted at him as he knelt on the wooden plank floor beside her. He couldn't resist leaning forward and planting a kiss on her white cheek.

"I've a note for you from Leah."

"Leah?" Anna cried.

"It was sent through Mr. James, the minister." Patrick held it up, and Anna held her breath as he unfolded it where she could see. "I'll read it to you."

"Yes, please!"

Clutching her hand in his, he began.

"There's a Negro women's Bible study near Frenchtown that reached out to Sandra, and she started attending. Finally, last week—I don't know when this was written." Patrick turned the letter over.

"Last week from whenever Mr. James wrote it. Last week, Sandra came to church for the first time with her children. I greeted each of them warmly and asked Leah and Jane particularly how they were. They knew that the Bulls worked with us to bring them to their mother. They said they were well, but Leah asked if I had heard from you (Mrs. Markland). I said I hadn't, and she then indicated a desire to send a message to you. After the service, I took out a paper and copied down the message she composed, which is as follows.

"Signed, Reginald James.

"Dear Mrs. Anna,

Jane and I miss you. We're happy here in Franklin County, but we miss you. I made a friend because when we met her, she had one of our dolls we made. I told her we made it and then we were friends after that. We don't have much time for sewing now, we are busy doing laundry all day, but Mama said maybe we can go to the Negro school next year. Jane and I try to follow the Bible like you taught us, and to always say our prayers. We wonder every day if you are well. We hope you aren't sick, and we always pray for you. The minister is sending this letter for me. I have to go now but if you can write us a letter, we would be happy to hear it. Someone at Mama's Bible study can read it to us. Love, Leah. Jane says love from her too. Love, Leah and Jane."

Patrick lowered the letter to see the tears streaming out of Anna's eyes. Pulling out his handkerchief, he used it to dab at her wet cheeks.

"Thank you, Lord," Anna whispered. "Sandra must be improving, if she's taking the children to church now."

"And the first thing Leah wanted to know when she went was how you're doing." Patrick brushed her hair behind her ear and placed the letter on the nightstand.

"Thank you for bringing it to me right away. Is there any news about your trial?"

"No, just a letter yesterday from Thaddeus that he expects it to be held next month. And I had a letter from Colm that Betha's been ill, but they aren't sure what she has." Patrick didn't repeat the dreadful word that Colm had admitted being his great fear. His stomach clenched at the memory of the letter and how rattled Colm sounded. It wasn't like him. Until she received an official diagnosis, he'd pray that it wasn't tuberculosis after all.

Anna's eyes slipped closed. "I wish I could meet them."

"You just rest and get well so we can get married." Patrick pushed to his feet and reached over to kiss her nose before turning down the lamp. "Do you need me to get you anything?" He shuffled toward the open door, feeling his way in the darkness.

"No, Mildred was just up a few minutes ago."

"Then I'll go back to playing in my mudpit in the cellar."

"I was wondering why you smelled like that," Anna said with a giggle.

Patrick gave one last grin at the darkness and gently shut the door behind him.

55

"Slavery, as it exists among us, must cease to exist." - Elijah Lovejoy

Patrick Gallagher extended his hand, and his wife placed her gloved hand in it to descend from the wagon to the frozen Cincinnati street.

Her blue eyes sparkled up at him. "What are you thinking about?"

"I'm thinking how long it's been since I was here. It's good to be back."

He followed her gaze to the sign above the door—Anti-Slavery Society.

"You're not thinking about the last time we came to a meeting together, when I lost my dinner all over you?"

"Nope." Patrick clipped the word at the end. "Doing my best here not to think about that at all." He shot her a wink and offered her his elbow as Uncle Charles leaped to the ground beside them.

Patrick hesitated before escorting Anna inside behind Uncle Charles. "Are you sure you'll be all right? If it gets too stuffy, we can leave right away."

"We can stand by the door where it's cooler," Anna suggested.

As soon as they stepped inside, they were accosted with hugs and congratulations by the Baileys and Mr. Pugh. David and Owen Nickens were there, and Patrick turned from greeting them to see a gaunt skeleton of a man.

"Marius!" Patrick almost didn't recognize him with the dark circles under his eyes and lines on his face. "I wasn't sure I'd see you."

Marius clapped him on the arm. "I just returned from a speaking tour, but I'm afraid a forced rest is in my future." His voice was hoarse, and Patrick had to strain to hear him in the crowded room.

Patrick decided not to tell him how terrible he looked. "I'm glad to see you alive. I'm coming off a rest period myself."

"I could say the same to you. I'll admit to feeling relief when I heard you'd arrived in Ohio. The news about Lovejoy sent us all reeling."

"I think it did for the whole country. Nearly every newspaper I pick up has talked about it. I keep praying that his death will wake our nation up from its complacent acceptance of evil."

Marius took a ragged breath. "I fear we are not yet at the worst in our conflict with slavery. The apathy, coldhearted indifference, and prejudice are so predominant that there seems but little hope."

The man's suffering went beyond the physical attacks. Patrick could but imagine the mental strain of his speaking tours and seeing such opposition on display around Ohio. "Having you around again brings us hope," Marius added. "Thank you for being here."

"Our hope is in the Lord." Patrick met his eyes steadily.

"Yes, and the Lord brings other saints alongside when we grow weary. Ever since God brought you all the way from a slave state to join our numbers, we've been encouraged that we are not forgotten. Uncle Charles told me the same thing when you were here during the riots."

Could it be true that even at his lowest, God had used him to bring hope to others? "God moves in mysterious ways," Patrick muttered under his breath. Aloud, he said, "I had a meeting with Dr. Bailey this afternoon to discuss joining him at *The Philanthropist*."

"Cincinnati will be very glad to welcome you and Mrs. Gallagher."

The title put a smile on Patrick's face, and he lifted a protective palm to Anna's back beside him. John Jolliffe called the meeting to order then, and Marius limped toward a seat at the front of the room, leaving Patrick back by the door with Anna.

"I want to open this meeting by reading a speech made at the Young Men's Lyceum in Springfield, Illinois, earlier this month by a lawyer named Abraham Lincoln," Mr. Jolliffe began.

Patrick watched Anna, distracted by concerns for her in this place that had made her sick before. She'd just recovered from a sick headache the day before they came to Cincinnati, and he would do his best to ensure she wouldn't spend their time in town holed up in their room at Rachel's. At least they didn't have to worry about Riverview Lodge, since Corydon's youngest sister and her husband had recently moved into Cleves and were managing the inn while they were away.

"A mulatto man by the name of McIntosh was seized in the street, dragged to the suburbs of the city, chained to a tree, and actually burned to death—and all within a single hour from the time he had been a freeman, attending to his own business, and at peace with the world," Mr. Jolliffe read.

Patrick snapped to attention, suddenly listening carefully to the words of this obscure lawyer.

"Whenever the vicious portion of population shall be permitted to gather in bands of hundreds and thousands, and burn churches, ravage and rob provision-stores, throw printing presses into rivers, shoot editors, and hang and burn obnoxious persons at pleasure, and with impunity—depend on it, this government cannot last."

When Mr. Jolliffe finished and folded the paper, Patrick joined in the thundering applause. Where was this lawyer and his eloquence when Elijah Lovejoy was being incriminated at the meetings of his anti-slavery society?

"We're pleased to have Mr. and Mrs. Patrick Gallagher with us tonight. Mr. Gallagher was at the warehouse with Elijah Lovejoy when he was murdered for standing up for the free press and abolition. Mr. Gallagher, we welcome you to share with us about the trials in Alton and any news you have about them."

Patrick ran his hand across Anna's shoulder as he brushed past her on his way to the front. "Thank you, Mr. Jolliffe. I'm grateful for the opportunity to be back. The trials of the mob that ruthlessly killed Mr. Lovejoy are evidence of the utter lack of justice and truth in our court systems. All the suspects, even those who proudly admitted to having fired one of the shots that struck Mr. Lovejoy at the time of his death, have been released with no fines or sentencing. It is with gratitude, however, that I can share with you that in the same vein, we received word this week that the charges against those of us who were defending the warehouse and press on the night of November 7 have all been dropped after an eleven-minute trial."

The crowd burst into applause again, and others were called on to give reports on recent events closer to the city. Patrick and Anna only stayed another hour before Patrick ushered her out onto the street, away from the overheating room. If anyone needed to be in contact with him in the coming days, they knew where to find him at Rachel's. Where, yes, he was staying in the front room *with* Anna and sleeping quite nicely.

"I have a new verse for you," Anna said once he'd handed her up into the buggy and wrapped the lap rug around her.

Patrick picked up the reins and clucked to the horses. "Yes?"

"It starts, 'Happy is he that hath the God of Jacob for his help, whose hope is in the Lord his God.' I read it this morning in Psalm 146 and thought it belonged on your promise list. But then it goes on to describe God with statements that could be viewed as promises—He keepeth truth forever. He executeth judgment for the oppressed. He giveth food to the hungry. He looseth the prisoners. And so on."

The air was frigid, so he was glad when Anna brought her warmth to him, snuggling into his side. "We can look at it tonight and add it to our list. God has done all those things, and He will do them again. It's good to remember that although we are told to do justice, feed the poor, remember those in bonds, and more, that it ends with Him, not us."

He would continue on this journey and in this work, clinging to God's promises, until, like Christian and Hopeful, he reached that glorious Celestial City and eternal glory.

"I knew you'd like that part. What do you think about the beginning? Does hoping in the Lord make you happy?"

Patrick wrapped his arm around her. Even with the grief that still overwhelmed him sometimes and all the uncertainty for the future—both for him and Anna and for the country as a whole—he had a lot to be happy about these days. Anna was right, though. None of it compared with the deep abiding hope that came from a power far greater and kinder than himself.

"Ah, darling, that is a promise that I can truthfully say has already come true."

Get the Bonus Epilogue!

The story's not over!

Scan the code to get the Sowing Hope bonus epilogue about Patrick, Anna, and their future family in your inbox

About the Book

I was fourteen the first time my dad took a road trip detour to the Elijah Lovejoy memorial in Alton, Illinois. Reading Lovejoy's quotes on the memorial, I was even then struck by the moral courage of the man. My sisters and I promptly named our pet rabbits Elijah and Joy.

While my family no longer remembers where my dad first learned about Elijah Lovejoy, there's no doubt that his interest in Lovejoy affected all of us. When my dad suddenly passed away in 2008, Rex Huppke of the *Chicago Tribune* wrote an op-ed telling about the electrical work my dad did in his home the week before his death. In the article, Rex relayed that my dad had told him a story to offer encouragement in a challenging time in his *Tribune* employment. It was the story of Elijah Lovejoy.

In the same vein, I retell Elijah Lovejoy's story to you now, extending to you the same encouragement. I suppose I was always destined to write this book, although it was only about five years ago that I realized it and came to feel that this was the book I was born to write. I didn't know until I started researching that this project would resurrect other long-forgotten names that even I hadn't heard before: James Birney, Marius Robinson, Jason Bull, David Nickens, and even Wesley Strother, the wagoner. A female with the last name of Williams owned the only known Black-owned boardinghouse in Cincinnati during this time. While I'm thrilled to introduce these real people to you, the book simply can't hold all the names and stories I wish I could tell. It will never be enough. The list of heroes of the free press, abolition, and the Underground Railroad in the 1830s is too great.

As much as absolutely possible, I gave historical figures their own words in dialogue in this book. Nearly everything Elijah Lovejoy said in *Sowing Hope* was from his writings or letters to his family. To a lesser degree, James Birney, Marius Robinson, Owen Lovejoy, and even John Lovejoy speak lines that are their actual words. The timeline of all their movements and the riots they endured is exactly accurate. In other words, this book is not based on the story of Elijah Lovejoy—it IS the story of Elijah Lovejoy. Patrick's decision to walk to St. Louis was a nod to Lovejoy, who did walk the entire distance from Massachusetts in 1827. When Lovejoy became ill on his trip to Cincinnati for the press, he recovered at the home of a friend named Banks in Louisville.

Patrick's article for *The Philanthropist* was written by John Graham of Ohio and appeared in the April 22, 1836 issue.

While the research done in preparation of this book was extensive, these four books deserve special mention for being especially invaluable, and I highly recommend them as further reading:

- *Memoir of the Rev. Elijah P. Lovejoy* by Lovejoy, Joseph and Lovejoy, Owen
- *Tide Without Turning: Elijah P. Lovejoy and Freedom of the Press* by Gill, John
- *Freedom's Champion—Elijah Lovejoy* by Simon, Paul
- *First to Fall: Elijah Lovejoy and the Fight for a Free Press in the Age of Slavery* by Ellingwood, Ken

Also deserving of special mention is *Sons and Daughters of Thunder*, a fantastic movie telling the story of Harriet Beecher Stowe and the Lane Debates. An interesting story all its own!

Many of the taverns on the National Road depicted here are real. While Benjamin Lundy's store in Mount Pleasant existed, I don't have proof that anyone still kept it open at this time.

Being such a personal book, I took joy in adding touches that are special to my family, such as naming Anna's inn after my Grandma June's cottage in Thebes, Illinois, and then featuring Thebes when Patrick's steamboat stopped there overnight in an era when it was known as Sparhawks Landing. And if you don't know who Ellis Dinsmore is yet, I recommend reading the Finding Home series for more of his story.

I'm deeply grateful for the assistance of my critique partners, all of whom have been with me for several books now. **Jennifer Q. Hunt, Amanda Chapman, Bonnie McGraw, David Wood, Rebekah Gwynn, and Scott Gwynn** have shown incredible patience and discernment working with this very stubborn author. Your investment in my work means a great deal to me.

A very special thank you to my sensitivity reader, **Tiffany Davis**, for ensuring that I was as respectful and truthful as I could be while discussing racial issues set in a difficult time period.

Thank you to my editor, **Jessica Barber**. I so appreciate you, the professionalism you brought to this project, and your campaign to reduce confusion and add clarity throughout.

Thank you to my cover designer, **Hannah Linder**, for nailing exactly what I was hoping for on the very first design you sent over.

Thank you to all the **Christian Mommy Writers** and to **my family** for your unfailing support, encouragement, and prayers.

Thank you to **my kids** and **my husband David**, without whom none of this would be possible. Thank you for so willingly coming along on this journey and your excitement about it. I know how blessed I am to have you.

And to **God**, the author of the most incredible stories. Because of what He has done in the lives of faithful men and women throughout history, I have their stories to share with you now.

I could not keep writing if it weren't for **my readers**, whose kind words, purchases, and recommendations to friends keep me and my writing going. Thank you for every review and share! You'll never know how valuable they are to your favorite authors.

About the Author

Heather Wood grew up in the Chicago suburbs, loving history, classic literature, writing stories, and Civil War reenacting. After obtaining her bachelor's degree in Bible/Theology from Appalachian Bible College, she settled in Virginia with her husband, David. Her early passions fuel her writing today, although she spends most of her days now working to infuse her love for God and good literature into the hearts of her four children.

I would love to have you visit me online at
my social media accounts @heather.wood.author or at
www.HeatherWoodAuthor.com,
where you can sign up for my newsletter and receive news of sales,
giveaways, and new releases in your inbox about once a month.

If you enjoyed Sowing Hope, please leave a review wherever you review books! Indie authors rely on reviews for our work to get noticed.

WEAVING ROOTS

GATHERING OF MERCIES BOOK 1

August 1827
Baltimore, Maryland

Betha studied the two-story brick building before her, praying that this wasn't yet another of Seamus's bad ideas.

"Are you nervous?"

Her nephew's voice pulled her gaze from the boxy red structure to the blue eyes tilted up beneath his plaid cap. A face that before much longer would stand eye to eye with her.

She smiled at how well Henry knew her, and wrapping an arm around him, she pulled him against her best mulberry-colored dress.

"Enrolling you in school oughtn't be too frightenin'." As long as they weren't making a mistake by sending him to the Oliver Hibernian Free School. It didn't matter how much she tried to convince her brother of the importance of a quality education for Henry; linen wasn't selling the way it used to, and the expense of a paid school would make things tight for them. A sacrifice Seamus wasn't as willing to make for his son as she was.

"Are you nervous?" Betha asked, turning the question around on Henry. Facing unfamiliar situations and people weren't her favorite things to do, but she wasn't the one starting a new school in a new city, and if she'd learned anything this year, it was that the ten-year-old by her side was far more resilient than she gave him credit for.

"I'd like to get it done with."

So he was nervous but carrying the brave face he'd worn since birth. Betha could only pray that this school gave Henry a new beginning as fresh as the one Seamus counted on Baltimore being for himself.

A shiny lacquered coach and four rounded the corner, and Betha pulled Henry out of the road, peering around the school at the affluent neighborhood beyond it. Despite its location, the building they now approached was obviously built more for function than to relay any grandiose sense of the high endeavor of education. Mounting the stairs, Betha felt the protective mother bear within her rise and surrendered Henry to the Lord. His new schoolmaster might be a strict, hardened old codger. He might hold Henry to an impossible standard or crush the boy's curious spirit. He might not see Henry as an individual in a crowd of rowdy boys. But at least he would never know of the circumstances of Henry's birth or call him names related to it.

No one in Baltimore would be able to hold Seamus's long-ago choices against Henry if Betha had anything to do with it. Not like New York had.

Betha sent Henry an affectionate smile. If he was going to allow courage to chase his fears away, she would do the same. She offered her hand to him. He took it, reminding her that despite what he often voiced, he was still her little boy. He still needed her. Betha didn't know what she would do if he ever didn't. Seamus might view Henry as the biggest mistake of his life, but he was the biggest blessing in hers.

"All the students here are Irish," she said brightly.

"I know, Ma. You already told me."

Betha reached for the front door and pushed it open. "It might be nice to have friends who are like you."

Henry shrugged like he didn't care either way. Betha didn't blame him with the way he'd been treated by so-called friends in the past.

A chair scraping across the floor greeted them as Betha closed the door behind Henry and turned around into a giant room filled with rows of benches. A man stood behind the desk, pulling his coat over white shirtsleeves.

"Good morning."

Betha lifted her eyes from the stacks of books and papers covering the desk to the face watching her approach. Well, she could check "old" off her list. His curious brown eyes didn't look hardened either.

"Good morning. We're here to enroll Henry in school."

"Excellent. Welcome to Oliver Hibernian." The teacher walked around the desk and extended his hand to Henry first. "I'm Mr. Gallagher, the boys' teacher."

Betha watched Henry straighten and his skinny little chest puff out as he gave a firm handshake like a man. "Henry Young."

Then Mr. Gallagher turned to her, and Betha took in the neatly combed brown hair, straight white teeth, and . . . dimples? Surely a man with dimples couldn't be a strict taskmaster of a teacher, could he? He was clean-shaven, but the shadow on his jaw and lines on the outer corners of his eyes told her he wasn't fresh out of college. Hopefully that meant he could hold his own in a classroom of energetic boys.

He reached his hand out to her with a real smile. "Colm Gallagher." His accent revealed that he was just as American as she was. Maybe he had never seen Ireland with his own eyes either. As far as Betha's da was concerned, those who had never stepped foot on the ancient land of Hibernia were lesser than. Which had always confused her, seeing as he was the one who brought Seamus and their mother to America before Betha was born.

"Betha Young," she murmured in response.

Mr. Gallagher released her hand and leaned back against the desk. "How old are you, Mr. Young?"

"Almost eleven, sir."

As if Betha needed to be reminded that he was growing up too fast. Especially when his birthday was still five months away.

"You've been in school before?"

"Yes, sir, in New York."

Betha supposed the teacher had to ask that one, as the school serviced poor Scotch-Irish neighborhoods, but at least he'd formed the question in a positive manner, assuming Henry had. Henry stood tall and brave, already so anxious to impress his new teacher.

Mr. Gallagher—or was it Colm, since he'd added that name just for her?—rounded the desk to rifle through his pile of papers. "I could place you in the level you were in in New York to start with, or if you're willing to undergo a more exacting evaluation, I'll place you in separate reading, writing, and arithmetic levels according to your abilities. That way you can simply continue your education from your current place."

"Do you do that for all your students?" Betha couldn't conceal her surprise. "Break up their academic level by subject?"

Colm didn't appear fazed by her challenge. "Yes, ma'am. I utilize the Lancaster education model, which allows for students to excel at what comes naturally to them while steadily working at what doesn't."

Whatever the Lancaster model was, it sounded newfangled, and Betha wondered what Seamus would think. But she wouldn't give away to Colm that she wished her teacher had used such a model when she was a child. Besides, Henry's dislike of writing made his eyes simply glow at the suggestion.

"I can do the evaluation, can't I, Ma?"

Betha looked to Colm.

"I could evaluate him now if you have time, Mrs. Young. It won't take long."

"Miss." Betha cringed at the implication left by Henry's address. Until now, she'd never felt obligated to correct the title he'd used for her since he was five. What compelled her to want to ensure this man knew the truth of their relationship? "I'm Henry's guardian, but in truth, only his aunt."

She noted with satisfaction that the information seemed to have pleased Colm, for he almost smiled. He stood blinking at her before Betha realized that she hadn't answered his actual question and he was still waiting.

"Yes, of course. We can do the evaluation now."

Betha wandered around the schoolroom to give them space while Colm pulled out his books and gestured for Henry to take a seat. Stopping by the window, she took in the view of church steeples and government buildings, the steady, articulated cadence of Colm's low voice wafting through the room as he quizzed Henry.

Somewhere out in Fell's Point, their neighborhood surrounding Baltimore's wharves, Seamus was looking for a flax supplier. Betha removed her bonnet from her black hair, breathing out a prayer that she and Henry would return home to good news and she could get the spinning wheel going sooner rather than later. Seamus hadn't seemed at all concerned about suppliers when he packed up his loom in New York.

"Baltimore is just as close to the Delaware Valley as New York is, Betha. It shouldn't affect our supply at all. Besides, Baltimore is half as big as New York and growing. It's the perfect place and time to establish our name."

Betha knew it was all just excuses to defend the decision he'd already made. When she'd reminded him that the new Erie Canal made New York a clearly more advantageous city for trade, he'd brushed off her concerns, pointing to the railroad Baltimore was planning to compete with the canal. It didn't matter, because they both knew cotton was overtaking linen in every market, and it wasn't a secret that behind her questions, she supported his reasons for moving. But someone had to ask them and keep Seamus's impulses in check.

She mindlessly stretched her fingers, glad for the forced break from spinning even as she welcomed the thought of returning to a normal routine. When had she ever had two whole weeks off since Ma died and Betha filled her place as the family's primary spinner? Back then, Betha wondered if she would ever be able to spin as fine a thread as her mother's nimble fingers could. Now there was no doubt that her mother would be proud of the quality of linen she and Seamus produced. Its quality had made the Young name respected in New York. Unfortunately, New York made it clear they would never extend the same respect to Henry.

Betha turned from the window when Colm and Henry's oral volley ceased and Colm came to his feet. She watched Henry beam as Colm shook his hand and said something she couldn't make out before turning his dimples on her.

"You have a bright boy here, Miss Young. He said you were the one primarily responsible for his education." He relaxed his stance, his hands in his coat pockets.

Betha dipped her head, self-conscious at the unexpected compliment. "I only helped fill in what was lacking."

"So many of our students come with little to no education, both immigrants and American-born. It's nice to have some well-educated students among them."

A thought struck Betha's mind, causing her brow to furrow. "Does the school serve both Protestant and Catholic children then?"

"All Scotch-Irish children." Colm used his whole torso to nod from the waist up. "The board is particular that the education doesn't exclude any student."

"How do you manage them all?" Was *he* Catholic?

"I manage," Colm said. He held her gaze, confidence emanating from his whole person and shutting down all of Betha's questions. He shifted his attention to Henry. "I'd like to consider you for one of my monitors. They each oversee a group of smaller boys working at the same level in a subject. Since you have an easy grasp of arithmetic, I think you could help others excel. Would you consider it?"

Henry's enthusiastic nod outpaced anything Betha had seen from him since before Seamus had him pulled from the New York school.

Colm remained as serious as a merchant striking a business deal. "Very well then. I'll announce my final monitor selections the first week of school. I look forward to having you in my class, Mr. Young."

"Thank you, sir."

Betha had grown so used to the tightness in her chest, she'd forgotten it wasn't normal until it unclenched, and she drew a deep breath for the first time in far too long. As she regarded Colm Gallagher and dipped her head in farewell, she felt the first flicker of hope fill her heart. Somehow she knew that this man was on Henry's side with her, and Henry had finally found a place to thrive.

As long as Seamus didn't mess anything else up for his son.

September 1827

Colm scratched one last name onto his list and leaned back from his desk to reread it. With the first day of the school year finally over, he had a pretty decent idea of who his monitors would be.

It was amazing what a person could learn in just one day of watching a group of children. The natural-born leaders emerged, for better or worse, and by the end of the morning's instruction, Colm had a feel for what to expect from his school year. After six years in classrooms, he was rarely surprised anymore.

His eyes landed on Henry Young's name and stopped there.

If there was a boy in his class that reminded Colm of himself, it was the serious Young boy. He had already shown himself exacting, conscientious, and eager to please. More than once, Colm had caught Henry's anxious eyes on him, as if asking, *Did I do it right, teacher?* If only he could warn the boy away from giving his allegiance too readily.

Colm shook his head, running his fingers across his forehead. Of course a student should seek to please his schoolmaster. It was the good and right order of things. It was also good and right that the schoolmaster should be worthy of that kind of respect. Not everyone was like Mr. MacMurrough. *He* wasn't. Please, Lord, let that much always be true.

Colm's mind wandered to Henry's pretty raven-haired aunt, wishing she had escorted Henry to school. Somehow in that first meeting, he'd gotten the impression that she was the type to hover over him, even if the boy was old enough to find his own way to school, but she hadn't. Would Colm's only interactions with her be reduced to school exhibition nights when all the parents were present for the children's recitations? It wasn't easy to find a good Irish girl who had decorum and all of her teeth. Betha had both, which meant that the Youngs were probably a merchant or craftsman family, not the typical shipbuilders and sailors of Fell's Point.

The front door banged open, breaking up Colm's thoughts. Betha Young's lovely image was chased away by that of his gangly brother filling the doorway.

"School's out, yet you're still here." Patrick pushed his coat open to rest his hands on his hips. His cap sat in its usual position on the back of his head, behind a mass of reddish-brown curls that had never truly been tamed in his entire life.

Colm dropped his pencil and cocked his head. "Yes, where there's quiet to get work done."

"Harsh." Patrick shot Colm a toothy grin. "Is the girls' teacher still here?"

"Miss O'Neill? I believe she's upstairs."

"Is she pretty?"

Colm narrowed his eyes. "Sarah O'Neill. You know her."

"Sarah?" A grimace crossed Patrick's face. "No then. Are you about done? I came to retrieve you."

"For what? I don't remember needing to be retrieved."

"For the freedmen society meeting." Patrick's eyes pleaded hopefully with Colm.

"I never agreed to go."

"You never agreed to go *yet*. I'm here to convince you."

"I don't have time for that, Patrick. I have responsibilities."

"You have excuses," Patrick returned. "Always more excuses."

"You have your causes, and I have mine." Colm gestured at the empty benches. "I cannot fix all the problems in the world, and neither can you. I'm doing the work I've been called to, and you need to accept that."

"Injustice is everyone's problem," Patrick shot back, his voice rising. "Where there are atrocities in a nation, everyone is affected. You can care and do something about more than one problem in the world at a time."

Colm sighed heavily. How many times had they had this exact same argument? "No, I can't. If I get involved with the freedmen society, I'll lose respect among the Irish. I won't be able to effect change from the outside any more than you could. On the inside, I can. I can teach the next generation that all men are created equal. But if I join the society, my students' parents will stop sending their children here, and I'll lose that ability to influence them for good."

"You make an awful lot of assumptions around here." Patrick scowled and started for the door. "It's really all a dung pile of your own fears. You can't influence anyone for good if you're too afraid to bring God into the classroom."

"I'm not afraid to bring God into anything," Colm snapped. "I simply teach to the specifications given by the founder, and that involves providing education for families of different beliefs."

Patrick stopped and turned back. "You're lying to yourself. And you only assume that supporting the freedmen society will lose your influence among the Irish. You don't actually know."

"I do know." Colm pushed down the ire rising in his chest as he came to his feet. "I do know, Patrick. I'm doing my job, and it's making a difference here. But don't let that stop you from doing what I can't."

"I wasn't planning on it." Patrick let the door slam shut behind him.

Colm let out a frustrated growl into the empty room and dropped into his chair. His brother was wrong about one thing.

Colm wasn't lying to himself. He knew the truth perfectly well.

He was only lying to Patrick.

Continue reading on Kindle Unlimited
or find the paperback on Amazon and HeatherWoodAuthor.com